BROTHERS BY GRACE

COMING OF AGE IN 1879

All scriptures referenced in this book are from the King James Version.

Publication date: September 2024

Illustration by *Halo's Design Studio*
Book cover design by Cherie Williams
Editor: Jessica Ryn

ISBN: 979-8-9874296-7-9 (paperback)
ISBN: 979-8-9874296-8-6 (eBook)
ISBN: 979-8-9874296-9-3 (hardcover)

www.CherieHarbridgeWilliams.com

ACKNOWLEDGMENTS

My sincere thanks to:

my husband, Conway Williams, for his unwavering support and
encouragement during the writing of this novel;

and my support team, women whose talents, wisdom, and prayers
were invaluable along the way:
Gail Anderson, Nancy Mills, Becky Paskvan, Jeanne Boyce,
Sara Bryant, Barbara Baranowski, Renee Pearison,
and Elizabeth Mitchell

When a fervent desire to excel calls to you,
embrace the instinct to rise above.

CAST OF CHARACTERS

Bartlett, Liam .... Undertaker in Lewisburg

Bishop, Jacob .... Solomon's friend and travel companion

Blackstone, Artemus .... Suitor of Marguerite Sterling

Bromley, Rev. Jonas .... Pastor, Cooper Street Baptist Church

Buster .... Boy who sheltered Solomon at Stratford

Creel, Benjamin .... Board member, Cooper Street Baptist Church

Davies, Brady .... Piano tuner

Ellsworth, J. William .... Owner of Ellsworth Piano Company

Grimes, Thaddeus .... Transportation from Selinsgrove to Lewisburg

Hawk, Emeline .... Solomon's mother

Hawk, Rev. Geoffrey Kingston .... Solomon's father

Hawk, Solomon .... Jacob's friend and travel companion

Kerr, David .... Purchasing agent, Chicago Opera House

Mayfield, Bradford James .... Solomon's grandfather

Mayfield, Harris .... Solomon's cousin

Mayfield, Maude .... Solomon's aunt

Mayfield, Peter .... Solomon's cousin

Mayfield, Virgil .... Solomon's uncle

McCreary, Col. Archibald J. .... Civil engineer, designer of cantilever bridge

Richards, Professor .... Professor of Architecture, University of Illinois

Rodding, Charles .... Registrar, University of Illinois

Schultz, Amelia .... University student

Schultz, Anna .... Amelia's mother

Schuster, Gerald .... Passenger on the stagecoach

Sterling, Marguerite .... Owner of the Sterling Mansion in Chicago

Thompson, Miss .... Piano teacher, Ellsworth Piano Company

Warren, Dr. Adam .... Veterinarian and piano customer

West, Hiram .... Ellsworth employee in Farm Implements

West, Victoria .... Hiram's wife

Wilcox, Paul .... Civil engineer in Chicago

TABLE OF CONTENTS

Chapter 1: Graduation Day

Friday, May 30, 1879

Solomon had waited for this day at the crossroads of relief and dread. It was his graduation from Yale—not something he had wanted to accomplish, but he had studied diligently to get good marks for his father's sake. His father was the Rev. Geoffrey Kingston Hawk, the dignified and revered pastor of St. Matthew's Church, the largest Protestant congregation in Bridgeport, Connecticut. He was a domineering man whose fondest dream was that his son would follow him in the ministry.

Sadly for Solomon, he was not so strong-willed. He had endured three years of study in a field where he had no interest or divine calling but where he would please his father. Now, there could be no putting it off. He had to either take his stand and declare his intent to follow his own interests or be bound to the life his father planned for him. His palms were sweaty; his breathing was fast and shallow.

Solomon took his place in line among graduation candidates who chatted excitedly among themselves, wishing he weren't so tall. He longed to hide his strained face from the joyous crowd around him. As the ceremony began, the graduates assumed the proper dignity. The line moved toward the stage at a turtle's pace, where Dean Avery Woodhouse presented each graduate with his diploma and shook his hand warmly. Solomon inched his way toward the dean, his stomach churning. At last, the moment arrived. Dean Woodhouse gave him a broad smile, shook his right hand, and laid the parchment in his left hand. "Congratulations, Mr. Hawk. Well done."

Solomon nodded a weak thank-you, then walked off the platform in his black robe and mortar board, diploma in hand. He had finally accomplished what his father had set out for him to do: graduate from the School of Divinity at Yale College.

As he walked off the stage, his parents met him, excited and full of congratulations. He smiled thinly as they unrolled the parchment to look at the evidence of his great accomplishment. The diploma was written in Latin: "Universitatis Yalensis—in Novo Portu in Republica Connecticutensi" over their son's name, Solomon Mayfield Hawk, in an ornate script. That was followed by a paragraph in the Latin text and the signatures of the college dignitaries. The year on the diploma was MDCCCLXXIX—1879.

Father was flushed with excitement. Solomon had never seen a grin that wide on his face.

The elder Hawk clapped him on the back. "Well, son, now you're ready to join me in ministry. Congratulations! I'll get you a desk set up at the church."

It was either now or not at all. Solomon took a deep breath. He tried to keep his hands in the folds of his gown to hide their shaking. "Father, I've just graduated. I only have book knowledge. I want to travel for a year and get to know the world from a different perspective before I start a ministry. I need time to get a different kind of education, a practical education, and round myself out as a person."

"Look, son, I can teach you everything you need to know about 'the world,' as you put it, and about people. You need to start earning an income. No, travel is nonsense. You'll start working with me at the church."

Solomon swallowed hard and gathered his courage before pressing on. "Father, I appreciate everything you've done for me, giving me an education and seeing to my needs, but I have to find out about life on my own."

Father's eyes hardened as he glanced at Solomon's mother. "Emeline, can you believe what you're hearing?"

Solomon took another breath. "I'm going to travel, Father. When I return, we'll talk about what I'll do."

Mother hesitated but then decided to speak. "Geoffrey, the boy has a point. He has no experience dealing with people as an adult or being responsible for his own needs. Some things can only be learned by doing for oneself."

Father's face reddened. "You stay out of this, Emeline. This is between me and the boy."

"Father, I'm twenty years old. I'm no boy. I need to make the plans that are best for me."

Before Father could answer, Solomon rolled up his diploma and walked away. He sensed the heat of his father's stare drilling into his back.

Father thundered, "If you walk away from your rightful responsibility, Solomon, you owe me three years' tuition!"

Other parents, standing in clusters around their graduating offspring, turned to stare at the man in the clerical collar shouting in anger. Solomon, his ears burning with embarrassment, kept walking.

He had already determined to find his way home alone to burn off some pent-up anger, even though his mother would be sick with worry. He was sorry about that, but the momentum he built in his defiance of Father temporarily overruled his concern for Mother.

Now, he faced the challenge of traveling the twenty miles from New Haven to Bridgeport without transportation or money. By the grace of God, he found a fellow graduate from Bridgeport and asked to accompany his family in their carriage. He wanted to be away from his father to think, to savor the fact that he had finally taken a stand, however wobbly his courage was.

He wasn't so foolish to expect this was the last of it. There would be further confrontations with his father. He prayed he could handle them. This was the opening of a new chapter in his life.

When he arrived home five hours later, the atmosphere was not what he expected. He found his mother weeping and his father trying to reason with her.

"What's wrong, Mother?" asked Solomon in alarm.

"A telegram came a few minutes ago," she said, sobbing. "Grandfather is dying."

His beloved grandfather. Solomon's world crumbled. "No!" His eyes prickling with tears, he sank to the settee beside his mother and laid his trembling hand over hers.

Rev. Hawk stood by the draped window, looking into the distance. "We need to plan our trip quickly. Lewisburg, Pennsylvania, is a long way to travel on short notice. Emeline," he said, turning toward his wife, "we must leave today. You need to pack some clothes for a long trip. We may or may not get to your father's in time to say goodbye before he passes, but I will send a telegram today and ask them to hold off reading the will until we arrive. Solomon will stay here and take care of the church for me. Solomon, you'll need to prepare a sermon for Sunday."

Solomon's stomach churned. "Father, I can't preach Sunday. I'm going to Pennsylvania with you to be with the family."

"You're not going with us. You're staying here. This is an emergency."

"Geoffrey, please!" pleaded Emeline. "Solomon's grandfather is dying. He's Father's favorite of all the grandchildren. He must go."

"I said he's staying here." Geoffrey's neck was red, and his veins popped out.

This kind of dictatorship had been going on all of Solomon's life, and he was not bending this time. His fury got the best of him, and he stood his ground. "No, Father. I'm going. If you don't allow me to go with you, I'll go myself and meet you out there. But I am going."

"I don't know what's gotten into you. If you insist on defying me, you will go alone. I'm not having it. As long as you live in this house, you will obey me or suffer the consequences."

Solomon held his tongue, his best strategy under the circumstances. Trembling, he turned and strode to his room. His hands shook, and his chest heaved with each breath. It would have been satisfying to slam the door, but that would only arouse Father's ire further. With the muscles in his arms pulsing, he closed the door with restraint, pulled his clothes from his bureau and stuffed them into his valise.

But, he was penniless. How would he get to Lewisburg alone with no

4

money? Why, that must be four hundred miles over mountainous terrain. It could take weeks if he went on horseback. Grandfather would probably be dead and buried by then. He sat on the edge of his bed and wept.

Mother argued with Father on the other side of the door, something Solomon had never remembered happening before. "Geoffrey, this is no time to impose your will on me! I'm losing my father. I'm out of my mind with grief. I need Solomon with us. I don't get any compassion from you, and I need someone to lean on for emotional support."

"That's just like a woman, all emotion, no reason. I say he's not going with us, and that's final. Now pack! Thanks to your ungrateful son, I must find someone else to preach on Sunday, and I'll send a telegram to your father's lawyer. What was that attorney's name?"

"I don't know. I can't believe you're more concerned about the will than you are about me and Solomon." She turned, sobbing, and went to the bedroom, probably to gather clothes to put in the trunk. Geoffrey left the house to run his errands. When the door latch clicked shut behind him, Solomon went to speak to his mother. He put his arms around her, and they wept together.

Solomon wiped the tears from his cheeks. "Mother, I need to talk to you about the trip. I need to be with the family, but I have no money. Do you have anything you could loan me?"

She put a hand to her mouth and lowered her head. After a moment, she nodded. "I have a little money I've been saving from the grocery allowance your father gives me. You take it. I don't know if it will get you there, but it's all I have." She opened her bureau drawer, lifted a bag of coins from under her dainties, and handed it to her son. "There's over forty-two dollars in there. I've been saving up for quite a while. But when Grandfather's will is read, I expect to have more. So please take this. I'll pray that God will multiply it as He did the loaves and fishes."

Solomon accepted the bag humbly, realizing what she was sacrificing to help him on his way. She couldn't defy her husband openly, as he was a hard man despite his profession tending God's business. His parishioners would be dumbfounded to learn what he was like behind closed doors. The church would not be well served for his personality to become known, so his wife and son kept it to themselves.

"Thank you. I'll be careful with it."

"It's your money now, Solomon. Spend it wisely, and God be with you."

"Goodbye, Mother. I don't know if I'll be ahead or behind you, but I plan to see you there. Take good care of yourself. My prayers are with you."

"As mine are with you, son. Goodbye."

He kissed her cheek, tucked the change bag into his valise, and left the house before his father returned.

Chapter 2: Heading for Stratford

How does one get from Bridgeport, Connecticut, to Lewisburg, Pennsylvania? Solomon carried his small valise to the stable behind the house and saddled Scout, one of Father's horses, planning to figure out the trip one step at a time. He prayed he wouldn't make mistakes that cost him time or money. He left the strongest horse for his father to hitch to the carriage but took the next best, a dapple gray. He strapped his valise behind the saddle.

"Come on, Scout," he said to the horse. "We're going to Lewisburg."

Lewisburg was hundreds of miles west, but Solomon pointed Scout toward Stratford to the east, where he could catch the ferry going west to New York. That would be his cheapest option for fast travel, but the hour was late. The ferry might have already started its last run. Scout galloped toward the docks six miles away, raising dust with every strike of the hoof on the dirt road. Solomon wanted to be well on his way when Father got home.

He wiped his brow in frustration. If he had to wait until the morning ferry, he could only hope Father would decide on another route. He dreaded an unpleasant and embarrassing confrontation with Father in public if they happened to be on the same ferry.

It had been a long day. It was almost as if he had become a different person since breakfast. He was now a college graduate and an outcast from the family. He worried about poor Mother, having to endure Father's tantrums to Lewisburg while he should be comforting her in her grief. He would never understand his father.

He hugged the horse with his knees, his body swaying in rhythm with its strides. He was lost in his thoughts until his belly complained, reminding him he hadn't eaten since breakfast. The general store in Stratford would be closed by now. He spoke to God about his hunger and asked for provision.

Solomon's anguish increased as time ticked by, and he became convinced he would be too late to get on the afternoon ferry. Worry overwhelmed him. He struggled to accept that he faced a day's delay when his overwhelming desire was to see Grandfather one last time.

The horse continued pounding the road toward Stratford. Solomon's thoughts whirled in a dozen directions. He was only dimly aware of the view of Long Island Sound and the waves splashing against the shore. He barely noticed the occasional fishing trawler or sailboat silhouetted on the horizon. He passed people out walking in the cool of the evening. Under other circumstances, this would have been a pleasant ride.

Approaching the town, Solomon came upon a barefoot boy of about twelve years old. He had tousled brown hair and a dirty face. The boy waved at him, carrying a bag in his other hand. Solomon pulled Scout to a halt and asked the lad what he wanted. The boy peered up at him with pained brown eyes and asked for a ride to his house in Stratford. "My feet are hurting something awful, mister, and I still have a mile to go. Can you let me sit behind you on your horse?"

Solomon gave the boy a friendly smile and lowered his hand. "Come on up," he said.

"Here, take my carrots first so I don't drop them while I try to climb up there."

Carrots? Solomon balanced the bag between his legs for safekeeping, then lowered his hand again and helped the boy up.

"Say, I haven't had anything to eat for a long time," he said. "Would you sell me two of those carrots?"

"I'd say I owe you two of them for taking me home," the boy said. "Just pick out the ones you want."

"You're an answer to my prayer, young man," Solomon said, reaching into the carrot bag. He took two and handed the rest of them to the boy.

8

Then he urged the horse on. "I'll eat my carrot and give one to the horse when I find a place to settle for the night."

"We have a barn out back. I'm sure Ma wouldn't mind if you stayed there. By the way, my name is Albert, but you can call me Buster. Everyone does."

Solomon smiled. "Nice to meet you, Buster. I'm Mr. Hawk."

"You mean like a buzzard? That's a funny name. But you can stay in our barn anyway."

"Thank you, but I don't want to impose on your family."

"No, it's all right. It's happened before. I'll introduce you when we get home. Ma will tell you to stay. You'll see."

Solomon's facial muscles relaxed in relief and gratitude that his needs would be met.

When they reached the boy's house, his mother wasn't there. "She must have gone to Granny's for a few minutes. That's all right. You can put your horse in that stall and sleep over here on this pile of hay. I'll get you a blanket."

"You're very kind, and I thank you."

Solomon removed his jacket, folded it neatly, and laid it beside him in the hay. Buster went inside the house and brought back a woolen blanket. He left Solomon to eat his carrot. The day had been long and hard. Despite his fatigue, Solomon lay awake, reviewing the day's events. He wondered what Father would say if he knew his Yale graduate son was sleeping in his clothes in a barn. He wondered how Mother was doing and prayed for her comfort. Finally, he drifted off into slumber.

An hour later, Solomon was awakened by a scream nearby. His eyes flew open to find a woman with a lantern in the dark barn. The harsh light in his eyes prevented him from seeing her face.

"Who are you?" she shouted. "You stay right there. I have a shotgun."

Solomon's heart pounded. "I'm very sorry to startle you, ma'am. You must be Buster's mother. He said I could stay in the barn tonight. He was going to tell you I was here. I'm waiting for the ferry in the morning."

The overwrought woman put her lantern down in the dirt and leaned the shotgun against the wall, blushing. "Sorry to have given you a scare. Buster's asleep. I was putting my horse away and took notice of that extra horse here. Not knowing who you were, I thought you were up to no good." Her hands trembled.

"I must have given you quite a fright. I'm very sorry. I'll get my horse and be on my way."

"No, no, no," she said. "Now that I know who you are, please stay and get some sleep. In the morning, Buster will bring you a bucket of water and a bar of soap, and I'll make you a breakfast of sausage and eggs before you go. We'll give your horse a share of oats. I believe in hospitality."

"Ma'am, that's more appreciated than you know. This has been the worst day of my life, and now I'm on my way to Pennsylvania, hoping to see my grandfather before he dies. He's very ill."

She tilted her head as her eyes filled with sympathy. "I'm sorry to hear that. You sleep well tonight, and Buster will wake you in the morning. You don't want to miss that ferry."

"Yes, ma'am. And thank you."

He dropped off to sleep again as she took her lantern and returned to the house.

Chapter 3: Preparing for a Long Trip

Back in Bridgeport, Rev. Hawk had asked every suitable replacement he could think of to preach for him on Sunday and had been refused each time. The reasons given were various.

Defeated and furious with his son, he headed the horse home, trying to decide what to do. He couldn't figure out why Solomon was bucking him. *Children today have no idea of the value of discipline and duty,* he thought. *They're soft; that's what it is. If I had spoken to my father the way Solomon talked to me today, my father would have beaten me.* His jaw set as images from his childhood played through his mind. *He beat me often when I was a boy, and I turned out fine as an adult. Maybe I was too soft on Solomon.*

Then, he came up with a brilliant idea. He congratulated himself on working out a solution.

"Emeline," he said as he strode through the front door. "Emeline, I want you to go to your father's with Solomon. I will follow on Monday. I couldn't find anyone to preach. This is Solomon's fault for ducking out of his responsibility."

Emeline paused in her packing and sucked in a breath. Geoffrey was confused at her hesitation.

"That won't be possible," she said. "Solomon left an hour ago. He went alone, just as you insisted."

"He what!" roared Geoffrey, his eyes bulging. "Now he's blocked my plans a second time. How did he get out of the house with no money?"

Emeline drew a long breath. "I believe he had some, maybe not much.

He will have to use his wits to get all the way to Lewisburg." She glanced at her drawer but kept her lips closed.

"Well, that settles it. We won't be able to leave today. I have to preach on Sunday. The church can't get along without me." He doffed his hat and threw it down on the table. "This is the devil's work."

***

Emeline retreated to the bedroom, shaking with silent sobs. She agreed with Geoffrey that this was the devil's work. Her grief and frustration were overwhelming, and now she was being delayed two more days.

Her heart was desperate to say a final goodbye to her father, but being angry with her husband took energy she couldn't spare. Anger only complicated things. She told herself that their delay was caused by his service to the Lord, which helped her past her anger. She was willing to do anything for her Lord.

At least I have more time to plan for the trip, she thought.

Geoffrey left again in one last effort to find someone to preach. When the front door opened and clicked shut, she lay across the bed, let down her guard, and allowed the tears to pour down her face. Exhausted, she fell asleep and was still there when her husband returned home.

***

Geoffrey entered the house with sagging shoulders. He took off his topcoat and top hat. As was his habit, he went into the bedroom to hang his coat in the wardrobe. He discovered his wife asleep on the bed in the middle of the afternoon.

"Emeline, wake up," he said.

She roused herself and sat up, still groggy. "What time is it?"

"It's time you should be making dinner."

"I'll see if there is something I can warm up."

There was a knock at the door, and Geoffrey opened it, seeing that Emeline's eyes were red and swollen, and her hair was untidy. She was not fit to see anyone, especially one of the parishioners. The visitor was a

12

plump middle-aged lady with a casserole.

Word spreads fast, he thought.

"Mrs. Leiterman, how nice to see you. Please come in."

"Rev. Hawk, I'm so very sorry about the impending death of your father-in-law. I brought a chicken dish for you so Mrs. Hawk won't have to cook tonight."

Geoffrey accepted the dish with a smile. "How kind of you. Mrs. Hawk isn't feeling well right now — the shock, you know. She will be most grateful for your thoughtfulness."

"I won't stay," said Mrs. Leiterman. "Please convey my condolences to Mrs. Hawk."

"I will."

Mrs. Leiterman turned and retreated down the walk. Geoffrey closed the door and put the casserole on a trivet on the dining table. "Emeline, there's no need to cook after all," he said. "Mrs. Leiterman brought dinner."

Emeline's shoulders relaxed. "I'll have to thank her later. Let's eat while it's still hot. I'm hungry, too."

The two of them seated themselves at the table. Geoffrey said the blessing, and they ate as two people sitting together but disconnected. They were about to finish when there was another knock at the door. "You need to get that," Geoffrey said, putting another forkful in his mouth.

"Geoffrey, I don't want to be put in any social situation right now."

She turned her eyes to him, waiting for a comment, but he only stared at her and kept eating.

***

Emeline sighed, put her napkin on the table, and went to the door. It was the deacon's wife with a pie in her hand.

"Mrs. Hawk," she said, "my husband told me about your father. My prayers are with you, and I wanted to do something else for you. Do you like cherry pie?"

Emeline lowered her eyes to hide her tears. "Yes, we do, Mrs. Carlson, and I thank you. That was very thoughtful."

"Are you going to your father's house?"

"Yes. And I apologize for my appearance," she said, blushing. "I'm just overcome with worry."

"Of course, Mrs. Hawk. I'll be leaving. Please know that you're in our prayers."

"I appreciate that, Mrs. Carlson. Goodbye."

She carried the warm pie to the kitchen and set it on the table. "Would you like some pie?" she asked. She tried to conceal her brokenness from Geoffrey but couldn't. Her eyes sagged. She could feel it in the care lines etching her face.

"Cherry pie? Yes, and then I'll have to go to the study and polish my sermon for Sunday."

Emeline sliced the pie and served a piece to her husband. She washed the few dishes and returned to the bedroom to relive memories of her father. And cry.

She remembered falling over a rock as a child, scraping her leg badly. Her father tied his handkerchief over her bloody shin, picked her up, and carried her all the way home. She remembered that as a schoolgirl, her father gathered her in his arms and prayed for her when a young man broke her heart. Her father had been her champion.

The sky was growing dark when Emeline approached her husband's study.

"I'm sorry to interrupt you, Geoffrey, but I need to know how we'll be traveling. Are we taking the carriage? It would help me pack if I knew what to expect."

"I think we should take the train. It will be the quickest way there."

"I've never been on the train. Do we take food with us?"

"I've never been on the train, either, but taking some food with us would be wise, just in case. Take some things that won't spoil quickly. Fruit, cheese, that kind of thing."

"Yes, Geoffrey."

"And take some bread and a canteen of something to drink."

"Yes, Geoffrey."

Emeline had all day tomorrow to plan. She would ask her husband's permission to stay home from church on Sunday and finish packing. The parishioners would understand her absence, and she didn't want to talk to people. She needed solitude. She and Solomon were so much alike in that way.

Chapter 4: The Young Preacher Meets the Blacksmith

Saturday, May 31, 1879

Buster arrived at the barn early the following morning, sloshing his wooden pail of water. In the other hand he carried a bar of lye soap and a towel. "Mr. Buzzard," he said, "it's time to wake up. Ma's cooking breakfast."

Solomon stretched and grinned at him. "Thank you for the water, Buster. I'll be in the house as soon as I get washed up. It shouldn't take long."

The boy left him in privacy. As Solomon lathered himself with soap, his thoughts returned home. *I wonder how Mother is. I wish I had a way to talk to her, but I suppose that will have to wait until I arrive at Grandfather's house. There's no way to contact her while we're traveling separately.*

Refreshed and dressed, Solomon knocked on the back door of the small cottage. Buster's mother opened the screen door and invited him to sit at the pine breakfast table. His stomach growled. The air was rich with the pungent aroma of sausage and eggs sizzling in the skillet. She put a full plate before him with a cup of coffee.

"You have a long day ahead of you," she said. "I'm packing a bag with garden vegetables and cheese. You take them when you go, but there's no hurry. The New Rochelle-to-Stratford doesn't come in until noon."

"I'm humbled by your kindness, ma'am."

"I'm trying to be the hands and feet of Jesus. I hope you get to see your grandfather before he passes."

She filled a plate for herself and sat at the table with Solomon, explaining that Buster had already had his breakfast and was at his chores.

Solomon said a brief prayer of thanks for the food and blessings on his hostess. "Do you know how to get to the middle of Pennsylvania?" He dipped a piece of sausage in his egg yolk and took a bite. Hot food had never tasted so good.

The woman sighed and lifted her fork. "No. I always wanted to travel, but it never worked out. My husband died in an accident at the docks when Buster was a little tyke. I'm needed here, so here I stay. But they say that if you get to New York City, you can go anywhere from there."

They made small talk while he ate. Solomon helped her clear the table. Then he took the bag of offered food with a grateful heart and said goodbye.

**

Solomon guided Scout slowly toward the docks, scanning the line of boats for the ferry that would carry him to New Rochelle. The sun shone brightly, and the cool air smelled of salt water and fish. The wide boardwalk was jammed with pedestrians carrying bags to and from passenger vessels. Further down, burly men carted loads of cargo from ship to shore.

Boats rocked gently at their moorings, most of them steamers and fishing trawlers. A fisherman sat on a dock mending his net while the crews of other boats scurried about shouting instructions at each other as they prepared to go to sea again.

Solomon was looking for only one boat — transportation west for him and his horse. When he got off the ferry, he would figure out what to do next. Traveling alone was both exciting and terrifying.

Soon, he spotted the ferry steaming toward one of the docks. It maneuvered into position slowly, rotating parallel to the pier at just the right second with a gentle bump. The deckhand hopped off, tied the boat to the cleats, and lowered the forward ramp, allowing a flood of passengers off. As soon as they were discharged, more passengers entered the ramp and paid their fare. The air was filled with chatter and laughter.

Solomon approached the ramp, wondering whether he'd be allowed on board with Scout.

"Sir, do you ferry horses?" he asked the attendant.

"Yes, sir, we do. The fare will be three dollars for you and the horse."

Solomon reached into his pocket and pulled out the three dollars, thinking that was a steep fare, but he had no choice. The attendant let him pass, and he urged the horse forward. Scout's hooves clicked over the wooden ramp.

Once on board, Solomon sat on a bench with his right knee bouncing up and down, eyes darting around to see if Father was approaching. Almost an hour passed before the boat was ready to leave the dock again. Solomon prayed fervently they would cast off soon. The longer they remained at the dock, the higher the chance that Father would show up. He glanced around the deck to see if there was a place to hide himself, just in case. Desperate to avoid a public scene, he sat on the other side of the wheelhouse and hoped Father would never spot him. His anxiety built.

He reached into his bag for a piece of cheese and popped it into his mouth, wondering how his mother would make the trip. He longed to be with her, but Father had made that impossible.

At last, all the passengers were on board, and the attendant raised the ramp. The ferry steamed away, heading into the deeper waters of the Sound. Black puffs belched from the smoke stack. Solomon was on his way at last, satisfied that Father didn't know where he was for the first time in his life. He relaxed and turned his face to the sun with a smile.

A variety of travelers mingled around the deck. Solomon was naturally timid, so he enjoyed retreating inside his thoughts, imagining why each person was on the ferry and where they were going. It was a game he played alone.

He spotted a young man about his age, dressed in laborer's clothes, hands rough with toil. The man had dark hair and a ruddy face. He was somewhat taller than Solomon. *Probably about six foot two,* he estimated. *I wonder where he's going. Maybe he has a job in New York.*

He shifted his attention to two women traveling together. They wore lace-trimmed linen dresses and carried silk parasols to protect their delicate skin from the sun. Their elegant hairstyles and the tilt of their chins betrayed their privileged status. Solomon presumed they were traveling to New York on a shopping expedition. A tall, well-dressed man in charge of their luggage joined them at the ferry's rail. *Ah, he must be their chaperone.*

An elderly couple sat on a bench at the side of the ferry. They held hands, chatting and giggling together. The plump little wife made liberal use of hand movements to help describe what she was telling her husband. Her white hair was pulled back in a bun, with stray wisps trailing at the sides of her wrinkled face. The white-haired gentleman held his cane with a trembling hand. They appeared to be having a great time together. Solomon's heart warmed at the sight of them. He hoped he would someday find a wife who would suit him like this gentle lady suited her husband.

Despite his angst, Solomon needed to get travel information from someone. The young man in dungarees—the one he noticed first—might be more approachable than some of the other passengers. The fellow stood at the rail, looking over the side. Solomon tied Scout to the rail and shuffled casually toward him.

"Nice day, isn't it?" he asked to see if the man was willing to converse.

"That it is."

"Do you know anything about transportation out of New York? I'm on my way to the middle of Pennsylvania, but I don't know how to get there."

The young man's eyes widened. "You got quite a trip ahead of yourself, sir." He extended his hand. "I'm Jacob Bishop."

Solomon shook his hand. "Solomon Hawk. Yes, I have quite a trip and very little money to get there. Any advice?"

Jacob gazed off into the distance as if pondering the possibilities. "I ain't been too far past New York, but I know there are three ways to get out of the city. You can either take a train or go on horseback, or you might be able to find a horse-drawn coach. A single traveler on horseback would need a pistol to defend himself from highwaymen."

Solomon shook his head. "I don't have a pistol."

19

Jacob continued. "The coach would take longer than the train, but it would be more comfortable. I've talked to people who've been on the trains. They tell some pretty bad stories. Fifty or sixty people packed in a car at one time, cooking their food on the train's heaters. They're overwhelmed by bad smells and soot from the engine. I couldn't recommend that for a gentleman such as you."

"If I could save days on the road, the train may still be my best choice," Solomon said. "My grandfather is dying. I don't want to miss being able to say goodbye to him."

"Your decision, of course, sir. I'm just telling you what people say . . . and I'm sorry about your grandfather."

Solomon nodded. "I shouldn't have brought my horse if I'm going to travel by rail or coach." Solomon worried that he had made a thoughtless decision.

The breeze blew through Jacob's hair, ruffling it. "If I was you, I'd find somebody to sell your horse to, seeing as you're short on scratch."

Solomon clapped Jacob on the back. "Fine idea, sir!" he said. "I'll miss him, though. He's a good horse. Say, do you need a horse?"

"Not now. I'm just as tight on dollars as you."

The two of them gave each other a wry grin and sat on a bench together, now feeling a sense of camaraderie.

"So, Jacob, what's your business in New York?"

"I don't have any business yet, Solly. I'm looking for work."

Solomon smiled at the familiarity with which Jacob addressed him. No one had ever given him a nickname before.

"You look like you've been working already. I see by your hands that you're no stranger to hard work."

Jacob self-consciously shoved his hands in his pockets. "Oh, that's in my Pa's blacksmith shop. My older brother will take over the smithy when Pa's too old to work. They don't need me there. And I'm looking to get away from Connecticut. My Pa wants to run my life, but I need to stand on my own and be a man. It's time I took on a man's responsibilities and fended for myself. I'll stay in touch with them by letter. And who knows, I may go back to the smithy someday, but right now, I want to get out there and prove myself . . . to me."

Solomon drew back in amazement. "Your story sounds just like my story, Jacob. Yesterday morning, I graduated from Yale College, and my father insisted that I work with him, but I can't bear the thought. As you say, I have to break loose and prove myself . . . to me." He paused for a moment. "But as soon as I got home from the graduation ceremony, we got word that my grandfather is dying in Lewisburg, so I need to get there as soon as possible. I want to be with the family, but Father won't allow me to go with him and Mother. He's angry that I refused to preach on Sunday as he demanded."

"What? You're a preacher?"

"I'm trained to be a preacher, but no, not really. I just graduated from Divinity School at the strong insistence of my father, but I don't want to be a preacher. I wanted to study architecture at the University of Illinois."

Jacob slapped his knee as if that were the funniest thing ever. "Here I am making friends with a preacher who doesn't want to be a preacher, and he's defying his Pa, the same as I am!"

Solomon grinned. "Well, you're a blacksmith who doesn't want to be a blacksmith. We have quite a bit in common, don't we?"

"Yes, I guess we do."

The two continued their journey shoulder to shoulder, swapping stories and taking in the passing scenery. After a couple of hours of talking and laughing together, Jacob spoke up. "I'm heading to New York to get away from home, but that's not where I want to settle. It's too crowded there. And I know we just met, but we seem comfortable. Would you like some company on your trip as far as Philadelphia?"

Solomon's face broadened into a smile. "Say, that might be a good idea. How about this? Since we've just met, we'll take it a little at a time. If we don't get on well, or if you want to take more expensive transportation than I can afford, we'll just part company at whatever point with no hard feelings. Would that work for you?"

A good-natured smile crossed Jacob's face. "That sounds fine. We'll go on together until one of us doesn't want to anymore or can't afford to anymore."

Solomon shook his companion's hand as if they had just made a major business deal. "It will be good to have someone to travel with."

The two young men stood at the rail, gazing into the water, watching the waves slap at the hull. They enjoyed the late afternoon, mesmerized by the constant whop, whop, whop of the paddlewheel.

After a five-hour trip, the boat pulled into the dock at New Rochelle. It was evening, and Solomon remembered he hadn't eaten anything since breakfast except for the vegetables and cheese he'd shared with Jacob. He was hungry but unfamiliar with his surroundings. Where could he sell his horse? Where could they get something to eat at a reasonable price? Where could they find safe lodging for the night?

"Jacob, we need to buy cheap food somewhere and find a place for the horse."

"I've been here before," Jacob replied. "A couple of blocks away, there's a stable where you can put up your horse for the night. I remember seeing an inn not too far from that. If it was earlier in the day, we could get food from a street vendor, but it's too late now. They've all gone home."

"You lead the way," Solomon said, thankful he was with someone with travel experience.

The two plodded up the hill toward the stable and led Scout in. The stable master was there with his young son, who shoveled hay in the stalls, but they were about to leave.

"Hello," said Jacob. "My friend here wants to put up his horse for the night."

"That's a dapper-looking horse, and we just happen to have a spot for him," the stable master said. He named a price and agreed to groom and feed him, all included.

"Actually, we're looking to sell him," Jacob remarked. "Would you know anyone interested in a fine horse like this?"

Solomon stood by, learning for the first time how to transact business.

The stable master changed his tack. "I might. But he looks a little long in the tooth. How old is he?"

Solomon's face fell at the negative comment, but Jacob didn't let it bother him. "We're not sure how old he is, but you can see he's well-nourished, cared for, and strong. He would make a good horse for someone who needs to get around town."

Solomon didn't know what a horse was worth, so he held his tongue while the dickering began. Jacob ventured a price, and the stable owner offered a lower price. The two went back and forth until they agreed on fifty dollars for the horse and twenty for the saddle. "Does that sound acceptable to you, Solly?"

"Yes, I'll agree to that," Solomon said. Whatever he could get would help with his trip, and if he tried to do the deal alone, his ignorance would make it impossible to get the best price. He was grateful for Jacob's ability to take charge of selling the horse. So far, Jacob was a godsend.

He unstrapped his valise from the saddle while the stable master pulled some cash out of his money belt. Solomon took his payment and patted Scout's nose for the last time. "Have a good life, boy," he said. He turned his head so his friend wouldn't see the moisture in his eyes.

Jacob put a hand of warning on Solomon's arm. "Count that money before we leave here. Make sure it's right." So Solomon counted it and confirmed it was correct.

He thanked the stable owner, and the pair took off on foot for the nearby inn.

***

The weathered sign overhead read 'The Hornsby Hotel' in gold leaf. The two men stepped inside the dim lobby where whale oil lamps flickered on tables. The walls were paneled with dark walnut wainscoting below pale flowered wallpaper, and a worn rug covered the floor. Through a side door, patrons lingered over a late dinner and a drink in the dining room.

"We'll reserve our lodging for the night before they run out of rooms," said Jacob, "then we'll eat."

They stepped up to the front desk.

"Two rooms, then, gentlemen?" the manager asked.

"One room, please."

Solomon turned to Jacob in surprise. "Are you sure?" he asked. "We would be more comfortable in two rooms."

"You said you were short on cash, Solly. But if you want a room by yourself . . ."

Solomon reconsidered. He guessed they could try it once. Since he

23

didn't know Jacob that well, he would have to guard his cash. "Let's get one room tonight. We'll find out if that works for us."

He was fully aware he was taking a risk with a relative stranger. He worried he was being foolish to save a bit of money, but stuck to his decision.

"That'll be two dollars," the manager told them. Each man took a dollar from his pocket and paid for the room. Solomon's hand quivered nervously as they signed the register.

"There's a bath down the hall," the manager said. "You each have fifteen minutes at a time out of courtesy to our other guests."

"Thank you, sir. Now, Jacob, let's get some dinner." Solomon said.

The front desk clerk waved them toward the side room. "You'll find hearty food in there, but the kitchen closes in half an hour."

***

The hotel's dining room also served as a gathering place to get a pint of ale. Bar stools were lined up at the long wood bar. The bartender was busy polishing glasses and serving drinks from the tap. Solomon and Jacob were greeted by the odor of stale cigar smoke and the malty scent of ale.

Eleven tables, each with matching chairs, were arranged on the main floor. Each table wore a white tablecloth and bore the dripping stub of a candle in a pewter holder.

A waiter led Jacob and Solomon to one of the tables and placed menus before them. Jacob's brow wrinkled at the confusing array of choices. He whispered, "I ain't never been in a restaurant before, Solly. I don't know how to order. Can you do it for me?"

"Of course." He scanned the menu. "Here we are, Jacob. Would you like chicken, steak, pot roast, or ham?"

"What's the cheapest?"

"Hmm. Looks like the chicken."

"Chicken it is."

When the waiter returned, Solomon ordered two chicken dinners with potatoes, buttered corn, and green beans with tea.

"This place is too fancy for me," Jacob whispered. "I don't think I fit in.

Just look around. It's so dark here they have to put candles on the table so you can see your food. And these chairs ain't like the plain wood ones back home. They're *padded*." Jacob scanned the room, marveling at one impressive feature after another.

Solomon eyed him with an amused smile.

"And look at that, Solly. Someone waxed up that floor 'most like a mirror. It's a wonder people ain't sliding onto their bums. How did they get that floor so shiny?"

"I don't know the answer to that, but I'll pay for your meal tonight in appreciation of your arranging the sale of my horse," Solomon said.

Jacob brightened. "Thank you. Much obliged."

The waiter brought linen napkins and cups. He poured the tea, offering them sugar and cream.

"Jacob," said Solomon in low tones, "we should enjoy this meal to the fullest. It may be some time before we get another one like it."

"We won't starve, Solly. There's ways of getting food. But that's still good advice."

After their meal, Jacob was surprised when Solomon left extra money on the table.

"What did you do that for?"

"It's called a 'tip.' The waiters aren't paid much, so when you eat at a restaurant, you leave them a little extra money for themselves. They could never live on what the restaurant pays them."

"Sounds like a strange way to do business."

Solomon chuckled. "I agree. But that's the way it is."

With weary bones, they climbed the stairs to their room. Solomon slid the key into the lock and pushed the door open with a squeak of the hinges. They surveyed the accommodations. Solomon's face fell. They would have to share a bed, which he had never done, and there was no privacy to undress unless they went down the hall to the bathroom. This wasn't the best situation he had ever been in, but it would have to do for tonight.

Jacob chuckled at Solomon's discomfort. "It'll be alright, Solly. I'm used to sleeping with my brother. Done it since I was a kid." He pulled off his drawers and shirt and slid in under the sheets.

25

Solomon took his valise to the bathroom, washed, and changed into a nightgown. He didn't think Jacob would steal from him, but he tucked his paper money under the drawstring of his underwear for the night and stashed the coins in the valise under his side of the bed. Then he knelt in prayer, thanking God for putting Jacob in his path but praying for protection from him in case he would prove dishonest.

As Jacob snored, Solomon took his security measures. He blew out the lamp and slipped into bed with his back to Jacob, hoping to get some sleep before tomorrow's adventure. But that was not to be. His mind raced.

First, he worried about how to reach his destination. Then, a hopeful thought formed in his head. Away from his father's grip, he began to revive his dream of attending architecture school. The idea took root in his mind, and he toyed with the possibility. As long as he had defied his father, he might as well go the whole way and continue to Chicago after seeing Grandfather. He couldn't imagine how to finance his dream, but his heart throbbed with excitement at the possibility. He breathed a prayer, asking for God's direction.

Chapter 5: Heading to Philadelphia

Sunday, June 1, 1879

Both young men were accustomed to early rising, Solomon to his classes and Jacob to his anvil. This morning was no exception. Jacob tossed his clothes on while Solomon dressed in his usual meticulous fashion. Breakfast in the restaurant was impossible since it was closed in accordance with the Sunday Blue Laws. The young men were obliged to find something to fill their stomachs elsewhere.

They struck out on foot, strangers in a city with rows of three- and four-story buildings towering over them on unfamiliar streets. The shops were all closed, but a few men loitered about, leaning on brick walls, sitting on the sidewalk, and following the pair with their eyes. Solomon shivered under their gaze despite the June warmth.

He found it strange not to attend church on a Sunday morning. This was the first time he could remember missing church for anything other than illness. He whispered a prayer asking the Lord for forgiveness.

"Jacob, do you have any idea where we should go next and how we should get there?" Solomon tried to recall the maps in his geography texts, wishing he had paid more attention to them.

"I'm not sure. I hear tell there's a turnpike between Philadelphia and Lancaster, but I don't know if that would get you to where you want to go." Jacob said.

"Do you have any idea how we should travel?" Solomon thought how foolish it was that a Yale graduate didn't know more about geography and transportation. Horseback and ferry were the only modes of travel he had known, other than his father's carriage.

Jacob shrugged. "I don't know. Let's walk down to the docks and talk to the travelers. We'll find someone down there who knows more than we do."

They grabbed their satchels and walked downhill to the water. Solomon, the more bashful of the two, was at a disadvantage. It was his nature to shy away from people as much as possible. *It would be a real blessing if Jacob would take the lead,* he thought. *Jacob seems comfortable talking to people, and he's a natural at turning on the charm.*

They spotted a well-dressed gentleman walking toward a boat with his trunk, and Jacob asked if he had time for a question.

"How can I help you?" the man said with a pleasant smile.

"You look like a man familiar with travel. If you were going to Lewisburg, Pennsylvania, how would you get there?"

"I don't know where Lewisburg is. That's a new one on me."

Solomon spoke up. "It's in the center of the state."

"Ah, that's a long trip. Depends on how much time you have. If it was me, I'd go southwest to Philadelphia. All the transportation runs out of there. You'll have to go through the Bronx to Trenton, New Jersey, and then to Philadelphia. You can get to Trenton by train or on the stage. The train station is five blocks from here. That's your fastest way to go, but if you prefer the stagecoach, it's two blocks past the train." The man pointed down the street.

"Thank you, sir, that's very helpful," Jacob told him.

"Oh, and once you get to Trenton, you can either go by train or catch a ferry down the Delaware River to Philadelphia."

"That's valuable information. Have a good trip, sir."

"Same to you." And the man continued on his way.

Jacob turned to Solomon. "We know what we have to do now. Let's go check out that train fare."

As they hiked toward the train station, Solomon said, "I appreciate your talking to that fellow and getting the information we need. You don't know how I hate talking to strangers. It was just some quirk that made me feel comfortable talking to you on the ferry. The hand of God, that's what that was."

"I don't know if God had anything to do with it," responded Jacob, "but it was a bit of good luck for me, too. You knew how to order a meal in that restaurant, and you knew to leave a tip. I would have been in a tough spot without you there."

Solomon chuckled. "I guess we have talents that complement each other."

Jacob stepped over a crack in the sidewalk. "I don't know what that means, friend, but it sounds like a good thing."

They continued walking, looking like an odd couple but feeling like friends.

***

Next to the train station, they found a farmer selling garden vegetables and other edibles from his wagon. They stopped to buy food for the journey, leaving there with a bag of bread, cheese, tomatoes, and jerky.

The train station was crowded with travelers headed in every direction. People of many descriptions milled about, several of them looking like they had nowhere else to go, looking like they spent time at the train station only to have a place to sit. Many of the occupants of the station house benches were unwashed. They wore patched clothing, carrying barefoot children and rag bags as luggage.

A few were of a higher social status, planning to travel in first or second class but uncomfortable in the train depot as if they didn't belong there. The general atmosphere was seedy and dirty.

The walls were covered with white shiplap paneling. A well-used brass spittoon sat in the corner. It was evident from the filthy, wet condition of the floor around it that it was the target of those whose aim was careless.

Solomon cringed at the conditions he found there. He trailed behind Jacob, worrying they might not be in time to say goodbye to Grandfather. His stomach tightened.

Jacob took no notice but strolled to the ticket window. "Friend, can you tell me the fare to Trenton and when the next train will leave?"

The clerk wore a green eyeshade visor like those used by telegraphers and accountants. He adjusted his spectacles and checked his schedule. "Yes, sir. The train leaves at 1:30 this afternoon. The fare is $3.50 for a Pullman, $2.25 for second class or a dollar and a quarter for third class. What'll it be?"

"I just needed that information. I'll confer with my friend and make a decision. Thank you. Oh, by the way . . . how long does it take?"

"With stops along the way, you'll spend all night on the train. It arrives at Trenton tomorrow morning at nine o'clock."

Solomon listened to the conversation, waiting off to the side, thinking this was the most distasteful place he had ever been. Jacob turned to him and said, "It's pretty high priced. I know you don't want to go third class. I can see it on your face. First class is three-fifty, and second class is two-twenty-five."

"I wonder what we should do."

"I'd suggest we go over to the stagecoach line and see what it costs to travel with people who use soap more often."

Solomon chuckled and picked up his valise. They began their short trek down the street.

The stagecoach office was more appealing. Ladies and gentlemen waited on upholstered benches for the coach to come in. Solomon nodded with relief. "This is more like it. I'll find a seat by the wall while you talk to the ticket agent." He carried their bags to a nearby bench and sat alone.

Jacob approached the ticket window. The agent was a short man with unkempt hair and a thin mustache.

"Excuse me," Jacob said. "How much is the ticket to Trenton?"

"$2.50 to Trenton, sir. We have two seats left on the next coach. It leaves in half an hour."

"When will it arrive in Trenton?"

"At 9:15 tonight. Would you like the ticket?"

"Not yet, sir. I need to talk to my friend. When does the one after that leave?"

"There's another stage tomorrow at the same time."

Jacob's heart sank. "Thank you. I'll talk to my friend." Deep in thought, he shuffled toward Solomon. He tried to keep a positive thought, but the news wasn't good, at least for him.

"What did he say, Jacob?"

"They have seats on the stage that leaves in half an hour. It's two dollars and fifty cents to Philadelphia. Would you like to go?"

Solomon pictured Grandfather lying in his bed. "I would. Let's go buy the tickets."

Jacob's eyes grew sad. "I can't afford the ticket. If I spend that much, I can't go any further." He hung his head. "It would be best for you if you went on without me. I know you need to get out to your family as soon as you can."

Solomon sucked in a breath. "I'd rather continue traveling with you. Let me pray about this for a few minutes. God will give me direction."

"Well, go ahead if that makes you happy, but I can't see that it will do any good . . . Wait, let me go back and talk to the ticket agent again. Be right back." He walked away while Solomon spoke to the Lord in his heart.

"Dear Lord, thank you for sending Jacob to help me. I ask for protection for both of us. But in the meantime, Lord, please help us get to Lewisburg quickly and within our budget. Somehow, someday, I'd like to repay Father for the horse and my tuition at Yale. And while you're at it, please protect Mother and Father as they travel."

He wished he could somehow find out if Mother and Father were behind or ahead of him. His dearest hope was that Father wasn't being too hard on Mother. Then Jacob returned.

"Solly, the manager wants to see you."

"The stage leaves in fifteen minutes."

"I know. But go talk to him. I'll stay out here."

"Watch our bags?"

"Sure."

Solomon had no idea what the manager wanted. He stepped over to the office.

"Please have a seat, sir," the manager said. "Now, the young man who was just in here—is he a reliable sort? I can see by your dress you're a man of quality, so I'm depending on you to tell the truth."

31

Solomon was taken aback. "I'm curious why you're asking me. Has he done something to make you mistrust him?"

"No, of course not," the manager said. "I ask for references from everyone who wants a job with the stage line."

Solomon stared at him with a blank expression. "He asked for a job?"

The manager was clearly impatient. "I can see this is a surprise to you. He's asking to be hired to ride shotgun on the stage. I don't want to hire a dishonest person or someone who may cause embarrassment for the stage line. I'll ask you again. Is he a reliable sort?"

Solomon grinned in amazement at Jacob's ingenuity in asking for work. "I can tell you that in the time we've been traveling together, he's been honest and has never tried to steal my money. He doesn't show any evidence of being a drinker. He's been helping me by making travel plans and giving me suggestions that make my journey more pleasant. I haven't known him long, but from what I have seen of him, sir, I can recommend him as an asset to the stage line."

The manager nodded. "On your say-so, I'm going to hire him. His timing was perfect. Our regular employee didn't show up for work today, and the coach is leaving in just a few minutes." He reached into his desk and retrieved a shaft of paper. "Please send the young man back in. You can purchase your ticket while I complete the paperwork for him."

Solomon stood and shook the manager's hand. He turned and entered the waiting room, motioning Jacob to return to the office. He laughed to himself. *Thank you, Lord.*

Stepping to the ticket agent's window, he handed over the two and a half dollars and pocketed his ticket.

Solomon lugged both bags outside. They bumped his legs as he trudged behind the other passengers: an older gentleman escorting two young ladies in stylish dress and another dapper gentleman traveling alone.

Coming from the office door, Jacob sauntered toward the coach with a wide grin, a shotgun in one hand and a mailbag in the other. He winked at Solomon and pulled himself onto the box at the front of the stage, leaving room for the driver.

Solomon chuckled and handed their bags over to be stowed in the boot at the rear.

The coach turned out to be a tight fit for travelers. It seated six, but Solomon was thankful there were only five. The tall man climbing into the stagecoach reminded him of his father. He was of the same age, dressed in a similar style, and removed his top hat. As soon as Solomon took his seat, the man placed his hat on the seat between himself and Solomon. Then he opened a book he had brought and began reading. Solomon was grateful for the barrier created by the top hat but wished he also had a book. Maybe he could pick one up in some store when they made a stop.

The young ladies settled on either side of their father on the forward-facing seat, their gloved hands folded in their laps and their eyes lowered. They were dressed in linen and lace, one in blue, the other in lavender. They both wore fashionable silk Gainsborough-style hats, one with a fabric rose attached to the underside of the turned-up side brim and the other ornamented with ostrich feathers. Sitting between them, their father was occasionally obliged to blow the tip of a feather away from his face.

Solomon gave a slight nod to acknowledge the man. He didn't want to invite conversation. He instantly regretted making eye contact with the fellow, who took it as a sign that Solomon would like to chat.

"I'm Gerald Schuster," the man said to Solomon, extending his hand.

"Solomon Hawk, sir. Nice to make your acquaintance." Reluctantly, Solomon shook his hand.

The man beside him kept his head down, reading his book through thick spectacles.

"How far are you traveling, Mr. Hawk?" Schuster inquired.

"To Lewisburg, Pennsylvania. My grandfather is dying." Solomon's heart ached to say that. He squirmed, trapped in this conversation. But he went along with it to avoid offending a passenger with whom he must spend several hours.

Schuster ignored his discomfort. "We're going to Chicago. My daughters are enrolled in finishing school there."

The young ladies raised their eyes to take a timid peek at Solomon.

"I'm sorry about your grandfather," Schuster continued. "Are you close?"

Solomon nodded, hoping that would be all he was required to say.

33

With a jerk, the coach pulled away from the station and rocked gently on its springs. The ladies picked up their fans and cooled their faces. Solomon thought it almost comical that when one did something, the other did it too, like two people sharing a single thought. He turned his head toward the window to conceal an amused smile.

The coach had little air movement from the windows. After a while, Solomon removed his jacket and prayed they would take a break soon. Facing the rear, he could only see where they had been, not where they were going.

The coach crossed a bridge over the Hudson River. Solomon craned his neck at the dark water flowing beneath them as the wheels rolled with a loud, hollow, rattling sound atop the wood planks.

They traveled through several small towns. The passengers listened to the rhythmic thumping of the horses' hooves pounding the dirt road. Dust rose and drifted into the coach. The travelers tried in vain to brush off their clothing.

Forested scenery flew by. Occasionally, the stage stopped to change horses. As the afternoon wore on, Solomon became hungry. He didn't know what he had done with the food they bought from the farmer. It was probably in Jacob's bag.

"It's getting toward dinner time," Schuster remarked. "Did you bring anything with you, Mr. Hawk?"

"We brought some food, but I'm not sure where it is right now."

"You said 'we,' but you're traveling alone."

"No, I have a traveling companion. It's Mr. Bishop, who's riding shotgun for the stage line. He was fortunate enough to get work to pay his fare."

Schuster snickered and leaned over one of his daughters, trying to look out the window. He strained to get a better look at Jacob. "That surprises me, sir. He doesn't look like a man of your social standing."

"No," admitted Solomon, "but he's honest and agreeable, which is more important to me."

Schuster muttered something in French, which Solomon recognized as "each to his taste." His opinion of Schuster dropped a notch.

"Father," one of the girls said, "I'm hungry. When can we stop for dinner?"

"I don't know, love. We'll have to be patient. The driver has a schedule to keep."

The coach bounced on, eating the miles across the uneven, rolling topography. Solomon's derriere rebelled against the hard seat, and his back ached. His thoughts turned to his parents. *I wonder where they are now. I wonder if they're ahead of me or behind me. I hope Mother is doing well.* Getting news about them would be impossible until he arrived at Grandfather Mayfield's house in Lewisburg.

The coach continued over the rough, hilly road to the next town. The weather had changed over the hours. A cool breeze blew in the windows, and the girls pulled their shawls around their shoulders.

At last, the driver called, "Whoa!" The carriage slowed down, stopping in front of a tavern where they could buy a meal and stretch their legs. The driver would change horses there.

"Forty-five minutes, folks," the driver called out. "Be back on the stage in forty-five minutes."

Schuster stepped out of the coach first, helping his daughters down. Solomon was next, followed by the mystery gentleman with the book. Jacob was already down from his perch, waiting for Solomon.

"I have our food in this bag, Solly," he said.

"Hang onto that," Solomon said. "I'll buy us a hot dinner in the tavern. There may come a day when there is no hot food available. We can use the jerky and cheese as snacks later."

"I'll pay for my grub this time," Jacob said, with enthusiasm in his grin. "I have enough money. And the driver will pay me for my work at the end of this trip."

Solomon clapped him on the shoulder. "As you wish, my friend. Let's go get some dinner."

Laughter, loud conversation, and clinking glasses greeted them inside the tavern. Young women tended the tables, taking orders and ignoring the local men who wanted to play slap and tickle. Their job was tricky, but Solomon said they did well with tips if they joked with the clientele without encouraging improper behavior.

Solomon and Jacob grabbed a table and received a menu. Solomon glanced at a neighboring table where Schuster sat with his daughters, ordering for them. They still weren't saying much. His eyes softened with compassion toward them, knowing what it was like to be under a father's thumb.

He and Jacob ordered ham dinners with fried potatoes, cabbage, and apple pie. Solomon was pleased that Jacob was more comfortable ordering for himself.

"I'd have a pint, but the driver advised me to take no alcohol on the trip," he confided. "I'll have one of those sissy cups of tea." He grinned.

Solomon took another forkful of his fried potatoes.

Jacob continued. "Say, those young ladies you're traveling with are easy on the eyes. Are they nice girls?"

"I wouldn't know," replied Solomon. "They're either repressed by their father, or they don't have a brain in their heads. They didn't say ten words the whole trip. And their father is a social snob."

"What a shame." Jacob finished off his cabbage and went for the dessert.

**

The passengers, having finished their meals, climbed back into the coach. One of the Schuster girls complained of a stiff back, but her father told her to hush. The taciturn man with the top hat boarded last, cleared his throat, and returned to reading. Jacob returned to his post beside the driver, and the coach lurched forward.

Solomon regretted not being able to buy a book, any book. Since he couldn't see where they were going from inside the coach, he was limited to side views as they passed fields and farms. Time dragged on and approached nightfall.

Mr. Schuster was clearly bored, too, and filled the coach with chatter to entertain himself.

"So, Mr. Hawk, are you married?"

"No. I just graduated from college and plan to travel, meet people, and experience the world. A wife isn't in my plans any time soon."

"That's a shame. There's nothing like a wife to make a man settle down and take responsibility."

Solomon gave him a thin smile. "I'm sure you're right."

"Now that you've graduated, what kind of work will you look for?"

"My father disapproves, but I want to study architecture at the University of Illinois in Chicago."

Schuster's laugh was derisive. "No wonder he disapproves. Anybody with half an imagination can put a house together. You don't need to pay a professional to tell you how to do it."

"*Chacun à son goût*," Solomon said, repeating the phrase Schuster had used to refer to Jacob. Then he bit his lip. He was sorry to have blurted out the first thing on his mind . . . but not sorry enough to apologize. Still, he didn't want to think of himself as a rude man. To his relief, Schuster pretended he didn't hear him.

"Why don't you take up something useful, like accounting, or medicine, or even farming? Those are honest professions."

Solomon shook his head. "I believe God created me to be an architect." He wished Schuster would stop talking. He was road-weary and irritated.

"So you're blaming the Almighty." Schuster snickered.

Trapped with a very unpleasant passenger, Solomon tried a different tack.

"Ladies, what are your names?"

Both girls raised their eyes as if surprised that someone was addressing them, not their father.

"I'm Lydia," said the one on the right, her eyes brightening.

The girl on the left squirmed and glanced at her father as if waiting for his approval to speak. He didn't respond.

She glanced back at Solomon. "Delores."

"Lovely names," he said. "What do you like to do in your spare time?"

Schuster spoke up and gave him a terse reply. "They follow domestic pursuits."

The girls resumed staring at their laps.

That ended the conversation, to Solomon's relief. He took advantage of the silence to retreat into his mind, wondering about his grandfather. Was he suffering? What was his mental state? Would he have the faculties to recognize Solomon when he arrived? His thoughts turned once more to his parents. He cringed at the thought of Father being too hard on Mother during their trip, especially since she was already under emotional stress.

He slouched over, leaning on the side wall of the coach, and napped.

They approached the Delaware River near Trenton as the sun dropped lower toward the tree line. "I wonder how we'll get across that river!" exclaimed Schuster.

The coach creaked to a stop. Jacob hopped down from his lofty seat and opened the coach door. "This is our Trenton stop, folks. If you're continuing to Philadelphia, you'll be crossing the river," he said, then turned to Solomon. "According to the stagecoach driver, the dock where the ferry comes in is a mile's walk north of here. The train station is just before that. We'll need to decide which one to take, but this is where we get off."

Solomon said a terse farewell to the Schusters, then turned to Jacob. "Have you been paid?"

Jacob grinned and patted his stuffed pocket. "Yes, the driver gave me an envelope."

The pair gathered their belongings and walked north along the meandering riverbank under overhanging trees. "Was it a good ride up there beside the driver?"

Jacob grinned. "Well, let's see. You paid for your trip, and I got paid to take it. I got to sit up top, where the view was grand, while you couldn't see ahead. And I had the companionship of a very agreeable driver while you were irritated by a boorish passenger. Of the two of us, I had the better deal by far."

Solomon nodded with a knowing smile. "It was by the grace of God that the stage line needed a shotgun rider today. You needed a paying job, so God delayed their regular employee somehow. That's the way He works."

Jacob rolled his eyes. "If you say so, Solly."

Darkness soon descended, and they lacked a lantern. Solomon's concern mounted. "Where can we find a place to sleep tonight? The sky is getting dark. I don't see any hotel within sight; in fact, I don't see any sign of civilization from here in the woods. Do you think we can get there without a lantern?"

Jacob's manner was calm and cheerful. "Probably not without tripping over tree roots and spraining our ankles in holes. Why don't we settle in here?"

"What?" Solomon couldn't believe his ears.

"Sure. I have a blanket rolled in my bag. We'll spread it on the ground, lay on top of it, and then cover ourselves with our jackets. In the morning, we'll wash in the river. We don't need any doors for privacy while we change clothes because there's no one around. Think of the money we'll save." He chuckled at the sight of Solomon's astonished face. "You've never done anything like that before, have you, Solly?"

Solomon took a deep breath and shook his head. "No, I haven't."

Jacob didn't wait for confirmation. He found a large, flat area behind some trees. He kicked away the sticks and stones and then spread his blanket. "Come on, sit here, and we'll eat the food we brought. It's almost bedtime, so we'll get a good night's sleep, take a nice bath in the morning, and be on our way. The ferry doesn't leave until mid-morning."

They munched on bread and jerky, talking about unimportant topics. Then Jacob stretched out on the blanket, put his jacket over his arms, and drifted into slumber.

Solomon sat in the dark with his back against the rough bark of an oak tree, listening to the sounds of the woods. Somewhere, an owl hooted while crickets and tree frogs kept up their constant buzz. In the distance, a train's whistle blew. Overhead, Solomon gazed at a crescent moon through the leaves and slapped at a mosquito. It was a clear night. A million stars glittered in the night sky. He was surprised he could enjoy the atmosphere of the woods. It was amazing what God had made.

Solomon resigned himself to the situation, which wasn't so bad after all, and crawled onto the blanket. He arranged some of his clothes as a pillow, covered his arms with his jacket, and dreamed he was a boy again, fishing with Grandfather.

Chapter 6: Rev. Hawk's Rough Start

Sunday, June 1, 1879

On Sunday morning, Rev. Hawk went to St. Matthew's Church early to prepare for the service and do a last-minute sermon review. He unlocked the carved wooden door and was greeted, as usual, by a heavy silence. He stopped to listen. *This is the only place in the world where silence is so profound it has an echo*, he thought.

As was his habit, his eyes swept the full view of the furnishings in the chancel. He so admired the magnificence and grandeur of it all! Why didn't Solomon share his love of this? The walnut communion table carried a hand-carved inscription across the front: "This do in remembrance of Me." He loved it all—the brass goblet and plate where the communion loaf would be placed, the brass candlesticks at either end of the altar table with tall beeswax tapers, the long walnut pews where the choir would be seated, and the polished pulpit where he ascended two steps and proclaimed the Word of God. He especially loved how the congregation hung on his every eloquent word.

He placed the round communion loaf on the plate and filled the cup with wine. The choir members arrived one by one, along with the music director. They dressed in their blue robes with white shawls fringed in gold. Entering the choir loft, they took their places under the large stained glass windows. The organist slid onto the bench before the great pipe organ, his feet feeling for their position on the pedals. He pulled the appropriate stops for the exact sound he wanted: diapasons, flutes, strings, reeds. He selected a wide range from the tiny two-foot flutes to the growling sixteen-foot diapasons. His hands hovered over the keys, and soft, worshipful music filled the sanctuary.

The parishioners began to arrive, and everything was ready.

***

At home, Emeline prepared for their long trip. She had a trunk packed with enough clothes for herself for a week. There was a larger Saratoga trunk filled with her husband's clothing, including hats and shoes, knowing he was very particular. He owned more shirts and shoes than most men, and everything needed to go. She had a satchel with foods that could be eaten with their fingers and several linen napkins that would serve them for a week.

She sat and waited for Geoffrey's return, her legs jiggling. They ate a quick lunch, and he struggled to get their heavy trunks into the wagon.

Geoffrey hitched the horses. That was when he discovered Scout wasn't in the stall.

"What happened to Scout?" he demanded of his wife.

"Solomon must have him. How else could he have begun his journey?"

The good reverend was off on another rant. "He's a thief! He stole one of my best horses."

"He's your son, Geoffrey. He has certain rights as a son. And you told him he would have to go by himself. What did you expect?" She was pushing the boundaries of what her husband would tolerate from her, but she was too stressed to care. He was always in a bad temper, no matter what she did. Her only concern at the moment was going to see her father.

To her amazement, Geoffrey sighed and spoke more gently than usual. "We need two horses for the wagon. I would have preferred to take the carriage. It's a more elegant mode of transportation, but we must take the trunks, so there isn't much choice. I also would have preferred to use Scout as one of the horses, but since he's not there, we'll have to use Sergeant. I'll see that Solomon returns the horse."

He helped her onto the wagon seat, and they pulled away from the house, expecting to be gone for two weeks.

41

"Do you have the route planned out?" Emeline asked. "Which way are we going?"

"We'll take the ferry to New York. From there, we'll head down to Philadelphia for the first leg of the trip. After that, I hope to leave the horses and wagon in the care of a stable and take a train the rest of the way. I don't know if a track has been laid to Lewisburg. If not, we'll have to figure out something else."

Emeline hesitated as a picture of her father as a younger man popped into her head. "I'm eager to get there, Geoffrey."

"Yes, I know, Emeline. We'll do the best we can."

The calm tone of his voice surprised her. It wasn't characteristic of Geoffrey. She wanted to talk to him about the way she felt. The parishioners confided in him, and he listened to them with sympathy, but the same privilege was never extended to her. She was afraid to start the conversation she longed to have, afraid she would chase his newfound calmness away and set him off again. Instead, she retreated inside her mind and concentrated on the clip-clop of the horses.

***

When they reached the docks, the area was crowded with people taking a stroll or catching the ferry for an afternoon excursion. Geoffrey tied the horses to a post. "Wait for me here," he told Emeline and approached the ferry attendant. The boat was in the dock with its gate down, passengers streaming onto the deck.

"Sir, I'd like to book passage for my horses and wagon," he said. "How much will that be?"

The attendant eyed his large wagon and two horses. "I'm sorry, sir; you can see there isn't enough room for your rig with all these people on board already."

"But this is an emergency. I'm Rev. Geoffrey Hawk of St. Matthew's Church," he said, assuming the man would recognize him. "My wife's father is dying, and we need to get to Lewisburg, Pennsylvania, as fast as possible."

"I'm truly sorry about your wife's father, Reverend, but you can still see it's impossible. These people have already paid their fare. I can't tell them to get off now. My only suggestion would be to leave your wagon and horses here and bring your wife and luggage aboard. That would be one dollar each."

Geoffrey caught his breath. He hadn't anticipated difficulty this early in the journey. "Let me consider our options," he said. "How soon do you leave the dock?"

"We're heading out in about forty-five minutes. Your other choice might be to wait until tomorrow and take the next ferry or continue to New York in your wagon. There's a barge that crosses the Hudson."

Geoffrey trudged back to the wagon, deep in thought. "Emeline, we have run into a snag. They don't have room on the ferry for our wagon and horses. They can take us and our luggage. Our other choice would be to wait until tomorrow—"

"No, Geoffrey, please! I can't wait another day! Father has been near death for two days already." Emeline's hand flew to her chest, and near panic crossed her face.

"Well, you're not strong enough to carry one of those trunks, and I can't handle them both. If you want to be on our way today, our only choice is to proceed in the wagon."

"Then I would like to do that. Please, Geoffrey."

"Against my better judgment, I'll agree to it. Let's be off, then." Geoffrey turned the horses back to the road, leaving the ferry to go on without them.

"Thank you," Emeline said. "I'm too upset to wait. I need us to make progress—any progress at all. I would have lost my mind if we had delayed another day."

***

The horses pulled them down the road, out of town, past beautiful scenery. They took a route that followed the coast. When the ferry passed them, Emeline's stomach knotted up. *We should be on that ferry,* she thought. It was especially tough when they drove through Bridgeport, the point where they started. However, there were some pleasant moments.

43

As the occasional ship appeared at sea with its sails unfurled, Emeline managed a smile. What a lovely sight! The cool breeze and the sea foam on the gray-green waves rolling in created a peaceful feeling in Emeline's soul. God was still in charge, and her father was in His care.

They bounced along for several hours, resting the horses only as often as necessary. Emeline's back ached, and she was hungry. "Geoffrey, the next time we come to a town, we should stop and eat."

"I agree." Geoffrey put his hand over his gurgling stomach.

It was another hour and a half before they found a hotel where they rented a room for the night. The restaurant wasn't serving dinner following the Sunday Blue Laws, and no porters were on duty. Emeline spread their cold meal on the bedside table while Geoffrey dragged their small bags and the Saratoga trunk upstairs, gasping for breath.

"I thought that would kill me," he said, "but I couldn't leave our valuables out there for thieves."

"Come eat, Geoffrey." She gave him a napkin holding a piece of cheese, bread, and some raw broccoli. "I brought strawberries, too."

"I hope you brought plenty of this," he said. "It's been a long day." He sat on one side of the bed to eat. She sat on the other with her portion of food.

That evening, there was nothing else to do but bathe and go to bed. Fortunately, the hotel's guest list was short that night, so Geoffrey took his time in the bath. Emeline was next. She had just gotten into the tub when there was a knock on the door, and a male voice said, "How long are you going to be in there?"

Startled, her heart pounded. "Give me just a few minutes, please." She rushed through her bath, fearing that someone might come in. When she returned to her room, Geoffrey was asleep in bed.

Monday, June 2, 1879

In the morning, they rose before dawn. Geoffrey told Emeline he was going down the hall to the bathroom.

"Hurry, Geoffrey," she begged. "I know how you like to linger."

When he returned to the room, she had their clothes packed and a quick breakfast of finger foods ready. As he helped Emeline into the wagon, she asked, "How far do we have before we cross the Hudson River?"

Geoffrey estimated they had another three-hour drive. The morning ride was pleasant. He thought Emeline was becoming accustomed to the idea that her father may be gone when they arrived. She became quiet, only falling into depression and grief for short periods during the day. At other times, she was beginning to be more like herself. What a relief. He didn't know what to do with an emotional woman.

It was late Monday morning when they arrived in New York. They found an environment much different than what they were used to. New York was a city of almost a million people. Many poor immigrants from Ireland and Germany lived in tenements. Women strung wet laundry on rolling clotheslines between buildings. The men with jobs rushed here and there; the unemployed searched the streets for work or handouts. Others sat on barstools. The city had a general aura of decay, discouragement, and poverty. Crime was high, and Geoffrey was concerned about his attractive, well-dressed wife.

"I want you to stay close to me for safety," he said.

"You needn't have told me that," she said. "I don't care to be around strangers in the first place, but now I'm worried about the rough men in the streets, making catcalls and whistling. I'm not used to this element."

Geoffrey glanced furtively at some of the characters loitering nearby. He spoke with more confidence than he felt. "Stick close to me. I'll protect you."

They dropped their trunks off at the train station. Then they found the stable about a half mile away and pulled the wagon in. Geoffrey spoke to the stable master. "My wife and I are on an emergency mission to join her family out west. Her father is close to death," he explained, "but I can't take my wagon. Can we leave it with you until our return?"

The man glanced at Emeline and back at Geoffrey. "Sorry about her Pa. That'll be a dollar per horse daily. We'll feed your animals and keep their stall clean. Your wagon will be here when you get back."

Geoffrey grumbled about the price but paid a week in advance.

After the half-mile walk to the train station, they bought first-class tickets and had a short wait until it was time to board. The conductor, in his gold-braided uniform with matching hat, stepped off the train and called, "All aboooard!"

The response was immediate. Travelers waiting in the station stood and swarmed through the door onto the train platform like a colony of ants. Outside, the third-class passengers gathered their bags and small children. They crowded into the cars at the end of the train.

As the Hawks climbed the steps to board, they were jostled by passengers carrying bags and reading materials. But once inside their coach, they found comfortable seating. Geoffrey slid over beside the window to watch the scenery pass by. Emeline took the aisle seat next to him. They sank into their chairs with relief. The upholstery was plush, and the walls were paneled with expensive wood veneer. Brass lamps lined the walls at intervals for passengers desiring to read after sunset. The couple settled in for a two-hour ride.

Geoffrey glanced around the rich wood and brass first-class appointments with a satisfied smile. "First class is worth the ticket price," Geoffrey whispered into Emeline's ear. "We don't have to rub elbows with poorly-dressed people, listen to their coarse language, and smell those odors."

She lowered her eyes and folded her hands. "Doesn't God love the second and third-class passengers as much as He loves the first?"

Geoffrey's jaw twitched, and his frown turned surly. "Of course He does, but it's much harder for people to love them. We humans don't have the capacity of the Almighty to love everyone." He nodded, thinking that should set her straight. He ignored her frustrated sigh.

The train strained forward as the boiler built up steam pressure, belching smoke and soot, then picked up speed. The soot passed over their Pullman coach and drifted back to the third-class cars, where folks were packed in with little room for moving around. Geoffrey smiled, leaned back, and closed his eyes.

Chapter 7: A Night at the River

Monday, June 2, 1879

Jacob woke early in the morning and nudged Solomon, who was still dozing.

"Wake up, Solly. I'm going to the river to take a bath. When I come back, it will be your turn."

Solomon sat up and groaned as he stretched, feeling stiff from the hard ground. "I could use a cup of coffee, couldn't you?

"As soon as we get our baths, we'll head toward town. It won't be long until we reach a restaurant." Jacob walked to the riverfront, stripped down, and picked his way among the larger, flat stones into the water. Goosebumps raised on his skin. It was colder than he anticipated.

Solomon was busy selecting clean clothes for the day and rolling up the blanket. "How's the water, Jacob?" he shouted.

Jacob called back brightly, "It's just fine." He chuckled, imagining Solomon getting into the chilly water and gasping. The cold wouldn't have been so penetrating if it weren't flowing so fast. Jacob crawled out of the water, patted himself dry with his dirty clothes, and then put on his clean ones.

"It's your turn, Solly." He clambered up the grassy bank and returned to their makeshift campsite.

Solomon laid his clean clothes over his arm. "Remind me to buy a bar of soap at the next general store we see." He walked to the river and stood behind a large tree. With his eyes darting about for any sign of someone

47

approaching, he removed his clothing self-consciously. He entered the water with a hearty splash and a gasp. "It's cold!" he screeched.

Jacob chuckled with satisfaction. *I shouldn't get such pleasure out of fooling him like that,* he thought, *but he needs to be toughened up.*

Solomon dressed and rejoined Jacob, still shivering from the chilly water. He wagged his head. "I know you didn't ask, but I forgive you, Jacob."

Jacob responded with only a chuckle.

Soon, they were dressed, packed, and on their way to the train station. Jacob would rather go by coach, but knowing Solomon was pressed to get to Lewisburg, he was willing to take the train.

It was a pleasant walk, listening to the birds chirping and enjoying the bright blue sky through the treetops.

"I know you wanted to travel with me only as far as Philadelphia," Solomon said, "but I'll be sorry to part company. What are your plans after that?"

Jacob grinned. "I've been thinking about that. Would you mind if I just continued with you? I enjoy your company, and I don't have any particular plans."

Solomon's eyes lit up. "That would be fine with me. But no more ice-cold baths. Agreed?"

Decision made. The two would be going on together. Solomon's steps seemed more energized.

***

The streets and sidewalks became busier as they approached the Trenton train station. Just beyond the station, Jacob spotted a general store, so they stopped to buy breakfast food and a bar of soap for later. They purchased their train tickets, rested on a park bench across the street, and ate breakfast.

At 9:30, a long whistle blast announced the approach of the train they would take to Philadelphia, so they gathered their belongings and moved to the boarding platform. Passengers stepped off the train and disappeared into the crowd. Then, it was time to board. Solomon and

Jacob had decided to compromise between comfort and price. With second-class tickets, they settled into their seats for the ninety-minute ride to their destination.

They still didn't know what to do after reaching Philadelphia. Aware of Solomon's urgency to get to his grandfather, Jacob feared they might have to part company. He didn't have enough money for another train ticket. Solomon sat with his eyes closed and head bowed. Jacob assumed he was praying and left him alone.

Who knows? Jacob thought. *He prayed before, and a miracle happened. Maybe there is a God. Maybe he has a pipeline to his God that I don't know about.*

Solomon opened his eyes and turned to Jacob. "Is this your first train ride?"

"Yes. This is amazing."

"Train is the way to go. Don't you agree? We pay a little more for tickets, but it saves having to pay for lodging for the extra days it would take to get there by stage."

"You could be right, but I admit I'm running short. I'll have to figure out where to get some extra money."

"We'll work it out." After a pause, Solomon turned to Jacob again. "I've been thinking about something, but I don't know if it would be possible."

"What's that?"

"After I see Grandfather, I'd like to travel on to Chicago and enroll in classes there. I want a degree in architecture. It's something I've always wanted to do, but I got interrupted by Father sending me to Yale. I don't know if I'm being foolish since I have no funds, but I believe God is urging me on, somehow."

Jacob's mouth dropped. "That's quite an ambition. What does an architect do?"

Solomon's eyes took on a sparkle. "They design buildings like houses, schools, hotels, anything that gets built. They put their designs on paper so the builder can build them to specifications. And they make an excellent living at it. I could expect to earn my tuition back in a year or two, and then the rest would be pure profit. I could work for another architect or set myself up in business in some city where a lot of construction is happening." He narrowed his eyes. "My big problem is the way I hate to talk to people. I wouldn't be any good at selling my services. I'd need to hire a guy to get my contracts for me. But once the deal was made, I could design beautiful buildings that would stand for a century." He stared into the distance with a grin, lost in his imagination.

Jacob gazed at his face with fascination. "Do you think your God could help with a project that big?"

"I'm asking Him. He says that if anyone lacks wisdom, he should ask of God, who gives freely. So, I'm asking for wisdom. And provision."

"Good luck with that, Solly. I'm still trying to figure out what I'd be good at and where I want to do it. There's nothing I have such a passion for. I envy you that." Jacob gazed out the window as the gently rolling hills went by. The trees wore their early yellow-green colors, just becoming darker summer green.

"Why don't you come with me, Jacob? You could find work in Chicago. It's a big city."

"Maybe."

When they arrived in Philadelphia, Jacob inquired at the ticket counter about the best way to Lewisburg.

"I'm not familiar with Lewisburg, sir, but there's a map on the wall over there." The agent pointed to the far wall. "You could work out how to get there by finding the town on the map and working backward to Philadelphia."

"Thank you."

Solomon and Jacob stood before the large wall map. It had been there so long it was curled and discolored at the edges. It took a few minutes before Solomon could locate Lewisburg, a small village. Once he found it, it showed no train track running near it. His heart sank.

"I had high hopes of reaching Grandfather's house by tomorrow, but I can see that will be impossible."

"Look here," Jacob said, his finger tracing a line on the map. "We could get to Harrisburg by train. That's a good-sized town. We may be able to find a boat on the Susquehanna River . . . is that how you pronounce that? It looks like a wide enough river that there would be boats. That would take us as far as this town up here . . . Selinsgrove. And that's only twenty miles or so from Lewisburg."

Solomon's eyes brightened. "I see what you're saying. We'll never make it by tomorrow, but maybe the day after. Let's get our tickets to Harrisburg."

Jacob swallowed, his heart sinking. "I'm short on scratch, Solly. I'll have to figure out how to get some cash. I guess you'd better go on without me."

Solomon sucked in his breath. "I don't want to do that, Jacob. You and I have been operating like a team this whole way. What one of us can't do, the other one can."

"I know, but you need to get to your grandfather. You can't wait while I earn enough to go."

Solomon searched his mind desperately, not wanting to part with Jacob. They had only known each other a few days, but they had a kinship Solomon had never known before. "Would you agree to a loan?" he asked. "I'll pay your way to Harrisburg, and then we'll try to find a way to get more money."

Jacob's face flushed with embarrassment. "I don't like to do that. I never borrowed money before."

"I only have this money because you sold my horse for me."

"It was your horse. Your money."

"I understand what you're saying. How about this—if you can't pay the loan back by the time we get to Lewisburg, I'll cancel the debt, and you'll owe me nothing."

Jacob's eyes dropped, and he scuffed the ground with his toe. "I don't like that, either. I like to pay my way."

Solomon pushed back his shoulders. "There has to be a solution. Let's go somewhere to get something to eat, and we'll work on a solution to this problem."

The two of them toted their bags down the street, looking for a place to buy some food.

As they walked past a bakery, the aroma of cinnamon wafted through the air. The apple fritters in the window caught Jacob's eye. "Look there, Solly. Those things look delicious. And look how big they are. We could get two of them for lunch."

Solomon nodded. "That would be quite a treat. I hope they keep us full until supper."

They stepped into the bakery and bought two fritters. Then, they found a bench across the street and enjoyed a sweet lunch washed down with water from Solomon's canteen.

"I'll bet the people waiting for a train wish they had something like this," Jacob said, licking his fingers.

"Yes, especially those women trying to control their children, running about the train station. I feel sorry for those ladies." Solomon took another bite of his pastry. The big, soft apple chunks in the sweet, cinnamon-flavored pastry were a delight. The two sat and filled their bellies until the pastries were gone.

"I have an idea," Jacob said with the hint of a smile playing at his lips.

"What's that?" Solomon leaned down, wiped his sticky fingers in the grass, and poured water on his hands.

"Those apple and cinnamon things were cheap enough. The people in the train station who don't have enough time to leave for something to eat—I'll bet they'd be willing to pay a little more to have the convenience of having food brought to them."

Solomon's eyes widened, and he grinned. "That would be worth a try. If we bought a dozen of those things and made a profit of twenty-five cents each, that would pay for your ticket to Harrisburg. And if we couldn't sell them all, we'd have them again for supper. Delightful idea. Let's go buy some fritters."

The two returned to the bakery, and Solomon purchased thirteen apple fritters, all the bakery had left. They hurried back to the train station. Solomon sat by the wall guarding their bags while Jacob walked the room, offering to sell the pastries. The scent of apples and cinnamon caught the attention of some of the hungry people. In ten minutes, he had sold all but one of them and earned enough to buy a second-class ticket to Harrisburg. Solomon and Jacob congratulated themselves and slapped each other on the back.

"Look what God helps us do when we stick together," Solomon said.

Jacob grinned. "Let's go buy our tickets."

They discovered that the next train to Harrisburg was leaving at two o'clock. They didn't have long to wait.

When they returned to their seats, Jacob broke the remaining pastry in two. "Here, eat this half. We don't want to carry a sticky fritter to our next stop."

***

A little before two o'clock, the conductor called for the passengers to board the train. Steam hissed and billowed under the engine, and the bells clanged. Solomon loved the conductor's snappy uniform and the scurrying of the porters as they stowed the luggage. He loved the whole train atmosphere.

They found seats in second class. "When do we arrive in Harrisburg?" Jacob asked.

"It should be about seven-thirty this evening after we make several stops. We'll have to find a hotel when we get there. Sleeping on the ground was fine last night, but my bones need a softer mattress."

They were both drowsy and drifted off into deep naps. Solomon roused first, then poked Jacob. "Wake up, man. You're snoring."

Jacob woke with a sheepish grin and scooted in his seat until he sat up straight. "Was I bothering the other passengers?"

"Just the angry lady behind us."

Jacob blushed and turned around. "Sorry, ma'am," he said.

She responded with a smile and a nod.

Jacob turned to Solomon. "How much longer until we're there?"

"Almost two hours."

The train rolled over the Pennsylvania hills. Often, the engineer sounded the horn in a long-long-short-long pattern as they approached crossings. Solomon loved that sound. He sat back in his seat with his eyes closed. Jacob sat by the window, enjoying the changing colors of the sky as the sun dropped in the west.

Since there were fewer towns on this leg of the trip, the miles seemed to fly by. It was near dusk when they arrived at the station in Harrisburg. The train's whistle sounded one long blast, the iron wheels screeched on the rails, and steam hissed from under the engine. The bell clanged. The two young men grabbed their bags and disembarked, looking around to get their bearings.

"Can you imagine traveling as many miles as we did today before there were trains?" Jacob asked in wonder.

Solomon laughed. "No wonder we're so tired. We've gone from New Jersey to halfway across Pennsylvania, all in one day."

"Look, Solly, there's a hotel down the street. Let's go there."

They began walking toward the hotel among the crowd of people leaving the train. Fearful they would not be able to get a room, Jacob urged Solomon to hurry.

Solomon had a better idea. "Look, I'll give you enough money for a hotel room; then I'll take both bags and free you up to run to the hotel."

Jacob agreed. Solomon fished a few dollars from his pocket and handed them to Jacob, who took off running. Solomon picked up both satchels and plodded toward the hotel, letting the crowd pass him. But the sign on the hotel door said, "Closed For Remodeling."

Solomon's heart sank. He searched the sidewalk for his friend but couldn't find him. Wait, there he was, ahead of him. "Jacob! Jacob," he called. The tall man with dark hair turned toward Solomon's voice, but it wasn't Jacob. Solomon had a moment of panic. How could they have gotten separated? There was another hotel in the next block but on the opposite side of the street. Maybe Jacob was there. Solomon picked up the two bags and made for the other hotel. His arms were heavy, and his back ached. It had been a long day. A crowd still surrounded him, some milling about the sidewalk, some walking toward the second hotel. They needed accommodations, too. He called Jacob's name as he walked but got no response.

When he reached the Barclay Hotel, he entered the lobby and sat in a chair to wait. A line of people queued up to register.

Jacob wasn't there.

One by one, the people got their room assignments and climbed the stairs. Several people were still in line when the front desk clerk said, "I'm sorry, sir. All of our rooms are full."

Solomon's breathing became fast and shallow. His hands trembled. There were no rooms available, and he still hadn't found Jacob. It was his fault. How foolish to suggest Jacob go ahead of him to get a room. They should have stayed together. What should he do? The last place he had seen him was on the way to the first hotel. Maybe he should go back there and wait. He stood, wrestled both bags again, and dragged them outside. If he could find his friend, Jacob would know where they could spend the night, even if it had to be somewhere on the ground.

He paced the sidewalk, scanning the crowd, his heart pounding. No Jacob. *I'd better go back to the first hotel and wait.*

He was so weary he didn't know if he could make it. He lifted both bags and started the walk back to the next block. Why couldn't things be easier? He was worn down physically and emotionally, still worrying about Grandfather. He had gone half the distance when he heard his name called.

"Solly," Jacob yelled, approaching from behind him. "Where have you been? I've been looking all over for you."

Solomon was so relieved he was giddy, not knowing whether to laugh or cry. The tension drained from his body. "Jacob. I was in a panic. I couldn't find you. Bad news: the hotel is out of rooms."

"That doesn't matter, buddy. I was almost first in line." Jacob held up the key. "We have a room on the second floor. Here, give me my bag. You don't need to carry both."

The two went through the lobby and climbed the stairs. The door with their room number opened to a spacious room with a soft featherbed.

Jacob stretched out on the bed, frowned, and sat up. "This sags in the middle. I'd never sleep if I had to lay here." He searched the bureau for extra blankets and made a pallet on the floor. "I'm sleeping here tonight."

Solomon, in his nightshirt, lay on the featherbed and found it was like the one at home. "I'm sorry this makes you uncomfortable. I'll sleep like a baby on it."

It was the best rest Solomon had since the trip began. But for Jacob, he had new thoughts in his head that excited him and kept him awake.

Chapter 8: Colonel McCreary

Tuesday, June 3rd, 1879

Solomon and Jacob woke before daybreak and hurried to pack their bags with little conversation. Solomon's mind was on his grandfather, but Jacob was fidgety and distracted.

Solomon paused in his packing. "Do you have something on your mind, Jacob?"

Jacob sat on the edge of the bed. "I had some thoughts, and I want to see what you think. This is just me thinking, you understand, and if it's crazy, I hope you'll say so with kindness."

Solomon's curiosity was piqued. "What could be so mysterious?"

"You said you want to go to architect school. How long would that take?"

"Three years."

"How would you support yourself all that time?"

"I hadn't thought that far. I know it wouldn't be easy."

"And what will you do when you become an architect? How are you going to sell your services?"

"I don't have an answer to that, either. I suppose I'll put some ads in the newspaper."

"Here's what I think. We're this far. After we see your grandfather, we could go on to Chicago." The words poured out of Jacob. "We could get an apartment together or stay in a boarding house. I would find work for three years to support both of us. Then, when you graduate and it's time to set yourself up in business, you could hire me to be your sales manager. I would go out and get business, and you would work, make a pile of money, and pay me a salary or a commission. We could work that out later."

Jacob's eyes were excited, and he was breathless after that speech. Solomon wore a smile. The idea captured his imagination. He swallowed as he gathered his thoughts.

"We need to ponder on this, don't we? There are so many ways it could turn messy, but if we went into it with clear heads and asked God for wisdom, it might work."

"It seems simple to me. How could it get messy?"

"We haven't known each other very long. What if, by the time we get to Chicago, one of us decides we don't want to spend three years with the other? What if we couldn't get work and ran out of money? What if one of us wanted to get married and move out of the apartment? What if you were unhappy with the amount I was paying you? And I still don't know how I would pay my tuition. That's a whole other question."

"I can see what you're saying." Jacob nodded.

"The other concern is, would you resent supporting me for three years? That doesn't seem fair."

"Look, Solly. Without taking this chance, my future is in a smithy, struggling to make ends meet. I would consider the three years an investment in a better life."

"I hadn't thought of it that way," Solomon said.

"If you prayed, would your God give you answers? He's bailed us out a couple of times already."

"Don't tell me you're beginning to believe in Him."

Jacob shrugged. "I can't deny your prayers change things unless those were just coincidences."

"They weren't. But so you'll know how I feel about your suggestion, it sounds like an ideal plan for both of our futures. We must keep an open mind and consider all the angles in advance. It's best to decide how to handle possible problems before one of us gets angry with the other."

Jacob chuckled.

"You know the first thing we have to do, Jacob, is get you a businessman's haircut and proper clothes."

"Hmm. I wonder what I'll look like in fancy threads." Jacob's eyes sparkled. "I'm happy that you're open to my plan. This will be good for both of us. It'll allow me to earn more money in the future than I could ever earn as a blacksmith or a longshoreman. This could be a way to earn real money and have a better life."

"And it gives me more time to work instead of trying to get contracts."

***

Downstairs, the lobby already bustled with guests checking out.

Solomon reached into his pocket. "I know you're short on funds, Jacob, and I still have some cash from selling Scout. I'll pay our expenses to Lewisburg. If we have to stay there for a while and earn some money, we can find work for a few weeks before we continue to Chicago."

Jacob blushed. "I would refuse to have you pay my expenses if we were only going as far as your grandfather's, but since we have longer-term plans, I'll make sure you're paid back when you're in school."

"This may work out just fine, Jacob." For a moment, Solomon retreated into his mind, thinking Jacob was the first friend he had ever been truly comfortable with. He had shared his dreams, and Jacob hadn't ridiculed him.

They checked out of the hotel. Next door, they entered the diner and received a menu.

"Flapjacks and coffee for me," Solomon said.

"Make that two."

After eating their fill, they walked to a general store two blocks away and bought soda crackers, cheese, and tomatoes. Solomon picked out a few pieces of hard candy to throw in.

It was a ten-minute walk to the dock where the steamboat to Selinsgrove waited. People were already aboard. Longshoremen loaded barrels of goods to be delivered upriver.

"I wonder what's in those barrels," Jacob said.

"I don't know about those particular barrels, but I know people ship all kinds of household goods. They also ship liquor. Lots of it."

Jacob laughed. "That's probably their best-selling item."

"Right. Let me tell you about a steamboat I heard about. It sank in the Missouri River when the hull got ripped open by a submerged tree. It was carrying tons of cargo. The crew worked furiously to offload the whiskey barrels while the thing sank. They managed to get it off, but the other cargo was lost."

Jacob chuckled. "I guess they had their priorities. Is that what you learned at Yale?"

Solomon grinned. "Education is a wonderful thing, Jacob."

The steamboat line sold tickets from a little shack at the river's edge. Jacob approached the ticket agent. "We'd like two tickets to Lewisburg."

"Sorry, sir. We don't go that far. Our northernmost point is Selinsgrove."

Jacob sighed. "Then we're going to Selinsgrove. We'll take two."

"Would you like on-board sleeping accommodations? Only five dollars extra."

"No, thanks." Jacob passed over the fare.

"The boat will leave as soon as the cargo is loaded. You can board now if you like."

"When will we arrive?"

"Since you're going upstream, this is a ten-hour trip, plus stops." We'll go part way today, spend the night at one of the stopovers, then finish the trip tomorrow."

Jacob's eyes cut to Solomon, who sucked in a breath. "Then that's the best we can do. Thank you, sir."

They took their tickets to the dock.

"I'm sorry we won't be able to get there today, Solly," Jacob said. His heart beat in sympathy for Solomon, who kept his head down. "I know you're disappointed. I hope your grandfather can last another day."

"We don't know if he's alive even yet," Solomon said. "I might have missed him already."

They crossed the long dock over the muddy riverbank to board the steamboat. It was small as steamboats go, with only two passenger decks. The rails were decorated with wooden scrollwork painted white. The red paddlewheel at the rear gave the boat its distinctive silhouette on the water. Tall black smokestacks stretched toward the sky near the bow, but Solomon was too disappointed to enjoy it.

"I can't stop thinking about Grandfather," he said with a frown. "I don't know if he's still alive. I so want to tell him goodbye before he goes and hear his voice one more time. I do love that man."

Jacob put a hand on Solomon's shoulder. "You should talk to your God about it, Solly."

Solomon's head turned toward Jacob. He nodded. "You're right. I will."

They strolled around the deck. "You know," Jacob said, "traveling the river is a new experience for me. What do you think we'll see along the way?"

Solomon shrugged. "I don't know what we'll see, but I'm disappointed there's no steam calliope. They say the showboats on the Mississippi River have calliope music as they travel."

"More of your education, I suppose. I never heard tell of a calliope."

Jacob's quip was intended to help lift Solomon from his melancholy but only drew a thin smile from him.

The pair took their bags and found comfortable benches overlooking the rails on the upper deck. They chatted and enjoyed the scenery as the great paddlewheel fought the current to make progress upriver. The muddy water swished along the sides of the boat. Crates of cargo were stacked here and there, and other passengers strolled the decks or leaned on the rails.

An older gentleman with a well-trimmed white beard and lively blue eyes sat on the bench beside theirs. He held a walking stick, which he placed between his feet and rested his hands atop the brass cap. Jacob turned his head toward the man. "Pleasant day for river travel, isn't it, sir?"

The man turned his attention to Jacob. "Yes, it is."

Jacob extended his hand. "My name is Jacob Bishop, and this is my travel companion, Solomon Hawk."

"Archibald McCreary here." He shook Jacob's hand. "Where are you headed?"

Solomon's head swiveled around. "Colonel Archibald Jackson McCreary?"

McCreary leaned forward to get a better view of Solomon. "Yes, sir. Have we met before?"

Solomon's eyes were now bright. "No, sir, but I've read about you. You designed that cantilever bridge across the Hess River."

McCreary grinned. "You're right. My reputation gets around more than I do. How did you come to know about my bridge?"

"I'm fascinated by the design process. Jacob and I are on our way to Chicago, where I intend to study architecture." His eyes sparkled.

Jacob nodded. "Sadly, his father disapproves, so he has a rough road ahead."

Solomon shot a glance at Jacob and then turned again to McCreary. "He does, but I intend to overcome every obstacle. I'm excited to get into design work."

Solomon was amazed at his courage in sharing so much with a stranger. His shyness had abandoned him at this rare opportunity, meeting a man of such accomplishment in the field he loved.

Jacob stood. "Trade places with me, Solly, so you can talk to Colonel McCreary without leaning over me."

The two traded seats while McCreary asked, "Why does your father disapprove?"

"For years, he's told me I'll go into the ministry and work with him at the church. He's a domineering man who expects to get his own way. But I've always wanted to be an architect."

"The ministry?" McCreary chuckled.

"Yes, I just graduated from Yale on Friday. But my grandfather is dying in Lewisburg just north of here, and I hope to say goodbye to him before he passes away." He hesitated, and his voice lowered. "I hope I get there in time."

McCreary's features softened in sympathy. "I hope so, too, son. But let me talk to you about architecture. I didn't take that route; my credentials are in civil engineering, and I make a very good living at it. Architecture is a related field and an honorable profession. If you're good, you can make your mark on the landscape wherever you work. You can build a good reputation and earn a very comfortable living. If you asked my advice, I'd tell you to go to the University of Illinois and work hard. That's the best school you could choose to study architecture."

Solomon listened with rapt attention. "How should I try to get my start in business? Should I hire on with someone else's architecture firm?"

"There's more than one answer to that question. If you get on with a firm with an excellent reputation and use it as a springboard for your own business, that's one way. But if you have confidence in your ability and a knack for attracting clients, I recommend opening your own office. That way, you rise or fall on your own. That's the best way to learn."

Jacob interjected a comment. "We plan to work together. I can sell anything to anybody, so I'll be in charge of getting the contracts."

McCreary nodded. "That would give Mr. Hawk more time to work." His attention turned back to Solomon. "You still need to socialize and meet people at parties and business events. If someone knows you personally, and at some point they decide they need an architect, you'll be first on their list."

Solomon nodded. Jacob poked his arm. "He's right, Solly. We can attend events together, so we both make contacts."

"Out of curiosity, sir, what are you doing on a steamboat on the Susquehanna River?" Solomon asked.

"It's a coincidence that I'm here talking to you," McCreary said. "If you know my work, you know I've spent a lot of time on the Hess River. Well, I was passing through this area and had a couple of days to spare. I thought I'd take a pleasure trip on an unfamiliar river to compare to the one I know so well. This river is more peaceful, and the scenery is greener. It has more foliage and fewer boulders on the shoreline than the Hess. This is a real treat."

"Oh, look over there," said Jacob, pointing to a barefoot boy on the shore pulling a fish out of the water. "Looks like he caught himself a decent supper."

McCreary chuckled. "Maybe his name is Tom Sawyer."

The young fisherman turned his head to watch the steamboat passing by and waved. They waved back. In the rear of the boat, the paddlewheel creaked and turned, and water sloshed over its blades. The sound was at once comforting and mesmerizing.

McCreary asked, "Do you plan to enroll for the fall semester?"

"Yes," said Solomon. "I don't know where I'll get the funds, and I don't know if they'll accept me. But that is my plan. And there will be more confrontations with my father, but Lord willing, I'll be able to stand up to him."

"Listen, young man. I can see in your eyes that architecture is your passion. Don't abandon that. You stay true to what God has placed inside you. This growing nation needs good architects. You can stand up to your father respectfully without giving in to him."

"Thank you for that advice, sir. I'll remember it when Father turns on the pressure."

"I have an acquaintance at the University. Find me on the boat again tomorrow. I'll try to claim this same seat, so look for me around here. I'll write a letter of introduction for you. You said your name is Solomon Hawk, right?"

Solomon's heart pounded. "That's right, Colonel. I can't thank you enough. That means more than you can know."

Overhead, birds cawed to each other, dipping and swooping.

McCreary stood and leaned on his walking stick. "And one more bit of advice. Don't stick to the tried and true if you have a better idea. Always try to imagine how something can be done better. Then, be adventurous enough to float your ideas to clients and let them decide. But if you do that, be dead certain your plans will hold up, just in case they go for it." His look was intense. "Do you understand me?"

Solomon returned his steady gaze. "Yes, sir, I do. Thank you."

"Good. I'm going to my cabin now, which I paid for in anticipation of an afternoon nap. Old men have their habits, you know."

"Rest well, sir."

"And you find me tomorrow, Mr. Hawk. I'll have that letter for you to take to Chicago." He turned and walked away, his walking stick tapping along the deck.

Solomon turned toward Jacob. "Can you imagine the odds of that happening? That man is the best engineer in the country. He's invented all kinds of things and built things no one dreamed of before."

"Yes, and he's taken an interest in you. I swear, you have the best luck," Jacob said.

"That wasn't luck. That was providence. That was what my Yale professors called a divine appointment. A meeting arranged by God." Solomon lifted his eyes skyward and whispered a prayer of thanks before leaning back to watch the scenery on the shore.

That evening, they disembarked to find lodging. They found a hotel near the dock where they spent the night. Early in the morning, they boarded the boat again.

Wednesday, June 4, 1879

"We have several hours before we get to Selinsgrove," Solomon said. "Let's find Colonel McCreary."

They climbed the stairway to the second deck and worked their way through groups of other passengers to where they had last seen the aging gentleman. He wasn't there yet, and other people had already claimed their benches.

They dropped their luggage beside them and leaned on the rail, shoulder to shoulder, to watch what was happening below. The deckhand loosed the ropes from the cleats, and the great paddlewheel began to turn. Inch by inch, they chugged toward deeper water, smokestacks belching.

Passengers walked the deck behind them in both directions, ladies in colorful, full-skirted dresses with parasols and men in suits or work clothing. Other passengers occupied the benches along the deck. When one couple left their seats, Solomon poked Jacob.

"Come on," he said. "Let's grab that bench before someone else does." They took their places and didn't move until McCreary arrived about ten o'clock.

"Good morning," he boomed. "How did you sleep? I had a delightful sleep in my cabin."

"We slept well, thank you," Solomon said.

Jacob glanced at the bench next to them, occupied by a young couple. He stood. "Colonel McCreary, please take my seat. I'll stand by the rail."

"Thank you, son." McCreary took the spot beside Solomon. The two made small talk for a few minutes. Solomon had a powerful urge to ask about the letter but couldn't bring himself to seem pushy.

McCreary smiled. "I'm sure you're wondering about the letter. I'm an old man, but I remembered to do it." He reached inside his coat pocket and pulled out an envelope addressed to the Dean of the College of Architecture.

Solomon took it with a wide smile. "There are not enough words for my gratitude, sir. This letter may open doors that might have otherwise been closed."

"I left my address in there. If that letter isn't adequate, contact me and let me know what you need."

"I will take you up on that offer if necessary. Again, thank you. I'm deeply grateful."

As Jacob stood by the rail, Solomon and McCreary chatted about various famous structures around the country and discussed which cities would suit Solomon after he got his degree. McCreary advised moving to a city undergoing a construction boom to get the best advantage.

Soon, the couple on the next bench got up and left, so Jacob took his seat there. After another pleasant hour, McCreary stood, wished them the best of luck in their new venture, and bid them happy travels.

Chapter 9: The Destination in Sight

The two young men scanned the shoreline ahead for any sign of a village. Selinsgrove couldn't be far. Solomon's energy level increased with the excitement of getting nearer Grandfather's house. When the steamboat rounded the final curve, Selinsgrove lay before them. Solomon cheered, throwing his arms in the air, and Jacob clapped him on the back.

"Almost there," he quipped.

They stepped off the steamboat onto the pier. A whitewashed wooden sign said, "Welcome to Selinsgrove." They trudged toward town with their possessions.

"Are you as tired as I am?" asked Jacob.

"I'm afraid so," Solomon said. "All this travel is catching up to me. It's almost twenty miles to Lewisburg. We'll either have to walk or find someone going by wagon. We could do five miles if we walked today, but our bags would slow us down."

"I'd rather not walk that far. Let's inquire at the general store," Jacob said. "Clerks talk to a lot of people during the day and know what's going on in town."

The Selinsgrove General Store was dusty and smelled of coffee beans. Once inside, the men approached the counter and dropped their bags to the floor.

"You gentlemen are traveling, I see," said the clerk. "What can I do for you?"

Jacob put on his best smile. "We're trying to get to Lewisburg as soon as we can. My friend here—his grandfather is dying, and he wants to see him before he passes."

The clerk nodded. "I'm sorry to hear the sad news."

"The problem is, we don't know how to get there. We came upriver on the steamboat, and we're now on foot. Do you have any advice? Do you know anyone going to Lewisburg willing to take passengers for a fare?"

The clerk rubbed his chin. "I could suggest my cousin Thaddeus. He might have some time to drive you there. It's a six-hour ride one way. I can tell you where to find him, and you can work out your deal with him."

Solomon's worried eyes lit up. "That sounds promising. We've been on the road for several days, so I don't even know if my grandfather is still living. I want to get there without delay."

"I hope he can help you," the clerk said. "He lives in the house behind the church. Go north three blocks. You can't miss it. His name is Thaddeus Grimes."

"Thank you, sir." Solomon and Jacob bought more food for the trip, not knowing if catching a ride with Thaddeus would work out for them. Then they hurried up the street to the church and found the house at the back.

A tall, thin man labored in his garden behind the house, his back bent to the sun. A ragged straw hat covered his head, and his hoe struck the dirt in a steady rhythm. He raised his eyes to see the two men approaching and wiped the sweat from his brow with his handkerchief.

"What can I do for you fellows?"

Jacob answered. "Your cousin at the general store said you might be willing to transport us to Lewisburg in your wagon for a fee."

A grin crossed Thaddeus' face. "I could take you there tomorrow. I'd have to stay the night, then return the following day."

Solomon's angst rose. "Please, we were hoping you could take us today. My grandfather is gravely ill, and I want to say goodbye to him before he dies."

Solomon's expression was so dejected that Thaddeus took pity on him.

"Even if we start now, it'll be late this evening before we get there. Is there a place I could spend the night?"

"You would be welcome to stay in Grandfather's barn with us."

They worked out a fee. As Solomon closed his eyes in relief, Thaddeus picked up his hoe and headed for the barn.

"Just in case we have to spend the night in the wagon, I'll put hay in the back. That may be more comfortable than the barn floor." Solomon and Jacob carried hay to the wagon while Grimes hitched up the horses.

"Climb aboard, boys," Thaddeus said. "This rig is headed for Lewisburg."

The boys climbed into the wagon and took seats on the hay bales. Thaddeus slapped the reins and yelled, "Hyaah!" The wagon jerked forward, then settled into a steady roll. Jacob and Solomon grinned at each other.

"We'll be at Grandfather's by tonight," Solomon said. His relief increased at the thought. "I wonder if Father and Mother are already there. I wonder if Grandfather is still alive." His joy of a moment ago faded, and he settled into a glum expression.

"Come on, Solly, let's enjoy the ride. There will be time to worry later."

"Give me just one more minute to worry about Mother. I'm certain her trip has been difficult, being Father's captive audience the whole way."

"It's not like you to be sour."

"You're right. I'm sorry. But you'll understand when you meet Father." Solomon stared into the distance and wagged his head.

"Are you boys doing fine back there?" Thaddeus asked over his shoulder.

"Yes, sir," Jacob answered.

Seeing that Thaddeus wanted to be a part of their conversation, they pushed their hay bales toward the front of the wagon to be closer to him.

The scenery as they drove was varied, with the river on one side and tall hills rising on the other. Wildflowers dotted the sides of the road. Grimes told them there was a dam ahead near Lewisburg. "Where are you boys from?"

Jacob said, "We're both from Connecticut. Solly here is a preacher, and I'm a blacksmith, but neither of us is happy with his lot. So after we visit his family at his grandfather's house, we're going to Chicago, where we plan to change our futures."

"That sounds ambitious. What's in Chicago for you?"

"Solly plans to study architecture at the University of Illinois. I plan to go into sales and bring in business for him when he opens his architecture firm."

"Best of luck to you. By strange coincidence, I took a preacher and his wife to Lewisburg two days ago. Would that be any relation to you?"

Solomon's back straightened, and he leaned toward Thaddeus. "What did they look like?"

The preacher was tall and wore formal clothing with a top hat. His wife was a real lady."

"That would have been my father and mother," Solomon said. "That's the first news of them I heard since I left home last week. Were they well?"

"Your poor mother was worn to a frazzle but otherwise healthy."

"I imagine Father was as overbearing as usual."

Thaddeus chuckled. "I wasn't going to mention it, but he was. I'm sorry to hear he's a close relative of yours. He wasn't a man I would want to spend much time with, begging your pardon."

"I took no offense at that. He's been a trial to me these many years, even though I prayed for patience and relief from him. But he hasn't changed a bit."

"I wouldn't be discouraged, son," Thaddeus said. "Sometimes God leads you through a trial, not away from it. As unpleasant as it may be, He does it for your good. My Clara was on her sickbed for two years before she passed away, and I prayed for her healing every day. I prayed for supernatural strength and endurance while I took care of her, doing her chores around the house while still doing my own work. It wasn't easy, and I often didn't do very well, but God was with me the whole way. He'll do the same for you. But you know that already, being a preacher."

Solomon's laugh was tinged with bitterness. "I graduated from Divinity School to satisfy Father. I never wanted to go there. And I don't feel a calling to preach . . . except from Father, of course."

Thaddeus sighed. "I'm going to stick my nose where it doesn't belong and advise you to do what God wants, not what your father says. You're a grown man."

"I appreciate hearing you say that, sir. It confirms what I was feeling in my heart. It takes away some of the guilt of defying Father."

Solomon's mind wandered back to one memorable day when he was fourteen. He had spent all summer observing architectural styles in Bridgeport and copying them into his sketch pad. He loved to sit on a hill overlooking the Sound, where he could enjoy the sun and the salt breeze. He penciled in house styles he had seen and experimented with variations until he had a beautiful original design he was proud of.

When Father discovered how he spent his time, he was furious and ripped up his summer's work, telling him that this nonsense would not help him in his ministry. Mother stood by helplessly, her strained face full of compassion. But, the only way to avoid his father's wrath and gain his approval was by forgetting what he was born to do and taking the path Father set out for him.

Now that he had reached a new level of maturity, Solomon could no longer live with that option. He regretted feeling angry and rebellious toward Father, but he had been pushed beyond what was tolerable.

The wagon bumped along as they enjoyed the scenery. Solomon was lost in his thoughts. The road took them past hills and valleys, through sunny patches of road and tree-shaded stretches, and followed the curves of the Susquehanna. The river was wide in some places, and in others, it narrowed somewhat.

Thaddeus glanced back over his shoulder. "Say, I hope you fellows brought supper with you."

Solomon pulled out the food they had bought in town. "We have some provisions here," he said. "Nothing fancy, but there's plenty of it."

They stopped the wagon beside the river near a willow tree, with its long, graceful branches drooping toward the ground and swaying in the breeze. It was good to stretch their legs. They gave the horses some oats and then sat on the ground with their supper.

"We'd better not linger here very long," Thaddeus said. "We still have a piece to go, and the sun will soon go down. We need to take advantage of whatever daylight we have."

They climbed back into the wagon and headed down the road once more.

As the sun dipped low on the horizon, shadows grew long. The temperature dropped. They finally arrived in Lewisburg after four full days of hard travel.

Solomon craned his neck, scanning the familiar buildings and streets he hadn't seen for several years. There was the old general store, then the barber shop where Grandfather once took him to get his hair cut the way he wanted it, much to his mother's chagrin.

"We'll go another half mile, then turn left."

"Yes," Thaddeus said. "I remember the route."

Solomon's heart thumped in his chest. Was Grandfather still alive? What kind of reception would he get from Father? What would they think of Jacob? He gripped the edge of the wagon so hard that his knuckles were white.

Thaddeus pulled the wagon up to the house. When they rolled to a stop, Solomon leaped from the wagon. "Give me a minute, then I'll come back for you," he said and ran to the door, giving it four sharp raps.

The door opened, and his mother rushed toward him with open arms. Her eyes betrayed her weariness. She was thinner than she had been at home.

"Mother!" he cried, embracing her. "I'm so glad to see you. I'm so glad you're safe."

Father sat in the room but didn't rise. "So it's the prodigal, is it?" he thundered. "Thanks to you, our trip was delayed, causing your mother extreme anxiety."

Emeline flinched at that interruption, then turned to Solomon. "How did you get here? Where's your luggage?"

"It's a long story, but I have two friends outside in the wagon. They need a place to stay tonight. I told them we could all stay in the barn. Wait, I'll get them and introduce you. You already know Thaddeus."

A smile lit Emeline's face. "So you met Thaddeus, too? Quite a fine man. And who is this?"

As Jacob approached, she turned to him with a congenial smile.

"This is my friend, Jacob. We met on the ferry from Stratford and traveled here together. I couldn't have made it without him. Fellows, please come inside and meet the rest of the family."

As they climbed down from the wagon, Solomon turned to his mother with urgency in his voice. "How is Grandfather? Is he still living?"

She lowered her voice, and her lip wobbled. "He is but continues to fade. He's been waiting to see you. Come. Your friends can wait in the parlor while you speak to Grandfather. There may not be much time."

Chapter 10: Farewell to Grandfather

After leaving Jacob and Thaddeus with his mother, Solomon went alone to his grandfather's bedroom. His legs were weak. He didn't know if he could keep his emotions in check. He didn't want to ruin his last moments with Grandfather by blubbering. He must control himself.

He tiptoed inside. His beloved grandfather lay in the bed, thin and pale, struggling to breathe, unlike the robust, cheerful man he had loved all his life.

"Grandfather, it's Solomon. How are you?"

A smile lit up the old gentleman's gaunt face. He reached out a frail, trembling hand, letting his grandson wrap both his hands around it. "Solomon, I've been waiting to see you. Please . . . close the door. I have something important I want to say." His breath came in gasps between words.

Solomon closed the door with a quiet click and stepped across the rug to Grandfather's side.

"Pull a chair over, boy. I want to see you." His eyes were tender as he rested them on Solomon. "Your father said you graduated from Yale with a Divinity degree."

Solomon managed a nod, and his heart grew heavier. "Yes, I did."

"I know that's not what you wanted to do. You always wanted to be an architect."

Solomon sighed heavily. "Yes, sir. I haven't convinced Father yet, but I won't spend my life preaching. God never called me to preach. I still want to go to architecture school."

The only sound in the room for a moment was Grandfather's tortured breathing. Then he said, "Open the bottom drawer of that chest beside you, Solomon. There's an envelope in there for you. And I caution you, do not tell your father you have it." He worked hard to take a deep breath as Solomon reached for the drawer. "I'm an old man with no future on this earth, so I will speak with liberty. I've always thought your father was a controlling, pretentious boob. You and your mother endured a difficult trial for many years. You handled it well, Solomon. God bless you."

Solomon turned to stare at the older man with a smile playing on his lips. "Thank you, Grandfather. I didn't think I'd ever hear you say anything like that. I admit I'm a little shocked."

Grandfather chuckled. His chest heaved as he sucked in another breath. "Do you have that envelope in your hand?"

"Yes."

"Put that in a safe place where *no one* will know you have it. I didn't make such a gift to your cousins. You have the most potential; I trust you to use it wisely. There's enough money to cover three years' tuition at the University of Illinois."

"Grandfather!"

"Lower your voice, boy. No one is to know about that. I don't have much time left. I want you to know I love and respect you. Now put your arms around an old man and give me a hug. Now that you're here, I can go in peace. Before this night is over, I'll be with Jesus."

Tears rolled down Solomon's face as he leaned over and embraced his grandfather for the last time. "I love you, Grandfather. I'll use that money to make you proud if you can see me from your new home in heaven."

"I know that, boy." He patted Solomon's back before the younger man stood. "I need to rest now." He closed his eyes and continued to suck in his breath.

Solomon leaned to kiss his Grandfather's forehead. "Goodnight, Grandfather." He put the money envelope inside his shirt and slipped out the door, wiping his cheeks with his hands. His parents sat in the parlor with Jacob and Thaddeus; the silence was heavy.

"How is your grandfather?" Jacob asked. His voice was low in reverence.

"He says he'll be with Jesus before the night is over. My word, I love that man."

Stiff and sore from travel, Solomon dropped into a chair and turned to his mother. "Is Uncle Virgil here?"

"Yes, they arrived yesterday—Uncle Virgil, Aunt Maude, and your cousins, Harris and Peter. They're down by the lake. Virgil and Maude are staying in the second bedroom while Harris and Peter sleep in the barn. There's room for the rest of you out there, too. I'm sorry there aren't enough comfortable beds in the house."

Thaddeus gave her a reassuring smile. "No need to apologize, Mrs. Hawk. There's enough room for the three of us in the wagon. I have plenty of hay to make comfortable beds."

"Mother, is there anything to eat here? I hate to ask, but we haven't had much today. We've been on the road for hours."

"Still mooching off your mother, are you?" Father snapped. "And what happened to the horse? Is he with you?"

"No, Father. I sold him in New York. I wasn't able to get him on the train."

Father went purple, and a vein bulged from his temple. "You what? Scout was my best horse. Now, you owe me the price of a horse. And since you're going to waste your education, you owe me for the tuition I paid to get you through Yale."

Emeline stood, stretched to her full diminutive height, and turned to her husband. Her face was resolute, and her eyes flashed with fury. Abandoning her restraint, she curled her small fists and gritted her teeth. "Geoffrey, shut up."

She twirled and marched to the kitchen, mumbling something about getting some leftover chicken to feed the newcomers. White-faced and looking shocked beyond words, Geoffrey stood and strode to the bedroom, where he remained for the evening. Solomon's face flushed red with embarrassment that the family's well-kept secrets were now on display to everyone else.

Emeline called the guests into the kitchen and asked them to sit at the table. They trooped in and took chairs at the wood table. It was covered with a red and white checked oilcloth. The iron stove stood by the wall, and an inside water pump was next to the sink. Her hands trembled as she put dishes before the men and placed the food on the table. She was distracted the whole time.

Solomon put a hand on her arm. "Mother, take a deep breath. Father will get over it."

"I'm not so sure, Solomon. He will make me pay for that somehow."

"Is it worth it?"

She giggled. "Yes."

Solomon paused and swallowed. "This may not be a good time to tell you this, but I'm not going back home. Not yet, anyway. Jacob and I are going on to Chicago when we leave here. We're going to make a future together." He chewed his lip. "And we'd like you to go with us."

Jacob and Thaddeus averted their eyes from the drama as they filled their stomachs with cold chicken and leftover vegetable dishes.

"Solomon, you're not coming home?" Tears formed in her eyes.

"I'm sorry, Mother, I can't. Father is so controlling I won't be able to be my own person unless I separate myself from him."

Emeline covered her mouth with her hand. Her eyes grew wide. "I'm losing my father, and now I'm losing my son. This is more than I can endure." She shook as the reality of his words closed in on her.

Solomon stood and wrapped his arms around her. "I'm sorry, Mother."

She pulled away from him, waving a hand in the air. "I understand, and I agree. The price you would pay to come home is too much. You do need a life of your own, son. But I shall miss you horribly." She burst into tears, covered her face with her hands, and dropped into the extra chair at the table, still trembling.

Thaddeus moved a bowl of potatoes out of her way and kept chewing. Jacob reached toward Emeline. "Ma'am, you would truly be welcome to come with us."

She dabbed at her eyes. "You are a kind young man, but my duty is with my husband. I only hope Solomon will see his way clear to come for an occasional visit."

"I'm sure he will, ma'am. Solly, we'll need to include that in our budget."

Emeline stopped her sniffling and lifted her head. "Solly? Did you call him Solly?"

"Begging your pardon, ma'am. I should address him with more respect."

She giggled. Then she erupted in gales of nervous laughter. She sank into a chair, still laughing. "No one has ever called him Solly before." She continued to giggle.

Thaddeus stood, his brow creasing and his eyes on Emeline with compassion. "Mrs. Hawk, let me get you a glass of water." He glanced at Solomon with a look that said, "Help her." Her laughing suddenly turned to sobbing. She crossed her arms to hug herself, rocking back and forth through her wailing.

Solomon came to her side, patting her arm. "Mother, take it easy. It's been a difficult and stressful week for you."

She put her hands over her face as she calmed herself. "I am so sorry—so embarrassed."

Solomon shook his head. "There's no need to apologize or be embarrassed. Do you think you should check on Grandfather?

"Yes, maybe I should." She rose, wiped her nose, and left the kitchen with as much dignity as she could muster.

Solomon lowered his voice. "I want to apologize to both of you," he said. "Mother never behaves the way she has behaved this evening. She's a dignified lady. I don't know what's come over her."

Thaddeus put his chicken leg down. "You don't owe anyone an apology, and neither does she. This was no doubt one of the worst weeks of her life. She needs room to grieve the loss of her father and son so she doesn't break down. I've seen people do that. It's ugly." He took another forkful of corn casserole.

Jacob nodded. "For my part, I was impressed that she was so kind to me, seeing as how we are so different. She didn't look down on me. Your father, on the other hand . . . well, let me say I understand your situation better now."

Solomon patted his shirt to make sure the envelope was still in place. "Someday, I hope to pay Father for the horse and tuition. That may take me a while, but that's my goal."

Jacob lowered his eyes to his plate. "What you do with your money is your affair."

"If you fellows don't mind, I'd like to check on Grandfather again; then, could we go to the wagon and settle in for the night? I want to leave the house before Uncle Virgil and his family return. It will be crowded inside if we don't."

"Sure, Solly. I'll put this extra food back in the icebox to save your mother some work; then I'll be out there."

After Thaddeus helped Jacob clear the table, they went outside to spread the hay. Solomon slipped into Grandfather's room and stood behind his mother's chair. He put his hands on her shoulders in the dim light of the bedroom. She reached up with her left hand and laid it on his right.

"How is Grandfather doing?" he asked in a whisper.

"He's asleep, still struggling for breath. I believe he's coming to the end."

Grandfather's chest rose and fell with jerky, uneven breaths.

"Why don't you sit in that chair, son? You may as well be comfortable."

Solomon took the rocking chair on the other side of the bed and leaned forward to touch his grandfather's arm. He wanted to pray, but he had no words. His chest ached.

"Don't you feel the presence of God here with us?" whispered Emeline.

"Yes, Mother, I do. I believe the angels have come for Grandfather."

The old man gasped heavily, once, twice, three times, then lay still, his breath gone.

"Father," Emeline cried. She leaned over him, held him, and kissed his face. Tears streamed down Solomon's cheeks and dropped on Grandfather's quilt.

"He's at peace now, Mother. No more struggling for breath. I'm sure Grandmother is meeting him at the gate of heaven."

She sniffed, and her voice cracked. "He only waited for you, son. He refused to go until he could say goodbye to you. Did you have a good talk with him this afternoon?"

"Yes, Mother. He wanted to give me some last-minute advice—" Solomon smiled through his tears— "as if the wisdom he gave me growing up wasn't enough."

"He was a good man and a good father. He loved God and his family." Emeline stepped back and sat in her chair. "We should cover him now. I'll tell your father and Virgil that he's gone. In the morning, we'll make funeral arrangements."

Emeline stood and leaned over his body. "Goodbye, Father," she whispered as she pulled the sheet over his face. Through tears, she said, "Let me hug you again, Solomon. We won't have many more chances after this."

Solomon's heart ached to bursting as he embraced his mother. "I'll go out to the wagon and try to get some sleep. I'll see you in the morning. Try to get some rest." With one last look at Grandfather's still form, he left the room and went to the wagon, heavy-hearted. His beloved grandfather was gone.

Jacob and Thaddeus were already bedded down in the hay when Solomon reached them. He made a spot near their feet and stretched out in exhaustion. It had been a very long five days. It seemed like a lifetime ago he held his diploma.

Chapter 11: The Funeral

Thursday, June 5, 1879

Emeline was still asleep when Geoffrey woke her. "Emeline, wake up. Virgil and I have work to do this morning. We need you to make breakfast."

She sighed and rolled out of bed. After they dressed and made their way to the kitchen, Geoffrey sat at the table while she cooked bacon and eggs. A few minutes later, Virgil came in with his appetite.

"Did you make coffee, Emmie?" Virgil asked.

A gentle smile lit her face. No one had used her nickname for many years. It gave her a warm feeling like she was home.

"I did. Just a minute, and I'll bring you each a cup." When the percolator finished its work, she poured two cups of coffee and carried them to the table. The men were in mid-conversation.

"I'll contact the attorney this morning," Geoffrey said. "Why don't you call on the undertaker?"

Virgil bristled. "Why are you so interested in the attorney? It was my father who died, not yours. I know all you're interested in is reading the will."

Geoffrey glared at him. "I can't believe you would accuse me of greed. All right, let's run those errands together. We'll go to the undertaker first so he can get started on the coffin, and then we'll see the attorney."

"If I have to have you along, at least I can keep an eye on you," Virgil muttered. Geoffrey acted as if he didn't hear. Emeline's cheeks burned with embarrassment as she poured the coffee.

"Why isn't Solomon up yet?" Geoffrey asked, turning to face Emeline.

"He's had a long, hard trip."

"And what about that ragamuffin he's traveling with? That fellow looks like he makes a living with his hands. And I don't hear a hint of education in his speech." He shuddered.

Emeline pursed her lips. "God loves him as much as He loves us. Solomon enjoys his company. I'm glad he had a companion for the journey."

"Hmpph. We'll be rid of that character when we take Solomon back home with us."

She gave him a cup of coffee without informing him of Solomon's plans and put another cup in front of her brother.

"Cream or sugar, Virgil?"

"No, thank you, Emmie."

Geoffrey downed his coffee. "Ready to go, Virgil?"

The two men left by the kitchen door, and Emeline kept them in view as they drove off in her brother's carriage. A few tears escaped her eyes, not only for the loss of her father but over Geoffrey's embarrassing lack of concern for anyone but himself. She cooked an egg for herself and sat at the table to eat.

Spotting her father's Bible on the table where he often sat, she picked it up. She opened to 1st Thessalonians, *"But I would not have you to be ignorant, brethren, concerning them which are asleep, that ye sorrow not, even as others which have no hope."* She bowed her head in prayer, thanking God for this lavish comfort. She had been taught from childhood that "them which are asleep" referred to the dead. She would see both her father and mother in heaven one day.

***

Emeline was still in the kitchen when Solomon came inside with Jacob and Thaddeus. The bacon was gone, so she whipped up some griddle cakes to serve with the eggs. She found some maple syrup in the pantry.

Thaddeus finished his breakfast and announced his intention to return to Selinsgrove. "I'll be heading home shortly. It was a pleasure to bring you boys here. If you're ever in Selinsgrove again, look me up."

Solomon thanked him and paid him for the trip, sad to see him go.

Maude entered the kitchen with her sons, Harris and Peter, both big, strapping boys a little younger than Solomon. Emeline informed them that Geoffrey and Virgil were out talking to the undertaker and the attorney.

"Any food left?" Maude asked.

"There are more eggs, and I mixed up some griddle cakes."

"Sit down, Emmie. I'll take over the cooking for my bunch."

Emeline smiled with gratitude and made room for her brother's family by retreating to the parlor and sitting in her father's favorite chair. After a while, there was a knock on the door. She opened it to a balding man wearing a canvas apron over his work clothes.

"Ma'am, I'm Liam Bartlett, the undertaker. Your husband came by and told me I was needed here. I'm truly sorry about your Pa's passing."

"My father is in the room there," she said, pointing at the bedroom door.

Bartlett wiped his feet on the mat inside the door, pulling his measuring tape and notepad from his pocket. "Thank you, ma'am. I won't be long."

As he was about his work, Virgil and Geoffrey returned. Geoffrey hopped out of the carriage and came inside, leaving Virgil to unhitch the horses.

"Since we're all here, we've arranged to have the attorney read the will this afternoon. Then we can leave as soon as the funeral is over."

Emeline's eyes grew large. "What? Will the will be read before Father is even in the ground? And you want to leave immediately? Please, Geoffrey, I want to linger with Virgil and Maude. It may be years before I see them again, and I need the comfort of my family."

"You know there is great urgency to get back home. I have important responsibilities. Of course, I could leave alone, and you could come later with Solomon."

Emeline sighed. Trouble was coming. "Solomon isn't coming home. He has other plans."

His head snapped toward her. "What plans? To waste his time running all over the country without a care in the world while I work? I don't think so. You stay as long as you like. I'm going back immediately after the funeral. You can come with Solomon."

"Geoffrey, I told you he's not coming home. Solomon is going to Chicago."

Geoffrey's face reddened, and the veins of his neck popped. "We'll see about that."

Emeline gave up. There was no sense trying to talk to him.

***

Solomon and Jacob were in the yard filling a basin with water from the pump when Geoffrey approached. "I need you and your two cousins," he told Solomon, ignoring Jacob's presence. "The undertaker needs help with your grandfather. And Virgil will help since he's the son. I'm stepping aside for this task."

Solomon fetched his cousins, and they trooped into the house. Jacob followed and took a seat in the parlor with Emeline. The undertaker was in Grandfather's room with Uncle Virgil. They had a leather stretcher supported by two side poles.

"Boys, I'm sorry about the loss of your grandfather," Bartlett said, his hands folded, looking each one in the eye. "I need help getting Mr. Mayfield's body to my wagon. Will you help me get him aboard the stretcher and carry him outside?"

The boys nodded silently, fighting tears.

"Virgil, I'll help you and one of your sons to roll Mr. Mayfield to one side. You other two fellows spread out the stretcher where he is now. Then we'll roll him back."

Virgil nodded, choking back his emotion.

The undertaker stood aside in respect. "Do you need a few minutes, sir?"

Virgil tried to gesture that he was fine but broke down sobbing. "You don't know what a fine man he was, sir. He was an exceptional father and grandfather."

The undertaker's eyes softened in sympathy, more than was required by his profession. He answered softly, "I'm sure he was, sir. I met him and Mrs. Mayfield briefly at the county fairground. That was the year she entered a berry pie and won second place. He seemed to be a fine man."

He folded his hands and waited while Virgil gathered himself. The boys sniffed and choked back their tears.

After listening to the undertaker's instructions, the four family members placed the stretcher under Grandfather's body. Virgil and the grandsons each grasped one end of a pole. The rest of the family made room while their dear patriarch was carried from his home for the last time. He was difficult to maneuver in the small parlor, and one of Virgil's boys bumped gently into the doorframe with the stretcher. Other than that, the only sound was sniffling.

The undertaker climbed onto the wagon seat, slapped the reins, and drove away. The family gathered in the living room, sitting wherever they could, not knowing what else to do. The house seemed hollow and deserted without his presence.

"What plans did you make for the funeral?" Emeline asked.

"We spoke to the pastor," Virgil said. "We'll bury him beside the church tomorrow morning. The pastor said to come to the cemetery at ten o'clock. He'll notify the church members as best he can. Word will spread quickly."

Emeline nodded.

The cuckoo clock ticked with relentless precision. Tick . . . tick . . . tick. To Solomon, the passing of time was like an insult without Grandfather. How dare time continue without that dear man?

Geoffrey broke the silence. "The attorney will expect us all at his office at two-thirty this afternoon."

A heavy, strained silence hung in the air.

Virgil pressed his lips together and left the room. Emeline and Maude headed to the kitchen to find something to make for lunch. The grandsons all went outside, taking Jacob with them.

**

That afternoon, Emeline tried her best to stay strong while the entire family loaded into Grandfather's wagon. They began the short trip to the attorney's house, where one room was used as his office.

Maude whispered to Emeline, "Reading the will before your father is buried seems obscene."

Emeline nodded, and tears stung her eyes. Maude's arm went around her sister-in-law's shoulder. Emeline's head hung low. She reached up and took Maude's hand.

Maude continued whispering. "I know you have a hard life. I pray for you often, Emmie. I want you to know that."

"It's not so hard."

"I hope you don't expect me to believe that."

"You're a good sister-in-law."

The wagon rolled to the attorney's office. When they reached their destination, they walked in together.

Four chairs had been placed in front of the attorney's desk for the two children of the deceased and their spouses. The grandsons stood behind their parents. Jacob volunteered to stay outside and watch the horses.

The attorney expressed his condolences, reached into his desk for a file folder, and pulled out a sheaf of papers. Arranging them fan-style, he cleared his throat and read, "I, Bradford James Mayfield, being of sound mind . . ."

After a few legal-speak paragraphs, he got to the meat of the issue. Mr. Mayfield divided his bank account, $1,750 each to Virgil and Emeline and $500 to each of the three grandsons. The house was to be sold, and the proceeds divided between Virgil and Emeline. The household goods and farming implements were to be divided between the brother and sister however they saw fit. Of his five horses, each grandson was to choose one with its saddle. The other two would remain with the carriage.

When the attorney finished, Geoffrey had the first question. "I thought he had more money in his bank account than that."

Emeline turned to him as her cheeks burned with embarrassment. "Geoffrey."

He ignored her.

"I've checked, Mr. Hawk. That amount is correct. Whatever else he had, he spent. His account at the bank is closed."

"It's Rev. Hawk, not Mr. Hawk."

"My apologies."

"Who is going to be billed for your fee?"

"Mr. Mayfield already paid me."

Geoffrey turned to Emeline. "When the bank opens in the morning, I'll check this out."

She closed her eyes and wagged her head. Virgil and Maude stared at Geoffrey in disgust. Solomon's cousins looked at him with questions in their eyes.

The attorney continued. "You can do whatever you like, sir. In the meantime, I have envelopes here with your cash distributions. The envelopes each contain the correct amount, plus a money belt. Mr. Mayfield was very thoughtful, knowing that some of you were traveling a great distance."

He handed envelopes to Virgil and Emeline first. Geoffrey took Emeline's envelope from her. "I'll take responsibility for that," he said.

She lowered her eyes, wishing he would have done that in private. "We'll discuss this later, Geoffrey," she whispered.

He handed the boys' envelopes to them. Solomon appeared surprised when his envelope contained the same amount as his cousins'. Emeline thought his reaction was significant. Later, she would have to ask him why.

"Let me have your envelope, Solomon." Geoffrey extended his hand.

"No, Father. I'll pay you for the horse now and reimburse you for my tuition later, but right now, I need the money to get where I'm going." He took four twenty-dollar notes from his envelope and handed them to his father. "This is for Scout."

Virgil turned to the attorney and said, "Thank you, sir. We appreciate all you did." He and his sons walked out, followed by Emeline and Maude, leaving Geoffrey alone with the attorney.

Virgil's eyes quizzed Emeline.

"You and the boys wait for me in the wagon," she whispered. "I'll wait for Geoffrey here in the hall." Virgil nodded and took his sons outside. Emeline peeked into the attorney's office to see what took Geoffrey so

86

long.

The attorney stood. He was a short man but exuded dignity and determination.

"Sir, I don't often stick my nose in my clients' personal business," he said, "but your wife is struggling with grief, and your behavior is an extra burden on her. As a man of the cloth, you should know better. My sympathies are with her."

"Thank you for your opinion." Geoffrey turned on his heel and exited the man's office. He found Emeline in the hall, listening, and scowled. He took her by the arm without a word and ushered her to the wagon.

***

Back at the house, Virgil and Emeline discussed the division of household goods. "Virgil, I can't carry anything big back home with me. You'll need to take it all. But I would love to have Father's Bible."

"Emeline," Geoffrey interrupted them. "You need to take what you want. We can crate up the larger things and put them on a train. We can use your Father's money to pay for shipping."

Emeline was still angry with him over his behavior at the attorney's office. Her arms and legs stiffened so much that she trembled. "Geoffrey, please stay out of this. This is between me and Virgil."

Geoffrey's mouth opened. Emeline expected a snappy retort, but instead, he made a strategic retreat in the face of losing control. Through tight lips, he said, "We'll talk about this later." He retreated to the bedroom and slammed the door.

Virgil led her to their father's bedroom. "Emmie, take a good look around. Maybe there's something small that you could put in your purse or your luggage."

Emeline put a hand on his arm. "Before we look, Virgil, I must apologize for Geoffrey."

"No need. But I'll tell you this: I'm the son, and Geoffrey is not. I would have confronted him earlier, but I didn't want to cause extra trouble for you."

Emeline lowered her eyes and nodded. "You're a kind and thoughtful brother."

They turned back to their task but hesitated to search the bureau drawers. They exchanged glances for reassurance. Emeline ran her fingers over the top of the bureau. "We were never allowed in Mother and Father's bureau as children, yet here we are, getting ready to search through his private things where we shouldn't be."

Virgil hesitated. "I feel the same way, but he's not here anymore, Emmie. We have to adjust to that fact."

"You're right. But it's a big adjustment." She opened a drawer and found a pair of pearl cufflinks, some shirts she thought might fit Solomon and an old quill pen and dry inkwell that Father had used as a schoolboy. "I'd like this pen and inkwell," she said.

Virgil nodded. "Take whatever you would like," he said gently. "I know you can't take much with you. I need to reimburse you for your share of the household goods. I'll give you a hundred dollars if you don't tell Geoffrey. I'll recoup the money by selling off what I don't want for myself."

"That's a very kind offer, and you're a wonderful brother. But I wouldn't know how to conceal a hundred dollars from Geoffrey . . . or even if I should."

Virgil peered into her eyes. "Emmie . . . I don't normally counsel women to hold anything back from their husbands, but you're in a different situation. You need some money of your own for emergencies. What will you do if Geoffrey dies and all the money is in a bank account in his name only? You won't be able to get it until it goes through the court. You'll be penniless, at least for a while." Virgil thought for a moment, then lowered his voice. "Tonight, when you change into your nightgown, leave your dress with Maude, but don't ask any questions." He put his arm around her shoulders and gave her a wink and a sly smile.

"All right, Virgil." Guilt stabbed at her for trying to hide something from Geoffrey, but she trusted her brother's wisdom; it was necessary to protect herself. She would wrestle through her guilt later.

She didn't know what she would accomplish by giving her dress to Maude, but she trusted Virgil. She slipped the cufflinks into her purse and left the bedroom carrying three shirts for Solomon, the quill pen, and the inkwell.

After the evening meal, the family sat together on the porch and reminisced about old times with Grandfather.

Emeline smiled. "Virgil, do you remember when we were kids? Mother bought us each a pair of ice skates. Father took us to the pond, but the ice had broken tree limbs. I remember when you tripped over one of the tree limbs and fell so hard your knee went through the ice. Father rushed us home in a hurry, didn't he?"

Virgil smiled wistfully and nodded. "He taught me to fish. Then he taught me how to clean and filet my catch."

"And Mother fried them in cornmeal breading," Emeline added. "They were delicious."

The conversation continued until the sun dropped behind the tree line. Darkness crept across the sky from the east until the stars twinkled brightly. Emeline said, "Father is up there, isn't he? I wonder if he knows we're talking about him."

Everyone stared at the sky, but no one answered.

Presently, they rose one by one and went inside to get ready for bed. Emeline slipped into her nightgown and took her dress to her sister-in-law's bedroom.

"Maude, Virgil said I was to bring you my dress tonight. I don't know why."

Maude had a sly smile on her lips. "He told me you're not to ask why. You can have your dress back in the morning. I'll take good care of it. I'm going to adjust the hem for you."

"There's nothing wrong with the hem."

"I know. I'm just making it better."

"Well, thank you for whatever you're doing."

She returned to the bedroom and slipped into bed with Geoffrey.

"What did you do with that dress?" he asked.

"I took it to Maude. She volunteered to mend it."

"Where is Solomon?"

"He and Jacob are sleeping in the barn."

"Hmph." Geoffrey rolled over and went to sleep. Emeline sighed with relief. She didn't want to be pressed for more answers. Her muscles relaxed, and she drifted into a fitful sleep, still dreading morning.

Friday, June 7, 1879

When Emeline woke, Geoffrey was at the desk with his open Bible, writing his sermon for the week they would arrive home. Without disturbing him, she slipped out to Virgil and Maude's bedroom and knocked on the door.

"Maude, are you awake?"

"Yes. Come on in."

Emeline opened the door. There was Maude, sitting on the edge of the feather bed, stitching the hem of her dress.

"I'm just about finished. A few more stitches . . ." She made the final stitch and bit the thread in two. "Here's your dress, Emmie. Wear it in good health." She grinned, and her eyes danced as she held out the dress.

Emeline reached for it. There was something different, something odd. She slipped it over her head. The dress bumped her back and legs as she adjusted it.

"What . . ?" She bent over and inspected the hem. To her astonishment, Maude had sewn folded paper into the hem. "What's in there?"

"Five-dollar silver certificates, twenty of them," Maude whispered. "You now own a hundred-dollar dress."

Emeline suppressed a giggle. "This is genius," she said. "There isn't much chance that they will be discovered, and they make the skirt stand out beautifully."

Maude beamed at her. "I know you, Emmie. I know you feel guilty about that, but please don't. Just be careful when you wash it."

"I will. How can I ever thank you?" She embraced her sister-in-law. It was the one bright spot in what promised to be a long, difficult day.

***

Breakfast for the entire group was a hasty affair of oatmeal and coffee. No one was in the mood for joking, so conversation was minimal as everyone prepared for the funeral.

"We're short on space in our carriage," Virgil said. "Geoffrey, take

Father's carriage for your family, and we'll meet you at the cemetery."

The two carriages made the short trip to the old cemetery beside Mr. Mayfield's church, a brown wooden structure that served a tiny congregation. A few of his lifelong friends were there, standing near the coffin. Most of them were well into their seventies. Pastor Zeigenbush waited with his Bible, and the undertaker stood beside the hastily dug grave. The ropes were already positioned under the coffin.

The gravel crunched under the wheels as both carriages pulled to a stop. The horses snorted and shook their heads as the families disembarked and walked across the soft, green grass to the gravesite.

The pastor lifted his eyes. "We're here to say goodbye to Bradford James Mayfield, but not the final goodbye, knowing we'll see him again. In this life, he was an outstanding husband, father, and grandfather. But his best role was as a saint of God. He taught everyone how to live by his example, and he will be rewarded for that in heaven."

Someone sniffled. The boys lowered their eyes and shuffled their feet.

After a few more words, the pastor read the 23rd Psalm from his Bible. "The Lord is my shepherd, I shall not want . . ."

Emeline's heart was grateful that she had been taught to trust God from childhood. *How do people ever get through something like this if they don't know Jesus?*

It was time to lay her father to rest. "Who will act as pallbearers?" the pastor asked. Virgil stepped forward and asked the three grandsons to each take a rope with him. With instructions given by the undertaker in low tones, they hoisted the coffin over the grave. Then, they let it down a few inches at a time, careful not to tip it too far. It wiggled back and forth as they let down the ropes, hand over hand. When the coffin reached the bottom of the grave with a dull thud, they released the ropes and let them fall. Emeline gasped at the finality of it and covered her mouth. Her knees sagged, but Geoffrey held her up.

The pastor finished by leading the group in the Lord's Prayer and reassuring them that though their loved one was absent from the body, he was present with the Lord. "God bless you all." He spoke to each family member one by one, then turned to go. Grandfather's friends gathered around the family, expressing their condolences.

So it was all over. There was nothing to do but leave. Emeline was devastated. What would happen now? Would Geoffrey insist on leaving immediately? Her stomach tightened. Lightheaded, she hung onto Solomon's arm. How could she bear to be separated from the son she loved so much? He was the only person on earth who loved her unconditionally. The only one.

Once they were back in the carriage, Emeline's breath was shallow, waiting for the arguing to begin. She dreaded the whole business. However, Geoffrey had softened his position.

"We'll get a good night's sleep, then we'll start for home in the morning. Virgil has agreed that we may take your father's carriage. We'll drive it as far as we can, then sell it if we can't take it all the way home. Solomon, I don't know your friend's plans, but you'll go with us in the morning."

"No, Father, Jacob and I are going to Chicago."

The strife that ensued was inevitable. Father's eyes narrowed, and his lips thinned into a cold line. "You're old enough that I can't force you to do what you're set against, but I can make you wish you had. If you don't come with us, you're no longer welcome in our home. Don't ever come back."

Emeline gasped. "Geoffrey, that's evil!" She broke down in sobs.

His head reared back as if he had been slapped. "You don't speak that way to your husband, especially when he is a man of God."

That was it. Emeline snapped. "You're not a man of God. You're a pretender. Furthermore, you're a poor father, and you're a poor husband."

Geoffrey stiffened for a moment, then swiveled toward her. "What has gotten into you?"

Emeline shouted at him. "My father has just died, and my son doesn't want to come home. Who knows when I'll see him again? I've had two losses of the people I love most, and you wonder what has gotten into me?" The pitch of her voice raised as she spoke until her tone was hysterical.

Jacob folded and unfolded his hands and then rubbed his knees.

Solomon gasped for air. "Mother, if Father doesn't want me ever to come home, please come with Jacob and me. I don't know when I'll be able to come back to Connecticut. It will be at least two and a half years until I graduate."

"Graduate," Geoffrey shouted. "You've already graduated. What nonsense is that?"

"I'm going to study architecture, Father. It's what God created me to do."

Geoffrey shut his mouth and kept driving. His lips were clamped tight, and his chest heaved as he breathed heavily through his nose. When they reached the house, he leaped from the carriage, shouting, "Solomon, take care of the horses." He strode into their bedroom and slammed the door.

Emeline sank to the sofa in the parlor. Solomon and Jacob soon followed her.

"What are you going to do, Mother?"

"I'll rest for a few minutes, then . . . then, I'll wash your clothes. I want you and Jacob to give me all your dirty things. The work will be therapeutic."

Solomon knelt by his mother's knee and stared into her face. "I wish you would come with us."

She leaned forward with trembling lips and touched his face. "I can't, son. You know I can't. I'm ashamed to admit I allowed myself to toy with the temptation. I've dreamed of living with you and taking care of you to escape...to escape...you know. But I can't." Tears streamed down her cheeks, and she wiped them away with the back of her hand. "Get your clothes and bring them to me. I'll look for Grandfather's washboard."

With heavy hearts, the young men gathered their laundry and brought it all to the house. After a quick nap, Emeline rose and spent the rest of the afternoon washing their clothes and hanging them on the line. Jacob helped as Solomon had other business to attend to.

Emeline was grateful for Jacob's company as she hung their shirts and pants on the line. "Where is your family, Jacob?"

"They're in Beacon Falls."

"So, not too far from Bridgeport. I'm sure your parents are proud of you."

Jacob sighed. "Maybe not so much, now that I've left. Pa wanted me to stay in the smithy."

She smiled gently. "Ah, a blacksmith. Well, I pray for success in your future, whatever it might be. And I'll pray for your parents. Maybe I'll be privileged to meet them someday. They raised a fine son."

They continued their task until all the clothes fluttered in the breeze.

"Your clothes will be dry in the morning," Emeline told Jacob. "I may not have a chance to iron them if Rev. Hawk insists on leaving early, but at least they're clean."

Jacob said, "Thank you, Mrs. Hawk. We're both grateful for your hard work on our behalf."

She turned toward Jacob, her face stricken with grief. "Take good care of my son, will you?"

He nodded. "We'll take good care of each other. We have some ambitious plans. And I'll remind him to write to you often."

***

While the laundry was being done, Solomon spoke to his cousin Harris. "Grandfather willed a horse to each of us, but if you don't need yours, I'd like to buy it. Jacob and I have a long way to travel. A horse for each of us would be a great help.

Harris nodded. "I can go home in the carriage with Father and Mother, so I don't need an extra horse. What do you say to ninety dollars for the horse and saddle?"

"Would you be willing to sell it for eighty?"

"Give me eighty-five, and the beast is yours." He grinned at Solomon.

The cousins shook hands, and Solomon peeled off the eighty-five dollars from his money belt.

Harris counted the money in his hand. "I know you gave your father some money, and now you must be down to a little over three hundred dollars. Is that enough to get you to Chicago?"

"I have Jacob with me. You'd be surprised at the ideas he comes up with to save a few dollars. Why, when we needed fare for the stagecoach, he got himself hired by the stage line. I paid for the trip while he got paid to go the same distance. Another time, we bought apple fritters and sold them at the train station to pay his fare. And once, we slept in the woods and bathed in the river to save hotel money."

Harris leaned back in a belly laugh. "He seems like an agreeable chap."

"He is. I'm very grateful for his friendship."

Solomon and Harris reminisced about their childhood visits to Grandfather. "Do you remember when we were boys, and Grandfather took us swimming in the river?" asked Harris.

"Are you talking about the time we found the rope hanging from a tree limb and swung out over the water to drop in? The water was ice cold." Solomon smiled wistfully, the images of the past playing through his head – skinny kids splashing in the buff, goosebumps all over their bodies.

"Yes. Remember the time I swung, but not far enough, and landed too close to the rocks near the shore? Thank God Grandfather was strong enough to carry me to the wagon with my broken leg."

"I remember that. Thank God he knew where the doctor lived."

"Thank God he knew where my pants were." Harris chuckled. "Otherwise, I would have gone to the doctor's without. One bright spot— when I went back to school in a splint that fall, I got a lot of sympathy from the girls."

"What about when we were little? He used to take us to the general store. We each got three coppers to spend any way we wanted. We bought so much hard candy; it's a wonder we have any teeth left."

"He spoiled us good, didn't he?" Harris said with a hearty laugh. "I bought so much licorice that summer I'm sure the storekeeper had to order another jar."

"And I loved those sour lemon things. I had to stand on my toes and reach way up to drop my coins in the shopkeeper's hand. My, what memories."

They returned to the house with their arms around each other's shoulders.

Once inside, Solomon sought out Jacob and took him aside. "Jacob, Grandfather gave me one of his horses, and I've bought Harris's horse for you. That means we can start our trip on horseback. We have transportation out of here. If Mother comes with us, I'll have to find a carriage to buy."

"Your mother says she's going back with your father."

Solomon's heart fell. "I strongly urged her to change her mind and come with us. He'll make her life miserable."

"Yes, I know. But are you surprised?"

Solomon sighed. "Not really."

Jacob gave him an encouraging clap on the shoulder.

Chapter 12: The Crisis

Saturday, June 8, 1879

Solomon woke early on Saturday morning, knowing this would be his last chance to spend time with his mother. His hands went to his chest. It felt empty and heavy at the same time. His eyes were puffy from lack of sleep. Jacob was still snoring, so Solomon had time to himself. In earnest prayer, he asked that his mother would change her mind and come with them. He prayed for a safe trip to Chicago. Fighting his anger, he prayed for his father's heart to soften. He prayed for godly wisdom for his father. Then he dressed and went into the house.

Emeline was in the kitchen cooking cornmeal mush. She had a pot of coffee percolating with a bubbling sound welcome to Solomon's ears. He helped himself to a cup.

"Mother," he said in a low, pleading voice, "please reconsider. If you come with us, we can live in peace without constant hostility and anger. Think about that."

She turned to him and placed her hands on either side of his face. "Solomon, I love you more than anything else in this life. Your offer is tempting, but my duty is with your father. It's a Biblical mandate. God will give me the grace I need to endure. He'll even give me the grace to flourish. You believe that, don't you?"

Solomon lowered his head. "I believe He can. I'm just not sure He will."

"The older you get, the more you will see that God keeps His word. My heart is breaking, dear son. I know it will be years before we're together again. Please write to me often and tell me what's happening in your life. You may even have a wife by the time I see you again. You may be a father. I don't want to miss out on my grandchildren's lives."

Solomon's mouth gaped open as he stared at her. "I don't plan anything like that until after school. I plan to go to school for two or three years, as long as it takes, and study hard. There will be no time to get married and become a father. As soon as I graduate, I'll come to see you. After graduation, we don't yet know where we'll live. Maybe we'll settle in Connecticut or Washington, D.C. It will be a city where construction is booming."

"You said 'we.' Are you including Jacob in this?"

"Yes. Jacob will find work while I study. He'll support us both for three years. That will be his investment in the future. My investment will be tuition and study. Then, when I get proven as an architect, he'll join me on my staff. He'll find clients for me. I'll pay him much more money than he could earn if he went back to being a blacksmith. That will make his first three years worthwhile."

"So you've had time to plan all this since meeting him a week ago? I'm astonished."

"Yes. I wish I had time to tell you about all the experiences we've had. It was the divine hand that brought us together. Jacob can do things I can't, and I can do things he can't. Our personalities fit together."

"I wish you well with your plans, son. You're bright, and you're a hard worker. I'm sure you'll have success. But please, keep me part of your life through letters."

"I promise, Mother."

As Solomon ate his breakfast, his father entered the room and took a seat. "What's your final decision, Solomon? Have you come to your senses?"

"I believe I have, Father. I'm going to Chicago."

Emeline shuddered and pressed her lips together. She filled a plate with cornmeal mush and set the plate in front of Geoffrey with maple syrup and a cup of coffee.

***

Emeline made breakfast for herself as Geoffrey choked down his food, seething in anger. He left the room, muttering about packing his trunk. He was perched on the edge of the bed reading a newspaper when Emeline finished breakfast and went to find him. "Pack your trunk, Emeline. We're leaving this morning."

She glared at him, fuming inside. "Geoffrey, you've had your way in everything since the day we married. I have bent to your will in every instance. Now it's your turn. You can give me some consideration while we're here. I'm not leaving this morning. I must tell you that Solomon invited me to go live with him, and I was tempted. You have a foul temper, and I'm tired of being intimidated by it. So, if you want to leave, go ahead. But I'm staying until this afternoon. I have unfinished business with my brother and his wife."

Geoffrey folded his newspaper, slammed it onto the bedside table, and lay on the bed with his back to her. Shaking, she left the bedroom and closed the door.

Maude was in the parlor. "Emmie, I'm going to walk to the general store to pick up some food for us. Would you like to go with me?"

"The exercise would do me good," Emeline replied. She picked up her bag and went with Maude.

"I heard the arguing coming from your room," Maude confided. "Is everything going to work out for you?"

"I believe so. Solomon asked me to go to Chicago with him, and I admit to being tempted. But I know it's wrong to leave my husband, so I'm returning to Connecticut with Geoffrey. I don't know when I'll see my son again." Tears flooded her eyes.

Maude patted her back. "I wish we lived closer to each other."

Emeline nodded.

***

Solomon and Jacob pulled the dry clothes from the line. They smoothed the wrinkles as much as possible and rolled them into their valises. "We should leave here as soon as we can. I want to escape my father's temper, but I need to wait until Mother returns from her walk. It would be cruel to leave without saying goodbye to her."

"We need to plan our route anyway. Do you have any idea how to get to Chicago from here?"

"I've been trying to remember the maps from my geography classes without success. So the best plan may be to return to Harrisburg, then take a train out west. That would be much faster and safer than horseback."

Jacob nodded. "We're not in such a hurry now. You said classes wouldn't start until fall. We can wait for a train that can take our horses, too."

Solomon had a sudden idea. "Before Mother returns, why don't we take you to the barber shop and get you a proper gentleman's haircut and shave?"

Jacob cringed. "I was afraid you were going to suggest that eventually. I was hoping it would be later."

"Come on, friend, you'll feel better with less hair."

The two walked a short distance to the shop displaying the red and white striped pole. Solomon escorted Jacob inside and gave instructions to the barber, who nodded and told Jacob to take a seat in the chair. He unfolded a sizeable white cape, gave it a sharp snap, and tied it around Jacob's neck.

"Hold still, now. I'm going to lather your face."

Jacob had clearly never had anyone do that to him before. "A man should do his own shaving," he grumbled.

"Hold still." The lather went on, thick and creamy. Jacob shifted in the chair as the barber used the strop to sharpen his razor.

"What are you doing?" His widened eyes betrayed fear and uncertainty.

"You want a good, sharp razor to cut your beard," the barber said. "A dull one will make the job difficult and painful. Now, hold still."

Jacob froze. The barber began at his cheeks and worked his way down to the jawline. He pushed on his nose a little while he worked on his upper lip.

When the barber finished the shave and wiped up the last remnants of lather with a towel, Jacob's face was smoother than he had remembered

100

since he was fourteen. His hands ran over his cheeks, and he broke into a grin. "That wasn't so bad."

"Now for the haircut."

The barber adjusted the chair so that Jacob was sitting erect. The snip-snip of the scissors around Jacob's ears made him nervous, but he endured, encouraged by the successful shave. Great chunks of dark, curly hair fell to the floor. Solomon stood nearby, nodding with a bemused smile. When he finished cutting, the barber parted Jacob's hair in the middle, applied a little hair oil, and combed it back on either side. He thrust a mirror in front of Jacob's face.

"How do you like it?" he asked.

Jacob tilted his head from one side to another and moved the mirror from right to left. "I look like a different person, don't I? I look more . . . important."

Solomon laughed. "Yes, you do. And people will take you more seriously, especially after we buy you different clothes."

Jacob stretched his legs to get out of the chair. "Don't go throwing your money around, Solly. You think it'll last forever, but it won't."

Solomon paid the barber. As the two young men strolled back to the Mayfield house, Solomon clapped Jacob on the back, grinning. "You look smashing, Jake."

Harris was the first to spot Jacob with his new look. "Jacob, what happened to you? The change is amazing." He walked all around Jacob, inspecting the haircut. "You look more professional."

Jacob's chest puffed out. "Thank you, Harris. I hope this gives me an edge when I look for a job in Chicago."

Peter was next. He came out of the house and stopped short when he spotted Jacob. "Jake, is that you?"

Jacob beamed and put his hands on his hips. "Yes, sir, this is the new Jacob Bishop. I expect to get a little more respect now that I look . . . respectable."

Peter chuckled. "I tell you what, if you were wearing a white shirt and new shoes, I'd hire you at the snap of a finger."

"I hope someone in Chicago feels the same way. Now all I need is that new wardrobe."

Emeline and Maude approached on the sidewalk, holding bags of food. "We're well stocked with enough food for everyone until tomorrow," Emeline said. "Solomon, can you help us put the groceries away?"

"Yes, then Jacob and I need to get on the road. We have a very long way to go. Do you have anything in those bags to make sandwiches to take with us?"

Emeline put her bags down with a heavy sigh and raised her eyes to her son's face. "Yes, son, I can make your sandwiches. I just wish you didn't have to go so soon."

"It could be two weeks before we get to Chicago. I have no idea how long it will take. And we need to find work before we run out of cash."

Emeline gave in to necessity. "I understand. I'll make a bag of sandwiches and put some apples and carrots with them. Do you have a canteen?"

"Yes."

"Make sure you fill it with fresh water."

On impulse, she threw her arms around Solomon and let the tears run.

"I know, Mother. It will be a long time until we see each other again. I'm sorry things worked out this way."

She wiped her face and turned to the bags of food. "I'll have your sandwiches ready in a few minutes."

Later, when Solomon and Jacob returned to the kitchen to get their sandwiches, Emeline focused on Jacob for the first time since his haircut. "Jacob, is that you? You look like a man of success."

He grinned at her. "When my calloused hands soften, nobody will ever know I'm only a blacksmith."

"I should say not. Maybe soon, you'll become a deal-maker. Sell those architectural deals, Jacob."

"Yes, ma'am, I intend to."

Solomon lowered his voice. "I'm here to say goodbye, Mother."

Emeline's shoulders sagged, and the tears trickled down her cheeks. She embraced her son, whispering, "My constant prayers are with you."

Solomon wrapped his arms around her back. "And mine with you."

"Are you going to say goodbye to your father?"

"No, I'm sure he'd rather not have to deal with that. I'll see him in three years unless he's still angry."

She nodded. "Say goodbye to your aunt and uncle and your cousins."

"We've already done that." Solomon's face was wet, and he pushed the tears away with one hand. "Thank you for the sandwiches . . . But, Mother, there's still time to come with us."

With a pained expression, she hesitated briefly, then shook her head. "My mind is made up."

Emeline followed the boys out the door with both hands over her chest, her eyebrows tented in grief and her face drained of color. Virgil, Maude, and their sons were in the yard to see Solomon and Jacob off. The two mounted up, waved, and started down the road.

"Goodbye, son! Goodbye, Jacob," Emeline called.

"Don't look back, Solly," Jacob said, but Solomon took one last look at his mother. She waved her handkerchief at him. He waved his arm and kicked his horse into a gallop, followed by Jacob. When they were out of sight of the house, they brought their horses to a brief stop. Solomon choked back a sob and gasped for air. "What kind of son am I to leave my mother with a tyrant?"

Jacob stared at him. "Are you thinking of going back?"

"How can I leave her to a life of misery?"

"Solly, let's get out of the sun for a minute. Come on, under those trees across the road. We need to talk."

They walked the horses to the shady area and dismounted.

Jacob got into Solomon's face. "Listen, if you go back now, how will that change your mother's situation? It won't. And you'll be putting yourself into a life of misery with her."

Solomon lowered his eyes as Jacob continued to press his point.

"Your mother could have come with us. She's staying because that's what she believes God wants her to do. She's putting God ahead of you."

"As she should."

"I don't know much about God, but it seems to me that He made children to become adults who leave home and make their own way, not stick to their Mama their entire lives. If you go back now, you'll never leave. You'll be stuck working with your father. You'll be forced to conform to his will every day, and you'll hate your life. Now, think about this. Is that what God wants *you* to do?"

Solomon's breathing slowed. He lowered his head and shuffled his feet.

Jacob persisted. "It's decision time, Solly. The decision you make right now will set the course of your life."

Solomon raised his eyes. "You have a way of cutting to the heart of a matter," he said. "Thank you."

They mounted up and continued their journey.

Chapter 13: Chicago Bound

The two trotted along the trail at a more relaxed pace, still not wanting to waste their days. They reversed their earlier journey. When they arrived at Selinsgrove on horseback, they boarded the paddlewheel boat with their horses and traveled as far as Harrisburg. From there, they booked passage for themselves and their horses on the train and were in Chicago within three days, even with all the stops. Thanks to Grandfather's money, they had the luxury of sleeping in the Pullman cars.

The train whistle blew one long wail, the steam whooshed from under the engine, and they stepped off the train in Chicago. The platform was longer and busier than any they had seen before, with people rushing in every direction. They stood together with their bags in their hands, staring at each other, wondering what to do next.

Jacob was the first to snap into action. "Let's get our horses. Then we'll buy a newspaper and look for boarding houses near the university. We'll do well if we can find a place to live by nightfall."

Solomon chuckled. "That seems ambitious, but we'll try."

At the livestock car at the back of the train, they retrieved their mounts. Then, they purchased a copy of the Chicago Daily Telegraph at a general store and inquired about directions to the university.

"You're on the right road for the university," the clerk said. "But it's about three miles from here. Once you get close, you can follow the signs to the main office."

"Thanks, friend," Solomon said. "Do you sell Chicago maps here?"

"Sorry, I don't. You'll need to ask the local folks for directions."

Solomon nodded and left with Jacob.

The ride to the university area took almost an hour. As they traveled, they passed some lovely homes.

"Look at that two-story house over there with the veranda that wraps around three sides," said Solomon. "I'll design houses like that when I graduate."

"I know you will, and I'll bring the business to you," said Jacob, his eyes sparkling. "There's nothing but blue skies in front of us, Solly."

They passed shops, banks, warehouses, and a train roundhouse. Solomon's mental creative juices flowed. His head turned one way, then another, trying to take in all the sights.

They found a boarding house to check in for some rest and to get their bearings in town. It was a third-floor walk-up with two beds and a dresser where they spent the rest of the evening scouring the want ads for a permanent place to live. It had been a long, exhausting four days since Grandfather's funeral.

Chapter 14: Discouraging Setbacks

The two men arose at daybreak full of energy. "This is the day we begin our futures," Solomon said with excitement in his voice. "After I register for the fall session at the university, I'll have time to look for a place to live while you look for a job. So where will we meet up? I know we have to check out of here, which leaves us without a base."

Jacob thought. "I believe we should stay here one more night. That way, we'll have a place to meet."

Solomon agreed. After breakfast, he took his letter from McCreary, mounted his horse, and headed to the registrar's office at the university.

The closer he came, the more his bravery left him. Was he on a fool's errand? Would the university take him seriously? He was here without Father's blessing, and despite their broken relationship, Solomon felt empty and abandoned without his approval.

He tied his horse to the rail and slowly ascended the brick steps. He was barely aware of the heavy aroma of jasmine filling the air from the delicate, star-shaped white blooms lining the pathway.

He stepped to the door, hesitated, then opened it. The squeak of the hinges seemed unusually loud. He entered and walked the granite-floored hall, following the sign to the registrar's office. To bolster his courage, he tried to imagine himself walking those halls to class in just a few weeks. His angst grew until he reached the registrar's door, which stood open. Light streamed through the windows on the opposite wall, lighting specks of dust in the air.

Mr. Charles Rodding, the registrar, was behind his desk. It was hard for Solomon to see him clearly, as he was backlit by the sun, but his silhouette revealed dark, bushy hair. He glanced up to see who had entered his office.

"What can I do for you, sir?" he asked.

Solomon adopted a confident smile as he tried to steady his shaking knees. "My name is Solomon Hawk. I'm here to register for the fall term in Architecture."

"Sit down, Mr. Hawk. I'm afraid I have some bad news for you. You see, our class roster in Architecture is full this year. But tell me a bit about yourself. Maybe I can suggest an alternative."

The news was given to him so abruptly that it nearly took Solomon's wind, and he took the chair across from Mr. Rodding's desk. He struggled to control his shock. From that angle, Rodding's face was in clear view, and he judged him to be a kind man.

"Architecture was all I came for, sir," Solomon said. "This is quite a painful disappointment. Last month, I graduated from Yale in a subject my father wanted me to study, but coming to the University of Illinois...well, sir, you don't know what I've been through to get here. My home is in Connecticut. My grandfather died after I graduated, and I traveled to say goodbye to him in Pennsylvania. It's been a long, hard journey, but here I am. I finally thought I had made it, only to be told—"

"I'm very sorry to disappoint you, son."

"Isn't there some way—"

Rodding shook his head. It was final.

Solomon's breathing went shallow. He would have to wait a year. That meant getting a job so his money would last. What could he do with a Divinity degree?

He mumbled a weak "Thank you" and left the office.

As he retreated down the hall, his footsteps echoed in his ears. They were the footsteps of failure. He had blown it. He had angered his father for nothing . . . crushed his mother's heart for nothing . . . raised Jacob's hopes for nothing. How stupid to imagine he could make a new life on his own. His head pounded like it was marching to a drumbeat.

In his anguish, he rode his horse back to the boarding house and stumbled up the stairs. He climbed into bed, pulled his knees up to his chest, and covered his head. This was too much. After all he had been through, after all Jacob had been through, this wasn't fair. He thought he was following God's plan for his life, but he had just been blocked. Was he wrong to think God was in this? He broke down in sobs.

In his brokenness, he silently breathed a prayer for help.

That was when he remembered the words of Archibald McCreary and the letter in his pocket.

He got out of bed with determination, washed his face with cold water, and took his horse back to Rodding's office at a gallop. He tapped on the doorpost.

Rodding turned his eyes toward the door. "You forgot something, Mr. Hawk?"

Solomon emboldened himself to enter. "Yes, I did. Mr. Rodding, do you know Archibald McCreary?"

Rodding's face took on a smile. "Yes, I do. We had him speak to last year's graduating class. While he was in town, he stayed in my home. He's highly honored around here and a very charming fellow."

Solomon reached into his pocket, pulled out the envelope, and handed it to the registrar. "Then you must be the man he wanted me to give this to."

With a puzzled look, Rodding took the letter. He unfolded it and read it silently, then raised his eyes to Solomon.

"He's very impressed with you, Mr. Hawk."

Solomon waited expectantly.

Rodding sniffed, then sighed deeply. "I would happily accept you with his recommendation if we had room, but I still can't. It's a matter of capacity. We don't have an extra desk, a drafting table, or tools for another student."

Solomon's hope was nearly gone . . . again . . . but he sat down and tilted his head. "Would it make a difference if I paid a year's tuition in advance?"

Rodding tapped his pencil on his desk while he thought. "Come again tomorrow, Hawk. Let me check with the president and treasurer, and I'll give you an answer then."

So there's hope. Thank you, Father, Solomon thought. Then, to Rodding, he said, "Thank you for your consideration. I'll see you again in the morning."

He rose and left, resolving to pray for favor with the university authorities during the day. *I'll take whatever answer you give me, Lord, knowing that Your will is always best. But I confess that my greatest desire is to enroll this term.*

That same morning, Jacob went looking for work, taking yesterday's help wanted ads.

The ads were full of possibilities. He scanned through for something suited to his skills. He applied first at the general store as a clerk, then at the upholstery shop for a job covering chair seats. He applied at a shoe manufacturer that needed someone to punch shoestring holes in the leather. They preferred a woman for that work, so he was turned down. He went to an enamelware factory next door to apply as a worker on the production line, attaching handles to pots. But after waiting over an hour for an interview, he was told they had just filled the position. Discouraged, Jacob returned to the guest house at lunchtime.

Solomon was there, waiting. "How did you do this morning, Jacob?"

Jacob's dead expression spoke volumes. "I wasn't so fortunate. I went to four places, but no one wanted me. I hope I can do better tomorrow. We can't depend on your Grandfather's money forever."

"Tomorrow is another day," Solomon said. "In the meantime, it didn't go easy with me, either."

Jacob's face fell further. "What happened?"

"I may not be able to enroll in school this year. They have a full class. But there's a ray of hope. I showed the registrar the letter from McCreary and told him I could pay a full year in advance. He wants time to consider my proposal. He'll give me the school's decision tomorrow. But if they still say no, maybe—"

Jacob sank to the edge of the bed and took a deep breath. "Ever looking for the bright side, aren't you, Solly? We need to face the situation as it is. What do we do now?"

"I've been praying about it—"

"We need practical help, not an invisible wish-granter," snapped Jacob.

"—and I don't want you to feel guilty if you decide to leave, but I hope you'll stay with me. I think we're suffering only temporary delays."

Jacob dropped his head. "Even if I wanted to go back to Connecticut—and I'm not saying I do—I don't have any funds. Alright, we'll give it a few more days. But we can't stay in this boarding house. This is too expensive."

Solomon nodded. "I agree. Right now, we need to find a cheaper place to live. Do you still have your newspaper?"

"Sure." They divided up the want ads and searched for available housing. Since school was not in session, most students were out of town, leaving many properties empty. They had their pick of the offerings.

"By the way," Jacob said, scanning down the ads, "if you're staying, so am I . . . even if you have to find work for a year before you get into the university. So we'll need a rental at a good price."

Solomon felt some tension melt away at Jacob's reassurance. "Let's check this one that says it's three blocks from the university," he said. "It's a reasonable price, and look, it's an apartment with two bedrooms, a parlor, and a kitchen. We would each have privacy. Even if you had a guest, I could study in my room without being disturbed."

"But here's another one, Solly. It's a detached house five blocks from the school, with one large bedroom, but it's almost half the price. It has an outhouse and a barn for the horses. It says the kitchen was recently remodeled."

Solomon sighed. "I'm reluctant to give up a private bedroom, and I hate that it's an extra two blocks to the university, but to save expenses, I'm willing to look at it."

They took the ride to the house on Howard Street. It was pleasant enough but plain, with no fence and no special features to make it attractive. Seeing that the owner lived in the house beside it, they knocked on his door first and explained their mission. He snatched the key from its hook and took them to the rental house.

"I've done a lot of renovating," he said. "I had some unruly young men from the university living here last year, and I swore I would never rent to

111

students again. What do you gentlemen do for a living?"

Solomon swallowed hard. Jacob spoke up. "We just got into town. I'm looking for work. I've done blacksmithing before, but I would prefer something in the sales line where I could make more money."

The landlord nodded. "You're right. There's no limit to what a good salesman can earn. And what about you, sir?"

Solomon hesitated. "I just graduated from Yale, and I want to continue my studies in architecture at the university. But I assure you, we're quiet, hard-working men, both of us. You won't have any trouble if you rent to us."

The landlord squinted his eyes and pursed his lips. "If neither of you is employed, how would you expect to pay your rent?"

Solomon said, "If we rent the house, we can pay you cash three months in advance. And we would take the house today."

The landlord raised his eyes, nodded, and said, "Let me show you around."

He unlocked the door and admitted the two young men. The parlor was roomy, and the kitchen was plain but clean and had the necessary stove and icebox. The house had one large bedroom. "Could you tolerate sharing a bedroom, Solly? It would save us a lot of money."

"Maybe. I'd still like to look at that other apartment."

The landlord said, "Let me show you the barn before you go. You know that if you rent an apartment, there will be noise and commotion from other tenants around you, and you won't have a private barn. You won't even have a private entrance."

"Good point." Solomon's eyebrows raised at that thought. Where could they keep the horses at an apartment?

After seeing the barn, Jacob turned to the owner. "Can you give us a moment, sir? We need to confer."

"I'll go back to my own house. When you finish talking, come let me know what you decide."

As he walked away, Jacob said, "Solly, I like it. It's a good price."

"I'm surprised you don't want to live in the apartment with plenty of close neighbors."

"I would like that if the price was right, but it's not. I'll depend on my work for friends."

"I want to find a church near here. There will be people you can meet there, too."

"Maybe, if I decide to go. What do you say about the house?"

"It feels right," Solomon admitted. "But how can I have privacy in the bedroom for study?"

"We don't have to do things like everybody else. I'll look for a day bed or oversized sofa to put in the parlor, and I'll sleep there."

"We'll have to work that out. Let's take the house. It's a good price, and I feel peace about it."

They went next door and settled the deal with the landlord. He agreed they could move in the following day.

As they left their landlord's home with the key in hand, Solomon had plans for the day. "Now, Jacob, we have other business to attend to. We need to find a clothing store. If we dress you properly, you'll be able to get a better job than punching holes in leather or putting handles on pots."

Jacob grinned. They mounted their horses and found a gentleman's clothing store nearby. When they left an hour later, Jacob wore a three-piece suit, shirt, shoes, and a new attitude.

"Tomorrow, Jacob, when you look for a job, you can look for a position in sales, and my prayers will go with you."

Jacob's smile went from ear to ear. He couldn't take his excitement off his face.

Over dinner at a nearby restaurant, Solomon said, "While you look for a job tomorrow, I'll go back to the university to get their decision. Then I'll look for furniture. Grandfather gave me some extra money. I'll buy only what we need."

They returned to the guest house for the last night there and pored over the Help Wanted ads. Jacob found three places within a reasonable distance that were looking for salespeople, and Solomon wrote down the names and addresses of some furniture stores.

Friday, July 4, 1879

In the morning, they checked out of their accommodations. Solomon returned to Rodding's office at the university while Jacob left on his horse to find work.

Solomon again tapped on the doorframe, seeing Rodding at his desk.

"Come in, Hawk," he said, smiling. "Have a seat."

Encouraged, Solomon entered and sat.

"Is there good news?"

"There is," said Rodding. "I spoke to the president and treasurer. They said they would approve your admission if the professors agreed to take on another student. I managed to get everyone to agree. We're going to make room for you. But let me caution you, Mr. Hawk. If I were you, I'd do my level best to excel at my studies. You caused several people to be inconvenienced."

Solomon grinned broadly. "I will do my very best, sir. Thank you so much. Where do I pay my tuition before someone changes their mind?"

Rodding chuckled. "I'll take it now if you're prepared to pay on the spot. There's another thing. Our librarian's assistant resigned suddenly, and he's short-handed, with a lot of organizing work to do over the summer. Are you interested in taking a part-time job?"

Solomon smiled as he reached into his leather money belt for his tuition money. "I am interested, sir." He counted out the bills and handed them to Rodding, relieved he wouldn't have to be responsible for carrying around those dollars anymore. "May I have a receipt before we talk about the job?"

Rodding was already writing it out. "You'll start tomorrow morning at nine o'clock and work until one o'clock each day. You'll be paid once a week."

"Perfect," replied Solomon. "I'll be there at nine in the morning."

He left the office with a cheerful step and went to the auction house to find some furniture.

***

While Solomon was learning his good news, Jacob was job hunting. His first stop was the McCormick Harvesting Machine Company. As he tied his horse to the rail, he hesitated. A strange feeling came over him, something entirely foreign. *Prayer works for Solly,* he thought. *I wonder if God would hear me.*

Thinking he had nothing to lose, he faced his horse where no one could see him and closed his eyes. *God, you probably don't know me. I'm Jacob, a friend of Solomon Hawk. I'm here to ask for a job, and I really need one to pay my way and support Solly while he works, but I've been turned down for other jobs. So, if you can hear me, would you help me get hired? Much appreciated, sir.*

He walked to the green-painted metal door of the building and stepped inside. The atmosphere inside spoke of the serious industry going on. The screeching of metal on metal in the back of the building and the shouting of workers pierced the thin walls. He found the receptionist. She smiled at him, oblivious to the muted racket, and studied the tall, handsome man standing there.

"What can I do for you?" she asked.

"I'm here to apply for the sales job."

"Let me take you to see Mr. McCormick."

They walked down a short hall to a small office. Paperwork cluttered the desk, and crates of metal parts were stacked against a wall. An ashtray overflowed, the stub of a burning cigar balancing precariously on its rim.

"Mr. McCormick, this gentleman would like to apply for the salesman's job."

"Fine, fine," bellowed McCormick over the din in the adjoining assembly plant. "Sit down here." He pointed to a dusty metal chair across from his desk.

Jacob leaned down to brush the dirt off the seat. He didn't want to get his clothes grubby on the first day he wore them. He took the seat he was offered and answered every question asked of him. He explained his background and presented himself well. After about twenty minutes, McCormick took him on a tour of the manufacturing plant. Jacob was fascinated. McCormick said he would like to hire him starting next week and explained how he would be paid on commission.

"I'll let you know by Monday morning," Jacob said, shaking McCormick's hand. "Thank you, sir." He put his cap on his head and left with his eyes sparkling. His confidence was restored. He didn't want to take the first offer if salesmen could find a job that easily.

The next stop was J. W. Ellsworth and Company. It was about a mile from McCormick's plant and gave Jacob a chance to think on the way. Maybe God had something to do with it; maybe He didn't. He chuckled.

He found the Ellsworth building and tied his horse in front. It was a long industrial building with stonework over the lower portion of one end where customers would enter. Shrubs were planted in front of the stonework. Jacob went through the door where the receptionist had her desk.

"Good morning," he said. "I'd like to apply for the salesman's position."

"One moment," she said, and walked to the next office down the hall to speak to Mr. Ellsworth. Then she stepped back into the hall, turned to Jacob, and motioned him to come. He walked toward her on the wood floor, hearing his shoes striking the boards.

"Come on in," called a voice from the other side of the door. "Sit down."

Jacob obeyed as the receptionist returned to her desk. He was face to face with a friendly, balding man dressed in a gray suit.

"Now, sir, tell me your name and why you'd like to be our salesman."

The two men chatted for about half an hour. Jacob learned some surprising details about the company and the pay scale.

"I like you, Bishop," Ellsworth said. "If you're interested in coming on staff with us, I'd like to offer you the job on a one-month trial period. If you do well, the commission increases, and you stay permanently. What do you say?"

Jacob swallowed and grinned. "That's tempting, sir, but I had another offer earlier this morning. I told him I'd let him know by Monday. I can give you the same promise. I need to think about which company I'd fit in."

Ellsworth frowned. "I see. What other company was that?"

"It was McCormick."

"Ah. Our competitor in the farm implement business. Well, you need the weekend to make your decision. I hope you decide in our favor. I need to get a salesman out in the field, and I can't wait forever."

"Of course. I'll let you know Monday, sir. And thank you."

116

Jacob returned to the rental house in mid-afternoon, excited to tell Solomon about his job offers. They sat chatting on the floor since Solomon's furniture purchases hadn't yet been delivered.

"I interviewed at three companies today, Solly. Two of them offered me a job, so now I need to choose."

"Which two are they?"

"The first is the McCormick Harvesting Machine Company, and the other is J. W. Ellsworth and Company. I'm leaning toward McCormick. They manufacture reapers and other farm implements. Ellsworth is different. You won't believe this, but they make reapers *and* pianos."

Solomon chuckled over the odd combination of products in one company. "There must be a story behind that. Maybe two families were joined by marriage and brought their businesses with them."

"If I go with McCormick, I can concentrate my efforts in one area instead of dividing my time. I can't imagine trying to go in two directions to sell such different products."

"I wish you the best. No, I'll go you one better. I'll pray that you make the choice God has for you; that way, you'll have His best."

Jacob opened his mouth to reply just as there was a knock at the door. Solomon jumped up. "I forgot to tell you I bought furniture and kitchen supplies this morning," he said. "And here are the delivery men."

He opened the door, and the auction house employees carried his purchases into the house. Solomon and Jacob positioned the furniture where they thought best. Within an hour, their rented house had become a comfortable home.

Monday, July 7, 1879

On Monday, Jacob went off to finalize his job situation. Solomon returned to the university to work in the library, shelving books and keeping records of titles coming in and going out. It was satisfying work for a few hours each week and would bring in some money.

Jacob came home at dinnertime. "Well, Solly, I have a surprise. I took the Ellsworth job."

"I am surprised. Why did you choose that one?"

Jacob blushed. "I admit I prayed about it. Maybe that's how I knew it was right."

Solomon smiled and nodded.

Jacob continued. "The pay is a little more, and they want me to concentrate on selling pianos. I won't be selling farm implements at all. That means I'll meet rich folks with enough scratch to buy pianos. Maybe they'll also need an architect. And I'll be working with churches and schools who want to buy a piano . . . maybe for their new building they'll be putting up."

As Jacob's reasoning and the reality of his decision dawned on Solomon, a slow smile lit his face. "That sounds like a wise move. Now, all we need to do is bring your vocabulary out of the smithy and into the business world."

Jacob's eyebrows pinched together. "What does that mean?"

Solomon patted him on the shoulder, amused. "It means you don't want to use terms like 'scratch' when you're talking with customers. Call it money or funds. It will just take a little practice."

Jacob sighed and lowered his eyes. "I'm trying hard, but sometimes I think I'll always be a blacksmith inside. Can I ever learn to talk right? Truth be told, I felt like a fake in these fancy duds today, pretending to be something I'm not. Do you think I'll ever really belong in your world?"

Solomon scratched his head. "I didn't know you thought that way, Jacob. I'm sorry I said what I did. But it's not very different from me. Father told me for years I'd be a preacher, and I'm struggling to convince myself that I made an honorable decision to be an architect. Sometimes, I feel like a little boy sneaking behind his father's back."

The two men gazed at each other's faces for a moment. Jacob spoke first. "So we're both going through the same thing. That makes me feel better. I didn't know you had doubts. I definitely see you as an architect."

"And I see you as a successful salesman. Look at the way you handled yourself on our trip. Look at the ingenuity you used to get us what we needed when there was no money. You're going to make it just fine, my friend. You have all the right personality qualifications, and yes, you belong in my world."

Jacob smiled. His eyes misted over for a moment before he cleared his throat. "What's for supper?"

It was Solomon's turn to blush. "I guess neither of us bought any food. We'll have to go shopping and see what we can find."

They hurried out before the stores closed. They bought the basics, then had a quick meal of eggs, toast, and coffee before turning in for the night.

Tuesday, July 8, 1879

The following day, Jacob's stomach fluttered as he approached the manufacturing plant of J. W. Ellsworth and Company. He dismounted and tied his horse to the rail. It was a sprawling building in a district of wooden warehouses. The stonework around the main entrance was designed to attract retail customers.

"Put on your business face, Jacob," he whispered. "Let's see how you are at selling pianos."

Inside, he went to the office of J. William Ellsworth, Jr. He took a breath, opened the door, and entered. "Good morning, Mr. Ellsworth." He radiated confidence despite his nervous stomach. He shook Ellsworth's hand in a firm grip.

"Good morning, Mr. Bishop. Are you ready to learn about pianos?"

"Yes, sir."

"Good. I'm turning you over to Miss Thompson, our piano teacher. She knows about the pianos. She'll give you an overview of the points you should make with a prospective buyer. Take some time to learn what she has to teach you, then tomorrow I'll give you a list of prospects, and you can contact them."

"Yes, sir."

Miss Thompson was an attractive young woman of about twenty-five years. Her long brown hair flowed over her shoulders in loose curls, and her brown eyes raised to meet Jacob's. "Would you come this way with me, Mr. Bishop? We'll start in the piano showroom."

She turned, and he followed her down a long hall. Her shoes tapped sharply on the pine floor.

"Have you worked here long, Miss Thompson?"

"Five years," she said, glancing back to make eye contact with him as she walked. "It's a great place to work. If you like sales work, I believe you'll enjoy it here."

"I hope so."

They continued down the hall to the door of the showroom. The room was also accessible from the street. Three different pianos were on display: two uprights and a baby grand. Miss Thompson's face brightened. "I love coming in here."

She swept to the piano nearest them, the one with the dark walnut cabinet. "This is a fine piano. Do you play?"

"What? Me, play piano? No, I'm sorry, I've never been that close to one."

She grasped one of his rough hands and turned it over. He flinched and tried to pull it back.

"No matter," she said. "I see you've been doing manual labor. Those callouses will take a little time to soften, but they will." She glanced at him and smiled. "Now let me tell you what a customer needs to know about pianos."

She seated herself on the round stool, launching into the sweet melody of *Für Elise*. Her hands floated over the keys. Jacob stood by attentively.

"Isn't that lovely?" she asked.

"Lovely. Yes," he said, noting that 'lovely' would be a term he could use with clients, even though it sounded too feminine to his ears.

"This tone is a result of many things," she said. "Let me show you the inner workings of an upright piano." She opened the top and gave Jacob a good view of the inside.

"That's amazing," he said. "So many parts! I never realized . . ."

"This large piece is called the soundboard. We make all our soundboards from high-quality spruce, known for its excellent resonance."

He hesitated. "Resonance?"

"Yes. I can see we have a lot of work to do."

Jacob flashed a smile at her. "Don't give up on me, Miss Thompson. I learn fast."

She smiled and nodded. "I believe you. But back to resonance. Another way to describe resonance is the way the piano sounds. A spruce soundboard makes that sound richer. It gives a rich, round sound instead of a flat, dull sound."

He nodded. "Resonance is how it sounds, and the sound comes from the soundboard. I need to write some of these things down. Do you have paper and pencil?"

"We'll just give you a quick overview this morning to give you background knowledge. After we're finished, we'll review it all again, and you can make notes then."

"All right."

"So play close attention," she scolded. "Now look at the upward curve on the soundboard. That's called a soundboard crown. It helps distribute the sound vibrations evenly and improves the sound. Moving on to the strings, you'll see eighty-eight sets of strings attached to the soundboard pins. Remember that number: eighty-eight. It's important. It's the number of keys on the piano, black and white."

"Eighty-eight. Got that."

"The strings come in different thicknesses and lengths. The long, thick strings create the lower notes, and the short, thin strings give us the high notes. Now look inside here, and you'll see the hammers. Watch what happens when I press the keys."

She played a quick C scale. Jacob stood mesmerized as the hammers struck the strings, creating audible vibrations that filled the air. "Do that again," he urged her, and studied the action more intently as she repeated the scale.

"Ah. Resonance," he said with a nod. "Round tones. Nicely distributed vibrations."

Miss Thompson raised her eyes to him, and her face crinkled into a smile. "Well said. I believe you're going to do well here, Mr. Bishop."

He beamed and stuffed his hands in his pockets.

"Now, the hammers are made from felt. The density and quality of the felt affect the quality of sound. If the felts are too soft, the tones sound dull and mushy. Too hard, and you get a harsh, unpleasant sound. You have to meet a happy middle. We've done quite well at getting the hammers right. We call them well-voiced hammers."

"Well-voiced hammers. Another term to remember."

"Step over to this other piano with me for just a moment. I want to show you something."

They went to the piano with a beautiful, carved mahogany cabinet. Miss Thompson pulled up the stool and played another rendition of *Für Elise*. The sound that came out of that piano was horrible. Jacob clapped his hands over his ears.

"What happened?" he asked. "That's a beautiful piano, but it sounds awful."

Miss Thompson giggled. "It does, doesn't it? That's because it's out of tune. Over time, especially if a piano is moved, the strings lose their tension. Then you have to have a piano tuner come and re-tune it, string by string."

Jacob's chin dropped. "You're kidding. That must take hours. And where do you find a piano tuner?"

"We have a man on our staff, an excellent tuner. He uses a tuning fork, but we can talk about that later. I'll introduce you another time. Right now, we still have some learning to do. Just one thing. If a customer asks how often he needs to have the piano tuned, we recommend it once a year as a general rule. Unless, as I told you before, it gets moved or is subject to wide temperature and humidity changes. Most folks know when a piano needs tuning just by listening to it."

"That's easy to believe."

The lessons went on most of the day, with Miss Thompson repeating the information and asking Jacob to treat her as a customer by explaining the features of the piano.

"Not bad for your first day, Mr. Bishop. I'm sure you'll do well. The more you talk about pianos, the smoother your presentation will become."

When Jacob left the piano shop, he had confidence and a head full of new information.

***

He arrived home to the aroma of beef stew filling his nostrils. "Doesn't stew take hours to cook?" he asked Solomon. "I thought you were working at the library today."

"I did." Solomon adopted a sheepish expression. "The librarian took pity on a newcomer and brought his wife's leftover stew for both of us."

It was a satisfying dinner and a relaxing evening as Jacob regaled Solomon with his new knowledge of pianos.

Wednesday, July 9, 1879

The next morning, as Solomon cooked omelets for breakfast, Jacob was eager to get to work and start selling. Yesterday had been a good day with Miss Thompson. He had learned a lot about pianos. She had even suggested that he learn to play to enhance his sales presentation, and she would teach him. That was a very appealing idea, even if he didn't know whether he had any musical talent. He wolfed his breakfast, then left.

As he tied his horse to the rail at work, he found himself humming *Für Elise*. He headed to Mr. Ellsworth's office.

"Reporting for duty, sir," he said with a broad smile.

"You're right on time," Ellsworth said. "Here I have a list of three customers interested in owning a piano, but they haven't yet committed. It's your job to get to know them, learn why they hesitate to buy and try to turn their objections into sales. Don't rush with this or make them feel pressured. Turn on the charm, boy. Lead them down a happy path to piano ownership. Appeal to their sense of snobbery, or whatever it takes."

Jacob burst into a hearty laugh. "I'm sure you're joking, sir. That's a good one."

"Not joking," Ellsworth said. "Some people only want a piano because their friends have one."

Jacob's eyebrows raised over his grin. "Good to know. I'll add that information to my list of sales pitches."

"You'll do fine. Now off with you."

Jacob took his list of prospective customers to the piano room to study them. He needed to decide which customer he should start with. First was Dr. Adam Warren. Second was Mrs. Marguerite Sterling, heiress to a modest typewriter fortune. Third was the Cooper Street Baptist Church, pastored by Rev. Jonas Bromley. Jacob rejected Dr. Warren as a first contact as he would be with patients during the day. Wealthy folks intimidated him, so he didn't want to approach Mrs. Sterling first. By process of elimination, he would try the church. He would pick Solomon's brain to get some background information and explore ways to approach Rev. Bromley. Solomon was well acquainted with preachers.

He mounted his horse. The air was warm and muggy. The clouds overhead warned of a storm coming, so he hurried to the university library, where Solomon was busy cataloging an order of newly arrived books.

"Can you take a break for a few minutes?" Jacob asked.

"Just a few." He made one last notation in a journal and turned his attention to Jacob.

"All right. Here's my situation. I need to go to the Cooper Street Baptist Church and talk to the pastor about buying a piano. How do I approach him? Will he have any concerns that I need to know about?"

"Good question." Solomon raised his eyes to an unknown point on the wall while he thought. "Alright, think of it from the pastor's point of view. First, you'll want to see the space where they plan to put a piano to give you a feel for the kind of piano they need. Is it a large sanctuary or a small classroom? Now, the pastor is probably working with a board of trustees, so it's not his decision alone. Think about how a piano could benefit the church. It would add to the enjoyment of the music and aid the congregation in singing and worship. Have you ever been to church, Jacob?"

"I went to Sunday School a few times as a small boy."

"You should attend a service so you'll have a better feel for the value of church music. Why don't you and I attend Cooper Street Baptist this Sunday?"

"I'll agree if it will help my research. Any more advice?"

"Find out if the pastor needs to convince an obstinate board who pinches dollars or if the board is agreeable to the purchase already. That will tell you how many people you have to convince."

"Hmm. There's a lot to think about."

"You're a natural at this, Jacob. Go. Relax. The pastor is just a man like you, but talk to him with respect, and you'll do fine."

Solomon returned to his work, and Jacob left with his head swimming with new information. He hoped the pastor would overlook the callouses on his hands and not think he was too lower-class to be taken seriously. He stopped by the general store and bought some lotion for his hands, telling the storekeeper it was for his mother. He also asked for directions to Cooper Street Baptist.

Outside the store, he stood close to his horse's side to shield himself from view. He opened the jar of cream and rubbed it all over his hands until his fingers were sticky. Then he rinsed off at the water pump in the alley and wiped his hands on his saddle blanket. *I wish I had my Levi's,* he thought. *I could've wiped my hands on my britches without a worry. I guess giving up comfortable trousers is the price of future prosperity.*

He mounted up and headed to Cooper Street.

Chapter 15: Jacob Launches a Career

Jacob's stomach fluttered as he approached the doors of the church. Its tall pillars and the majestic sweep of the roof with the soaring steeple filled him with awe. He had never been in such a place as this.

Opening the heavy wooden door, he stepped out of the sunlight and entered a large, cool vestibule. The sanctuary was visible through a second set of doors. Rows and rows of oak pews lined up before the imposing pulpit. The wood floors were polished and worn smooth over time by the feet of many worshipers. Jacob marveled at the sunlight flooding through the stained glass windows, splashing color on the pews and floor.

The atmosphere was different in this building—holy, somehow. The silence had weight. Jacob tiptoed to the door of the sanctuary and studied the room. There were more pews behind the pulpit. It was a mystery to Jacob why anyone would want to sit there. *People probably sit there only if the other seats are all taken,* he thought.

As he soaked in his surroundings, footsteps approached from behind, echoing off the walls, and he turned to face the pastor. He was a middle-aged, robust-looking man with dark hair and a friendly smile.

"Good morning, sir," said Pastor Bromley. "What can I do for you?"

Jacob's feeling of awe was interrupted. He turned on the charm and extended his hand for a shake. "Good morning. I'm Jacob Bishop from J.W. Ellsworth. I came to see if I could help you with a piano."

The pastor nodded. "I'm glad you're here. Come to my office."

He turned, and Jacob followed him to a side room. A bookcase loaded with leather-bound volumes stood against the wall. Beside it hung a framed picture of a long-haired fellow holding a lamb. The room was dominated by a broad mahogany desk faced by two red wingback chairs. The next thing to catch Jacob's eye was the colorful Oriental rug. As small as it was, the entire office spoke of wealth and discriminating taste.

Jacob took a seat in one of the wingbacks. *Very comfortable,* he thought.

"I was in your piano showroom a week ago," the pastor said. "We're looking for a piano for the sanctuary. We now have a pump organ, but a piano would add volume and versatility. We have a man in our church who's a skilled pianist. He'd like to use his talents to the glory of God."

Volume and versatility, thought Jacob. *Good to know.*

"Is your board agreeable to this purchase?" he asked.

"Most of them want to proceed with this sale, but you've touched on a major snag. One board member insists that we don't need a piano. He's holding us up since we must have a one hundred percent vote, a mistake made by those who drafted the by-laws. The fellow's name is Benjamin Creel. Please don't spread this around, but I wish he had never been elected to the Board. He's held us up on more than one issue."

"I'm sorry to hear that," Jacob said. He leaned forward and folded his hands. "So let's pretend for a minute you didn't have anything holding you up, and let's talk about what you'll want to buy when Mr. Creel changes his mind."

The pastor grinned. "Going on faith, are we? Good suggestion. I like that."

Jacob returned his smile. "Could I see the spot where you want to put the piano, just to get a feel for the space?"

"Sure." The pastor stood and ushered Jacob back to the sanctuary. "It's the space up there on the platform to the left of the pulpit. You can see how the domed ceiling over the platform will add to the acoustics. It will send the sound right out to the congregation."

Acoustics. Jacob tucked the word into his mental filing cabinet, meaning to ask Miss Thompson about it later. He surmised it might be related to 'resonance.' The two proceeded up the center aisle until they were on the platform.

"This is a large space," Jacob said. "You have room for a grand piano here. Is that what you're looking for?"

"No, there's not enough room for that. You see this hatch?" Pastor Bromley reached down and grasped a handle screwed to the floor. When he gave it a mighty tug, a six-foot section of the floor opened on a hinge, revealing the sunken baptistry. "We have our baptisms here. We can't put anything on top of this."

Jacob's eyes widened. "Tell you the truth, Pastor, I never laid eyes on anything like that before."

The pastor chuckled. "Where do you attend church?"

Jacob stammered, then corrected himself. "I, uh . . . my friend and I just moved to town. We haven't found a church yet."

"Well, I invite you to try us. I think you'd like to worship here."

"We'll be here Sunday." Jacob thought it would help sales to attend the church, at least for a time or two, until the piano was sold.

"Good. We look forward to meeting your friend. What did you say his name is?"

"Solomon Hawk."

The two returned to the pastor's office and sat opposite each other.

Jacob leaned forward. "Can you tell me about Benjamin Creel? Maybe I could help change his mind."

"Ah. Mr. Creel." The pastor clasped his hands behind his neck and tilted his head back, gazing at the ceiling. "Mr. Creel is the son of one of the founders of this church. I don't mean this to be unkind, but his attitude is that he owns it. Do you know what I mean?"

"I'm beginning to understand."

"He doesn't want us to spend a dime more than we have to."

"But this church . . . your office . . . it looks like a lot of money has been spent on it. And I hope you don't think I'm being critical. I'm not."

"Yes, but that was before Benjamin was elected to the Board. He was always loud when expressing his opinion, but he didn't get a vote until a couple of years ago. Then, he got enough relatives together to vote him in. Now, they're sorry they did."

Jacob chuckled. "And how long is his term?"

"He'll be on the Board for another year. I don't want to wait that long to get our piano if I don't have to. It's been a matter of prayer and will continue to be."

"Did you see a particular piano at the showroom that you liked?"

"You have that walnut and another mahogany, but I'd like one made of oak to match our pews. Can you get one like that?"

"Being a new salesman, I'll have to confirm it, but I believe they can make a piano from whatever wood you like. I'll find out and let you know on Sunday."

"Thank you, Mr. Bishop. I'm grateful to you for coming and discussing this. I look forward to seeing you again."

The men shook hands, and Jacob left with energy in his steps. *That went better than I had expected.*

He was ready for lunch. Knowing there was little food in the house, he did some shopping at the butcher's and took his purchases home. When Solomon arrived, Jacob was wielding a spatula before a skillet of sausages.

"Hey, Solly, how was your morning?"

Solomon stretched his arms. "My back is stiff from reaching high and low to put books where they belong, but I got a lot done today. How did you do at the church?"

"I feel encouraged." Jacob flipped the sausages. "The pastor has an issue with one member of his Board, so I'm glad you told me to ask about that. By the way, we're attending Cooper Street Baptist Church this Sunday."

Solomon chuckled. "I'll look forward to it. I've never been to church anywhere except my father's church and the chapel at Yale."

"Now I have a new problem. I need to talk to a rich lady. She has a pocket full of rocks, and she's thinking of buying a piano."

Solomon leaned back in a hearty laugh. He pulled out a chair and sat at the kitchen table. "That's a colorful turn of phrase. Let me give you a few terms to replace 'pocket full of rocks.' You can say she's wealthy, well-off, well-heeled, or blessed with substance, but don't say 'pocket full of rocks' in her presence. And don't say she has plenty of scratch. Wealthy people are sensitive about that kind of thing. They take it as disrespectful. And above all, they want to be respected."

Jacob tilted his head and peered at Solomon. "Is your father wealthy?"

"Wealthier than average, I'd guess."

"So when you defied his wishes—"

"Yes, that was a hard blow for him to take. He demands unquestioning respect, especially from me and Mother."

Jacob nodded and flipped the sausages again. "These links are ready. Are you hungry?"

"You bet!"

Jacob filled two plates and sat at the table with Solomon. He stabbed a forkful of well-cooked meat and wrapped his mouth around it. "So, how do I show respect to a well-heeled lady?" he asked through his teeth. He swallowed his food and lifted a glass of water to his lips.

"You'll need to be sensitive to her moods. For instance, a raised eyebrow could mean you just offended her. Try to figure out what you did and back out of it some way. Try to make her comfortable in your presence, not like she's pressured to give up money she doesn't want to spend. She needs to feel safe around you. Try to learn why she's thinking of a piano and play up to that need in her life."

Jacob nodded, still chewing his sausage. He swallowed. "Why do you think she might want a piano?"

Solomon gestured, waving his fork in the air. "Oh, there could be many reasons. Wealthy people are often very sociable, so maybe she likes to host parties and wants some background music. Or maybe she has a son or daughter who wants piano lessons. Or maybe she's interested in home decorating and thinks a piano would look good in her parlor. She could even want a piano only because her friend just bought one. Could be any reason, according to her whim."

Jacob put down his fork and wiped his mouth with his hand. "I'd better be going. I want plenty of time to spend with her this afternoon if she's willing to talk."

"Wait, Jacob. Here's a napkin for your hands and face."

Jacob took it, wiped the grease off his fingers and swiped at his mouth. "Thanks, Solly. See you later."

***

Full of energy, Jacob mounted his horse again and headed to Mrs.

Marguerite Sterling's address. He tied his horse to a post and walked up the wide stone walkway. He had no idea what to expect when he rapped on her door. The house was the largest he had seen, almost as big as a hotel. The outside was limestone and had pillars beside the main entrance, supporting a balcony off the second floor. The front windows beside the main entrance were glazed with leaded glass sparkling in the sun. It was landscaped with cedars and beds of flowers designed by a gardener with the heart of an artist.

A woman dressed in a gray linen dress and white apron answered the door.

"Mrs. Sterling?" Jacob asked.

"And your name is—"

"Jacob Bishop. I'm from the Ellsworth Piano Company."

"Step inside, and I'll see if she's available," the woman replied. She disappeared into an adjoining room for a moment, then returned. "Please come this way. Mrs. Sterling will see you now."

Jacob followed the woman into a library room with floor-to-ceiling bookshelves. A large table stood in the center of the room, holding a floral centerpiece. It was ringed by comfortable chairs. The lady of the house, a petite woman of about thirty-five years, sat in a wheelchair with an open book on her lap. She had intelligent eyes and dark hair framing her face. This was not the elderly matron Jacob had imagined her to be. She raised her eyes and gave Jacob a polite smile as he approached. She stretched out her hand, so Jacob took it and squeezed it warmly.

"My name is Jacob Bishop, ma'am. Thank you for seeing me."

"You're welcome. Pull a chair over, and we'll talk. I don't get to talk to people often since I broke my leg. I'll be glad when it's healed."

"How did you do that?" Jacob asked.

"Oh, I was putting a large pot of flowers on my front step to brighten the entrance when I stubbed my toe on something. Probably a crack between the paving stones. Anyway, I tripped and lost my balance. It's a good thing Gloria was on duty that day. She came running and went for the doctor. The worst of it was when I dropped the pot. It broke, and the most beautiful flower arrangement I ever made fell to pieces." She wagged her head at the sad memory of that day.

Jacob's eyes ran around the room. Fresh-cut flowers and potted ivy filled every empty spot.

"I can see you like a beautiful room. This room is so lovely, so peaceful." *There, I got to use the word 'lovely.'*

"I'm pleased you noticed. Would you like a cup of tea, Mr. Bishop?"

"Yes, if it's not too much trouble. With sugar, please."

Mrs. Sterling called Gloria and asked her to bring two cups of tea with sugar. "If there are any lemon cookies left, bring them, too."

Gloria hurried off to do her bidding.

"Now, Mr. Bishop. You came here for a purpose."

"Yes, ma'am. I understand you're thinking of buying a piano. Is that right?"

She leaned back and met his eyes with hers. "I was, but now, with my broken leg, I don't know if I should. I couldn't use the sustain pedal without causing myself pain."

"Oh, so you're the musician in the house," Jacob said. "How long have you been playing?"

She smiled. "I started lessons when I was eight years old. I studied piano for six years and became quite accomplished. I miss having one, although I would be playing for my own amusement most of the time. Since my husband died, I haven't had too many guests."

"I'm sorry to hear about your husband. How long ago was that?"

"Two years. I still miss him something awful."

Compassion filled Jacob's heart. He gave her a sympathetic smile as Gloria brought a tray with the steaming teapot, cups, and a plate of frosted, pale yellow cookies. She placed it all on the table and poured the tea.

"Mr. Bishop, would you mind wheeling me to the table? We can sit together and have our tea and cookies there."

They spent a few minutes enjoying their refreshments and getting to know one another. She spoke about how her life had changed since her husband's death. The people in her social circle invited her to their parties less often, especially since the accident with her leg, and she stayed home most of the time. She enjoyed decorating the house. It was sad that few people came to see it.

"But what about you, Mr. Bishop? Did you grow up in Chicago?"

"No, ma'am, I just arrived here with my friend, Solomon Hawk. He's studying architecture at the university. When he opens his business, I'll be lining up his clients."

Mrs. Sterling nodded. "I'm sure you'll be successful."

"This house is so beautiful," said Jacob, glancing around the room. "If you had a piano, where would you put it?"

She grinned. "Wheel me into the hall. We'll go to the great room, and I'll show you where I would put one if I had it."

Jacob shoved the last bite of his cookie into his mouth. As he pushed her wheelchair, she asked, "How long have you been playing?"

"Piano?" he asked. "I'm sorry to say I've never learned, but Miss Thompson at the piano store intends to give me lessons."

"I saw your hands," she said, and he pulled them back to get them out of sight. "Don't be embarrassed. You have strong, muscular hands. You'll be able to play those dramatic octave runs that most women struggle with. Men with strong hands make excellent pianists. Practice will limber them up."

Jacob's brows raised in amazement. "Hmm. Good to know."

"Turn left here," she said, and they entered the great room with a massive stone fireplace, polished parquet floors, and soft upholstered furniture arranged in conversation groups. Tall French doors at one end allowed sunlight to flood in. Jacob gazed upward at the heavy wooden beams crossing the high ceiling and then down at the art objects around the room.

"I've never seen brass sculptures like you have on this table," he said, "and look at this pottery! It's huge and blends well with the colors you've chosen."

She placed her elbow on the armrest of her wheelchair, rested her chin on the back of her hand, and grinned at him. "It's unusual for a man to notice things like that," she replied. "I'm impressed."

"You have enough room here for several couples to dance without crashing into one another."

Mrs. Sterling laughed. "We had dances here when my husband was living. It was wonderful fun. And I think the record is ten couples dancing

133

at one time. They had to step carefully."

Jacob observed her eyes roaming the room as if remembering some previous gala.

"And over here, Mr. Bishop. Here's where I would put a piano if I had one." She pointed to the far wall opposite the French doors.

"But there's no wall space," Jacob said. "Where would it go?"

"You see that ugly plaid chair?"

"I see a plaid chair, but it's not ugly."

"Well, it would have to go, and I would put a piano against that wall. It would have to be an upright to preserve the most floor space for dancing."

Jacob took a few steps further into the room. Putting his right hand over his heart and stretching out his left arm, he spun around to some imaginary music. "Can't you see this grand room filled with guests dancing to the piano music?"

Mrs. Sterling giggled with delight. "Oh, you're taking me back a few years. It was so much fun at our parties. If I had another one, I would also want to hire some violinists. They could play waltzes with the pianist . . . Mr. Bishop, if I buy a piano after my leg heals, would you promise to come to my first party and dance with me?"

Jacob grinned. "Yes, I promise. It would be a real pleasure. It would get you back into the social life you've missed since your husband died." He stood gazing around the room with a wide stance and his hands on his hips. "What kind of wood would you choose for the piano?"

"That's an interesting question." She glanced around. "I think a nice, dark mahogany piano with carvings on the legs would look perfect here."

He turned toward her. "We have such a piano in the showroom, you know. It needs tuning, but any piano we deliver will need tuning anyway. If you like, I could try to hold it back and not sell it to anyone else until you're ready for it."

She beamed at him. "I'm still picturing you dancing in the silence . . . Mr. Bishop, if you can arrange to get a woman in a wheelchair to your salesroom, I'll look at it. If I like it, I'll buy it now and have plenty of time to plan a party while my leg heals."

Jacob's brain went into high gear. "Give me the afternoon to arrange a carriage to pick you up tomorrow morning. I'll lift you in and out of the carriage and have another wheelchair for you at Ellsworth's while you test the piano. How does that sound?"

She beamed. "I look forward to it."

He grasped her hand and then left her house, wondering how he could keep the ambitious promise he just made. He mounted his horse, went home, and dashed inside to talk to Solomon.

"Solly, I'm in trouble. I hope you can help me," he said.

Solomon turned to him in alarm. "Is that wealthy lady angry with you about something?"

Jacob laughed. "Quite the contrary. She wants to buy a piano if I promise to come to her party and dance with her."

"What?" Solomon's eyebrows raised, his chin dropped, and the corners of his mouth turned up in amusement. "So what's the trouble?"

"She's in a wheelchair. I promised to arrange for a carriage to pick her up tomorrow morning, take her to Ellsworth's, and have another wheelchair waiting for her there."

"Whew. Let me think. You can probably rent a wheelchair from the medical supply house on the other side of the university. And you can probably borrow a carriage from Mr. Ellsworth since he knows it will be used to make a sale. But we'd better hurry to the medical supply house before they close. Do you have enough money?"

"Probably. Do you have any extra, just in case?"

"A little."

The two men left for the medical supply house together on their horses. Once there, they paid to have the wheelchair delivered to Ellsworth's first thing in the morning. Then Jacob went to the office to arrange to use the carriage. All was settled.

Thursday, July 10, 1879

The following morning, Jacob went to work early to ensure the plan was in place. The wheelchair was there, waiting by the front door. Jacob asked Miss Thompson to be on hand to demonstrate the piano. Then he took Mr. Ellsworth's carriage and traveled the two miles to Mrs. Sterling's house.

When he rapped on the door, Gloria asked him to come in. "Mrs. Sterling will be ready soon," she said. "She's finishing her breakfast. Would you like to wait in the great room?"

Jacob said he would. He strolled to the room he had enjoyed yesterday and stood by the large French doors, his hands clasped behind his back. The garden was lush with oaks, maples, and yellow-green ferns. Multi-colored zinnias were in bloom throughout the garden.

How pleasant it would be to live in a home like this, he thought. *If I work hard for Solomon, maybe I could have a smaller version someday.* He chuckled, imagining his Ma and Pa visiting him in such a fine home. *What would they think?*

"I'm ready now," the feminine voice behind him said. He turned to see Mrs. Sterling in her wheelchair, wearing a lace-trimmed blue silk dress with a matching wide-brimmed chapeau.

Jacob took one look, and his eyes widened. "A lady who looks like you shouldn't hide herself from the public." He regretted his impudence as soon as it was out of his mouth. "Mrs. Sterling, forgive me. I didn't intend to be so personal."

She came close to choking, trying to stifle a giggle. "You're forgiven," she said. "Now, let's go look at a piano."

He wheeled her down the hall, through the foyer, and out the door. Gloria accompanied them as they took the front steps one at a time. Bump . . . bump . . . bump. When they reached the carriage, Jacob said, "Mrs. Sterling, you would be easier to carry if you'd hold your hat."

She removed it from her head. "That's not a hat. That's a chapeau. Here, Gloria, hold this 'hat' for a minute."

Gloria reached for it, her lips twisting in an effort to hide a smile.

Jacob leaned over to pick up Mrs. Sterling, who wrapped her arm around his neck for support. He blushed, lifted her, and deposited her on the carriage seat. Gloria observed all this with an amused grin. She handed the chapeau back to Mrs. Sterling.

"I'd tell you to keep that bothersome bonnet here, Gloria, except I'll need it to keep the sun off my face." She positioned it back on her head while Jacob went to the other side of the carriage and climbed in.

"Ready?" he asked.

"Let's go."

He slapped the reins, and they were off. They chatted for thirty minutes until they arrived at Ellsworth's.

"Stay here until I get some help," Jacob said.

"Trust me; I won't run off."

Jacob ran inside to get the wheelchair and pushed it to the carriage. Then, Mrs. Sterling leaned toward him with her arm ready to hang onto his neck while he scooped her out of her seat. With great care, he placed her in the wheelchair. He checked to make sure her dress wouldn't get caught in the wheels and pushed her through the door.

Once inside, she wheeled herself to the mahogany piano Jacob had told her about.

"This is a beautiful instrument," she murmured with reverence, running her hand over the cabinet. "May I play it?"

Jacob's heart sank. "First, let me explain that this piano needs tuning. It sounds terrible right now, but once it's inside your home, our tuner will come and put it to rights."

"I just want to feel the action. I don't want a piano that's too stiff or too loose in the keys."

She wheeled herself into position at the keyboard, but the wheelchair was lower than the piano stool. "Oh, this is awkward," she said.

"I can help you sit on the stool if you like," Jacob offered.

She nodded, and he slid the stool to her. Then he helped her stand on her good leg and transfer to the stool.

"Now, this feels better." She placed her hands over the keys and began the first measures of the Blue Danube Waltz.

"Oh, you were right. That sounds horrid." Her hands dropped to her lap. "I so wanted to hear how it would sound."

"Come over here to this other piano," Jacob said. "It's in tune, and the action is the same. The soundboard and strings are identical to the one you're playing. Only the cabinet is different."

He helped her roll on her stool to the other piano. Once again, she began the lilting notes of the Blue Danube Waltz. "Now, this is a tune you can dance to, Jacob," she said. "I like this. The tones are round and pleasing, and the action of the keys is well-balanced. Are you sure the mahogany piano will be this good when it's set up in my home?"

"I give you my word. An excellent pianist deserves an excellent piano."

She blushed at the compliment as she finished the Blue Danube, then launched into a sweet rendition of "I Dream of Jeannie With the Light Brown Hair." Smiling, she ended her mini-concert and spun on the stool to face Jacob. "I must have a piano, and I'd like that mahogany one, conditional on its sounding and feeling proper when it's been set up at home."

"Wonderful," he said. "Let's get you to Mr. Ellsworth's office, where he'll write a receipt for your payment and schedule delivery."

As he lifted her back into the wheelchair, she said, "Don't forget, you promised to come to my party and dance with me."

"I look forward to it."

He pushed her into Ellsworth's office. They scheduled the delivery and tuning for the next day.

Jacob returned her to her home and drove back to the store to speak to Mr. Ellsworth.

"Any suggestions on my first sale?"

"You did a fine job of it. I was impressed that you went out of your way to get a woman in a wheelchair into the store. Now, tell me about Rev. Bromley."

"He wants the piano, but one board member is blocking his path. I plan to attend the service there this Sunday. Maybe I can meet the stubborn board member and determine what it would take to win him over."

Ellsworth nodded. "That's good. And what about the third lead I gave you, Dr. Adam Warren?

"I haven't met him yet. I figured that he would be with patients during the day. I'll have to meet with him during the evening or on a weekend."

Ellsworth wagged his head. "I should have told you he's a veterinarian. He treats mostly large animals. You'll have to find out from his wife where he is at any particular time, then meet him at whatever farm he's visiting."

Jacob's mouth formed an "O," and he nodded. "I'll visit his wife on Monday. I want to be at Mrs. Sterling's house when her piano is delivered tomorrow and watch the piano tuner at work. That way, I'll have first-hand experience when I talk about it with future customers. Sunday, I'll be at church, then Monday, I'll try to see the doc."

Miss Thompson entered the room. At the sight of Jacob, her face lit up. "Mr. Bishop, good to see you. When are we starting your lessons?"

Jacob turned toward her. "Are you busy now?"

She grinned. "I'll meet you in the piano room in a few minutes."

Jacob went to the well-tuned piano and sat on the stool. It was too high for him, but he found that it was attached to three legs by a large screw. By turning the seat round and round, he could lower it. He chuckled to think what fun it would have been as a child to spin round and round on a seat like that. While he waited, he became adventurous and pressed one of the piano keys.

Miss Thompson came in with a music book in her hand. She pulled another stool to the piano and handed the book to Jacob. On the first page, there were horizontal lines with square shapes splashed on them. Most of the squares were attached to little poles pointing up or down, and some poles had flags. This was going to be like learning Chinese.

"Now, Mr. Bishop, for your first lesson. We'll get to those notes in a minute, but you must first learn the hand position. You don't lay your fingers flat on the keys like this." She stretched out her fingers to demonstrate. "You curl your fingers around so they strike the keys more on the tips." Again, she showed him with her fingers. "Now, lay your hand over mine and curl your fingers over . . . just so. You see? That's how you need to hold your hands."

Jacob tried to conceal his blushing. He had difficulty concentrating as she explained the position of middle C, but he wanted to learn. A half-hour later, his head was stuffed with more new knowledge. He didn't know how much more he could remember in so short a time.

Friday, July 11, 1879

The following day, Solomon was at the library reading a list of instructions left for him by the librarian. The job was beginning to grow on him. He thought it was perfect. Since it was during the summer, there were few students on campus. He was the only person in the library most of the time, and the solitude was like a tonic for a shy, retiring person like him.

He gazed up at the tall bookcases lining the walls, then down at the stack of books that needed to be set in their proper places. He grinned, then picked up one of the larger volumes and climbed the rolling ladder attached to a rail on the top shelf. When he reached the right level, he pushed the ladder to the left until he found just the right slot, brushed off a bit of lint, and slid the book into its home space. Perfect. He loved riding the ladder back and forth across the bookshelves. He had half a dozen more books to go. Then, he would have time to dive into the textbooks he had bought for the fall term. He would get a head start on reading.

In the quiet of the library, his thoughts turned to Mother. He wanted to make her proud with his studies. He breathed a prayer to keep her safe and happy.

***

That same morning, Jacob left the house after breakfast. He hurried to Mrs. Sterling's house and arrived ten minutes before the delivery men. Three muscular men pulled up with the piano loaded in the wagon. Their first task was to remove the plaid chair to make room for the piano.

"What do you want us to do with this chair, ma'am?" one of them asked.

"Do whatever you like. I just want it out of the house."

They moved the chair out, arguing in low tones about which of them would keep it. Then they went for the piano. After a mighty struggle, they carefully slid the piano out of the wagon on a ramp.

"Watch it, fellows," Jacob said. "You need to move it a little to the right to get it off the wagon."

One of the men snapped at Jacob. "Get out of our way, man. You think we haven't done this before? You'll distract us and make us drop this thing."

Jacob apologized and stepped back. Lesson learned.

Mrs. Sterling told the men where to position the piano in her great room, then wheeled herself back several feet to check it from a different perspective.

"That's the perfect place for it, isn't it, Mr. Bishop?"

"Yes, it is."

"Now I need something on either side of it to fill in the space. When my leg heals, I'll go shopping."

Jacob consulted with the delivery men and learned the tuner wasn't coming until after lunchtime.

"Mrs. Sterling," he said, "the tuner won't be here for a while. I'll head to the office and come back later with him."

"Please, Mr. Bishop, why don't you stay and have lunch with me? Gloria has prepared a light chicken lunch, which we could eat in the garden. It would be a waste of time for you to go to Ellsworth's only to turn around and come back."

Jacob was touched by the offer, and his stomach growled. "Chicken sounds good," he said. "I'll wheel you out to the garden."

A table with two wrought iron bistro chairs waited under the giant oak. Jacob moved one of the chairs aside and pushed the wheelchair to the table while Gloria brought their lunch with a pitcher of lemonade.

"Join me in saying grace, Mr. Bishop." Mrs. Sterling bowed her head and said a brief prayer of thanks, then picked up her fork.

"Someone told me your family made typewriters," Jacob said, slicing off a bite of chicken.

"My husband's grandfather had a hand in its invention and development," she replied. "It was only through the efforts of ambitious salesmen like you that they are now common in offices everywhere." She took a sip of her lemonade and swatted a fly. "You see, Mr. Bishop, you're in a profession that has the potential to change the world. Salesmen make the wheels of commerce turn, you know."

"And I hope to do just that," he replied. "My roommate, Solomon Hawk, is studying architecture. When he opens his business, I'll be the front man, selling his skills. Poor Solly, he's the shy sort. He doesn't like mingling with people."

Mrs. Sterling chuckled. "It's tough to be in business if you don't like being around your customers. But if I hear of anyone getting ready to build a house, I'll remember you."

They lingered over a pleasant meal and finished just before the piano tuner arrived.

***

Brady Davies was a slight, balding man who moved with energy. He introduced himself as the piano tuner and then set about his work with determination. Jacob noted every movement as Davies ran his fingers up and down the keys, frowned, and then opened the top of the piano, exposing the strings. He pulled various tools from his leather bag: tuning fork, wrench, rubber mutes, tweezers, and felt strips. He struck the tuning fork, listened to the resonance, and applied his wrench to the A string pin. It took several strikes and turns of the wrench before he was satisfied that the string was on pitch. Then, he tuned all the A strings before moving on. A considerable time passed before he was happy with the pitch of all two-hundred-sixty-four strings. As a final test, he sat on the stool and played a quick melody.

"How does that sound to you, Mrs. Sterling?" he asked.

She smiled and nodded her approval. "That's good. Thank you, Mr. Davies. I'll call for you again next year."

Jacob turned to her. "Thank you for purchasing your piano from Ellsworth's and allowing me to watch the piano tuner. I'll be going now, but let me know when you have your party."

She beamed at him and offered her hand, which he took. "Thank you, Mr. Bishop. I will."

Chapter 16: Cooper Street Baptist Church

Sunday, July 13, 1879

On Sunday morning, Jacob and Solomon were off to Cooper Street Baptist Church. Solomon went to worship; Jacob went for research. He planned to do whatever he had to do to wangle an introduction to Benjamin Creel. Maybe he could get to know him and learn his motivations. The two entered the sanctuary and found a pew about midway up the aisle. Other worshipers greeted them and introduced themselves. Jacob soaked in the unfamiliar atmosphere until the choir entered in their robes and filed into the seats behind the pulpit. Jacob smiled, realizing that those pews were reserved for the choir.

After Pastor Bromley's opening prayer, an older man stood to lead the congregation in singing, "Holy, Holy, Holy! Lord God Almighty." Everyone turned to page fifty-nine in the hymnal, and there were those printed lines with square dots attached to poles. Jacob had only a second to marvel at them before the Estey pump organ sprang to life in reedy tones, and the congregation joined in with enthusiastic singing.

The organist pumped the two pedals with the energy it took for a brisk walk. At the same time, he increased the volume by pressing the knee paddles to either side. Jacob's mouth dropped in astonishment. *That fellow sure is busy. He must be exhausted after the service,* he thought.

Solomon leaned over to whisper in Jacob's ear, "The pump organ is very limited. You can't vary the volume or the sound very much. My father's church has a pipe organ, a thousand times better than that."

Jacob whispered back, "Would a piano help?"

Solomon nodded. "Yes, a good pianist would fill it out . . . give it depth and feeling." He went back to singing.

Jacob thought that over for a moment, then joined in the hymn.

After the sermon, the pastor announced a brief get-together in the basement fellowship room for visitors who would like to stay and meet him, his wife, and the board members. The ladies' missionary guild would serve coffee and cookies.

"Excellent opportunity for me," said Jacob. "Solly, I know that's not something you like to do, but it would mean a lot if you would go with me. We won't stay long. I might be able to meet Mr. Creel and feel him out without telling him I sell pianos."

Solomon agreed to stay for a short while, though a look of worry entered his eyes. Jacob understood that look, knowing that Solly had been dreading the whole business, preferring to get home to his books. The two descended the stairs to the basement room where the meeting was held. The space had short windows high above the ground level to let in the light. Still, oil lamps were added to make the room feel more welcoming. Three pleasant older ladies stood behind a table serving cookies, tea, and coffee.

Pastor and Mrs. Bromley were there, as well as three members of the Board, including Benjamin Creel. Four other visitors also came to the meeting. Everyone stood in a circle and introduced themselves. Solomon shuffled his feet and was clearly miserable. Then, they picked up their refreshments and mingled among the group.

Jacob gravitated to Mr. Creel, while Solomon stayed aloof. "Mr. Creel, I understand you're on the Board of Trustees," Jacob said. "I've never been part of a church before, so I don't know what a board does."

Creel, approaching sixty years old, was dressed like a man of means. He stretched to his height of five foot eight and locked eyes with Jacob, who was taller by six inches. "We're the advisory board for the pastor," he said. "We keep a close eye on the budget."

"That sounds like an important assignment."

"I should say it is, especially in a church of this size. We're prominent in the community, so we don't want to make mistakes with our money.

What about you? You say you've never been part of a church before."

"No, I just came here from Connecticut. My family never took me to church, but now I live with my friend, Solomon Hawk. His father is the preacher at a large church where he was raised. I thought I'd see how I like it."

"Well, you'll find a church home here. I hope you come back. How did you like the service?"

"It was interesting. During the sermon, I learned some things I didn't know before."

Creel slapped him on the back. "Then the pastor is doing his job. Welcome to Cooper Street Baptist. I hope you and your friend will come again." He moved on to talk to another visitor.

Jacob caught the pastor's attention and shook his hand. "Thank you for this opportunity, sir. I'll talk with you later."

Chapter 17: A Date with Miss Thompson

October 1879

Summer gave way to autumn, and classes began at the university. Solomon enjoyed his morning walk to school. On this particular Tuesday, the air was crisp and damp, his path carpeted with soggy leaves in shades of brown, orange, and yellow. He tugged his knitted cap, a recent gift from Mother, down over his ears. Countless oaks, maples, and pine trees lined his path, their trunks in shades of gray-brown to black.

The wind coming off Lake Michigan blew without ceasing. It whooshed through the tops of the trees, filling the air with orange leaves from the maples and dark reddish-brown leaves from the oaks, the last trees to give up their summer foliage. The leaves spun like toy tops, swooped and dived, then swirled again as another gust blew in. Bending into the wind, Solomon hugged his textbooks under his double-breasted coat to protect them from possible rain.

As his boots traced a path through the sodden leaves, Solomon anticipated the day's classes with a smile. Two dozen serious-minded students occupied each class as the professors explained the study material. Another larger room held drafting tables. There, the students would learn the vital art of putting designs on paper in standardized form. This was the world of rulers, protractors, and drawing compasses. This was a welcome change from the homiletics class at Yale. Solomon thought he might enjoy the company of some of his fellow students when they became acquainted, but there was no need to rush that.

He promised himself he would write to Mother when he returned home. He needed to know she was doing well. Otherwise, his time was spent on his studies and his few hours of work in the library each week. As he quickened his stride, his brain danced with the intricacies of drafting, the mechanics of materials, and architectural styles.

***

Solomon's class schedule created a significant change at home. The young men kept such staggered schedules that they were rarely home together. It worked fine for Solomon, who buried himself in his books, but it was hard on Jacob, who craved company and conversation. Even though he was becoming acquainted with a few more people at Cooper Street Baptist, he hadn't found anyone he cared to spend leisure time with.

In search of casual friendship, he asked Miss Thompson if she would like to see a matinee on Saturday and have dinner with him at a local restaurant.

She hesitated. "My aunt and uncle both got cholera from eating at a restaurant two years ago. The symptoms were horrible. We weren't sure Auntie would survive. They had to boil their water, and the doctor gave them some medicated powder to mix in. You can understand why I'm reluctant."

Ah, she had prodded Jacob's instinct as a salesman to overcome objections. He couldn't stop himself. "I agree there's been a problem with restaurant food, but I did some scouting around. There's a restaurant with a good reputation called The New York Kitchen, and I asked to take one of their menus." He pulled the paper menu from his pocket and unfolded it. "Look here. It says plainly they don't take scraps back into the kitchen and re-cook them. And they ask that restaurant patrons report anything suspicious to the owners. They don't tolerate such behavior from their staff."

Miss Thompson took the menu and opened her spectacles, shoving them onto her face. She peered at the menu intently. "I see. At least they're aware of the problem and work to prevent it."

"Yes. Have you ever heard of anyone getting sick at the New York

Kitchen?"

She gave him a crooked smile. "No. How could I? I don't know anyone who ever ate there."

"So, will you go with me? I'll borrow a horse and carriage and pick you up at two o'clock."

She turned her attention back to the menu. "Oh, look, Mr. Bishop. They have beef stew with potatoes." She lowered her head. "I might as well confess I've never been to a restaurant. I won't know what to wear or how to order my food."

Jacob chuckled, remembering his first clumsy experience in a restaurant with Solomon. He wanted to make the most of this opportunity. "I'm a man with experience, you know. I've been to a few restaurants. I'll order for you. Just wear what you wear to church on Sunday. I like that fancy hat you wear with the blue ribbons. I don't think anyone there will look better dressed than you."

He studied her expression. *I believe I've appealed to what motivates her,* he thought.

She glanced at the face of the tall man and wagged her head, trying to hide the smile spreading across her face. "All right. You've sold me. I'll go with you and have a good time. But, Mr. Bishop, can you afford a matinee and dinner both? We could skip one or the other."

He raised his eyebrows but tempered his scolding with a gentle smile. "Miss Thompson, that was an impertinent question. But the answer is, I'll be able to afford it by Friday. I sold two pianos this week."

***

Jacob spoke to Mr. Ellsworth about the loan of his carriage. The man couldn't deny a favor to his star salesman.

On Saturday, Jacob took the carriage to pick up Miss Thompson, dressed in her finery. He took her to see Sarah Bernhardt in the stage comedy "Frou Frou" at the Columbia Theatre. Their tickets gave them seating in the one-dollar section. Neither Jacob nor Miss Thompson had ever seen such rich, colorful costumes made of expensive silks and brocades nor such elaborate stage sets.

Jacob observed Miss Thompson during one of the funnier scenes. Tears rolled down her cheeks as she leaned forward, laughing. She glanced at him at that moment, and her eyes met his. He was caught staring and didn't know what to say, so he leaned close to her ear and said, "Miss Bernhardt isn't very pretty, is she?"

"But she's funny. And she looks very intelligent."

The man in the seat behind them hissed, "Shh!" That ended the conversation.

At the end of the play, they took the carriage to the New York Kitchen, which advertised itself as "The Leader of Low Prices for First-Class Victuals." The restaurant had a capacity of one hundred twenty-four diners. There were few vacant tables. An army of servers scurried about, taking orders and refilling glasses. It was an enjoyable meal with decent food. They topped it off with apple pie.

Miss Thompson stood to put on her cloak. "It's been a lovely evening," she said. "But I'm getting a chill. Would you mind taking me home?"

"Not at all," Jacob said. "It is getting colder. It's time we end the evening before one of us catches a vapor."

He escorted her to the carriage, drove her home, and walked her to the door.

She giggled. "Thank you again for a wonderful time. It's been memorable."

"You're welcome." Jacob was in an awkward spot. He shook her hand, thinking this was probably not an appropriate goodbye, but he didn't know what else to do. He waited while she stepped inside. Then he returned the carriage to Mr. Ellsworth's barn, retrieved his horse, and went home.

When he arrived, Solomon was at his desk in the bedroom with a heavy textbook.

"Can I get you a cup of coffee, Solly?"

Solomon raised his eyes and reluctantly bookmarked his spot in the text.

"Thanks, Jacob. That sounds good. How did your afternoon with Miss Thompson go?"

"We had a good time. Neither of us had ever been to the theater before, and she had never been to a restaurant. I left a tip, just like you taught me."

Solomon grinned. "Good for you. She must think you're a *bon vivant*."

"I never heard those words before, but I think you mean a fellow with some experience." Jacob poured water into the percolator and set it on the stove.

"That's right." Solomon bit his lip for a moment before peering at Jacob. "Is Miss Thompson someone you want to pursue a relationship with?"

Jacob shrugged. "She's plenty nice, but she's a couple of years older than me."

"That means nothing."

"I don't know if I could warm up to her enough to spend a lifetime with her. But I'll take her out again if I don't meet anyone I like better. She was nice company."

Solomon raised his eyebrows. "I'm no expert on the ladies, but you should be careful with her feelings. If you spend time with her, she could develop emotions for you that you may not return, so be aware. If she tries to get too close, it may be time to talk with her and explain that you don't want to get as involved as she does. That could end your friendship . . . and cause trouble at work."

Jacob's eyes widened. "Oh." That had never crossed his mind. He would need to watch his behavior around her when he was taking his piano lesson. It might be best to let some time pass before he asked her out again, if he ever did. He poured the coffee and took a cup of the brew into the bedroom for Solomon.

"Thanks for the advice, Solly. I think I'll make up my bed and get to sleep early if you don't mind."

Solomon nodded and went back to his books. When Jacob opened his eyes two hours later, Solomon's lamp was still lit.

***

The following afternoon, Solomon arrived home before Jacob. He walked toward the kitchen to start supper but changed his mind and went to check the letterbox first. The metal lid squeaked in the cold as he lifted it. He reached inside and found a letter from his mother. He ripped open the envelope with care lest he tear the precious letter.

"*My dear son,*" he read. "*You must know how much I miss having you here with me. Your bedroom is so empty. Your winter clothes are in the closet where you left them when we got the news about Grandfather. I'm sorry you don't have them there. I hope you got the cap I knitted for you and are staying warm.*

Father has been coughing a lot and seems tired. I'm sure it's just a vapor, and he will recover soon.

I'm doing well. I'm singing soprano in the church choir now, and we are starting rehearsals for our Christmas music. I guess the director thinks we need plenty of time.

I was thankful to hear you were able to enroll in classes. I believe you will have great success as an architect. God has blessed you with tremendous artistic talent. I hope someday I will see a house that you designed. That will thrill my soul.

Please say hello to Jacob. God bless you both. I pray for you both every day. Know that I love you."

The letter was signed *Mother* in her graceful, elegant hand.

As he read, her gentle voice spoke every word in his head as if she were in the room with him. A tear dropped on the paper and blurred the ink in a tiny spot. Solomon dabbed it off with his handkerchief. He couldn't wait to answer her.

In the kitchen, he peeled two large yams and cut them to boil, then slapped a slab of ham in the skillet. While they cooked, he sat at the kitchen table with paper and pen.

Dear Mother,

I was happy to receive your letter today. Yes, I have the cap you knitted. Please forgive me for not thanking you sooner. It keeps me warm as I walk to school.

I'm sorry to hear about Father's health.

Jacob excels at his job as a piano salesman, so we don't lack anything.

I enjoy my classes. This semester, I'm learning about the properties of wood, metals, and concrete that go into building construction. Drafting is my favorite class. And we're studying the different architectural styles. It's quite interesting.

The university library hired me part-time. When I'm on duty, I can find a quiet table and study if I finish all my assigned work early, so it's the perfect job.

We live in a small house within walking distance of my classes. We share the kitchen, laundry, and cleaning duties. He is an agreeable soul to live with, but since we now have separate schedules and see each other less, he yearns for someone to talk to. He took one of his co-workers to the theater and a restaurant the other night. I'm not sure that was a good idea, but I'm glad he had a chance to get out.

Mother, I want you to know how much I love you. You are still welcome to come to Chicago and live with us anytime. Jacob agrees. I long to see you again.

I hope Father isn't still angry. Tell him I said hello.

   With much love,
    Solomon

He folded the letter and slipped it into the envelope, certain of two things: Father was still angry, and Mother wasn't coming. It broke his heart.

Chapter 18: Jacob's New Wardrobe

November 1879

Jacob's piano lessons with Miss Thompson continued, and he made good progress, but their relationship had changed. She was more informal, almost possessive, and sat closer to him when he played. She sometimes reached out to touch his arm or shoulder. He was stumped as to how he should handle it. He continued to endure it and tried to demonstrate the formality he wanted to keep by his actions. She was slow to catch on.

He had another excellent week, selling two pianos. He said nothing to Miss Thompson about his sales, but she found out from the bookkeeper. She even hinted that she had never been to Haverly's Theatre and would like to go some time. He didn't respond. By the weekend, she was moody and quiet.

The following week, Mrs. Sterling's housekeeper came to the piano store and asked for Jacob.

"Hello, Gloria. What can I do for you?" he asked.

The girl smiled. "Mrs. Sterling plans to have some people in for a party next Saturday night," she said. "She would like you to come as you promised."

Jacob's eyes lit up. "I take it, then, that her leg has healed."

"Oh, yes. She's getting around quite well."

"Please tell her I look forward to being there."

Gloria smiled, nodded, and left.

Jacob was surprised at how excited he was to think about Saturday's party. He told himself, *a new wardrobe is what I need, and maybe a new haircut.*

That evening, as he and Solomon were having supper, he said he would be home late on Tuesday after his shopping trip.

Solomon grinned. "Do you want me to go with you?"

"I think I have enough experience now to choose my clothes, but you're welcome to come if you like."

"No, if you don't need me, I'd rather study. The semester finals are coming up, and I need to concentrate. But I hope you enjoy your shopping trip."

The following day after work, Jacob rode to a local men's store and told the salesman he wanted something to wear to Mrs. Sterling's party.

"Ah, a party at the Sterling mansion. Impressive. You will need something special for such an occasion," he said. "Step over here, and let me show you a three-piece suit in one of our finest fabrics."

He showed Jacob a rack of suits and chose one he guessed to be the correct size. Jacob took it to the dressing room and tried it on. The sleeves and pants were too short for his lanky frame. The salesman pulled others off the rack. After several tries, he found one that fit perfectly with a striking cut. The price was higher than Jacob planned to pay, but he was impressed when he studied his reflection in the full-length mirror. The black suit with his dark hair added drama to his appearance. He smiled and nodded.

"I'll take this one," he said.

"What about the shirt? We have a good selection if you'd like to look."

He chose a white shirt and a red ascot.

"And what about shoes, sir? Do you have shoes that will look good with this suit?"

"No, nothing that would do it justice. What do you have to show me?"

After he purchased the shoes, he chose a bowler hat. He left the store with a thin wallet, but there was no doubt he would attract attention in his new outfit.

His next stop was the barbershop. The barber styled his hair by parting it down the middle, combing it to either side and sweeping it behind his ears. He left short curls in the back.

"Look at this," the barber said, handing him a mirror. "You'll be the sensation of the party in that haircut."

Jacob held the mirror, turned to the right and left, and checked out the sides and back. A wide grin spread across his face. "Thank you, sir. I believe I'm ready for the Sterling mansion."

***

The next day, Jacob counted three days until the party. At work, his co-workers complimented his new haircut. Miss Thompson was impressed.

"That's a great haircut. What made you change your style?" she asked.

Without thinking, he said, "I'm going to a party at the Sterling mansion this Saturday."

She hesitated. "Who are you going with?"

"No one," he said. "I'm going as a guest of Mrs. Sterling."

Miss Thompson raised her eyebrows. A frown clouded her expression. *She's jealous,* he thought. *Now, what do I do? What will be the outcome of this?*

"Miss Thompson," he said gently. "I need to speak to you honestly."

"Don't bother," she quipped, turning on her heel to walk away. She didn't show up for his piano lesson that afternoon and avoided him the rest of the week.

Mr. Ellsworth learned of his plans and asked him to come into his office. "I hear you're going to the Sterling party this Saturday."

"Yes, sir. I bought some new clothes to get ready."

"You can't go on horseback to a party like that. I won't be using my carriage. Why don't you take it?"

Jacob's jaw dropped. "That's a very generous offer, sir, and I'll take you up on it."

Mr. Ellsworth rummaged through his desk, then returned his attention to Jacob. "On Friday at the end of the workday, I'll ride your horse home, and you take my carriage. You can return it to my house and get your horse after Saturday night's party. Mrs. Ellsworth and I will need the carriage to go to church on Sunday morning."

"I can't thank you enough. I'm looking forward to this party."

"No wonder. Mrs. Sterling was known for her fabulous parties before Mr. Sterling passed away. I guess she's trying to reclaim that lifestyle."

Jacob grinned. "It's an Ellsworth piano that will help her do it."

Saturday, November 8, 1879

When Saturday arrived, Jacob had the Ellsworth carriage at home. He fidgeted and paced all afternoon, checking his pocket watch every few minutes. He planned to leave the house at about five o'clock to be at Mrs. Sterling's house in time for the party. Giving himself plenty of time, he bathed and put on his new shirt, ascot, three-piece suit, shoes, and derby hat. Then he knocked on the doorframe where Solomon was concentrating on his textbook.

"Solly?"

Solomon tore himself from his reading; then, his eyes bugged out. "Jacob. You look amazing. Turn around and let me see the back."

Solomon stood and took a few steps forward while Jacob turned.

"What do you think?"

"Very nice. Quite a fine fit. You were fortunate to find something that fits you so well." Solomon brushed a bit of lint from Jacob's collar. "I couldn't have picked out anything better for you. That red ascot is perfect for a bit of color."

Jacob grinned. "I think I'm beginning to fit into your world."

Solomon nodded. "You fit into my world better than I do. You'll be a big success, my friend. I hope you have a good time tonight. What did Miss Thompson say when she found out?"

Jacob's jaw twitched. "She hasn't spoken to me since, and she skipped my piano lesson."

"I'll pray that your job won't be affected. But if you don't think you want to get involved with her, it's better to let her down sooner than later."

"It wasn't my purpose to hurt her, but I'm relieved she's figuring it out. Well, I'll be off now. You can go back to your studies, and good luck."

Chapter 19: A Party at the Mansion

Jacob wiggled into his overcoat, positioned his bowler on his head, and stepped outside. Darkness had already descended, and snowflakes fluttered down in the glow of the gaslights. He drew his fur collar around his neck, covered his knees with a lap blanket, and slapped the reins. The horse stepped forward smartly, pulling the carriage to Mrs. Sterling's party.

At the mansion, warm lamplight glowed through the windows, revealing people milling about in the great room with drinks in their hands. His heart beat a little faster. He smiled and strode to the door, giving it a sharp rap.

Gloria answered his knock and gave him a welcoming smile. "Come in, Mr. Bishop. Mrs. Sterling is waiting for you in the great room."

He handed her his overcoat and bowler, adjusted the lapels of his new jacket, straightened his ascot, and made his way into the great room. When Mrs. Sterling spotted him, she stepped toward him with bright eyes. She wore a stylish satin dress with a white bodice and flowing skirt made of copious amounts of black satin, swishing as she walked.

"Mrs. Sterling, it's good to see you out of your wheelchair. I wondered what you looked like upright."

She giggled. "And Mr. Bishop. I've never seen you looking so magnificent. Come with me. I want to show you off to some of my friends."

She put her hand in the crook of his elbow and ushered him into the crowd toward a middle-aged couple chatting near the fireplace. "Mr.

Bishop, I'd like you to meet Mr. and Mrs. Brickell. He's the Supervisor of the Cook County Building Department. Mr. Bishop works with an architect, Mr. Solomon Hawk."

Brickell thrust out his hand. "Good to meet you, Bishop, but I don't believe I know Mr. Hawk."

Jacob shook his hand. "Good to meet you, sir. You don't know Mr. Hawk yet because he's still in architecture school. But I can tell you, he will be one of the best. His designs are impressive."

"I hope they're also cost-effective. An impressive design isn't worth the paper it's on if it's too expensive to build." Brickell took a sip of his drink.

"Yes, sir. I'll be sure and pass on that message."

"Tell the young man to come by the office to meet me. It's always good to get to know up-and-coming architects."

"I will do that."

Brickell led his wife away to talk to someone else while Mrs. Sterling smiled up into Jacob's face.

"My, my, you look good. Do you know that?"

Jacob blushed. "You do, too, ma'am."

"Do you mind if I call you Jacob?

"No, ma'am, I don't mind."

"Let's get you some eggnog, Jacob."

She led him to the buffet table, loaded with beverages and holiday goodies. Jacob spotted plates of cookies, vegetable trays, nuts, and candies. An attractive young girl, a uniformed server, poured each of them a cup of nog and grated a bit of nutmeg on top.

Jacob raised the cup to his lips, and his eyes widened. "I've never tasted this before. This is delicious."

"It's a Christmas thing, Jacob. It's a little early for it, but it was something I wanted. Now, let's meet someone else. There's Mr. Townsend over there, the fellow in the brown suit. That's his wife beside him. You should meet him. He's the architect who designed the warehouse on Fremont Street." She pulled Jacob toward the man and his wife. "Mr. Townsend?"

Townsend turned toward them as his wife spotted a friend and walked the other way.

"Mr. Townsend, I want you to meet Mr. Jacob Bishop. He works with a gifted architectural student you'll want to snatch up after graduation, or he'll run circles around your firm. His name is Solomon Hawk."

Townsend scowled and cleared his throat. "That's quite a boast, Mrs. Sterling. Good to meet you, Bishop." He thrust out his hand for a friendly shake. "Is your friend as good as she says he is?"

"You'll have to see his designs. I believe you'll be impressed. Of course, none of them have been built yet."

"You tell the young man to come see me when he can and bring some of his drawings. If I'm looking for another architect when he graduates, I'd like him to apply."

"Thank you, sir."

Townsend turned toward the buffet table.

Mrs. Sterling grasped Jacob's arm again. "Come sit with me, Jacob. I want to talk to you. It's important."

Jacob had no freedom to circulate among the other guests. He was a captive of this woman, as beautiful as she was. He allowed himself to be led to a club chair near the fireplace. She sat in the matching chair next to him while groups of people in the crowd continued their conversations within inches of them. The fire snapped and crackled, sending sparks and live ash up the chimney.

"Jacob, I should have invited your friend, too. I didn't think of it in time. I want to discuss something with you: You know I love decorating. I've done every room in this house to my satisfaction, and I want something else to work on, so I've bought a piece of land to build another house. I plan to hire a staff and turn this mansion into a bed and breakfast to increase my income. This property would make a perfect bed and breakfast, don't you think?"

Jacob was taken aback. *She wants another house?* He gazed at the room he and the other guests were in. Conversations around them competed for his attention, but he needed to hear what his hostess had to say. "Yes, I suppose it would make a fine bed and breakfast. It has enough bedrooms and a large dining room. So, where did you buy your land?"

She leaned closer to his ear to shout over the general din of the party.

"It's a couple of miles north of here. I bought eight acres on a private lake. It has woods and a walking path." Her eyes lit up as she talked, and she gestured to accompany her description. "I want a smaller house to live in, something cozy and inviting. I don't want more than three bedrooms, but I want a modern bathroom on each floor. I want a laundry room where my housekeeper can wash clothes, iron them, and hang them to dry inside when the weather is poor. I want a parlor with a fireplace and a comfortable kitchen. Oh, and a dining room. But that's all I want inside. Outside, there needs to be a balcony overhanging the lake. What do you think? Doesn't that sound exquisite?"

A man squeezed between them and another couple, brushing against Mrs. Sterling's foot, which she jerked back.

"I'd say," Jacob said. "I've never seen a house like that."

"No, it will be one of a kind. And I'd like Mr. Hawk to design it."

Jacob's jaw dropped. He blinked, and his eyebrows raised. "I'm not sure he's ready for an actual project to be built."

"Would you bring him by one day next week so I can discuss this with both of you?"

"Of course. I believe his classes end early on Thursday. I could bring him by at about three o'clock."

"That's perfect. Now, let me get the musicians started. I want the first dance with you, Jacob. Agreed?"

Jacob swallowed. "I've never danced with a lady, but—"

She smiled and walked away as he closed his eyes and shook his head. This was an excellent chance to make a fool of himself and embarrass her. His stomach did a flip-flop.

Her voice carried from across the room. "Ladies and gentlemen, we have Mr. Thomas Good on the piano and two violinists from the Chicago Philharmonic Orchestra. They're here to play some dance music for us. I hope you enjoy it. I have the first dance with Mr. Jacob Bishop. He's the handsome man over there. Jacob, I'm ready for you to join me." She reached her arms toward him in a dramatic gesture.

The crowd opened a way for him to cross the room, and he approached his hostess for the Blue Danube Waltz.

"I hope this isn't a mistake," he whispered.

"No problem," she said. "Put your right hand on the small of my back and take my right hand with your left, like so. Now dance the way you did before I bought my piano."

He followed her lead and discovered that he could do a fair job of dancing despite the difference in height between the two. She was shorter than him by ten inches, but her personality made her larger than life. As they twirled to the music, he breathed in her perfume. Many people stood near the walls, watching them dance. He had never before had so many people give him so much attention. He smiled broadly and gazed down into Mrs. Sterling's face. She wore a pixie grin and eyed him with delight.

After the dance, Mrs. Sterling left him and worked the room like the perfect hostess, making everyone feel comfortable. Jacob visited the punch table and picked up a dessert plate, piling it with cut vegetables and cookies. He hadn't been alone more than a minute when he was approached by an attractive young woman with long, flowing copper-colored hair. She was dressed in green velvet and struck up a conversation.

"Hello, Mr. Bishop. I'm Amelia Schultz," she said. "How long have you known Mrs. Sterling?"

"Not long. I met her when I sold her that piano you hear."

"You're a salesman? Well, never mind. You're a fabulous dancer."

Jacob chuckled. If only she knew the truth. "Thank you."

"Would you dance with me the next time?"

She had asked a direct question, so Solomon was obligated to tell the truth. "I would, but you'll find out I'm not such a fabulous dancer."

"I'll take my chances. When they announce the next dance, find me."

"I'll do that, Miss Schultz."

Jacob popped a carrot stick into his mouth, scanning the crowd to see if he recognized anyone else. His height made it easy to see over everyone's heads. He thought he spotted Benjamin Creel, his nemesis from Cooper Street Baptist, who prevented a piano purchase. He took a bite of a cookie and headed for Creel.

He bumped into him gently, on purpose. "Sorry, sir. Oh, it's you, Mr. Creel. So good to see you. How are you?"

"Ah, Mr. Bishop . . . the beau of the ball. How long have you known

Mrs. Sterling?"

"Since I sold her a piano. Are you and Mrs. Creel doing well?"

"We were until I looked out the window. Look out there, Bishop. Snow is coming down by the wheelbarrow load. We'll have to leave early."

Jacob stared out the window. Yes, the snow fell wet and heavy. It had already coated the ground. He would need to get Mr. Ellsworth's carriage to him before it got too deep. He turned back to Creel.

"Rev. Bromley tells me you're reluctant to buy a piano for the church."

"Well, I'm considering it. The pump organ seems inadequate, but I'm not yet ready to say yes."

"What would it take to convince you?"

"Don't push me, Bishop. This isn't a decision entered into at a party."

"Sorry, sir. Just know that I'll be ready whenever you are."

"I'll ask the pastor to contact you if I change my mind."

The musicians began another dance number, and folks paired up with their partners. Jacob scanned the crowd for Miss Schultz, spotted her, and approached. "May I have this dance, Miss Schultz?"

She smiled, stepped toward him, and he took her hand. They waltzed to a song Jacob recognized from his piano lessons.

"It's a Chopin waltz," he said.

"Yes, and it's lovely." They swayed with the music. "By the way," she said, "if you should want to contact me for any reason, I'm a student at the university. I think I met your friend, Mr. Hawk. He's the shy type, isn't he?"

Jacob chuckled. "That would be an understatement."

"He's quite dapper but not as handsome as you."

Jacob was caught unprepared for a way to respond, but the perfect reply popped into his head: "Why, Miss Schultz, you make me blush." It was the truth.

She gazed up at him with a Mona Lisa smile.

His head spun. *This girl throws me off balance. I've never met anyone like her.*

When the music stopped, he said, "Thank you for the dance," and returned her to her friends. Then he peered out the window to check the depth of the snow. It was piling up quickly. *I hate to leave so soon. It was just getting good.*

His hostess was in conversation on the other side of the room, drink in hand. He hurried to her through the crowd as quickly as possible, weaving his way carefully to avoid bumping anyone's drink. "Mrs. Sterling, I need to be on my way. The snow is falling hard, and I promised to return the carriage to Mr. Ellsworth tonight. But thank you for inviting me. I enjoyed it."

She rose from her seat. "Oh, I'm sorry you must leave so soon. But thank you for coming, Jacob. I don't blame you for leaving early. Some of the other folks are going, too. Do be careful out there in the weather, and I'll see you and Mr. Hawk on Thursday." She pressed his hand between hers, then walked with him to the door where Gloria waited with his overcoat and derby.

Mrs. Sterling lifted her chin and smiled at him.

"Goodnight, Jacob."

He gave her a last smile, nodded goodbye, and stepped into the snowy night. The air was cold and moist. After brushing two inches of heavy snow off the carriage seat, he hopped in to take the reins. His body heat melted some snow he had missed, which soaked into his trousers. It was like sitting on a wet ice cube. Within twenty minutes, he was at Mr. Ellsworth's house, putting the carriage and horse away. Then, he switched to his own horse and rode home, shivering.

When he arrived, Solomon was studying by the light of two oil lamps.

"You're home earlier than I expected," he said.

"Yes, there's a bad snowstorm out there. I wanted to beat it." He took a deep breath. "I have something to talk to you about."

Solomon wore an amused smile. "What? Did you get into some kind of trouble at the party?"

Jacob grinned. "Judging by Mrs. Sterling's behavior toward me, I think it would have been easy to dip my toes into trouble if I had wanted to, but I managed to avoid it. Mrs. Sterling bought some land and wants to build a new house. She has definite ideas about it. I get the impression she's accustomed to getting what she wants. And here's the thing: she wants you to design it."

Solomon's eyes widened in shock and alarm. "What? I can't do that. We haven't yet studied site analysis or roof structures. That comes next term.

"Well, you can tell her that in person. We have a meeting with her next Thursday at three."

Solomon put his head in his hands. "Oh, no. When we talked about bringing in business after I graduated, I had no idea you would get started early. What will I do?"

Jacob took the extra chair in the room and leaned toward Solomon. "You'll meet her at three o'clock on Thursday and explain why you can't design her house yet. Or, maybe you can design part of it, and she can hire out the parts you can't do to someone else. Or maybe she can't get her money in order as fast as she thinks, and there will be delays until you're ready. Who knows? But don't you see, Solly? This could be a great opportunity for you. At least talk to her."

Solomon's forehead creased in worry. Then he raised his head, and his eyes brightened. "Wait. The professor announced a design competition last week. I didn't intend to enter, so I ignored it. Interested students can submit a design of their choice by the end of May. It will be judged on the materials used and the unique design. Of course, it has to be sound in structure, and it has to be practical for the use it's designed for. I didn't plan to enter since I still lack some of those classes, but you're right. By the time the design is due, I will have that knowledge. I could use Mrs. Sterling's house as my entry." His face lit with a smile, and he nodded, his brain spinning design ideas as he stood there.

"What's the prize for winning?" Jacob asked.

"The university will send the winner on a trip to Philadelphia for a private tour of the First National Bank, designed by John McArthur, Jr. It's a magnificent two-story building with a palazzo façade, columns, cornice and roof balustrade, the whole package. Do you know the architect got a fee of $3,500 to design that building?"

Jacob whistled. "It would take a hard-working blacksmith four years to earn that much."

"But you haven't told me about the party. What happened?"

Jacob squirmed. "The snow was coming down like gangbusters, so I couldn't stay as long as I planned. But while I was there, Mrs. Sterling took charge of me. You know, she was very possessive and introduced me to a lot of folks at the party. I had the first dance with her—"

"What? You know how to dance?"

"I do now. Then I danced with a pretty redhead named Amelia Schultz."

"I think I know Miss Schultz. She comes into the library and checks out math books. How did you like her?"

"She was a little pushy, but that may not be bad. I like a girl with spirit. She's pretty enough. I think she charmed me with those cute freckles."

"Well, I'll leave you to work out your love life on your own. I need to go to bed."

"Sleep well, Solly."

"You too."

***

An hour later, Solomon still stared at the ceiling, wide awake. *What if Jacob falls for a girl and marries her? Will that end our plans? Will we still be friends?* He wrestled with the thoughts swirling in his head until he remembered his only option was to leave Jacob in God's hands. He rolled over and went to sleep.

Chapter 20: Mrs. Sterling's Lake Home

Thursday, November 18, 1879

By Thursday, the sky was still overcast with cold, gray clouds. That afternoon, Solomon and Jacob mounted their horses and rode to the Sterling mansion, the horses' hooves clopping through the dirty, gray slush on the roads. Solomon's stomach was churning in anticipation of the meeting. As usual, the housekeeper answered Jacob's knock and let them in.

"Mrs. Sterling is in the study," she said. "You can leave your boots here in the foyer." She waited while they removed their wet boots, then led them up the carpeted stairs. The carpet was luxurious under their stocking feet.

"Welcome, Jacob," Mrs. Sterling said, reaching for his hand. "And this must be Mr. Hawk. Please sit down." Three comfortable chairs faced each other in a triangle formation.

"I'm pleased to meet you, Mrs. Sterling," Solomon said.

The room was spacious and lined with shelves containing books and souvenirs of travel. The book titles he could read would have been of no interest to a woman whose passion was decorating, so this must have been her late husband's study. The desk was polished walnut of the finest quality. He brought his attention back to Mrs. Sterling.

"Jacob raves about your design skills," she said. "I'm sure he told you I bought a piece of land and want to build a smaller house for myself."

"He did."

"Are you interested in doing the design work?"

"I may be, as long as you understand that nothing I have designed has been built yet. I'm still learning. On the positive side, I'm getting outstanding marks in my studies. And the professors will double-check everything I do."

"Yes, I understand all that. And you must understand that I don't intend to pay top dollar under those circumstances, but I will pay a fair fee."

Solomon smiled. "Yes, ma'am. That sounds fine."

"Did you bring samples of your work so far?"

"Yes, I did."

He passed over a folder of designs. She opened it and examined one page after another, nodding and smiling. "I like your style. There's a certain flamboyance here, and that's what I'm looking for. What I want is something that no one else has. It needs to be innovative but elegant." She closed the folder, handed it back, and focused on Solomon. "I want to be your first client, Mr. Hawk. Please understand that if we can't work together to get a design I love, I'll pay you for whatever work you've done, but I won't build it. I'll look for another architect and start over with him."

"That's more than fair. I'll do my best. Let me get my paper and pen to take notes as you talk." He opened the folder and pulled blank paper from underneath his design work. "Let's talk about the lot where the house will sit."

"You'll want to see it for yourself. I have a man downstairs with the carriage. He'll drive us there, but first I want to describe the house to you. Then, when you see the property, you can envision it."

Solomon nodded.

"I want a house no more than half the size of this mansion, something cozy and inviting. It can't look like a widow's cottage. It needs to have a sophisticated look."

Solomon wrote, 'Cozy—sophisticated.'

"I'd like three bedrooms, but no more than that." She smiled. "Too many bedrooms lead to too many guests."

Solomon glanced at her in amusement and kept writing as she

continued.

"I want a modern bathroom on each level and a private one adjoining my bedroom, where I can bathe in privacy, even if I have visitors. I want a fireplace in my bedroom and a small pot-belly stove in each of the other bedrooms. Do you have all of that so far?"

Solomon had been writing so fast his hand cramped. "Just a minute . . . Yes, I have it."

She continued. "I want a laundry room where my housekeeper can wash clothes, iron them, and hang them to dry inside the house if the weather is poor. I don't want any laundry dripping in the kitchen. I want a parlor with a fireplace and a large window with seating where I can read in the sunlight. The parlor doesn't need room for the piano because I'll leave it here at the bed and breakfast. There will be a well-appointed kitchen. Oh, and a dining room with seating for maybe ten people. But that's all I want inside."

"Do you have any special requests for the exterior?"

"Oh, yes." Her eyes sparkled, and her face became animated. "That's where there will be a spectacular feature no one else has. It will be a spacious balcony overhanging the lake with room for seating. But we can't put any columns or posts in the water. Chicago ordinance."

Solomon raised his eyes toward her. "That's an unusual request, which I don't believe has ever been done for a residence. I need to see the property."

"Of course. This would be a good time to go."

The three of them descended the stairs. They dressed in their winter gear and ventured into the slush outside. Mrs. Sterling took Jacob's arm as they walked along the stone promenade to the waiting carriage. "Let me hold onto you so I don't fall, Jacob," she said. Jacob helped her into the carriage, and the two gentlemen sat on either side of her.

It was a half-hour ride to her property. Upon arrival, they remained in the carriage at the street level as she described where the boundaries were. It was a wooded property sloping down to the site where she wanted the house, then falling at a steep angle to the lake. "When you approach from the road," she said, "the highest level is forested with pines, oaks, and maples. You should see it in the spring! Someday, I'll have someone tap those maples for me and get the syrup."

They found a cleared entry and rolled down toward the lake on a gravel driveway. The land at the homesite was pocked with the muddy prints of deer and dogs. It was too soggy from the recent snow to get out and walk around, so Solomon stood in the carriage and scanned the property for the best view. "You'll need a surveyor to come out and set boundary markers. Once we agree on a design, we'll know where to cut trees."

"I anticipate the house will sit close to the water, so the balcony won't have to be too large," she said.

"That will depend on the soil analysis, whether the soil here can support a house without letting it sink. The balcony will have to be a cantilever deck." They discussed the water level of the lake, erosion issues, and other subjects that clearly didn't hold Mrs. Sterling's interest. She told them she wanted to concentrate on the house's appearance and said she would leave the related problems to Solomon. Then they returned her to the Sterling mansion.

"I have to tell you, "Solomon said on the road home with Jacob, "that project would challenge an experienced architect. An engineer should design that deck. It will take a lot of steel."

"You can always tell her you can't do it, but think about where you can get the expertise before you turn it down. You could make a good reputation for yourself with this job. A little fame wouldn't hurt at all. Can you hire an engineer to work with you to design the scary parts?"

Solomon laughed. "'Scary parts' is correct. But I'll consider that. Before I turn her down, I'll see what I can do."

Solomon began working on a house plan, sketching one design after another when his schoolwork was complete.

Chapter 21: Amelia

November 1879

Jacob continued to sell pianos, placing them in homes dotting the Chicago map. It helped that Christmas was not far off. Folks were buying them for their offspring, hoping to introduce them to the music arts and hoping their darlings would exhibit some musical talent. Others bought them for their entertainment value at holiday parties.

Jacob made an appointment with Benjamin Creel and used his most passionate reasoning. After an hour of back-and-forth discussion and negotiation, Creel finally agreed that the church should have a piano. He said it would add new life to the Christmas music.

Miss Thompson had discontinued Jacob's piano lessons and was keeping herself aloof. That relieved Jacob, even though he was sorry their relationship wasn't as comfortable as it used to be.

After Thanksgiving, Mr. Ellsworth announced a company Christmas dinner in the ballroom of a local hotel on December 13th, the second Saturday of the month. All the employees were invited to come and bring a guest. That included everyone from the Farm Implement Division and the Piano Division. Men who assembled reapers, men who built pianos, the tuners, the delivery men, the salesmen for both sides, the piano teacher, and the people who worked in the back office would all be there. It promised to be a grand occasion.

Jacob took the news to Solomon. "Solly, there's a big company Christmas dinner at the Royal Oak Hotel. Would you like to come with me?"

"No, thanks, Jacob. I'm not the party type, and finals are coming up. And I'm still working on Mrs. Sterling's house plans."

"You need to get out more and meet people. You'll never be successful in business if you don't have connections with the right folks."

"I know, Jacob, but I'm putting that off until I'm out of school and we decide what city we'll settle in."

"All right. I guess I'll look up Miss Schultz and see if she wants to go with me."

"If she comes into the library tomorrow, I'll schedule an appointment for you to talk with her."

"Thanks."

***

Solomon continued his intense research at the library. He read everything he could find on cantilevered structures but was still uncertain whether he could do it right. Then, he had an inspired idea: he would write a letter to Colonel Archibald McCreary, the civil engineer he met on the ferry. This famous engineer had built the cantilever bridge over the Hess River. He had shown kindness once; perhaps he would be willing to give a student some pointers again.

The following day, Miss Schultz entered the library to return her books and find something for light reading. Solomon was at the library's check-out desk when she came in.

"Mr. Hawk, you look tired today. Were you up too late studying last night?"

Solomon nodded. "Yes. Not only that, but I have a job for a client. I'll be glad when the finals are over. By the way, Jacob Bishop mentioned that he'd like to talk to you. Could you meet him in the library tomorrow at about this same time . . ." He checked his pocket watch. ". . . say, three o'clock?"

Her eyes betrayed her interest. "I'm meeting another friend at two o'clock. I'd have to cut that meeting short to make it. Could he meet me at three-thirty instead?"

Solomon lowered his head and smiled, suspecting she didn't want to appear too available. "I'm sure he won't have any problem with three-thirty."

He watched her walk away, wondering how this girl would affect his friendship with Jacob.

***

Another day passed. Jacob browsed the library shelves shortly before his appointment with Miss Schultz, but she wasn't there. She dropped in ten minutes late without offering an excuse or an apology.

"Good to see you, Miss Schultz. Would you like to sit with me at one of the tables for a few minutes?"

"Certainly."

Jacob guided her to a table where they could have some small amount of privacy. He pulled a chair out for her, then seated himself, trying to calm his jiggling knee.

"Thank you for coming. I wanted to meet you here for a special reason."

"What is that?"

"I'd like to invite you to a Christmas dinner given by the company I work for. It's a fancy affair at the Royal Oak Hotel on the second Saturday of this month. Would you like to go with me?"

"I don't know you very well . . ." Her mouth objected, but her eyes danced.

"Then we should take a walk and get to know one another. Would you like to walk to the delicatessen down the street? I'll buy you a sandwich."

"It's too early for supper, but maybe by the time we get there . . . well, why not?"

As they passed the check-out desk, Jacob leaned toward Solomon and whispered, "I won't be home for supper."

They took a brisk walk in the cold air. Their noses and cheeks were red when they reached Steinberg's Deli six blocks later. This was one of Jacob's favorite places. He loved the yeasty aroma of freshly baked bread mixed with the pungent scent of pickles. He loved the displays of baguettes, exotic meats, roasted red peppers, salads, dressings and dips, olives, and cheeses—things that weren't available back home in Beacon Falls. They chose a table and ordered hot sandwiches with tea and coffee.

Jacob asked Amelia about her studies.

"I'm learning bookkeeping," she said. "I don't plan to stay in school long enough to graduate, but if I know how to keep books, I'll be able to get a good job. Then I'll support myself if I'm single or help my husband in his business if I'm married."

"That's good planning," Jacob said. "It sounds like you have your future covered."

"I intend to. What about you? Do you plan to be in sales forever?"

"Yes, but not in piano sales. Solomon and I have plans. When he graduates, he's going to open an architecture business. But since he's so shy, he needs someone to help him get clients. That will be me. I used to be a blacksmith, but by working with Solly—"

"A *blacksmith?* Are you serious? You don't look like a blacksmith."

Jacob grinned. "If you had seen me six months ago, you would have believed it. My hands were dirty and calloused, my hair was long and curly, and my clothes were ragged from working over fire and iron. I have a much easier life now, selling pianos. And I meet much more interesting people."

She chuckled. "A blacksmith. All right, Mr. Bishop, tell me about the Christmas party."

"I'll pick you up in a carriage and take you to the hotel. It's a fancy affair, so you can wear a dress like you wore to Mrs. Sterling's party. They'll serve a catered dinner. Mr. Ellsworth will give a short speech and pass out awards. Then there will be an orchestra and dancing."

"I love to eat, and I love to dance. I'm not too keen on the middle part."

"That's the price of the dinner, sitting through awards. Who knows? Maybe I'll get one."

"Then I'll go with you."

Jacob's heart leaped.

Chapter 22: A New Job Offer

Later that week, Jacob received a note from a courier that Mrs. Sterling needed to see him.

If she wants to talk about her house, she needs to contact Solly, not me, he thought. But after work, he took his horse to the Sterling mansion.

Gloria let him in and took him to the great room, where the lady of the house waited for him with a cup of tea.

"Jacob, I'm so glad you got my message," she said, reaching for his hand and pulling him to the chair beside her. "Is Solomon busy working on my house plans?"

"Oh, yes. He's doing extra research to make certain the front deck will be safe for you and your guests. And he's working on some floor plans I think you'll like. He hasn't finished the exterior yet, except for the deck."

"Then he's coming along fine. I have two things I wanted to talk to you about. First, I'm planning a Christmas party on the second Saturday of December, and I want you to come."

Jacob put his hand to his forehead. "Oh, no, I can't come that day. Mr. Ellsworth is having a dinner dance with an award presentation, and I'm obligated to be there. I'm sorry."

Mrs. Sterling pressed her lips together. "That's a big problem. I wanted to announce that you'll be managing my bed and breakfast."

"What?" His eyebrows knitted, and he frowned. This didn't make any sense. "I already have a job, as you know."

"If you leave Ellsworth's, I'll guarantee to match your pay and give you bonuses for booking the rooms. A man of your sales talent is hard to come by. I don't think Ellsworth pays you enough."

Jacob chuckled. "You don't even know what I'm getting paid."

"Yes, I do. I asked. The man in the back office had no problem telling me what I wanted to know. Now, if I had been any average person unknown to him, it might have been a different outcome."

"Yes, money does more than buy things," Jacob said dryly. Irritation at her unfair advantage rose in him, but he pushed it aside in favor of his curiosity.

"It would mean leaving Ellsworth's and managing Sterling Mansion as a bed and breakfast. We would change it from a private residence into a hotel. I would live in the hotel for a year while my house is under construction."

He frowned. "I'm not sure I would make a good manager."

"Of course you would. I would be there to train and assist you. You would hire staff—someone for the front desk, someone to clean rooms, and someone to cook breakfast. We would hire a carpenter to build a front desk and make an elegant sign for the lawn. And we would have to make a good working budget. I'm not doing this to lose money. It must make a profit."

"I appreciate the offer, but I can't give you a definite answer without considering how it would affect my long-range plans."

"Really? And what are your long-range plans?"

"I think I told you. In two years, when Solomon graduates, we'll leave Chicago. We don't know where we'll go yet. It will be a city with a lot of building activity, probably closer to Connecticut, where our families live. He'll open an architecture business, and I'll sell his services."

"I see."

"So if you still want to hire me, knowing I won't be here for more than two years, I'll let you know."

"No one knows for sure what the future holds. You may be here forever. Think about it."

"Yes, ma'am. I'll give you a decision within the next few days."

"I hope you'll give me a favorable response. Now, what about that party? Can you come if I have it on the third Saturday?"

"Yes."

"Good. Then it's settled. I'll send out invitations for the third Saturday. And Mr. Bishop, this is not an event to bring a date." She stood, and Jacob took that as his cue that the conversation was over.

"Solomon will show you some drawings as soon as he has them ready," he said.

"That's fine. I'll see you later."

Outside, as he mounted his horse, his eyebrows raised. He shook his head to get some clarity. Things had happened so fast he hadn't had time to process the information. *My present pay plus bonuses for filling the rooms. It might be a good thing. But Mr. Ellsworth wouldn't take it well. I'll talk it over with Solly.*

The wintry sky was already growing dark, so he hurried home.

***

"Solly?" Jacob said as he opened the front door. Solomon was, as usual, seated at his desk with an open book in front of him.

He raised his head. "Oh, good, you're home. Do we have anything for supper?"

Jacob hung his overcoat and derby in the closet. "I'll make some soup, but we need to talk. Can you come in the kitchen for a few minutes?"

Solomon left his desk and entered the kitchen. He set the table while Jacob chopped vegetables and started the soup. "What's up?"

"I've had a job offer."

"You don't say. Does it pay more than the piano company?"

"Yes, in bonuses. Here it is: Mrs. Sterling wants to convert the mansion into a bed and breakfast. She'll live in the master bedroom until her house is built. She's a smart lady. The plan will give her more income to pay for her new house."

Solomon snickered. "I should think she doesn't need any more money."

Jacob shrugged. "Appearances may not tell the whole story. She may be flush, but on the other hand . . . maybe she's short on scratch." He grinned at Solomon as he reverted to his old terminology.

176

Solomon smiled and rolled his eyes. "You could be right."

"I would hire the staff and run the house according to a budget. She wants to make sure she's making a profit."

"She's been a little possessive of you recently. Do you think she would try to take over your life? Would she make demands on your time that you're unwilling to give up?"

Jacob drew a breath. "I'd need to bring that up with her. She would have to know that I'm not available at her whim. That brings up something else that was odd. She asked me to come to a party on the third Saturday of December and specifically told me not to bring a date."

Solomon grinned. "You need to be careful around her. If you want some advice from me, here it is. You'll need to set some boundaries. You'll need to spell them out on paper so you both know what to expect."

"Boundaries. That's a good term."

"Jacob, I'm going to suggest something you may not take seriously, but I hope you do. You need to pray about this and ask for God's direction."

Jacob was annoyed that the conversation had taken a turn. What began as a practical problem got sidetracked to a spiritual solution. He tilted his head. "Are you serious? Ask someone I can't see or hear?"

"I do it all the time, Jake. I don't ever make a big decision without doing it."

"I know you're committed to God, but I can't see that for myself. Not yet, anyway. It doesn't make any sense."

"Then I'll pray on your behalf. I'll pray that He'll open good opportunities for you and close the ones that would be bad for you."

"Well, your prayers can't hurt anything, can they?" Jacob was relieved Solomon didn't push his opinions on him further.

Solomon reached for a knife to peel a potato. "So tell me, how do you feel about the offer?"

"I keep thinking about the kinds of people that would pay to stay in a mansion like that. They would be wealthy folks from out of town where we may someday live. I would meet them, have a chance to talk, and maybe make some contacts. If nothing else, I would become more comfortable talking to folks of that income level. You know something, Solly? I found out people like me, and most of the time, they wouldn't guess I'm just a poor blacksmith."

Solomon burst out laughing. "You used to be a poor blacksmith, but those days are gone. You might not fit in with your old friends as well as you used to. You're one of us now."

The chopped beef and onions sizzled in the pot, sending an inviting aroma into the air. Jacob stirred the savory mixture. "Hmm. That's an interesting idea. You may be right. That's a big accomplishment, but in some ways, it's a little sad."

He poured broth into the pot over the meat and added the chopped vegetables. "We'll eat soon," he said.

Chapter 23: The Ellsworth Party

Saturday, December 13, 1879

On the second Saturday of the month, Jacob rented a carriage to take Miss Schultz to the Ellsworth party. When he arrived at the rental agency to pick it up, they only had a big two-seater that would hold six passengers.

"I want a smaller carriage for this event," he said. "I'm taking a young lady to a Christmas party, and I'd like her to sit close to me. Do you know what I mean?"

The dealer chuckled. "Yes, and I'm sorry. If I could rent you a small carriage, I would, but this is the only one I have left. If you had been here an hour earlier—"

Jacob sighed, paid the fee, and took the oversized carriage with two horses. The only other option was to take the girl on horseback. That was out of the question.

"Make sure you have it back by tomorrow at this time, or there will be another day's rent."

"Yes, sir."

Jacob returned home, dressed in his best, and went to pick up Miss Schultz. He cut a handsome figure. His black suit and dark hair gave him an aura of sophistication he didn't yet fully possess.

Miss Schultz met him at the door, her red hair arranged in curls on the back of her head. She wore the dark green velvet dress with a matching hat. The hat featured a modest feather on the brim and sat tilted forward on her head to avoid crushing her hairstyle.

"You look lovely," he said when she opened the door. His heart beat a little faster.

"Thank you, Mr. Bishop. Please come in."

She introduced him to her parents while she wrapped herself in her hooded winter cape. "I'm ready now."

He helped her into the carriage and took the seat beside her. They rode the half-hour to the Royal Oak Hotel, making small talk and watching their breath form clouds. The horses clip-clopped on the brick road, tails swishing, as their path took them in and out of the circles of yellow light cast by the gaslights along the street.

When they arrived at the hotel, people were streaming into the ballroom. It was decorated with candles, oil lamps, and cedar boughs trimmed with red ribbons. A giant Christmas tree adorned with white ribbons and glass ornaments dominated the corner of the room. The tables bore white tablecloths, polished silverware, and fine china. Crystal wine glasses stood ready at each plate.

Miss Schultz sucked in a breath. "Look at this room! Look at the poinsettias and candles on each table. Have you ever seen anything so beautiful, Mr. Bishop?"

"They must have spent hours decorating," he said. "If you don't mind, I'd like to call you Amelia. Why don't you call me Jacob?"

"I'd like that."

Good. That was the first step toward being more comfortable, Jacob thought.

They found the place card with Jacob's name in a decorative script and took their seats. It was near the stage. Other people found their places.

"There must be seventy-five people here," Jacob said, swiveling his head to take it all in.

"I counted eighteen tables when we came in," she said. "If four people are at each table, that's seventy-two, so you were very close."

"You counted the tables?"

"I'm sorry. I'm a math girl. I love numbers."

He smiled at her. "That's not a bad thing. It just surprised me, that's all. Do you calculate things all the time?"

"Oh, yes. I calculate prices per ounce at the general store, I calculate what marks I have to earn on each test to maintain my grade at an A, and I calculate how long it will take me to save up for something I want. But so far, I've never been able to calculate the number of stars in the sky."

Jacob laughed. "That one may take you a while." He beamed at her as a smile lit her face. *What a beautiful smile to get lost in,* he thought.

Another couple arrived and sat at their table. He was a short, middle-aged man with a prominent nose and heavy eyebrows. His wife, a chatty brunette with gray strands at the temples, accompanied him.

As they took their seats, the man thrust his hand toward Jacob. "I'm Hiram West, and this is my wife, Victoria. I work in the Farm Implement Division. How about you?"

"Nice to meet you, Hiram. I'm Jacob Bishop, and this is my friend, Amelia Schultz. I sell pianos."

"Oh, you folks aren't married," said Victoria.

Amelia blushed. "We haven't known each other long."

Victoria leaned toward Amelia and said in a stage whisper, "He sure is a handsome devil."

Amelia shot a look at Jacob and blushed again. Jacob pretended not to hear.

Mr. Ellsworth took the podium and called for silence. When the room settled down, he said, "We have a wonderful evening planned, so let's get started with dinner. Bow your heads, and we'll say grace."

Scores of people bowed their heads while Mr. Ellsworth thanked the Almighty for such a good year in business, for all of his loyal employees, and for the food they were about to receive. The crowd said, "Amen."

Servers came through the doors bearing trays loaded with small bowls of cold beet and onion salad. They placed one of the bowls in front of each person. Hiram and his wife peeked at Jacob and Amelia from the corners of their eyes, observing how they spread their napkins in their laps. Then, they followed suit. Jacob lowered his head and smiled to himself. It hadn't been that long that he was in their position, not knowing the finer points of dining in public.

Another waiter came by to fill their glasses with wine from a carafe.

Jacob asked for water instead.

Amelia's eyes widened. "Don't you want some wine, Jacob?"

"Not tonight," he said. "I used to drink a lot of ale, and I didn't like myself much after that."

She chuckled. "At least get them to put a slice of lemon in your water."

More servers came, removed the empty salad bowls, and put down plates of roasted chicken with mashed potatoes, gravy, and buttered carrots.

Hiram hailed a waiter and asked for more wine.

"What kind of work do you do in the Farm Implement Section?" Jacob asked, cutting his chicken into bite-sized pieces.

"I've been at it long enough to know how to do it all," Hiram said. "So they move me from position to position. If somebody is sick and can't get to work, I do their part of the build until they get back. The job I like best is the painting. Once the reaper is all assembled, or whatever piece of equipment we're building that day, the equipment is moved to the paint shack. The painters spray it and get it ready to sell. I like to do that."

In the meantime, Victoria was filling Amelia's ears with details about her children, their runny noses, rashes, and behavior problems at school. Amelia barely got a word in. She could only nod as she ate her meal.

For dessert, they were served devil's food cake with chocolate icing, a sprig of spearmint, and a cherry. "Oh, look," Amelia said. "They made it look like mistletoe."

Dropping to a stage whisper again, Victoria said, "Since it's mistletoe, maybe Mr. Handsome over there will kiss you by the end of the night."

Amelia blushed and ducked her head. "Please, Mrs. West, we're not ready for that."

Victoria cackled. "I'd like to be there peeking through a keyhole when it happens."

Amelia rolled her eyes and glanced sideways at Jacob with an "I'm sorry" look. Jacob's heart went out to her. The unseemly tone of the conversation wasn't her fault. She was trapped at a table with a coarse woman who had no sense of propriety.

"This cake is delicious," Jacob said. "You ought to eat yours before it dries out, Victoria."

Mr. Ellsworth stood again and tapped on the podium. "Ladies and gentlemen, please give me your attention."

The buzz of conversation slowed, then stopped.

"We've had an outstanding year at Ellsworth's," he said, "and it's all due to you hard-working employees. So we have a few awards to pass out."

A uniformed hotel employee wheeled a squeaky cart full of plaques across the stage to within Ellsworth's reach. He droned on about outstanding work, naming top employees from the Farm Implement Division and the Piano Division. The crowd was polite enough to clap after the presentation of each plaque. Jacob observed his coworkers' bland expressions. They, like him, wished it would be over soon.

"This last award," he said, "is for outstanding sales in the Piano Division. Mr. Jacob Bishop has sold more pianos in five months than our former salesmen ever sold in nine months. So, Mr. Bishop, would you come and receive your award?"

Jacob stood slowly as his tentative smile grew to a grin. He ignored his napkin falling to the floor and walked to the stage. The audience applauded politely while Hiram whistled and stomped at their table. Jacob chuckled. Ellsworth shook his hand and awarded him a beautiful walnut plaque with the Ellsworth logo. A brass plate read, 'Jacob Bishop, Salesman of the Year, 1879'. "This is for outstanding sales, Bishop, helping us turn a good profit. Do you have anything you want to say?"

Jacob was caught off guard. "A salesman should always have something to say, so first, let me thank Hiram West for his enthusiasm." He paused as a ripple of laughter went through the crowd. "I'll admit this surprise has me speechless. For me, it's been a long, hard road to get here. My family is back in Connecticut. Ma and Pa will be proud to hear about this." He turned the plaque around to see it better. "Just let me say I'm grateful for the opportunity to learn the piano business and improve my sales skills. You're a good man to work for, Mr. Ellsworth."

Ellsworth beamed at him while the crowd applauded again. As Jacob left the platform with his plaque, a pang of conscience stabbed him. He had just received a high honor at work, and he was thinking of quitting.

He had never pictured himself as disloyal, but . . . but there was no time to think about that now. He had to think of Amelia.

Ellsworth continued. "Now, let's dance off these heavy dinners. We have a string quintet here from the university who will provide music. The dance floor is now open."

The director raised his baton, and the orchestra began a Strauss waltz.

Servers swarmed in to remove the plates and silverware, leaving the drinking glasses.

"Amelia, may I have this dance?" Jacob asked.

She smiled and moved to the dance floor with him. "I'm relieved to be away from the Wests for a few minutes," she said.

"I'm sorry you had to endure all that. Some first date."

"Oh, did you expect a second?" She gave him a coy smile.

He only grinned, feeling her back muscles flex under his hand as they swayed to the music. He inhaled the scent of perfume in her copper-colored hair and gazed into her hazel eyes. Her green velvet dress followed the curves of her slender body. "You are quite beautiful," he said.

"Thank you, Jacob. You are, too. All the ladies say so." She gave him a sly grin.

Jacob chuckled and wagged his head. Then he glanced around. The dance floor was getting crowded. "I wonder how many people are dancing."

Amelia gave him a twisted smile. "If you give me a minute, I'll calculate the area of the dance floor and multiply by the number of dancers per square yard."

"Don't bother, Miss Numbers. Let's *(two-three)* just *(two-three)* dance *(two-three-one-two-three)*."

She giggled as the string quintet began another waltz.

They bumped into another couple, and Jacob turned to apologize. It was Miss Thompson, glaring at him. "Oh, Miss Thompson, it's you. I'm sorry we bumped into you."

She said nothing but moved on. He suspected Miss Thompson had purposefully bumped into him.

"Who was that?" Amelia asked.

"That was a fellow employee and my former piano teacher. She's been mad at me for weeks."

"Whatever for?" They continued to sway in time to the music.

"She expected me to do something I couldn't do in good conscience. She's a person who likes to get her way."

"Who can blame her? I like to get my way, too."

"I hope you're reasonable about it and don't mind giving other people their way once in a while."

She gave him a smile that made him melt. "I don't mind. I like give-and-take." They danced until they could dance no longer. They found their table for a rest, and to their relief, Hiram and Victoria were elsewhere. Maybe they had left early to tuck their unruly children into bed. Amelia's elbow rested on the table, and she leaned her head on her hand.

"You look tired, Amelia. Are you ready to go home?"

"Give me a second to have another sip of this wine. It's been a great evening, Jacob. Thank you for inviting me."

"And thank you for coming."

He picked up his plaque and slid into his overcoat while Amelia wrapped herself in her cape. His arm went around her shoulders as they walked to the door.

***

Back home, Solomon was aware of the lid on the letterbox squeaking open and closed outdoors but didn't check it immediately, being immersed in his studies. After he had a light supper, he went to see what was there. It was a letter from his father. Solomon frowned and took it inside.

He tore open the end of the envelope and slid the letter out. His hands shook, and his stomach was already churning as he unfolded it, spread it out, and leaned over it with his hands palm-down on the table. He read,

Dear Solomon,

Your mother says you are enrolled in architecture school. So you

finally got your own way. I'd like to know where you got the money since you still owe me for your tuition at Yale. Your mother is upset about this, and I think you owe me the courtesy of a reply.

   Sincerely,
      Father

Anger spread from the pit of Solomon's stomach until his entire body was consumed with it. This was a poor reaction—even the devil would agree—but he wanted to stay angry for a while. He was still in that state when Jacob reached home. Solomon was pacing restlessly, and his face was red.

"Solly, what's wrong? You're agitated."

"I got a letter from Father today."

"Oh?"

"He didn't ask how I was or how my studies were going. He didn't say how his health is or how Mother is. All he wanted to know was where I got the money to attend architecture school and why I hadn't reimbursed him for my tuition at Yale. He says I'm upsetting Mother."

"Having met him, Solly, I'd say he's the one upsetting your mother."

"Of course he is. I wish she would leave him, but I know she won't, out of a sense of duty."

"You said she's doing what God tells her, the same as you. So you can't blame her."

Solomon stopped pacing and turned to Jacob in surprise. "You're right, Jake. You're right."

"Are you going to answer your father's letter?"

"Right now, I'm too angry, and I don't see any point in it. It seems rude not to, but it would only give him fuel for another round of criticism. So, no, I won't answer his letter."

"Good man. I'm proud of you."

"Did you enjoy the party?"

Jacob smiled and showed him the plaque. "I got this award and had a great time dancing with Amelia. I plan to ask her out again. She's easy to talk to and very pleasing company."

Solomon took a breath. "Good for you. I know you need someone to talk to since I'm not available for much chatting."

186

"Yes, and she's prettier than you, too."

Solomon recognized the joke, but it fell flat. He turned to go to his bedroom, thinking his comment to Jacob was hypocritical. He wished Jacob would forget about girls until they were established in their work.

Solomon tossed all night, alternately stretching out on his back and then curling into a fetal position, struggling with what he should do about his father's letter.

As they dressed for church the following morning, Solomon said, "I've changed my mind. I'm going to answer Father's letter."

"What? You said it wouldn't do any good."

"It wouldn't if I said what I wanted to say. But I prayed about it. I believe God wants me to remind Father that he raised me to follow God's leading, and God doesn't want me in the pulpit. He wants me to be an architect. So how could I do anything else?"

Jacob leaned back and laughed. "That'll get him."

Solomon's eyebrows raised. "I'm not telling that to 'get him.' I'm telling him that because it's the truth."

"Honest? You heard God tell you to be an architect?"

"Not with my ears. But His Spirit communicates with me on a spiritual level."

Jacob stared at him. "I wish I could believe that, but that sounds like a story you made up."

"I hope you will believe it someday. I didn't make it up. It's in the Bible, and I'm living it in practice."

Jacob made no reply as they put their coats on to go out.

"Solly, I still have the carriage I rented for last night's party. I don't have to return it until this afternoon. Let's drive it to church this morning."

"That sounds good."

The weather was biting. They pulled their overcoats closer, thankful that the carriage's landau roof protected them from the wind. The two horses pulled the carriage over the brick street, clip-clopping along while their breath steamed in the air before them.

As they traveled, Jacob asked about Mrs. Sterling's new house. They discussed the features of the second floor, the elevator access, and the roofing materials.

Solomon sucked in a breath of ice-cold air and shivered.

Jacob asked, "Did you write a letter to Colonel McCreary?"

"Yes. I haven't received a reply. He may be traveling. Or maybe he read it and doesn't have time to answer. I couldn't blame him."

"Have faith, Solly. I believe you'll get a reply. He was very helpful before."

When they reached the church, they pulled in, tied the horses to the hitching post, and hurried into the worship service.

The music started with the organist playing an introduction to "O Come, All Ye Faithful." When the piano joined in, adding its mellow tones to the metallic, reedy tones of the pump organ, the congregation's voices lifted. A huge grin lit Jacob's face, and his chest swelled. The piano gave the music an extra burst of energy, an almost magical quality. He leaned toward Solomon's ear as the congregation sang and said proudly, "Well-voiced hammers."

"What?"

"I said, 'well-voiced hammers.' On the piano. Round tones."

Solomon's mouth formed an O, and he nodded with a smile. Then he shoved the hymnal toward Jacob and pointed at the music as if to say, "Sing."

Chapter 24: The Decision

Tuesday, December 16, 1879

For the next two days, Jacob wrestled with the decision of whether to stay at Ellsworth's or take the job offer from Mrs. Sterling.

"What do you think I should do?" he asked Solomon before supper.

Solomon shrugged as he added vegetables to the pot. "When I have a big decision to make, I ask God. He knows better than we do with our inability to see the future."

Jacob sighed and stared at Solomon. "That's irritating. I ask you for advice, and all you tell me is you'd go to God if you was me. Don't you have anything better than that? I need solid advice."

Solomon sighed. "All right, let's try another approach. How do other people make decisions? I suppose they look at the benefits and disadvantages of both options, then toss a coin."

"I know you meant that as a joke, but there's probably a lot of truth in it."

"Are there any factors affecting your decision that stand out as a potential problem?"

"My biggest concern is whether I'm good enough to manage a business. What happens if I can't keep within a budget and Mrs. Sterling goes bankrupt? I'd be out of a job, and the guilt from knowing I had ruined someone financially would be overwhelming."

The stew boiled and sent steam rising. Solomon reduced the heat and gave Jacob a crooked smile. "Don't worry about Mrs. Sterling going bankrupt. Her attorney will probably open a corporation to conduct business at the mansion, so even if the corporation goes bankrupt, she's still good personally."

"So that's how things work."

"In that case, you might be able to get hired at Ellsworth's again."

"Possibly, but that's not guaranteed. He's proud of me now, but he might not like me so much if I tell him I'm leaving."

"Have you done any research? You could ask around at the hotels. Find out their level of occupancy and where they do their advertising. You could ask them how much they pay their employees and where they buy their supplies."

"That's a good idea. While I'm out making my sales calls tomorrow, I'll stop at some of the hotels and ask questions. Good idea, Solly. Thanks."

***

When Wednesday morning dawned, Solomon had no classes until January, so he had a free day. He grinned at the man in the mirror as he shaved, relishing the prospect of a rest. However, most of the day was spent doing laundry for himself and Jacob. He worked on Mrs. Sterling's house plans while the wet clothes dripped from lines strung through the parlor.

***

After the day's work, Jacob bounded into the house, finding Solomon cooking sausage and sauerkraut.

"Solly," he shouted. "I made great progress today." He bombarded Solomon's weary brain with details he had learned about the hotel business, then announced that he wanted to try his hand at management. He planned to resign from Ellsworth's.

Solomon set the table and served the meal.

"It sounds like you have enough information to work out a budget."

"Probably," Jacob said, scooping up some sauerkraut off the serving

190

plate, "but I don't know how to do it."

Solomon grinned. "Isn't your Miss Schultz a numbers person?"

Jacob's eyes lit up. "Aha! I believe you have a great idea there. But I can't ask her to help me without paying for her work, and I can't ask Mrs. Sterling to pay her for something she's paying me to do."

"You could take her to a matinee and a dinner as payment."

A slow smile spread over Jacob's face. He shoveled his food down as quickly as he could. "Good supper, Solly. Thanks. I'm going to Amelia's house to see if I can make a deal with her."

"But it's after dark," Solomon protested.

"I'll take a lantern. I want to get things moving. I want to impress Mrs. Sterling."

"I wish I could make things happen as fast as you do," Solomon said, gazing around the dirty kitchen. "Maybe I should take a lesson."

Jacob grabbed his overcoat and a lantern. He was out the door in a moment as Solomon put a pot of water on the stove for dishwashing.

***

Jacob mounted his horse and left at a trot. Thankfully, it didn't take too long in the cold air to arrive at the Schultz home. When he rapped on the door, Mr. Schultz answered.

"Jacob, what a surprise," he said.

"Mr. Schultz, I apologize for arriving without an appointment. Is Amelia home? I want to talk to her about a business deal, and there is some urgency."

Mr. Schultz tilted his head. "A business deal? I'll call her to the parlor. You can talk here."

"Thank you, sir. That will be fine."

Mr. Schulz called Amelia to come, then sat down himself. When he opened his newspaper, it became clear that he planned to stay there to listen in. It didn't matter to Jacob. There was no need for privacy.

When Amelia entered the room, her eyes lit up. "Jacob, what a surprise."

Jacob laughed. "That's exactly what your father said. I apologize for coming this late, but I want to see if you'd be interested in a business proposition."

"Really? What could that be?" She sat on the Chesterfield sofa next to him.

Jacob explained that he planned to resign from Ellsworth's to manage Mrs. Sterling's bed and breakfast. He told her about gathering all the information needed to create a budget. "Do you know how to do budgets?" he asked.

"Of course. It can't be done quickly unless you've dug deeper than I think you have. What does this little job pay? I don't want to spend time doing it for free."

Jacob glanced sideways at Mr. Schultz, who tried to hide a crooked grin. *He must think I can't see him behind that newspaper.*

"How much would you charge for something like this?"

"It depends on how long it takes. For an average job, I'd say I'd need to be taken to the theater for a matinee, then to a nice restaurant for dinner, and maybe dancing. And I want to sit in the three-dollar section at the matinee."

Mr. Schultz coughed and tried to conceal his amusement. He rattled the newspaper and turned a page.

Jacob beamed. "That's exactly what I thought, only I wanted to sit in the two-dollar seats." His eyes sparkled, hoping she would respond well to his teasing.

She grinned. "No, I'm holding out for the three-buck section."

"Fine. Is it a deal, then?"

"Deal." She thrust out her hand for a shake. Jacob had never shaken a woman's hand to confirm a business deal. When he reached out for her hand, he spotted Mr. Schulz's smirk.

"When can we get started?" he asked.

"What about Friday? I don't have classes that day."

"We could work on it in the morning before I see a client on Friday afternoon. Then, I have an appointment with Mrs. Sterling on Saturday, followed by an evening event. We could do the matinee and dinner the Saturday after Christmas. How does that sound?"

"That will be fine. Do you want to meet at the university library, say, nine o'clock on Friday morning?"

"That sounds good."

She smiled. "Don't forget to bring all your notes. I'll bring a columnar pad, pencils, and plenty of erasers. We'll need them for our work."

"Thank you, Amelia."

He stood.

"I'll see you Friday. Good night, Mr. Schultz."

On his way back home, he reflected on what had just happened. *I'd love to be a spider on the wall and hear what Amelia and her father are talking about right now.* He chuckled, lifted his lantern to light the way, and urged the horse home.

***

Jacob woke energized on Thursday morning. He hadn't given Mrs. Sterling his decision yet, so he fried some eggs for himself and Solomon and then left for the Sterling Mansion.

When he knocked on the door, Mrs. Sterling answered. "Good morning, Jacob. Come on in."

"I'm surprised you answered the door. Is Gloria working today?"

"No, Gloria is sick. I sent her home. It's just you and me today."

Jacob swallowed hard, remembering how possessive she had been and wondering if that last comment suggested trouble ahead. If so, he didn't dare accept the job. She led him to her library, where he had first met her in her wheelchair.

They made small talk for about ten minutes. The conversation carried no hint of anything suggestive, so Jacob relaxed.

"Have you thought about my proposal?"

"Yes, I have, and I'd like to accept your offer."

She leaned back in her chair, grinned widely, and clapped her hands. "That's great news. I prayed you would give me that answer."

"I have some questions we need to discuss," he said, switching to a business attitude.

"I'd say there are many things we need to discuss. What are the things on your mind right now?"

He told her about his concern over the timing of his resignation from the Ellsworth Company. He also said they would need to set boundaries on their work relationship so he wouldn't be called out twenty-four hours a day. He told her he had been doing some research and would have a preliminary budget ready for her review on Saturday.

Her eyebrows raised. "That's quite a mouthful, Jacob. I can see we'll have to have some give and take in our relationship. For instance, if you're the manager of the bed and breakfast, you *will* be on call twenty-four hours a day. That's the nature of the job. You would only be called out for emergencies, however. I promise not to call you if an issue can wait until morning. Can you live with that?"

Jacob's mouth formed an O as he gained a better understanding of the nature of the job. *Of course,* he thought. *Guests may sometimes have needs after office hours.* "Yes, that wouldn't be a problem."

They discussed staffing details in that meeting. Since some people in Chicago were beginning to put telephones in their homes, and the more prominent businesses all had them, they determined the telephone would be a necessity in the mansion and Jacob's home. They would offer Amelia a job checking guests in and out, recording payments, making reports, and depositing the rent money in the bank.

Mrs. Sterling nodded. "Amelia Schultz. She's a very bright girl, and she's all business."

Jacob grinned. "Yes, she is. She'll do us a good job."

"I think that's all for today, Jacob. Once I approve your budget, you'll go on salary. Is that acceptable?"

"I'll put in my notice to Mr. Ellsworth when you hire me officially, so give me two weeks after that."

"Agreed. Our next meeting will be next Saturday morning at ten o'clock. Come with that budget in hand. I may yet be able to announce you're my new manager. Oh, and ask Mr. Hawk to come too, bringing his plans."

Chapter 25: Mrs. Sterling's Plans

Friday, December 18, 1879

On Friday, the postman dropped mail in the letterbox by the door. Solomon was alerted by the squeaking of the rusty letterbox lid, so he went out to get it, hoping it wasn't from Father. It wasn't. There was a letter in the familiar bold hand of Colonel McCreary. Solomon dashed back into the house and sliced the envelope open with the engraved silver letter opener his mother had sent for his birthday.

His face lit as he read the Colonel's words.

Dear Solomon,

Your project sounds fascinating. If I could be there myself, I would love to get involved in the design of that balcony. It would be a similar project to the bridge over the Hess, only on a much smaller scale. I've never done anything like that on a residential property.

However, I'm currently involved in another project. You need to consult a civil engineer who can guide you in areas where you still lack training. Such a man will be qualified to test the soil for the foundation and retaining wall, and he'll calculate the steel requirements for the cantilever balcony.

I am proud of your progress, Solomon, and I am even prouder that you dare to take on such a challenging project. Don't botch it up.

Yours truly,
Col. A. McCreary

Solomon's heart beat faster, and he laid the letter down with a shaking hand. What an honor to have personal guidance from such a famous engineer. *Thank you, Lord.*

He was not surprised at McCreary's suggestion. He would locate an engineer with a good reputation and find out what it would cost to hire him. That would prepare him to talk to Mrs. Sterling.

The library had a list of Chicago engineers. Not wanting to waste any time, Solomon mounted his horse. When he arrived at the library, Jacob and Amelia were huddled at a round table in intense discussion.

"Jacob, you look stressed," he said.

Jacob wagged his head. "This is harder than I expected. Our erasers are almost worn out, and our calculations are shocking. I've never been responsible for that much money. I don't know how to make the bed and breakfast pay that much. And where can I cut expenses to increase profits?"

"It gets even worse," Amelia said, amused. "To make it work, you have to include reserves for replacement of major items like roof, kitchen appliances, and that sort of thing."

Jacob sighed. "This may never work," he said.

"It will if we find the right combination of room revenue and cost. Come on. Stay with me."

Jacob peered at Solomon again. "What are you doing here?"

"I came to see if I could get the name of a good civil engineer in Chicago."

"Good luck."

Solomon walked to the reference room as Jacob and Amelia ducked their heads and resumed their discussion. He remembered a book listing Chicago businesses with addresses. If a company was progressive enough to have a telephone, its number was listed.

He located the directory and searched for civil engineers. The sheer number of engineering firms surprised him, but none of the names were familiar.

Heavenly Father, please lead me to the right engineer, he whispered. He ran his finger down the list of names and stopped at the name of an engineer who had paid for an ad. The fellow's name was Manfred Gebaur.

Hmm. A German engineer. His lower lip jutted out, and he nodded approvingly, writing the contact information in his notebook. The ad gave the names of well-known commercial clients whose buildings he had designed. But Solomon continued through the list.

The next name he stopped on was Paul Wilcox, a specialist in bridges and retaining walls. Solomon had a gut feeling this was the one. He jotted down the address, located it on the map of Chicago on the library wall, and wrote the directions to his office.

Outside, he stepped into the stirrup and swung his leg over the horse's back. "Let's go," he said, shifting his weight forward. The horse wasted no time getting him to where he wanted to go.

The address listed for Wilcox was a house in a residential neighborhood. It was an imposing three-story Victorian home with turrets and bay windows. Set on a hill, it overlooked the neighborhood. It was painted in a buttery shade of yellow trimmed in white, except for the green door and shutters. A flight of brick steps led to the front porch. Solomon stared at it in admiration. He tied his horse, grabbed his notes, and climbed the stairs.

At his knock, a matronly woman wearing a white apron over her black dress opened the door and invited him in. "I'm here to see Mr. Wilcox if he's available," Solomon said.

"Right this way."

The engineer stood before his drafting table in a room adjoining the hall, concentrating on his latest project. He was a solidly built man of average height. What little hair he still had was turning silver. He worked in his stocking feet near the radiator.

"Excuse me, sir. My name is Solomon Hawk. May I have a moment?"

Mr. Wilcox turned his head enough to stare at Solomon.

"Now that you've interrupted my train of thought, let's sit at my desk." His voice was commanding and conveyed irritation.

Solomon muttered, "Sorry, sir," in embarrassment. But then he reconsidered. *Wilcox is being rude and unprofessional. Maybe he's under a lot of stress.*

Wilcox padded to his desk in his socks and dropped heavily into the rolling oak chair. He waved Solomon into the smaller chair on the opposite side.

"What can I do for you?"

"I'm an architectural student at the university, and I've already been given my first job. It involves a retaining wall and cantilever balcony, so I need an engineer."

Wilcox paused for a moment and narrowed his eyes. "What you've described seems pretty heavy for a student," he said. "What makes you think you can handle it?"

Solomon squirmed, being put on the spot, and gathered his courage. "I can handle it, except for the parts that require an engineer. Would you like to see the preliminary plans?"

"Who's the client?"

"Mrs. Marguerite Sterling."

The atmosphere in the room changed at that magic name. Wilcox sat up and leaned forward. "Let me see the plans."

Solomon spread out his drawings. Wilcox pored over them, asking questions about the property's location and Solomon's choice of materials. "Ah," he said. "You've put in an elevator. Why did you do that?"

"When I first met Mrs. Sterling, she was in a wheelchair with a broken leg. She recovered, but she could eventually need one again. And she lives alone with no one to help her up and down stairs."

Solomon perceived that Wilcox's respect for his work increased as they talked. Finally, the engineer leaned back in his chair and clasped his hands behind his head.

"I'd be interested in bidding on this project," he said. "How soon do you need me to quote a fee?"

"I'm seeing Mrs. Sterling in the morning. I'd like to have something to tell her then."

He whistled softly. "You should have contacted me sooner."

"Yes, sir, I realize that, but I just got a letter from Colonel McCreary recommending that I hire a local engineer. Up until then, I thought I could work it out myself. I admit that's a beginner's mistake."

Wilcox's eyes widened. "Are you talking about the same Colonel McCreary who designed that bridge over the Hess?"

"Yes."

"You know him personally?"

"Yes, I met him on a ferry on the Susquehanna. We were able to spend several hours together. He wrote a letter for me that got me admitted to the university."

Wilcox sat at his desk with his legs crossed, swinging his foot and thinking. His jaw twitched. "If he should come to town sometime, maybe you could introduce me."

Solomon smiled. "I'd be happy to."

"All right, back to the Sterling project. I want to look at the property before I give you a quote. Are you prepared to take me there now?"

"I came on horseback. If you have a carriage— "

"Of course. Come on." Wilcox tugged his boots onto his feet and slid his overcoat on. "The carriage is out back. Bring the plans."

Solomon gathered up the plans and scurried behind Wilcox, who was surprisingly quick for a man of his husky build.

They climbed into the carriage and took off on their mission with Solomon directing the way.

Arriving at Mrs. Sterling's property, Wilcox hopped out, shielding his eyes from the bright sun while scanning the wooded land that sloped toward the lake.

"She wants the house close enough to the lake that her balcony hangs over the water," Solomon said.

"We may have to talk her out of that. It will depend on the quality of the soil. You're right; she'll need a retaining wall." He trod over the land near the lake to get a preliminary feel. "She'll need someone to clear a lot of these trees. I have contacts with men in that business."

Wilcox took a notebook from his pocket and jotted notes on the property's topography and types of trees. "Let's go back to the office, and I'll give you a quote."

They rode silently while Wilcox chewed on the problem. When they reached the office, he gave a higher quote than Solomon expected. "That fee includes the soil test, the cost of the land survey, the design of the retaining wall, and the design of that cantilever balcony. You and I will collaborate on the balcony design, since it will be anchored by the house."

199

"Thank you, sir. I'll see Mrs. Sterling in the morning and tell you what she says."

Solomon tied his plans into a roll and went home.

***

Jacob arrived home later with a budget ready for Mrs. Sterling's review. He had a reasonable estimate on paper of what it would cost to run the bed and breakfast and how much they would need to charge the guests per night to cover the expenses. He would suggest to Mrs. Sterling that they offer free incidentals like evening snacks. If they added that small expense, they could raise the price high enough to make a profit. He would also suggest offering laundry service for guests' clothing for an extra fee. And they would make the great room available to folks wanting to rent it for parties and wedding receptions. Jacob was excited and eager to explain all this to Mrs. Sterling.

Saturday, December 19, 1879

In the morning, Solomon and Jacob rode to the Sterling Mansion for their meeting. Mrs. Sterling led them through the entrance hall, where two workers hung cedar boughs and large silk bows. They had already placed a candle arrangement with Christmas greenery on the hall table.

"Fellows," she instructed the workers, "when you finish here, decorate the great room. You'll need to start with the fireplace."

"Yes, ma'am."

She invited Jacob and Solomon into the library, where a parquet table with four chairs was positioned in the center of the room.

"Jacob, sit beside me so I can see your numbers while you talk," she said. He took the chair beside hers while Solomon seated himself on the opposite side of the table.

Jacob opened his file folder and laid out the plan, explaining the cost of hiring a cook, housekeeper, groundskeeper, bookkeeper, and Jacob's salary. He also laid out each employee's duties. He gave her the numbers for all other expenses and showed her the bottom line. To him, the numbers were shocking. His eyes followed her reaction carefully as he talked. She surprised him when she didn't flinch, but he carefully hid his emotion.

"It looks like you've done a thorough job, Jacob, but what if something unexpected happens? How will we cover it?"

Jacob flipped a page in his budget. "We have a line item in the budget for emergencies; for instance, if a guest somehow damaged a room so bad I couldn't handle it all myself. Then repairs and labor would come out of that emergency fund."

She nodded her approval. "Where did you come up with these numbers? Did you estimate?"

"I estimated where I had to," Jacob said, "but I talked to other hotel owners about how much they pay for consumables. I estimated how long a housekeeper would take to do laundry and clean a room when a guest leaves and how many eggs, pancakes, and other staples it would take to serve breakfast to a full house."

Mrs. Sterling beamed. "This is good work, Jacob."

Solomon waited patiently while they discussed the details of running a bed and breakfast. It took them almost an hour. Finally, Mrs. Sterling turned to him.

"What do you have for me, Mr. Hawk?"

He stood to spread his plans over the table, then walked around the table and stood beside her chair.

"Here's the plan for the front elevation," he said. He waited while she took in the impact of the pillars, multi-paned windows, double entry doors, and the arched window over the door.

"That's lovely," she said.

"And this is the first floor," he said, pulling out another page and leaning over to point at the features as he explained the layout. "There's plenty of room to entertain a few guests but not as many as you entertain here. I think you'll enjoy the fireplace on the north wall and the window wall with double doors on the lakeside. You go through those doors onto the cantilever balcony. Now, I've spoken to an engineer who tells me that the condition of the soil will tell us how far we can build out over the water."

Her back stiffened, and she spoke firmly. "I want that balcony to extend over the lake far enough that you won't see the ground under you when you sit there. That's not negotiable."

Solomon glanced at Jacob with his mouth open. Fortunately, she couldn't see his expression from her seated position. He spoke confidently despite having serious doubts about whether it could be accomplished. "Well, you can build anything you want if there's enough steel. The engineer will be doing the specifications for that, so we'll tell him that's your dream, and he should make sure you have it."

Mrs. Sterling absent-mindedly tapped her fingernails on the table and continued studying the first-floor plan.

She moved her hands over the drawing. "I see you have the kitchen off the hall between the foyer and dining room. Obviously, the kitchen will be closed off to view with doors."

"Of course."

"Let's see . . . there are two small bedrooms with a shared bath along the opposite side of the hall. But wait, what is this little room beside the stairs at the end of the great room? I didn't notice it before."

"That's the private electric elevator. If you're ever in a wheelchair again, as you were a few months ago, you'll be glad to have an elevator."

Her face lit up. "That's perfect. No one else has an elevator right in their home. It has to be decorative. I want to choose the one I want."

"Naturally." Solomon pulled another page out and laid it over the ground floor plan. He reviewed each feature with her, including the radiators for heat rather than outdated potbelly stoves. He showed her the upstairs master bedroom, private bath, and the double doors that would open onto a small private balcony, giving her a wonderful view of the sunset over the lake. He suggested having a small table and chair there to take her tea.

"Ooh," she said and stood to get a better view of the entire plan. Her eyes were bright, and she was grinning. "Jacob, can't you just see this? I can put potted plants on my private balcony."

Jacob smiled and nodded.

"Mr. Hawk, there's a change I'd like to make. I don't need a bedroom that wide. Can you extend the closets from where they are and run them to the back of the bedroom so I'll have more storage space?"

"If you like."

"And I want an archway to visually separate the bedroom from the sitting room."

"That can easily be done." Solomon made some notes in his notebook.

"Where will we do the laundry? I don't see a place for that."

Solomon drew a fourth sheet from under the pile and placed it on top. "It will be in the basement, with doors directly to the outside."

"That's good, but please add a chute where we can toss laundry from upstairs."

Solomon made more notes. "Also in the basement are the utilities— the boiler for the heat and the marble fuse mount for electricity. Is there anything else?"

She clapped her hands. "Oh, it will be lovely to have electricity. And what about the roof? What do you recommend to cover the roof?"

"You have your choice. You can use asphalt shingles, embossed tin shingles, wood shakes, slate . . ."

"Slate. I want slate."

"That's a good choice for a long-lasting roof, although it will add to the construction cost. We'll have to ensure the load-bearing walls are beefed up enough to hold that weight."

"Work up an estimate on that, will you? I might want to change my mind and have asphalt shingles. I don't want to go crazy with costs."

He scribbled more notes.

Beaming, she said, "I'm satisfied with your plans and the changes we discussed. There may be more changes as we go along. What is our next step?"

"The engineer needs to go to work doing a land survey and soil analysis so we'll know which trees to remove and where to locate the house. He'll also design the retaining wall and work with me on the cantilever balcony. I have a quote here for his fee." Solomon gave her the amount of the engineer's fee and told her how much he would charge for his own fee.

Mrs. Sterling opened her mouth, changed her mind, and closed it. "That's more than I expected," she said.

Solomon took a deep breath, trying to figure out what to say next, but Jacob intervened.

"Mrs. Sterling, there's more work involved in this than appears on the surface. You're asking for a one-of-a-kind home that will be the envy of everyone in Chicago. I'm sure newspaper reporters will be there taking photos. The whole city will follow the construction as your house goes up." He tilted his head and gave her a warm smile. "Creating something spectacular takes time . . . planning . . . even inspiration. I can only imagine what it will look like when you're done decorating! It will be even more beautiful than this mansion. But there is still work that needs to be done. If you're concerned you're not getting a good deal, you should ask around town and see how much other architects will charge."

Mrs. Sterling picked up the plans, gazed at Jacob from the top of her eyes, and smiled. "That's why I'm hiring you to manage my bed and breakfast. I couldn't have had a better demonstration of your sales skills."

"So, do you agree to Mr. Hawk's fee?"

She gave him a sly smile. "I've already checked with other architects. Yes, I agree. I'm excited to begin construction."

Solomon was tempted to wonder if he should have asked for more. It was too late for that. He chuckled and shot a glance at Jacob. "There's a lot of preparation to do before the foundation can go in. I'll keep you informed. I'll make another appointment to discuss the location of electric outlets and plumbing in a few days."

The meeting was over. As Jacob and Solomon walked to the road to mount their horses, Solomon clapped his friend on the shoulder. "Thank God you were there, Jacob. I would have made a mess of it when she balked at the fee."

Jacob grinned. "I'll expect my commission, Solly."

Chapter 26: The Announcement

Saturday, December 19, 1879

It was after dark when Jacob knocked on the mansion's door, noticing a large Christmas wreath had been placed on it since morning. It was decorated with pine cones, greenery, and mistletoe. He breathed deeply. The aroma took him back to the Christmas trees of his childhood.

Gloria opened the door and invited Jacob inside.

The flames dancing atop the candles on the hall table spread a welcoming glow. Yule decorations throughout the house completely changed the atmosphere from earlier in the day. The music from the great room reached his ears.

He handed his overcoat and bowler to Gloria. "It sounds like Mrs. Sterling hired extra musicians for the party."

"Yes," she said. "We have a harpist and violinist from the opera house to play carols with the pianist throughout the evening. Mrs. Sterling is waiting for you."

Jacob thanked her and proceeded down the hall. The musicians played "Bring a Torch, Jeanette, Isabella."

When he entered the great room, Mrs. Sterling swept toward him in a red satin dress that must have had yards of fabric in the overskirt. It sat atop a lacy white underskirt. She was radiant. Other guests had already arrived and stood chatting with glasses of eggnog or wassail in their hands. He glanced at the buffet table with its cheeses, cut vegetables, cookies, fudge, and petit fours, all artistically arranged on silver salvers.

"Come, Jacob," Mrs. Sterling said. "I want to introduce you to some of my friends."

She drew him toward two men who were engaged in conversation.

"Mr. Dawes, I'd like you to meet Mr. Jacob Bishop, an up-and-coming young man who has agreed to join my staff. Jacob, this is Mr. Charles Dawes. He's an attorney currently managing William McKinley's campaign for president."

Jacob's heart leaped. A blacksmith never expected to meet such an important gentleman. He thrust out his hand. "I'm pleased to meet you, Mr. Dawes."

"And I, you," Dawes said. "Marguerite has told me a lot about you. She has great plans, and you're an important part."

"I hope I don't disappoint her. What are you doing in Chicago? Do you have business here?"

Dawes chuckled. "I'm trying to find a venue for a McKinley victory party. We anticipate a win once the ballots are counted. Besides, after the election is finalized, I'm considering opening a new bank in Chicago. I have some backers, and I'm making some contacts here."

"I wish you the best of luck, sir."

Dawes nodded his thanks.

Mrs. Sterling laid her hand on the arm of the man Dawes had been chatting with. He was a thin fellow who had never spent much time in the sun. "And this is Mr. Ralph Clarkson," she said. "He's a portrait artist of great fame who just returned from Europe. He's visiting Chicago, so I invited him to share our Christmas fest with us. Mr. Clarkson, meet Jacob Bishop."

"Good to meet you, Bishop," he said, shaking his hand. He took a sip of his wassail. He was near Jacob's age, perhaps a little older.

Jacob asked, "So you're visiting. Where are you heading next?"

Clarkson leaned in as if to share a secret. "Actually, after seeing Chicago, I have a mind to settle here. I think I could make a good living doing portraits in this city."

Jacob raised his eyebrows and nodded. "You're probably right."

"Mrs. Sterling has agreed to let me do her portrait," he said, smiling at her.

"Ah, and she'll be a perfect subject," Jacob said. "I'm sure it will be a beautiful painting."

"Come, Jacob," she said. "Let's go meet some other people."

They moved through the room, meeting men and women from different stations in life. Jacob found all of them interesting.

After some time had passed, Mrs. Sterling asked the musicians to stop for a few minutes. She picked up a crystal wineglass by the stem and tapped it with a spoon to get everyone's attention.

"Ladies and gentlemen, thank you all for coming. I have a formal announcement if you'll give me your attention." After the chatter of the crowd stopped, she continued. "Some of you know about this, but others may not. I recently bought a lake property and will be moving out of Sterling Mansion as soon as I can build a new house."

There was murmuring among the crowd, as some were surprised she would leave the historic mansion. Jacob overheard one gray-haired woman turn to the lady beside her and wonder if Mrs. Sterling had financial problems. He rolled his eyes.

Mrs. Sterling continued. "This will be an excellent move for me. As you know, my late husband left me this mansion, which is much too large for one person. I plan to turn it into a bed and breakfast, a vacation location for visitors to Chicago. Why should I be the only person to enjoy the elegance and history of this beautiful home? But I wanted to leave it in such a way that the mansion would not leave the Sterling family." Applause rippled through the crowd.

"Further, I've hired Mr. Jacob Bishop, the handsome man I introduced to most of you, to manage the bed and breakfast for me. Jacob, would you like to say a few words?"

Jacob grinned at the crowd and stepped beside Mrs. Sterling. "You caught me off guard, Mrs. Sterling, but let me urge all of you to come to the Sterling Mansion Bed and Breakfast for a night or several nights. We'll open in about thirty days. When you stay here, you'll enjoy comfortable beds, attentive service, free breakfast, and a free evening snack with a glass of wine or juice. And you don't need to bring a whole trunk full of clothes. You can use our in-house laundry service, which is available for an extra fee."

As the crowd applauded again, Mrs. Sterling shouted, "Now, let's have more music. The dance floor is open. Ladies, I'm sorry, but I have dibs on Mr. Bishop for the first dance."

She grabbed his arm and pulled him to the dance floor while the musicians played a variation of "O Little Town of Bethlehem" as a waltz in three-quarter time. *Could this be part of my new job,* Jacob thought, *or am I just being put on display?* Either way, he enjoyed dancing, so he put his right arm around her, grasped her hand with his left, and took the lead.

"What do you think of the party, Jacob?" Mrs. Sterling asked.

"I'm a little overwhelmed with the famous people you have here. How did you meet them?"

"I met them here and there. A lot of them were friends of my husband when I married him. It would help if you got used to this. This will be your life from now on."

"Remember, I told you that Solomon and I are leaving here in two years."

"We'll see."

They spun around the dance floor until the music ended, and Mrs. Sterling returned to circulating among the crowd. She made sure the drinks were replenished.

Jacob didn't have time to rest. He was approached by one woman after another, asking for a dance. He danced with ladies young and old and charmed them all.

When the crowd began to thin out, he found Mrs. Sterling and said he must leave to go home. "Thank you for a wonderful evening," he said.

She beamed at him. "I'm giving you two weeks to work off your time at Ellsworth's, then I'll expect you here."

"I'll be here. And Merry Christmas, Mrs. Sterling."

Chapter 27: Leaving On a High Note

Jacob dreaded going to work on Monday morning. It was time to put in his resignation. He approached the head office with slow steps and tapped on the door.

Ellsworth's face broke into a smile. "Come in, Bishop. You're just the man I wanted to see. Have a seat."

Jacob sat. "I have something I need to talk to you about."

Ellsworth said, "In just a minute. First, I need to tell you about a new prospective client. The opera house is considering buying three pianos, a full-size concert grand for the stage and two baby grands for rehearsal rooms. He's hesitant to commit, so I'll give you the name of the fellow in charge of purchasing, and you can go see him."

"All right. But I need to tell you that I was offered another job. And I accepted it."

Ellsworth's face went blank, like a deer staring at a flame. He tilted his head. "What?"

"I'm sorry, sir, but I accepted another job. I'm giving my two weeks' notice."

Ellsworth shook his head to clear his thoughts. He straightened his back. "How can you do that? You just got an award for Salesman of the Year." His voice took on an edge. "Are you going to work for a competitor?"

"No, sir, I wouldn't do that. Mrs. Marguerite Sterling has offered me a job running the mansion. She's turning it into a bed and breakfast."

Ellsworth nervously tapped his pencil on the top of his desk. "That's a hard blow to our piano business. You realize that, don't you?"

His eyes pierced Jacob's composure. Jacob shifted in his seat.

"Sir, you can hire other people, but I'm the only person who can improve my future. This opportunity means more pay and contact with people I would never meet otherwise. Why, the other night, I met William McKinley's campaign manager and a host of other well-known people. Those contacts could be valuable in the future."

"Look, Bishop, I'll give you a raise."

"I'm sorry, sir. I've already committed to the new job. I've already started working on the budget on my own time. Please understand. I'll give my best effort to selling pianos for the next two weeks, but then I'll work with Mrs. Sterling."

Ellsworth pressed his lips tightly and drew a deep breath through his nose. His expression tightened. "All right, Bishop. I see that I don't have a choice. Here's the information you'll need to go to the opera house. See the purchasing agent, Mr. David Kerr." He passed a scrap of paper to Jacob with the address.

"Thank you, sir. I'll go there now."

He left the office, relieved to have escaped so easily. *Thank God Mr. Ellsworth isn't the type to explode in anger!* Jacob paused, realizing he had just thanked God for something. He didn't remember ever doing that. *Is my thinking changing?*

At the library, he consulted the Chicago map and plotted his route. It took him about an hour to reach the opera house. Inside, he asked for David Kerr and was directed to his office.

The door was open, so Jacob rapped on the door frame.

"Come in," said Kerr. "What can I do for you?"

Kerr was a well-dressed man in his late thirties with dark hair, wearing a white long-sleeve shirt, spectacles, and thoughtful expression. Black suspenders held up his trousers.

The desk was a fantastic clutter of papers. *How in the world does he ever keep track of his tasks?* He extended his hand for a shake.

"I'm Jacob Bishop with the Ellsworth Piano Company. I understand you're thinking of buying three pianos."

"Yes, we are, but I've already been talking to the salesman from your competitor, the Julius Bauer Company. He's given me some good prices on their pianos."

"Would you mind interviewing me, too? It never hurts to get all the information you can before making a major purchase."

"I can give you a few minutes, but please be brief. I'm in the middle of ordering costumes for the summer opera."

Jacob sat in a chair across the desk. "I don't know much about the opera house business," he said, "but I would assume that your success rises and falls on the quality of your performers."

"Of course."

"And the only way to attract quality performers, and the only way to attract an audience willing to pay the higher prices, is to have quality instruments. Would you agree? You need expertly-built pianos with spruce soundboards that have a good crown. That's the way to get the best resonance from the instrument. You also need well-voiced hammers. The felt covering the hammers can't be too soft or too hard. At Ellsworth's, we've found the perfect balance that creates round, mellow tones pleasing to the ear—tones that carry well through the auditorium and into the box seats without sounding mushy or tinny."

Kerr nodded, familiar with the terms Jacob used. "But what about price?"

Jacob gave him the retail price of a concert grand and two baby grand rehearsal pianos. "They all have the same touch, so the performers won't be surprised when they leave the practice room and sit down to play in front of the audience."

Kerr blew a puff of air from pursed lips, then said, "That's a fair amount more than the other quote I got."

Jacob smiled confidently. "But you're buying three pianos, so I'm sure I can negotiate a discount with Mr. Ellsworth. Why don't you come to the showroom and listen to the professional tone of the pianos? Comparing price is one thing, but what do you think management will do if you buy inferior pianos to spend less, and you lose business as a result?"

Kerr nodded thoughtfully. "You have a point. I'll come tomorrow to hear the pianos. Say, ten o'clock?"

"I'll meet you in the piano showroom."

He placed his card on Kerr's desk and left the office. He had one other customer to visit, then planned to go to the print shop. He had some ideas for advertising the bed and breakfast and needed prices.

***

Meanwhile, Solomon worked furiously on the changes Mrs. Sterling requested on her house plans. Then, he began making preliminary plans for the electric wiring and plumbing. When Jacob entered, he was leaning over his new drafting table, studying the possible locations for electric outlets in the kitchen.

Solomon glanced at Jacob coming in the door. "Welcome, Jake," he said. "You got a package from your mother today."

"Where is it?"

"On the lamp table in the parlor."

Jacob tore open the package and found a pair of hand-knitted socks. "Bless her," he said, holding the soft socks to his cheek. "I need to thank her. Say, do you need me to cook supper today?"

"No, there's a pot of last night's stew in the icebox. We can heat that."

Jacob paused as if remembering something.

"Did you ever answer your father's letter?"

"Yes. I did it just as I said. I told him that God called me to be an architect."

"Did you ever get a reply?"

"No."

Since Solomon was involved in his project, Jacob retrieved the pot of stew from the icebox and lit the stove.

***

In the morning, Jacob waited in the showroom at ten o'clock. Kerr rushed in a few minutes late, eager to listen to the pianos. Jacob had requested that Miss Thompson be present to play for him, but she had an excuse to

212

be doing something else.

Jacob welcomed Kerr, made some small talk, and then launched into his sales spiel. He opened the top of an upright and showed him the soundboard with its crown and the strings for each tone. They stepped over to the baby grand. Jacob lifted the top and explained how the open "lid" helped distribute the sound through the room.

"I'd like to hear it," Kerr said.

"Our piano teacher isn't here, but I've had a few lessons. Hold on, and I'll get a stool."

"Oh, I know how to play," Kerr said, grinning. "Gimme a stool, and I'll dazzle you."

He sat at the piano and launched into the toccata section of Bach's Toccata and Fugue in D Minor. Jacob stood with his mouth open, watching in awe as Kerr's fingers danced rapidly over the keys, occasionally crossing his arms and playing the bass with his right hand while his left hand was busy with sixteenth notes. When he was satisfied, Kerr stopped playing in the middle of the piece.

"That was amazing," Jacob explained. "I've never seen a piano played like that."

"Thanks. You were right; it does have a great tone. And a nice touch. I like the touch. That's the baby grand. Do you have a concert piano I can try?"

"No, the concert grand takes up too much space for us to keep one here. But it will have the same tone and touch as this baby. We guarantee that. And another advantage of buying from us is that we have a staff piano tuner. I've seen him at work. He's a perfectionist. You need that before a performance."

"Did you work out a discount with Mr. Ellsworth?"

"Yes, I did," Jacob said. "He gave me some figures to quote to you." Jacob handed him a paper with the discounted prices.

"I like your pianos," Kerr said with a frown, "but that figure would bust my budget. Can't you do any better than that? There's no sense buying the best pianos available if they send us into bankruptcy." He twirled around on the stool. "If you give us a good price, Ellsworth's name will be mentioned in all our printed programs."

The two men went back and forth and finally arrived at a figure slightly higher than the bottom dollar that Jacob had negotiated with Ellsworth. Kerr agreed to take possession of one of the baby grands immediately, then the other two pianos in sixty days, giving Ellsworth time to manufacture them.

Ellsworth was ecstatic. "Three pianos at one go! We've never done that before. I can't afford to lose you, Jacob. Is there a possibility that you could deal with some of our more difficult clients even after you start working for Mrs. Sterling?"

Jacob grinned. "I can't promise one way or another in advance. I don't know what my workload will be. But I'd surely be interested in trying. You know how to reach me."

When he received his commission from this sale, he planned to buy a small carriage. A carriage was so much more sophisticated than riding horseback, and it would allow him and a lady friend to go somewhere together.

The image of Amelia Schultz's face materialized in his mind. He hadn't seen her for a few days.

Chapter 28: Sterling House Bed and Breakfast

January 1880

After Christmas and the turn of the new year, the weather deteriorated severely. The temperature dropped, and snow covered the ground. When classes resumed, Solomon bundled up in his Inverness coat, scarf, and knitted cap for the walk to school. It was good to look forward to classes again.

The snow fell softly. The naked branches of the trees had a wild beauty as they were silhouetted against the overcast sky. The only sound was a horse and carriage passing him in the street. Clip-clop, clip-clop. Bells jingled lightly on the harness.

Solomon stuck out his tongue to catch a snowflake as he walked and smiled as the cold dissolved in his mouth.

His thoughts turned to Mrs. Sterling's property. Fortunately, the design work was done except for the inevitable changes so that he could return to his books with his typical concentration. He was eager to get the survey so they would know which trees to take down, but the loggers couldn't cut trees in the sub-freezing chill, and the masons couldn't build a retaining wall in a frozen lake. Work had come to a standstill.

That afternoon after classes, Solomon rapped on Mrs. Sterling's door.

"Come in and let me take your coat," Gloria said. "Mrs. Sterling is in the library."

Solomon knew his way and entered with a spring in his step.

The two of them had a lengthy consultation. They came to a final decision on the wiring and plumbing.

"I've hired a contractor, Solomon," she said. "He's been building homes for twelve years, so he knows what he's doing. Everything is in place, waiting for a break in the weather. You're probably as excited as I am to get this project going."

He grinned. "That I am."

***

Jacob dove into his assignment at the bed and breakfast enthusiastically. He hired a housekeeper and put her to work cleaning the mansion from top to bottom. He hired Amelia to establish a system for checking the guests in and out and tracking reservations. She would also account for funds, see that Jacob stayed within budget, and deposit the money in the bank. A carpenter was chosen for his artistry in wood to build a front desk and create an appropriate sign for the front lawn.

"All of this is useless if we don't fill the rooms with guests," he said. "I need to figure out how to attract people willing to pay for accommodations."

Jacob printed fliers and took them to the country club and opera house. He carried a supply to a newly established travel agency. There were no winter cruises on Lake Michigan, but he obtained the cruise line's mailing list by promising the manager two free nights at the mansion. Amelia mailed fliers to all the cruise customers. Jacob placed a big ad in the newspaper advertising a venue for parties and wedding receptions in the great room.

Within a few days, letters, phone calls, and telegrams came in with reservations. "Mrs. Sterling," he shouted with excitement. "We have our first reservations. One couple wants to come in on the twentieth of January for three nights. Another couple has booked the great room for their twenty-fifth wedding anniversary party on the third Saturday of February. We need to hire a cook."

Mrs. Sterling grinned with delight. "It's beginning to work, Jacob."

Chapter 29: The Design Contest

Despite being back in school, Solomon was determined to calculate the design requirements for Mrs. Sterling's balcony himself for two reasons. First, he wanted to enter the design contest. He would need to be able to say he had done the design work personally. Second, he wanted to compare his calculations to the engineer's to see how close he was. He stayed extra hours at the library studying cantilevers.

By mid-February, he had come up with figures that he believed were accurate and completed his design work. Since the plans he entered in the contest were not expected to be built, he didn't need to wait for the soil samples. He had two sets of plans, one marked "Contest" and the other marked "Sterling."

Tuesday, May 25, 1880

By late May, the engineer's work was complete, the trees had been removed, and the foundation had been laid.

Solomon had worked hard for two weeks to finish his contest plans. He submitted his entry to Professor Richards, who was in charge of the university's design contest. He was confident that he had a good chance of winning.

The following day, he was called to the professor's office after classes.

"Professor Richards?" he said, tapping on the door frame.

"Mr. Hawk, please come in."

Solomon took the chair opposite Richards' desk.

"I want to talk to you about your plans."

Solomon held his breath and smiled, expecting to be congratulated.

"Mr. Hawk, you have done incredible work on these plans, and your execution is excellent. That's why I wanted to tell you why you won't win the contest."

Solomon's eyes widened, and his mouth dropped. He cleared his throat. "That's not what I expected when I came here." His voice was gruff.

"I don't suppose it was. Mr. Hawk, your design is impressive, but it's impractical. No one would have a house built like this. It would be ridiculously expensive."

"But it's being built right now."

"Please don't insult me, Hawk. That's impossible. The glass walls, the cantilever deck, and that slate roof—no one would build this house."

"Would you like to go see the progress to date?" Solomon asked.

Professor Richards studied his face. "Are you joking?"

"No, I'm not. The client is Mrs. Marguerite Sterling. She's turned the Sterling Mansion into a bed and breakfast and is building this smaller home for herself. It's on the edge of a lake."

Richards was still scoffing. "And how did she choose a student architect to develop such a design?"

"My friend, Jacob Bishop, manages her mansion. Through him, she reviewed my portfolio and asked if I would handle the design of her house. Of course, she's not paying top dollar for my work, but it's quite a triumph on my resume."

Richards closed his mouth. "Actually, I would like to go see it. Can we go now?"

"Certainly. But I don't have a carriage."

"We'll take mine. It's parked out front. Let's go."

On the way to the Sterling property, they chatted about the details of the house.

"Why did you include the elevator in a private house?" asked Richards.

Solomon chuckled. "The first time my friend met Mrs. Sterling, she was in a wheelchair with a broken leg. A woman living alone would be in a difficult position if she couldn't climb the stairs to her bedroom and had no one to help her."

"Good thinking since she can afford it. Not many people could."

"That's true. Anyone else would have to sleep downstairs on their sofa."

The horse trotted along until they reached the property. Solomon pointed down the hill toward the lake. "There it is," he said.

A large pile of stone had been delivered to the lakefront to be used in the retaining wall. The contractor and some workers were there digging the footing.

"I'd like to speak to the contractor," the professor said.

They took the carriage down the hill and caught the eye of the contractor, who waved and called, "Come see the work in progress, Hawk."

Solomon introduced Professor Richards. "I entered the design of this house into a contest, but the professor had a hard time believing it was actually being built." He grinned.

Professor Richards blushed. "I'm sorry I gave you that impression, Mr. Hawk. It's just that the design was so fantastic—"

The contractor laughed. "You were right about that. It's not feasible for the average person, but our Mrs. Sterling is not the average home buyer. This house is pushing my limits, and I've been building houses here in Chicago for more than a decade. Getting the contract on this house was a real triumph. I'll get a lot of free advertising from this project."

After walking around the lot for a few more minutes, Richards was ready to return to his office. "I apologize, Mr. Hawk. Your design is by far the best of the entries. I'm going to give it a special category award. It went far beyond what was expected."

"Thank you, sir."

"You'll be going to Philadelphia for a private tour of the First National Bank. We'll provide you with a round-trip train ticket, first class, and three nights' lodging at a hotel near the bank. But I'd appreciate it if you'd keep this quiet until the awards ceremony at the end of the month."

"I won't let the news leak out."

"Fine. I predict you'll become one of the nation's finest architects. I'll be proud to say I was one of your professors."

"Thank you, sir, but please don't puff me up too much. God gave me the talent, ability, and inspiration for this project. He even provided the tuition to come to this school."

"Is that so?"

"Absolutely. I'll tell you about it sometime."

***

After the June awards ceremony, Solomon said goodbye to Jacob and boarded the train for Philadelphia. He took a private tour of First National Bank, continually asking questions and making copious notes. That evening, he carefully recopied the notes into chart form at his hotel. He spent the following day touring the city, including the Liberty Bell and other historic sites, before returning to Chicago.

Upon his arrival, Mrs. Sterling wrote a check for the first half payment for his design services. He had never had so much money at one time. He paid Jacob his commission, then sent most of the remainder to his father to cover his Yale tuition.

As he wrote the check payable to Rev. Geoffrey Kingston Hawk, a weight lifted from his shoulders. *I'm finally free from Father,* he thought. *It seems like he was someone I used to know, not like he's currently part of my family.*

His thoughts went to his mother. She was still under Father's thumb. He appealed to the Almighty to care for his mother and comfort her. He picked up his pen to write her a letter, planning to mail it when he mailed Father's check.

He began writing:

Dear Mother,

I hope you're doing well. I pray for you daily.

I'm getting along fine. If you remember, I told you I was hired for my first design job. Construction is moving along, and I'm enclosing a newspaper photo. The design has brought me a lot of local fame. I also won an award from the school. As a result, I've been offered other jobs, but I'm selective about what I accept so my studies don't suffer.

Just think, I'll have my degree in less than two years. Jacob and I will decide where to live, and I'll open my own business.

Speaking of Jacob, he's now running a successful bed and breakfast. He manages to meet some famous people and enjoys his work.

I'll see you as soon as possible, Mother. As always, the invitation still stands.

Your loving son,
Solomon

He folded the letter around a five-dollar bill and stuffed it into the envelope. He put her letter and the other envelope containing his father's check in the letterbox and put the flag up.

Chapter 30: A Shocking Change of Plans

Summer 1882

O ver the next two years, Solomon continued to study hard and work on design projects. Jacob's business skills increased. The bed and breakfast became highly successful, enjoying an outstanding reputation among businessmen, vacationers, and cruise customers arriving in town early for their Lake Michigan cruise.

Solomon's claim to his mother that he'd been offered other jobs was an understatement. He was in such high demand that Jacob suggested raising his rates to eliminate the less lucrative offers. He was meeting with so much success that he was tempted to leave school ahead of graduation to take on more projects. He had already cut down his class load in favor of design projects, so he wasn't ready to graduate in June with the rest of the class. He would need to wait until December.

Jacob stepped in and convinced him to finish his studies. "What do you think God would have you do, Solly? Cut your education short to make a few bucks? Think about it."

"You're right, Jacob. Just one more semester."

"Oh, I meant to tell you," Jacob said. "I'm taking Amelia to dinner tonight, so I won't be here for supper."

Solomon raised his eyebrows. "Again? You've been out three times this week."

Jacob sighed. "Look, Solly, I have to live my life. I can't sit around here doing nothing while you stick your nose in your books and ignore me."

The two men stared at each other.

"I'm sorry, Jacob. You know how it is."

"Yes, I do." Jacob put on his coat and left.

Solomon sank into the kitchen chair and put his head down. *I didn't want him to leave with that hanging over us. I wish things could go back to normal without Amelia.*

Still, Solomon recognized that Jacob was not the same man as when the two met on the ferry from Connecticut to New York. He was now rubbing shoulders with the upper class, and his dress and speech patterns had conformed to theirs. He had over two years of business experience, first as a piano salesman and now as a hospitality manager. No one would ever believe he was a former blacksmith; in fact, he remembered Jacob telling him that the smithy was like a distant memory.

He sighed deeply and opened his textbook.

August 1882

As Solomon's December graduation approached, Jacob reviewed his options. He was still managing the Sterling Mansion. *Solly doesn't need me like he did,* he thought. *He wants to go home to Connecticut, but I don't belong there. I belong here in Chicago with Amelia. I can't see spending the rest of my life without her. I want to marry her if she'll have me.*

After work that day, he went downtown to a jewelry store and bought a modest engagement ring with a row of tiny diamonds on a narrow band. As he handed the payment to the jeweler, his heart raced. He couldn't wait to see the look on Amelia's face when he gave it to her. Oh, Amelia . . . her red hair, snappy wit, the way she thought in numbers. He loved everything about her, including her freckles.

He bought some ham and cabbage at a restaurant and took it home to share with Solomon. As usual, Solomon was at his drafting table, concentrating on a new design.

"Have you had your dinner, Solly?" he asked.

"No, I've been working on this pesky front elevation the client requested. He doesn't know for sure what he wants, so I've been modifying my modifications."

Jacob chuckled. "I brought some food. Take a break and join me. I have some news."

Solomon laid down his pencil wearily and shuffled to the kitchen. "Didn't you say you were eating with Amelia tonight?"

Jacob put plates and silverware on the table. "I'll see her later this evening. I wanted to tell you that I'm going to ask her to marry me."

Solomon's jaw dropped. He opened his mouth to speak, but it was many seconds before the words came out. "I shouldn't be surprised. It was bound to happen eventually. Is she willing to move with you when we decide where to go?"

Jacob stared at the floor. "I don't know. I haven't asked her."

Solomon's brow creased. "Don't you think that's important?"

"Sit down and have some cabbage." Jacob handed him a serving spoon, and he dipped some of the steaming vegetables onto his plate. "We need to talk about the moving thing." Jacob took the spoon and dished up some food for himself. "Want some salt?"

Solomon took the salt shaker. "What do we need to talk about?"

Jacob took a deep breath. "When we talked about moving after your graduation, you needed me to sell your services, and I needed you to help me escape the blacksmith mentality. My word, that seems like fifty years ago now."

"And so?" Solomon's eyes drilled into Jacob.

"You don't need me anymore, Solly. Your reputation is enough to get you more work than you can handle. You know how to ask for high fees. You don't need me now."

Solomon's face paled. His voice softened. "And you don't need me, either. Is that what you're saying?"

Jacob sighed. "Think about it. Right now, my income is higher than yours. That won't be true once you graduate. You'll be able to spend all your time working then. But I'm already making enough money to support a wife and family comfortably. Amelia wouldn't need to work if she didn't want to. We belong in Chicago. This has become home, and Amelia's family is here. I know you don't want to stay here. This is too far away from your mother. I know you want to be within a day's train ride of her where you can check on her regularly."

Solomon turned away with a stricken face.

"We'll still be friends," Jacob implored. "We can talk on the telephone and write letters."

"I need some time to process this," Solomon mumbled. "I never imagined we would part company just when our goal was so close to being met."

"I'm sorry. I didn't think you'd take it this hard."

"Please reconsider, Jacob. Amelia might like living back east."

"I need to follow my heart. Amelia is my heart. You haven't had the experience of being in love with a woman yet. You're single-mindedly chasing your goal. I understand that. But the natural path is for a man to get married and have a family. I want to do that. And I enjoy my work at the mansion. It's what I want to keep doing."

Solomon stared at his plate. "I understand."

Jacob peered into his face. "Are you sure?"

"Yes . . . I'm not hungry." Solomon stood and left the room. He went to his bedroom and shut the door.

Jacob's heart grieved for his friend, but he was compelled to take his own path. He picked at his cabbage, threw out the rest, and left to find Amelia. He needed the comfort of being in her presence.

***

Solomon lay in bed with his arms cradling his head. So many emotions swirled inside him he couldn't straighten them out. Anger that Jacob was abandoning their dream? Certainly. Grief that he was losing his friend? Of course. Fear that he wouldn't be able to run a successful business without Jacob? That was a given.

The shock that his life was out of control was paralyzing. He could imagine his father's triumph when he failed. The possibility of being unemployed and having to move back home with his parents made him ill. *Failure.* It played over and over in his head.

Then, God's presence invaded his spirit, and he let the tears flow. *Fear not; I'm with you,* the Spirit impressed on him—not once but several times. Finally, Solomon relaxed, closed his eyes, and slipped into sleep.

***

Jacob groped in his pocket to ensure he had the ring with him. It was time. He rapped on the door, and Amelia let him in. Her parents were in the parlor, occupying comfortable chairs as they read. As usual, Mr. Schultz had the newspaper in front of his face, and Mrs. Schultz flipped a page in her novel.

She waved the book at Jacob. "Hello, Jacob. How nice to see you."

Mr. Schultz lowered his paper enough to nod and acknowledge Jacob's presence.

"I'm surprised to see you this evening," Amelia said.

"It's been an upsetting dinner with Solomon. I wanted to talk with you."

"Would you like to sit on the sofa?" she asked.

He tried to signal with his eyes that he would *not* like to sit there, but she didn't take the clue. She took his hand and led him to the couch.

Mrs. Schultz glanced at him. "Have you read this novel that just came out, Jacob? It's called "The Sorrows of Satan." It's quite fascinating. Some Englishwoman wrote it."

Mr. Schultz cleared his throat. "I wish you wouldn't read such trash, Anna. That stuff gets stuck in your head. You know what the Bible says, 'You are what you read.'"

"The Bible doesn't say that."

"It must say it somewhere."

They both went back to their reading. At any other time, Jacob would have found that conversation funny, but he had other things on his mind.

He fidgeted in his seat. Finally, Amelia suggested they go to the kitchen. "We can talk privately there, and Mother made some pudding today. Would you like a bowl?"

"That sounds good. I didn't eat much."

The two left the parlor, and Jacob sat at the kitchen table. Amelia scooped the pudding into small bowls and then pulled out a chair for herself. Jacob was about to open his mouth when Mr. Schultz shouted from the other room: "I'd like some of that pudding, too, and bring a bowl for your mother."

Amelia sighed, produced two more bowls, and carried them to the parlor.

"Thank you, dear."

"Sure, Mother."

She returned to the kitchen and sat down again. "Did you want to talk about anything in particular? Why was your dinner with Solomon so upsetting?"

Jacob's voice dropped to a near-whisper. "I'm sure I told you before that our plan was for me to support him for three years while he went to school, and then we would move to another city where I would sell his services. It was a great idea at the time because, as you know, I was only a blacksmith, and I needed a way to improve myself."

Amelia rolled her eyes. "You a *blacksmith.* That's still hard to imagine."

Jacob continued: "As we planned, I supported him for a while until he found himself in demand as an architect before he graduated. He's paying his expenses and my commissions already. He has enough experience now to make his way without me." He paused and peered into her eyes to gauge her reaction. "So I told him I was staying in Chicago after he graduates."

Amelia's eyes widened, and she broke into a smile. "You're staying here?"

"That's my plan. I'm earning more money now than I ever dreamed, and I'm spending my time with a different type of people—people with wider horizons and a more modern outlook. I want to marry you and stay here with you, Amelia."

She gasped. "Jacob . . . was that a proposal?"

"Yes." He fished in his pocket for the ring. The tiny stones caught the light and sent a sparkle into Amelia's eyes. He swallowed, his hands trembling. "I'll have to ask your father first, but if he says yes, are you willing to spend the rest of your life with me?"

Shaking, she lifted her left hand and let him slip the ring on. "Yes, of course I am."

Her father shouted from the parlor, "I'll say yes."

The couple's eyes widened. Jacob whispered, "I didn't know his hearing was so sharp."

"Mother," she shouted, jumping up and running into the living room. "Jacob and I are getting married."

Both parents laid down their reading material and embraced their daughter while Jacob entered the room. They were smiling. He would make a good husband.

The questions came fast. "Have you set a date?" "Where will you live?"

Amelia held up her hands, hoping to stop the questions. "We don't know. We don't know. He just asked me. That's something we'll have to decide."

Mr. Schultz turned to shake Jacob's hand. "Welcome to the family, son."

Jacob broke into a grin. "Thank you, sir."

He turned to Amelia. "I know it's muggy outside, but would you like to take a drive in the carriage? It would give us a chance to talk through some things."

"The air movement will cool us as we drive. Give me a minute."

Soon, she returned wearing a bonnet to protect her hair. They headed out to the carriage, and he helped her in.

They took a short drive along the lakefront and enjoyed the steady crashing of Lake Michigan's dark, foamy waves against the shoreline.

"Jacob, I don't want to be the cause of a rift between you and Solomon. If you want to go with him to sell his services, I'd be willing to go, too."

"That's good to know, but I like managing the mansion. I like meeting accomplished people from all occupations. I've learned to fit into that world. Wealthy people like and respect me. I still can't get over that. *Me!* And I like and respect them, not for their money, but because they lead such interesting lives. I feel like I belong in that world, Amelia. Am I seeing it wrong?"

"No. I've seen you grow and change since I've known you. You were once a little uncomfortable in social situations. I suppose it was how you grew up. You didn't know what was expected. But now, you're the self-confident man who makes other people feel comfortable. I like that about you. So, when do you want to get married?"

"I'd say we could get married as soon as we find a house. You couldn't live with me and Solly. I don't even have a bedroom to myself. I sleep in the parlor. And I don't want to live in the same house as your parents. I want some privacy. Just you and me."

"That sounds perfect."

He wrapped his arm around her shoulders and leaned over to kiss her. She turned her face toward him and returned the kiss.

"Can we turn around and go home? My arms are getting hot from the sun."

"Sure."

After Jacob dropped off his fiancée, he returned home, partly joyously but partly with a heavy heart. He hated disappointing Solomon. After all, they had been close friends and had grown together over the past three years, both changing for the better. He remembered how he had been accepted by Solomon's family, except for his father, when his grandfather died. Images of the long, arduous trip to Lewisburg and the comfortable train ride to Chicago played through his mind. Those experiences would always be a part of him. But it was time to move forward with his life.

He opened the door to a dark house. Solomon had already gone to bed and shut his door. There was nothing to do but spread a sheet on the daybed and try to sleep.

Chapter 31: Jacob and Amelia

In the morning, Jacob was roused by the rattling of skillets and the aroma of bacon, eggs, and coffee. Solomon was at the stove, spatula in hand, filling two plates with a hot breakfast. He was already dressed for school, but his eyes drooped as if he hadn't slept much.

"Morning, Solly," Jacob said, testing Solomon's mood.

"Good morning. Did you sleep well?" It was a question he asked every morning.

"I slept pretty good. Amelia accepted my proposal."

Solomon's congratulations lacked enthusiasm, but he managed a smile.

"That's the saddest smile I've ever seen, old man. I wanted you to be genuinely happy for me."

"Give me some time. I'm still adjusting."

Solomon sat at the breakfast table with Jacob and said grace, then picked up his fork. "Are you working at the mansion today?"

"Yes, but I'm taking a long lunch to look for a house. If you don't have any classes, would you like to go with me?"

"I would. I want to spend as much time with you as possible while I still have the chance. Will you pick me up in your carriage?"

"Yes. Can you bring a copy of today's paper from the library? We'll have a look at the ads."

At half past twelve, Jacob pulled his carriage up to the library, and Solomon stepped inside. "I found a couple of possibles for you," he said. They read the ads for a few minutes, comparing locations and prices. They inspected two houses before Jacob needed to return to work.

"I liked that second house best," he told Solomon. "Don't expect me for supper. I'm going to take Amelia to look at it. As soon as we rent a house, we can get married."

Solomon nodded. "That one was very nice. It was the kind of house a woman would like."

Jacob had a sudden pang of conscience. "Solly, I'm not putting you in a bind, am I? I mean, you can afford the rent on our house by yourself, can't you?"

Solomon nodded. "Yes. My design fees are plenty to cover the rent and other expenses."

Jacob nodded, relieved. He returned Solomon to the university for his afternoon class.

That evening, he took Amelia out for dinner and then drove her to the house he liked. The owner met them there and let them in. Amelia went through the cozy one-bedroom house, loving every detail. They rented it on the spot, and Jacob paid the cash for the first month.

Amelia's energy overflowed as they returned to the carriage. "We need furniture now, Jacob. What will we do?"

He patted her knee as they drove down the cobblestone road. "Solly told me to take the living room furniture. He never sits in the living room, anyway. But he's keeping the bedroom and kitchen things."

"So we'll need bedroom furniture and kitchen supplies."

"Tomorrow evening after work, we'll try to find what we need. Now, my love, when do you want to get married?"

Amelia giggled. "We can have the ceremony any time we want now, can't we? Mama and Papa will want to be there. Let's do it Saturday morning."

"Maybe Mrs. Sterling will let us use the great room."

Amelia's eyes lit up. "Yes. We don't need to dress it up fancy. It's already beautiful. I'll ask Pastor Bromley if he can be there at ten o'clock."

By Saturday morning, their house had been furnished enough to move in, and the wedding plans went smoothly. It would be a private affair with only Amelia's parents and Mrs. Sterling as guests. Amelia's closest girlfriend, Iva, would serve as a witness along with Solomon.

Saturday, August 19, 1882

Jacob arrived alone at the mansion half an hour before the ceremony to make sure he would be on time. Mrs. Sterling met him at the door and invited him into the library to chat until the rest of the guests arrived. At nearly ten o'clock, she rose. "I suppose we need to go to the great room now, or everyone will wonder where you are."

The pair began the walk down the hall. "By the way, Jacob, I have mixed feelings about this wedding," she said, looking down at the floor. Her forehead wrinkled, and she hesitated. "There was a time that my heart longed for you to find me attractive and that I would be the one wearing the bridal gown today."

"What?" he asked, his mind not registering the full import of what she said. His eyebrows tented. "I was aware you treated me differently from other people, but I didn't know—"

"There was the age difference. I wasn't surprised it didn't work out. By the way, I trust you never to tell anyone what I just told you. I just needed to get that off my chest. We can forget it now and go back to normal."

Jacob's first reaction was confusion. Why would she get that emotional over a man from such a different background? And why would she blurt out her feelings like that? His second reaction was irritation. What an inappropriate thing to tell a man minutes before he was to take a bride.

"You can trust me never to tell anyone." He continued walking down the hall with her, his lips pressed together in a frown.

***

As it was a hot summer's day, a fire in the fireplace would have been intolerable. Amelia had requested that an arrangement of asters, daisies and Queen Anne's lace be placed there instead of logs. Jacob noted that this was an effective way to decorate the great room for future summer parties.

The pastor took his position in front of the flowery fireplace with Jacob and Amelia in front of him, Solomon to Jacob's left, and Iva to Amelia's right. Mr. and Mrs. Schultz sat in club chairs behind the wedding party with Mrs. Sterling.

Amelia wore white lace and a waist-length veil over her copper-colored hair. To Jacob, she was the most beautiful woman in the world. They stood to face each other with bright eyes as if they were the only people in the room. His conversation with Mrs. Sterling was forgotten.

The pastor led them through their vows and then pronounced them man and wife. The bride's parents and maid of honor were thrilled.

Solomon shook Jacob's hand. "I'm sorry to lose you, old friend," he said, fighting back the mist in his eyes.

"Solly, we'll always be friends. Not like before, obviously, but we've been through a lot together. You're like a brother to me. Give us a week for a honeymoon; then we'll have you over for supper. Does that sound good to you, Amelia?"

The new Mrs. Bishop smiled and took Solomon's hands warmly. "You're welcome in our home any time, Solomon." She gave him an impulsive hug. "After a week, anyway."

"You two have a wonderful honeymoon. Do you plan to travel?"

"No," said Jacob. "We'll be at home, relaxing. We spent all our money on furniture."

"Well, blessings on your marriage. I'll see you in a week." Solomon clapped Jacob on the shoulder and left to return to his empty house.

Mrs. Sterling approached the couple and congratulated them. "You'll both be back at work a week from Monday, right? You'll not leave me in the lurch?"

Amelia laughed. "No, ma'am. We'll be back. We just need the week to adjust to married life."

"Then, congratulations to you both. I'll see you a week from Monday." Mrs. Sterling retreated to the office, saying she needed to make sure things were orderly. She would handle the front desk herself for the week.

Amelia's face turned toward Jacob. "Did you think she didn't seem quite like herself? I wonder what's wrong."

Jacob replied, "It's probably nothing." He watched their employer's back as she left the room. He determined that Amelia would be better off if she never learned of Mrs. Sterling's earlier confession.

Amelia's parents were the last to make a fuss over them. "We have a gift for you," Mrs. Schultz said. "We hired a photographer to make a portrait of the two of you, with you in your wedding gown."

"Thank you, Mother," Amelia said, hugging both parents. "Where does he want us to stand?"

"He's waiting for you in the garden."

Jacob and Amelia entered the garden through the French doors. The photographer was set up under a shade tree, his large-format camera perched on a tripod, and aimed at the curved concrete bench.

"Do you want us to stand?" Jacob asked.

The photographer studied them with a practiced eye. "No, the height difference between you wouldn't make a pleasing photo. So, Mr. Bishop, I'll have you sit on the bench, straddling it, with Mrs. Bishop in front of you, backed up to your chest. That's fine. Now, both of you turn your faces this way. Good. Mrs. Bishop, tilt your head just slightly to the left so I can see Mr. Bishop's face clearly."

The photographer ducked under the cloth covering the camera. There was a pop and a blinding flash. They blinked rapidly, trying to clear the spots before their eyes.

The photographer kept up his rapid instructions. "Mr. Bishop, would you kindly step out of the photo? The parents want a bridal portrait of Mrs. Bishop alone." Jacob stood and joined his in-laws.

"Now, Mrs. Bishop, I'd like you to stay in that position with your knees to your left. Stretch out your left arm to touch the bench. Like that, yes. Now, turn your head to the right. Look to your right and down. Arch your back. Good. One more thing: with your right hand, grasp some of the lace in your skirt and lift it slightly. Keep your eyes on your hand."

Again, he ducked under the cloth.

Pop! The flash bulb went off again. "Beautiful. Thank you." Turning to Amelia's mother, he said, "I'll have this film developed and some proof prints ready for you by Tuesday."

Amelia rubbed her eyes. "Is it over?"

It was. The happy couple said goodbye to her parents and took off in Jacob's carriage.

***

Solomon unlocked his front door and went inside. The living room was bare since Jacob had taken the daybed and other furnishings. This wasn't the way things were supposed to be. He and Jacob should be thinking about where they would move after graduation. He hadn't realized before how much he took Jacob's presence for granted. Now, in his grief, he turned to God. He went into his bedroom, sat at his desk, and prayed with his head in his hands.

In a few moments, God's presence surrounded him, comforting his spirit. He wasn't surprised; he had known that peace before in difficult circumstances. His heart was still heavy, but he thanked God for peace as he returned to his drafting table.

His mind soon began to review the list of cities where he could make a good living, but since Jacob wasn't coming, he only wanted to be where he could keep an eye on Mother. He wrote her a letter, telling her he would return to Bridgeport after graduation. If he found reasonable prospects there, he would rent a house and set up shop. If he saw a lack of construction, maybe there would be better prospects in Hartford, not too far away, or even across the Sound in Long Island. But first, he would check out the possibility of staying in Bridgeport. He had people there.

With the decision settled, he returned to his design work.

The following day, he went to church alone. Jacob's voice haunted his mind when the congregation stood for a hymn, and the piano joined the organ. 'Well-voiced hammers' echoed sorrowfully through his mind.

He was relieved the following month when he returned to school and had new challenges to occupy his mind. This semester was his last, and the professors tackled the more intricate engineering problems. He was ahead of the other students since he had already been intensely involved in designing Mrs. Sterling's cantilever balcony.

He remembered the letter of encouragement from Colonel McCreary and how surprised he was to learn that McCreary had no formal training in engineering. He didn't know if that was the truth or merely a rumor. If he had been confident that McCreary had no degree, he would have been sorely tempted to leave the university and return to Connecticut. But he was this close; leaving now would be a shame.

Requests continued to come in for his design services, but he was careful not to accept any work that would last beyond graduation. Once that diploma was in his hand, he wanted to be free to leave.

It became a habit to have supper with Jacob and Amelia once a week, but it wasn't the same. He didn't have a chance to discuss things with Jacob without Amelia's presence, so their relationship became more of a surface friendship. There was no tension between them, but there weren't any close confidences, either, as there had been. Solomon found himself fighting loneliness and depression; he had no other close friends. His only solace was his books.

Chapter 32: Going Home

December 1882

As the months passed, Solomon adjusted to living alone. He did well in his studies and finished the design work he had accepted. As a result, his bank account was healthy. That was good; he would need the money to travel and to establish a new office . . . somewhere.

Ceremonies were scheduled in December for the small graduating class of the University of Illinois School of Architecture. Solomon was again approaching graduation with a mixture of victory and dread. He was graduating with honors, but it meant saying goodbye to everything he had been familiar with for three years. The best part was that he was returning to Connecticut to explore the next phase of his life.

He carefully listed everything he would need to do before moving. He sold the drafting table, which was too large and expensive to transport. The last item on his list was his horse. He hesitated and lifted his pencil. Then, with a firm hand, he crossed 'horse' off his list. She had been Grandfather's, so he paid the railroad to transport her back to Bridgeport.

During his last meal with Jacob and Amelia, they bubbled over with excitement.

"We have something to tell you, Solly."

Solomon peered into Jacob's face, then Amelia's, wondering what was so wonderful.

"Amelia is . . . no, *we* are having a baby!"

Solomon grinned. "Congratulations, both of you."

"Something else," said Amelia. "We would like you to be the godfather."

"That's a big responsibility," said Solomon. His heart swelled, touched at the honor being offered. "But for you—of course. Your little tyke can call me Uncle Sol."

"Amelia will leave her job to stay home with the baby. I'm so proud. Solomon, you can't imagine the feeling until you experience it."

Solomon chuckled. "Maybe I will someday. Jake, I'm truly happy for you both. When do you expect this miraculous event?"

"We calculated that the child will probably come next June. Of course, that's only a guess."

"Let me know when the baby comes," Solomon said. "When I get to Connecticut, I'll send word where I am and how you can reach me by telephone."

"Yes, please do that, Solly. We're friends for life, you and me."

After dinner and a long chat, the men hugged each other for the last time, clapping one another on the back. Amelia observed them quietly from across the room, her hands folded, compassion in her eyes.

"I'll miss you, Jacob," Solomon said gruffly. "I'm thankful we had those years together."

"So am I, my friend. Knowing you has changed my life drastically. I hope we'll see each other again."

Solomon nodded with teardrops blurring his vision. "Maybe I'll come back for a visit and stay at the Sterling Mansion."

"No, you won't. If we have a bigger house then, you'll stay with us." Jacob choked back his emotion.

Solomon's voice dropped to a whisper. "Thanks, Jake. You're the best friend I ever had." After throwing their arms around one another, Solomon turned and left. It was a difficult parting for both men.

Monday, December 18, 1882

Solomon tossed in his bed that night, dealing with emotional upheaval. In the morning, he packed his clothing and architect's tools. Jacob had agreed to sell the bedroom and kitchen furnishings for him, so he had no loose ends. He arranged for a hansom cab to take his luggage to the train station, and then accompanied it on horseback so he could check the horse into the livestock car. This would be a much more comfortable trip than the first trip he had made.

His mother was thrilled he was coming but told him in her last letter his father wasn't feeling well. Father had been confined to bed for two weeks with a heavy cough.

At that news, Solomon struggled with guilt. He was relieved his father couldn't berate him when he got home, but the proper response would be sorrow that his father wasn't well. How sad it was that he had only resentment toward Father. The ill feeling hung over him constantly, shadowing his life.

He sank into the plush seating in first class but still fidgeted, unable to relax.

The conductor came down the aisle. "Tickets, please."

Solomon offered his ticket, and the man punched it with a sharp click before handing it back. Then the train's whistle blew long-long-short-long, and the wheels strained to turn on their rails. Solomon turned his face to the window and said a sad goodbye to Chicago, his second home.

I would have given anything to have Jacob here to see me off, he thought, *but he's working. He has his responsibilities now*. His heart ached.

As the train rolled down the track and the city scenes changed to farmland, Solomon gave in to exhaustion and went to his assigned Pullman bunk for a nap. The gentle rocking of the coach and his restlessness the night before lulled him to a deep slumber. He slept through two stops until his empty stomach woke him up.

He sat up and rubbed his eyes. *They'll be serving dinner now.*

He climbed out of the Pullman, stretched, and followed his nose to the dining car. Dozens of people were already there. Chatting, laughter, and the clink of silverware met his ears. Only one vacant table was available. He headed for it and claimed his seat.

He picked up a newspaper someone had left on the chair and glanced at a front-page story. Since President Garfield had been assassinated in September and Chester Arthur succeeded him, other news lately had paled by comparison. He searched the paper for something interesting to read.

The steward came to take his order as the train rolled on, rocking gently from side to side.

"I'll have the fried chicken dinner," he said. "And please bring me a cup of tea with sugar."

He was relieved that no one had asked to take the other seat at his table. He enjoyed his solitude until he was halfway through his meal. A middle-aged, well-dressed man came and asked to join him.

Reluctantly, but not wanting to be rude, Solomon nodded.

"You're Solomon Hawk, the architect," the stranger said as he pulled out the chair. An excited smile covered his face.

Solomon raised his head in surprise. "Yes. And you are—"

"I'm Dr. Paul Sayers, a surgeon at Presbyterian Hospital in Chicago."

Solomon offered his hand for a shake. "How did you recognize me?"

"Are you kidding? Your picture has been all over the papers since you designed that house for Marguerite Sterling."

Solomon chuckled. "I guess it has at that."

The doctor leaned forward. "Look, Mr. Hawk, I'm going only as far as Columbus, but I want to talk to you."

The steward came and offered Dr. Sayers a menu. "Something to drink, sir?"

"Cup of coffee. Black, please," he said, then turned back to Solomon. "My wife and I plan to build a new house on two acres with a beautiful stream running through the back. Other than that stream, the property is fairly level. We want you to design it for us. Can you do that?"

"The house will be built in Chicago?"

"Yes."

"I'm so grateful for the offer, but I'm afraid I can't do it. I'm on my way to Connecticut to open an office there. I've left Chicago behind me."

Sayers raised his eyebrows. "Why can't we have an engineer do the site work and send you the reports? You could do the design work from Connecticut. We can send the work back and forth by courier and communicate by telephone. Once your plans are done, we'll turn them over to the contractor. If he has questions, he can call you."

Solomon sat back in his chair. "That's a surprising idea," he said. "I never imagined working long-distance that way. Let me consider the possibilities. It would add a layer of expense, of course, and probably some delays. Have you considered that?"

"Yes." Dr. Sayers chuckled. "We're not in a big hurry, and the delay would be worth seeing our friends envious that Solomon Hawk designed our home. That's worth a lot to me and even more to my wife." He pressed his lips together in a crafty-looking smile. It was clear to Solomon that the good doctor expected to get some benefits from his wife for hiring him.

Solomon's lips turned into a smile, making wrinkles at the corners of his eyes. "Here's my situation: I'll need at least a month to get settled and set up my office. I don't even know what city I'll be settling in."

"I'll give you my address and telephone number," Dr. Sayers said. "You can stay in touch as you make your decisions. I want to give you a retainer to guarantee you'll call me."

Solomon took a deep breath. "A retainer? Dr. Sayers, I'm interested in this job, but this is moving a little too fast. I need some time to consider how this would work, say, overnight, and give you my answer in the morning."

"That won't work. I'm getting off the train at Columbus in an hour, according to the train schedule. Let me give you the retainer. If you decide you can't take the job, you can return my check."

The steward brought Dr. Sayers' coffee and took his order for a steak and baked potato.

Solomon smiled, yielding to the offer of more work under experimental circumstances. "We should be thankful for the invention of the telephone, even if long-distance calls are expensive. Alright, I'll agree to that arrangement," he said. "Tell me how to contact you."

Dr. Sayers' face broke into a wide grin. He pulled his business card out of his pocket and slid it across the table, then wrote a check for the retainer.

"I'll give you my mother's telephone number," Solomon said. "I'm going there first, and even if I don't stay in Bridgeport, she'll know where I am."

The doctor's steak dinner was delivered to the table, and he attacked it with gusto. Solomon lingered there, enjoying conversation with his new client until both men were finished eating.

"I can't wait to tell my wife I ran into you on the train, and you're going to be designing our house," Sayers said. "This has been more than good luck."

Solomon chuckled. "You're right about that, sir. Only God could have arranged this meeting."

They shook hands and parted, promising to be in touch within a month.

Solomon tucked his retainer check into his pocket and returned to his coach, well-fed and now wide awake. Dinner had been an encouraging turning point in his thinking. Even though he would miss Jacob, he could still be successful on his own. As he breathed a prayer of gratitude, one of God's promises popped into his mind: *I will never leave you or forsake you.*

Chapter 33: Bridgeport

Tuesday, December 19, 1882

Three days later, after an uneventful trip, Solomon stepped off the train at the Bridgeport depot, luggage in hand. It was all he owned in this world, except for his horse, his education, and his God-given talent, which would determine the course of his future. It had been three and a half years since he left in a hurry.

It was still the same; nothing had changed.

Solomon's chest swelled with joy as he spotted Mother at the far end of the platform in her silver fox coat and hat, waving a white glove at him. *She's still an attractive lady. Father should be proud.* He grinned and strode toward her at a brisk pace, carrying his luggage. He dropped his bags as she approached and threw his arms around her.

"Solomon, my son," she cried as tears ran down her cheeks. She wiped them away with a gloved hand.

"I don't want your tears to freeze to your face, Mother. Do stop crying."

She laughed. "Bring your bags and come home at last, son. You look good, and the past three years have treated you well. Father will be glad to see you."

"I know better than that, Mother. How has he been?"

"He's not been well for some time, and the past two weeks, he's been confined to his bed, poor man. He's quite frustrated."

Solomon resisted the evil temptation to chuckle but allowed himself an amused smile.

"I have a cab waiting, Solomon. Come on home."

"I need to get my horse first. You take the cab, and I'll follow right behind you."

The cab driver dropped Emeline in front of the house. Solomon dismounted and stood with her, replaying the good and bad memories in his head. He remembered the day he left in a panic with Mother's forty-two dollars in his pocket and hundreds of miles to go, without even knowing how to get there. He had come a long, long way.

He followed his mother up the walk and entered for the first time since the day he graduated from Yale. Now, there was a Christmas tree in the parlor, and she had decorated the fireplace with cedar boughs and red bows for the holiday. The house was warm and welcoming.

"Take your things to your room and go see Father."

Solomon's face fell. He deposited his bags on his bed, paused, and reluctantly entered his father's room. He barely recognized the man lying there. This was not the strong, forceful man who had ruled Solomon's life with an iron will. This was a sick man, thin and helpless under quilts.

"So the prodigal comes home at last," he rasped at the sight of Solomon.

Solomon hesitated and flicked a piece of lint off his sleeve. Then he raised his eyes. "Did you get the money I sent to reimburse you for my tuition at Yale?"

"Yes. Thank you."

There was an awkward silence while Solomon took a chair beside Father's bed. He was surprised at the unaccustomed courtesy in his father's expression of thanks.

"What does the doctor say about your illness?"

"He's unsure what it is but thinks I'll be fine when it runs its course. He's seen people with bad coughs make complete recoveries."

"That's good."

"If you had been here, you could have covered for me in the pulpit."

Solomon sighed. Nothing had changed. "If I had been here, the people of the congregation would not have been well-served. God does not want me in the pulpit. I'm an architect, Father. Not only that, but I'm well-paid and well-known in Chicago." Solomon's voice softened. "It would mean a lot to me to someday hear you say, 'I'm proud of you, son.' But just so you'll know, if I never hear those words from you, I can be happy and successful without it."

The Rev. Geoffrey Kingston Hawk went into a coughing fit, then wiped his mouth with a shaky hand. His eyes were red-rimmed.

"Solomon, the Lord has been dealing with me on my sickbed." More coughing.

"How so?"

"This is difficult to say. He has shown me I was too harsh with you and your mother."

Solomon stared at him, barely able to believe his ears. He waited for Father's next words.

"I need your forgiveness."

Solomon's chin dropped. Emotions swirled through him. He resented the difficulties Father had caused him for years. Even his request for forgiveness had been in the form of a demand. Solomon didn't want to offer forgiveness. But hadn't Jesus forgiven him? After a few seconds of battling his dilemma, he still couldn't bring himself to say the words. Not now. He steeled himself.

"I'm sorry you're sick, Father. I pray you'll get better." Solomon rose and left the room, angry with himself for his own weakness and angry with Father for asking for forgiveness. He wanted his father to face the consequences of his bullying over a lifetime. Guilt overwhelmed him. He wanted to be a bigger man than this, but he couldn't manage it.

He joined his mother in the kitchen without mentioning what had just happened.

Emeline poured a cup of tea for him. "The doctor says he'll get better, but he's only getting worse. I don't know what I'll do if he never recovers. It's taxing to wait on him hand and foot all day."

"You've done that since the day you married him."

"Mmm." She nodded, raised her cup to her lips, and sipped it. "So, what are your plans now?"

Solomon smiled, willing to change the subject even though the issue of forgiveness was still nagging at him. "I met a doctor on the train who gave me a retainer to design his house. We agreed that I would start within a month. So I must decide what city I'll live in, find a house with suitable office space, buy furnishings and a drafting table . . . "

Mother put her hand on his shoulder. "I get the picture. I've been praying you'll settle in Bridgeport. But what are the other options?"

"My other option is the closest city I can find to make a good living and still be near enough to you that I can visit often."

She nodded her head and smiled into her teacup as she sipped. "What do you need to get started?"

"A nap. And then a newspaper. I want to see if there's enough building activity around here to require my services . . . although, if I can do a good job designing a house in Chicago from here, I could design buildings anywhere."

"Go take your nap, then. I have today's newspaper here on the table. It's yours whenever you want it."

Solomon drained his cup and slipped into his bedroom. It didn't seem the same. He had left it as a young graduate of Yale, having to battle his father's will, and re-entered as a respected architect with confidence and experience under his belt. He stretched out on top of the quilt, folded his hands under his head, and stared at the ceiling. His father's coughing reverberated through the walls, piercing his heart with guilt.

He found he wasn't ready for a nap, so he dropped to his knees beside his bed and implored God to help him forgive his Father and show him the right city to settle in. He was prepared to relinquish his desire to live near his mother if God directed him elsewhere, but he reminded the Almighty of his personal preferences. After lingering in worship, he prayed for his father's recovery and then returned to the kitchen.

By then, Mother was preparing a chicken casserole with rice and cheese.

"Your father can only eat soft food without making his throat worse. I hope he can tolerate the chicken, but if that's too much, he can manage the rice and cheese. And I'll take him some hot tea with honey and lemon."

Solomon set two places at the table while she talked.

"Do you still like string beans? I'll cook some of them for us."

He walked to the stove and peered into the pot. "Yes, I do. You know,

246

in Chicago they call them green beans. Jacob and I learned to like cider vinegar on them."

Her eyebrows raised. "Do tell."

"Try it, Mother. You'll be surprised."

***

Emeline prepared a tray with Geoffrey's dinner and carried it to his bedroom. She helped him sit upright, propped him on pillows, and put the tray on his lap.

"Will you stay with me while I eat?" he asked.

"I can if you like. Solomon and I will eat when you're finished." She resigned herself to staying and sat in the chair beside his bed.

With a shaking hand, he dipped his fork into the casserole and tried to lift it to his mouth. Most of the food fell back to the plate, and he had only a few grains of rice when he wrapped his lips around the fork.

"Emeline, help me with this."

He must be worse. It must have grieved him to ask for help, she thought. She took the fork from his hand and scooped up some of the casserole. She placed it in his open mouth and waited patiently as he chewed a little. When he swallowed, pain distorted his face.

"My throat hurts. Can't you give me anything softer?"

"I can give you some pudding. I made it this morning."

He nodded, holding his hand to his throat.

She removed the plate of chicken and rice and took it to the kitchen.

"How is Father now that he's eaten?" Solomon asked.

"He didn't eat but one bite. His throat is too painful from coughing. He asked for pudding."

She scooped some pudding into a dessert cup and took it to her husband with a spoon. He was dozing against the pillow.

"Open your mouth, Geoffrey."

He opened his eyes and mouth, and she gave him a spoonful.

"This will give you some strength," she said. "It has milk and eggs in it."

He managed to take three more spoons but then waved the rest of it away. "Tea," he whispered, grasping his throat.

She held the cup to his lips and tipped it into his mouth too fast. He coughed and sputtered.

"I'm sorry, Geoffrey," she said, gently wiping his chin with a cloth. "Let's try it again."

The second try was successful, and the warm, soothing liquid with honey slid down his throat.

"I'm tired. I need to sleep."

She rearranged his pillow and helped him lie flat on the bed. He was snoring before she left the room.

"We can have our dinner now, Solomon," she said, entering the kitchen.

She filled their plates and sat at the table with her son. He said grace, and they dug in for a hearty meal.

"I've been looking at the paper, Mother," he said. "There's a moderate amount of commercial building going on here but a good amount of residential construction. I need to check with some of the contractors and find out if they're building the type of house I could get involved in or if they're the cookie-cutter variety being thrown up without an architect."

Emeline pierced a piece of chicken from the casserole and put it in her mouth. Solomon had her full attention.

He asked, "Do you know of any churches or businesses needing a new building?"

With her mouth full, she shook her head.

"Pass me the salt, Mother."

She handed him the shaker. "Oh, I just remembered that the city is discussing a new school building. The town is growing so fast that they need another one to house all the students. P. T. Barnum just built the hospital in town. Too bad you couldn't get in on that."

"I was too busy getting my degree, but it would have been something to work with him." Solomon grinned at that idea.

Mother shifted in her seat and hesitated. "I have a suggestion, so please hear me out. I'd like you to use this house as your new office. We have an extra bedroom that's big enough for your drafting table. Father won't object in the condition he's in."

Solomon patted her hand. "Mother, that's a tempting offer, but I don't think it would be good for either of us. When Father recovers, he'll be a tyrant again, and I can't afford that distraction to my work. And besides, someday, I'll want a wife and a family like Jacob. I need a place to grow my business and be my own man without Father's interference. It may be in Bridgeport, or it may be somewhere else. It's too early to say. But thank you for the offer."

Mother stared down at her lap. "I understand. Do you think you'll be able to get along without Jacob?"

Solomon's eyes crinkled in a smile. "I had that same question when I boarded the train in Chicago. But God showed me that He's my partner, whether Jacob is with me or not. He provided a client right there on the train, and we worked out a deal without Jacob. So yes, I'll get on without that guy, as much as I miss him. We both did a lot of growing in the past three years."

Wednesday, December 20, 1882

After breakfast, Solomon entered his father's bedroom on a mission. "Father," he said, jiggling his arm to wake him.

"Hmph?"

"Father, I'm going to work today, but I wanted to talk to you first."

Geoffrey rolled onto his side and searched Solomon's eyes.

"You asked for my forgiveness, but I couldn't do it right then. I'm sorry, Father. I've worked through it with God, and now I can tell you this: I do forgive you."

Tears flowed down Geoffrey's cheeks as he went into another coughing spell. He held his hand to his painful throat and mouthed the words, "Thank you, son."

Solomon took one of his hands and squeezed it. His heart was full as he left the room, but it was time to get to work. He called a cab, took a file folder with sample plans and newspaper photos of some houses he designed, and left to visit contractors' offices.

That day, he learned a lot from the contractors. He learned who was building and how much they were spending. He listened to rumors about future projects in Bridgeport and the surrounding towns. Still, it was not enough to convince him that Bridgeport was the town he should settle in without looking around further.

While he was out, he stopped and bought a bottle of perfume for his mother as a Christmas gift and a package of cotton handkerchiefs, each with an embroidered "H," for his father.

Solomon attended church with his mother on Sunday. Being around folks he had known all his life was a joy. It was good to worship in the sanctuary of his boyhood. He was at home here but didn't know if it should remain his permanent home. He raised his voice in the hymns, with Jacob's whispered "well-voiced hammers" echoing in his head.

The guest speaker filling the pulpit for Father brought a heart-warming Christmas sermon.

Monday, December 25, 1882

Solomon was thrilled to be spending Christmas Day with his family. It was the best Christmas he could remember. At last, there was peace with Father. Mother roasted a small turkey to a golden brown, adding potatoes, gravy, and corn. They gathered in Father's bedroom to open gifts, but Father didn't have the strength to open a package. He fell asleep after Emeline opened his handkerchiefs for him and tucked one under his pillow.

She turned to Solomon with weariness in her eyes. "I count it a blessing that his coughing eased up today."

"You need some rest, Mother. Go ahead, take a nap. I'll clean up the kitchen for you."

On Tuesday, Solomon headed off to the train station for a trip to Hartford via New Haven. Traveling could be accomplished in two hours, with stops along the way. Emeline would remain in Bridgeport to care for Geoffrey.

Solomon picked up a copy of the Hartford Weekly Times on the train and studied it the entire trip. By the time he stepped off the train, he was familiar with some of the projects under construction. He hired a cab to take him all over the city, visiting job sites and talking to contractors with the confidence born of experience. He left his business cards everywhere he went.

This city could be a more promising location, he thought, *except I would miss being near the Sound . . . and Mother.*

He found a hotel for the night and returned to Bridgeport in the morning.

"Hartford may be my next home," he told his mother when she picked him up at the train station. "But I'm not sure yet."

"You need to pray for God's guidance."

"I have been. He'll put me where He wants me."

The rest of the week, he toured projects and talked to people along the coast from New Haven to Stamford, leaving his business card. Nothing seemed right to him except Bridgeport. He had the idea to open a temporary office in his hometown and, like Abraham, be willing to move if God told him to go.

He remembered a three-bedroom house for rent near the downtown business area that would make a good home office. He would set up a reception room and filing cabinets in the parlor. He would hire a competent young lady to answer the phone and handle correspondence. The largest bedroom would be used for design and drafting, and the other two would be his living quarters. He signed a lease with the property owner and went on a furniture-buying trip. Then, he had a telephone installed. His mother was ecstatic that he would remain in Bridgeport.

"Mother, do you know any young women who could answer the telephone for me and handle my correspondence?"

She pondered for a moment. "I know two girls at the church you could interview. One of them, Betsy Farnham, just graduated from secondary school. She's interested in finding a job. The other one, Sarah Carson, is quite shy but pretty. Your clients would find her charming."

Solomon laughed. "I have enough shyness. I don't need anyone else in the office with a problem like mine. I'll interview Miss Farnham and see if she would be a good fit."

The next day, as Solomon worked on writing an ad, Miss Farnham knocked on the door. Solomon invited her in. She was a tall, dark-haired, no-nonsense girl with bright brown eyes.

She looks intelligent enough, Solomon thought. "Please have a seat, Miss Farnham, and thank you for coming. My mother tells me you're interested in working outside the home."

She took the chair beside the desk and turned her eyes on him. "Yes, sir, I am."

"Do you have a beau? I only ask because if you're considering marriage, you might quit just as you have learned the job well."

"No, sir, I'm not thinking of getting married. Perhaps someday I'll meet the right gentleman, but I'll be very particular."

Solomon nodded. "Do you know how to use a telephone?"

"No, sir, but I'm smart. I'm sure I could learn." She glanced at the contraption on the desk, standing there like a cold black post with a mouthpiece at the top, an earpiece hanging from a hook on its side, and a rotary dial at its base.

"My clients will be very demanding. They will require perfection in my work and yours. I need someone who will pay attention to details and help me to satisfy their needs. My reputation as an architect depends on it."

"I think you will find me satisfactory. I'm neat and organized, and I pay attention to what's going on."

"Then I think you might do well. Before we discuss salary, do you have any questions for me?"

"Yes, sir. What does an architect do?"

Solomon smiled. "That's a fair question." He pulled out files of his former work and showed her the plans and photos. Her eyes lit up.

"That's fascinating," she said. "I would like to learn more about this business."

"That's good," Solomon said. They discussed the work hours and pay rate. She agreed to begin work the following day.

Solomon was free to begin advertising in the newspaper. He made the rounds of the engineers' offices and the real estate professionals. He took contractors to lunch, met the owner of a nearby blueprinting service, and talked to well diggers, loggers, and electricians. He would have preferred Jacob to do that, but it was up to him now. He smiled to himself, proud that he was gaining the confidence needed to tackle these tasks.

He had Miss Farnham telephone Dr. Sayers in Chicago to give him the new contact information. Other work trickled in. He made enough in design fees to cover his expenses, but it would have been better with Jacob. His local fame had brought work in Chicago, but the same was not true in Bridgeport.

His mother came two or three times a week, bringing lunch. They laughed and chatted about the latest news among the church folks, and she kept him abreast of his father's illness. Father was not improving. Day by day, he was getting worse. The doctor admitted he was stumped.

Chapter 34: Tragedy to Victory

June 1883

O ver the next months, Father's health see-sawed between improving and growing worse, but the overall trend seemed to be a gradual decline. Solomon saw his mother struggle with the effort of caring for an invalid while trying to keep her spirits up.

"Mother, I don't know how you're doing this," he said one day. He wished he could help her more, but his work took all his time.

"It's by the grace of God," she said. "This isn't going to last forever. Either he'll improve, or . . ." her voice trailed off. She appeared to be continually exhausted, never getting enough rest.

In late June, Solomon received a telephone call from Jacob. His voice was hysterical, raising the hairs on Solomon's arms.

"Jacob, what's wrong?"

What came through the telephone was anguished groaning. "It's Amelia, Solly. She went into labor the evening before last and had a lot of trouble delivering. The doctor couldn't help her. She died in childbirth an hour ago." He choked back a sob.

Suddenly, it was as if the earth disappeared from under Solomon's feet. He couldn't think straight, and tears flowed from his eyes. Here he was, hundreds of miles away, when his friend needed him.

"And the baby came stillborn. She was a little girl, a perfect baby with ten fingers and ten toes." Jacob's voice broke in deep sobs. "She had red hair like her mama. We would have named her Estelle. My Amelia! I can't believe she's gone."

Solomon's heart broke for his friend. "Jacob, I'm sorry! I'm so sorry."

Jacob still needed to talk. "I held Estelle's little body and kissed her, but the nurse took her away from me. I didn't have more than two minutes with my daughter. *Two minutes,* Solly. It should have been a lifetime."

Solomon paled. "What are you going to do?"

"I don't know. Amelia died only an hour ago. The undertaker just took her and the baby."

"Call Pastor Bromley. He'll come help you."

"I called Amelia's parents. They took the news rough." His voice cracked. "And now I have to call Mrs. Sterling."

Solomon was stunned. He had never had to deal with the death of someone young before. It defied the natural order of things. Young people shouldn't die.

While he was sure God could heal Jacob's heart, he couldn't imagine how or how long it might take. "Jacob," he said. "God is equal to the task of giving you peace. I'll pray for you. I wish I could come, but I'd never make it in time."

"I know, Solly. The distance is too much. I've missed you, really missed you."

"And I've missed you. Why don't you come for a visit after the funeral? It would help you heal."

"Maybe Mrs. Sterling will give me time off to do that. I still have to hire someone to replace Amelia." He broke into inconsolable sobs again.

As soon as their conversation ended, Solomon mounted his horse and rode straight to the church. He stepped inside the large, quiet sanctuary and knelt before the altar, shedding tears, pouring out his sorrow to God, and asking for help for Jacob. He asked for direction for himself. And he asked that whatever the outcome of this tragedy, God could use it for good. After his spirit calmed, he stood, returned to his office in deep sadness, and continued his work.

***

Jacob's heart was ripped in two. His closest confidante was hundreds of miles away, and his wife—his beautiful, copper-haired Amelia—lay dead at the undertaker's. Her wedding dress was still in the wardrobe, and now she was gone. He had no one to turn to for comfort, no one who knew him as intimately as she did. He lifted her framed photo off the wall, her bridal portrait, and clutched it to his chest, sobbing.

The worst thing was the guilt. It was the seed he had put in her body that had caused her death. If they had never married, she would still be alive. How could he live with that? His anguish was overwhelming.

That evening, he stopped at the nearby pub and sat alone. He ordered a pint, then another, then another.

"Hey, buddy," the bartender said. "We're closing. You have to go."

Jacob looked up at him with red-rimmed eyes. He could barely focus on the man talking to him. "What about the others?"

"You're the last. Everyone else has already gone."

Jacob struggled to his feet and stumbled outside to his carriage. He curled up on the floor with his lap blanket, and cried his heart out. He was too drunk to go home and didn't want to be there, anyway. Amelia's clothes were there. The blanket she had started for the baby was still on knitting needles on the parlor table, and the baby's cradle waited empty beside their bed. How could he go home and face all that?

The morning light was dawning when he woke up, stiff and sore, in his carriage. He had a ferocious headache. He returned home, splashed water on his face, and went to bed. He slept all morning until someone knocked on the door.

He sat up, rubbed his eyes, and went to open it. "Yes?" he said.

It was Rev. Bromley. "I came to see what I could do for you, son. I can't imagine what you're going through. May I come in?"

Jacob's soul was numb. He didn't care if the pastor came in or not. He didn't care if he lived or not. He opened the door wider, and the pastor stepped inside.

"Have a seat," Jacob said.

"I came to pray with you."

"Solomon said he'd pray for me, too, but if there is a God, why did he let Amelia die?" He broke down in sobs once again. "Amelia believed in Him. Why didn't He help her?"

"I know you can't appreciate this right now, but God's ways are higher than ours. Amelia and your baby are enjoying one another right now in heaven."

Jacob's voice raised in anger. "But I got left behind. I wish I'd died, too."

He bent forward, shaking, covering his head with his hands.

The pastor laid a hand on his shoulder. "You were left behind for a reason. God has plans for your life." His voice softened. "Besides . . . are you ready to die? Would you have gone to heaven if you died?"

"I don't know."

"Jesus said you have to be born again to see the kingdom of God."

"I don't even know what that means."

"It means that you believe that Jesus died to save you from the power of sin. It's all about trusting Him. Agree with God that you've sinned, just like everyone else has, and ask His forgiveness. It's the only sure way to happiness and eternal life in heaven with Amelia and the baby."

There was silence while Jacob tried to focus on the conversation, but his mind was still suffering shock. "I can't think about that right now," he said.

"That's fine. You have a funeral to prepare. We'll talk again later."

"Can you help me plan the funeral? I don't have any idea what to do."

"Of course. We'll plan a nice funeral, then share the details with Amelia's parents and the rest of the church. Lots of folks will want to be there to support you in your grief."

The pastor took Jacob to talk to the people in charge of the cemetery and pay for someone to dig the grave. They went to the undertaker's and paid for the coffin, deciding that baby Estelle could be buried in her mother's arms. Amelia had cousins who would be honored to serve as pallbearers and lower the casket into the grave. Pastor Bromley would say a few words at the graveside. Then they went to the Schultz home and gave her parents the details.

The Schultzes were numb with grief. They hugged their son-in-law through tears.

"Jacob," Mrs. Schultz said through sobs, "you're the only family we have now. You'll always be a part of us."

Rev. Bromley prayed with them, then left. Jacob lingered in their home for a while. They were his family in Chicago, and he loved them. Amelia's death seemed to solidify his status with them.

Later, they went together to Clark Brothers Grave Markers and ordered a concrete headstone engraved with the names of Amelia Bishop and infant Estelle Bishop. Jacob made sure it would say that Amelia was Jacob's beloved wife and Estelle was his beloved daughter.

The funeral was scheduled for the next day.

***

At ten o'clock, a crowd of Schultz family members and church friends gathered around the grave singing "Blessed Assurance." Jacob's former coworkers at Ellsworth Piano Company were there, including Mr. Ellsworth, Miss Thompson, and the piano tuner. Mrs. Sterling was also there in a black dress. Pastor Bromley spoke of Amelia's life, her marriage to Jacob, and their plans for a family. He said Amelia had trusted Jesus as her savior and would be ready when the Lord returned. He read portions of scripture from 1 Thessalonians 4 slowly and clearly:

"But I would not have you to be ignorant, brethren, concerning them which are asleep (that is, those who have died*), that ye sorrow not, even as others which have no hope. For if we believe that Jesus died and rose again, even so, them also which sleep in Jesus will God bring with him."*

Here, the pastor paused, smiled, and raised his voice. *"For the Lord himself shall descend from heaven with a shout, with the voice of the archangel, and with the trump of God: and the dead in Christ shall rise first.* (That means Amelia and the baby will rise first.) *Then we which are alive and remain shall be caught up together with them in the clouds, to meet the Lord in the air: and so shall we ever be with the Lord."*

He lowered his voice, his eyes locking onto Jacob's, and he nodded, confirming what he had just read.

Jacob listened intently, and in a sudden flash of understanding, his eyes were opened. The words burned in his heart. He wanted that hope, too. Maybe they could all meet the Lord together as a family.

After the casket was lowered into the ground with Amelia and the baby,

Jacob and the Schultzes were surrounded by well-wishers. He was desperate to speak to Pastor Bromley right then, but so many people wanted to offer their condolences that he couldn't leave. From the corner of his eye, he saw the pastor climb into his carriage and drive away. At that moment, Mr. Ellsworth had his arm around Jacob's shoulders, giving him encouraging words. Jacob couldn't be rude. Anxiety rose in his stomach.

He stayed at the gravesite only as long as necessary, thinking to return later when he was alone. As the crowd filtered away, he dashed to his carriage and drove to Pastor Bromley's house, beating on the door like a wild man.

Mrs. Bromley opened the door, alarmed. "Jacob, what are you doing here?"

"I need to see Pastor Bromley."

"He went to the church to work on his sermon."

"Thank you, ma'am. I hope I didn't alarm you."

He was off the porch in a flash and leaped into the carriage, slapping the reins and urging the horse toward the church. He entered the now-familiar foyer with the fifteen-foot ceilings he had first seen as a piano salesman. The cool air inside was refreshing. He stepped to the pastor's office and rapped on the door frame.

With his head in his notes, Pastor Bromley raised his eyes to see Jacob standing before him, his face pale from grief but otherwise clear-headed.

"Jacob. What a surprise. Are you all right?"

"Yes, sir, but I need to talk to you. I hope I'm not interrupting. It's urgent."

"Please have a seat. What can I do for you?"

"That scripture you read from the Bible. I understood it, and I want that hope. What do I have to do?"

Pastor Bromley's eyes softened. "Do you believe in God? Do you believe Jesus was the Son of God, that He died for your sins and rose again?"

"Yes."

"Then let's pray and tell Him that."

The two men knelt together and thanked God for Jacob's new spiritual understanding. He acknowledged his sin before God and received forgiveness and acceptance. As the load of guilt was lifted from him, he sensed more freedom than he had ever known. It didn't reduce the pain of Amelia's death and the loss of the baby, but his torn heart found peace in his grief. His gratitude overflowed.

The pastor put an arm around Jacob's shoulders. "Congratulations, man, you're in the family of God. So welcome home."

Jacob's heart was whole. He wanted to go home and make a long-distance call to his dearest friend.

After going through the operator, Solomon's phone rang, and a young lady's voice said, "You've reached the office of Solomon Hawk, Architect."

The operator signaled Jacob to go ahead.

"I'd like to speak to Solly, please . . . I mean, Mr. Hawk."

"One moment."

Jacob fidgeted until Solomon took the phone.

"Hey, this is Jake. First, I want to tell you that I've been to see Pastor Bromley, and I've come to trust God completely. It was like my eyes were opened during Amelia's funeral. It was amazing. He says I'm a new creation."

"That's great news, Jacob! I can't tell you—"

"Give me a few weeks to get myself straight, Solly. I just buried my family, so it's possible I'm not thinking right. But if I wanted to come to Bridgeport and work with you in a few months, would you still have me?"

"Without hesitation, brother. Come to Connecticut whenever you're ready. The two of us will be dynamite together."

Chapter 35: The Rescue

Time went by for Jacob almost mechanically. He was grateful for God's comforting presence, but he still grieved for his wife and child. Day after day, he put one foot in front of the other, doing what was necessary, even though he had lost interest in his work. He found it gut-wrenching to find a replacement for Amelia early on as the mansion's bookkeeper and front desk clerk. He hired a pleasant widow in her forties, Eloise Kemper. She was an efficient woman who kept accurate records and was a blessing to the bed and breakfast.

With her skills to rely on, Jacob fell into a routine and thought about staying permanently, but his thoughts of Solomon made him want to return to Connecticut. Little by little, his interest in his work was rekindled. He was in a constant tug of war with himself, trying to decide whether to leave or stay.

Mrs. Sterling was still planning parties, holding them in the great room of the mansion while living in her lake home. Clients also booked weddings and anniversary parties in the great room. Occasionally, someone had a birthday party there, usually an elderly family member. Jacob bought an easel with a sign saying "Private Event" to keep guests of the bed and breakfast from intruding on private parties.

Since he was single again, Mrs. Sterling insisted he attend every party she held, meet the guests, and dance with her. He enjoyed the distraction from his loneliness and meeting the parade of famous people who attended every event—that is until one particular party became pivotal in Jacob's relationship with Mrs. Sterling.

"I'm having another party in early November," she told him. "You're welcome to come, but it's not required."

Jacob thought that was odd. He took that as a signal that his privileged status with her, as unearned as it was, may be forming cracks. He had never known why she treated him with such deference in the past (except that she was attracted to him), nor did he understand why things were changing. Since he had nothing else to do that evening, he came to the party to mingle and discovered she had a charming gentleman with her. She hung on his arm.

"Jacob, I'm glad you came," she said when she spotted him among the guests. "I'd like you to meet Mr. Artemus Blackstone. He owns several hotels between here and Washington. Artemus, this is Jacob Bishop, the manager of the mansion."

They shook hands. Jacob was surprised to see her with a man he didn't know but hid his astonishment well. "Good to meet you, Mr. Blackstone. Where are your hotels located?"

Blackstone raised his chin slightly. "I have them in the larger cities— Cincinnati, Philadelphia, New York, Boston, and, as she said, our nation's capital."

"You must do quite a bit of traveling. Thank God there are trains now, or you would never get around to all those hotels."

"Yes, of course," Blackstone said. "Marguerite, my throat is dry. Is there something to quench my thirst on that table over there?"

"Of course, Art. Let me show you what we have." She took his arm again. They turned away from Jacob and worked their way through the crowd to the refreshment table.

Jacob lounged by the wall with a drink in his hand, analyzing this new wrinkle in his relationship with Mrs. Sterling. Was his favored status being replaced? He observed Mr. Blackstone as he and Mrs. Sterling lifted drinks, chatting and laughing. He watched as she led him around to each guest as she had done at previous parties with Jacob. He wondered if Blackstone planned to buy the bed and breakfast to add to his other properties but rejected that idea as unlikely. Mrs. Sterling would never sell the historic mansion.

Jacob was caught off guard at this turn of events but recognized that she had a right to do whatever she wanted. He left the party early and went to the Schultz's home to relax in their company.

The next day, her attitude toward him seemed to revert to normal, as if nothing had happened. But Jacob's attitude had shifted just slightly off-center. Somehow, his trust in their relationship had soured just a little. He wondered if his job security was on the line.

In December, as the Christmas decorations were going up, Mrs. Sterling approached Jacob and told him she planned a New Year's party. "This is going to be a special event," she said. "Some important guests will be there, so I want you to help plan it."

"Do you have a guest list?" Jacob asked.

"A partial list," she replied. "But I plan to keep the list open until mid-December. Right now . . . let's see . . . there's Mr. Terence Powderly, the mayor of Scranton, Pennsylvania. I believe he's interested in labor issues. Then, Mr. and Mrs. Frank Butler will be passing through Chicago at that time. When I found out they made reservations here, I jumped at the chance to invite them to the party. You know Mrs. Butler as Annie Oakley."

Jacob's eyebrows raised, and he smiled. "She has quite a reputation. I hope you don't ask her to demonstrate her shooting skills in the great room."

She chuckled. "I hope she doesn't offer. And currently, last on the list is the gentleman I've been seeing lately, Artemus Blackstone."

Jacob turned to her. "Yes, I met him at the last party. How long have you been seeing him?"

"Not long," she said. "Probably three months. We see each other only once a month. The rest of the time, he's on the road, checking on the chain of hotels he owns. I booked him a room here from December 30th through January 3rd."

"That's odd. I didn't see that reservation."

She blushed. "No, I just slipped it in. It's a complimentary reservation."

"What?" Jacob's jaw dropped. "For New Year's Eve? You know that's one of our busiest times. "We could rent that room to someone else at our highest holiday rate."

Her lips formed a thin line, and her eyes drilled into him. "Jacob, I own this mansion. If I want to put up someone and make a gift of it, that's my business. I don't do it often. I just wanted to spend New Year's with a friend. I suppose you'll be celebrating with the Schultzes?"

"Probably." Jacob walked away, wagging his head at her poor decision.

***

The Christmas season was a trial for Jacob. He saw a jewelry box in a store that he thought Amelia would like for Christmas and then remembered she wasn't with him. He left the store with an aching heart. He mailed gifts to his parents in Beacon Falls and made a long-distance call to Solomon to wish him a Merry Christmas.

He attended the Christmas Eve service at Cooper Street Baptist with the Schultzes. Mary and Joseph, angels, shepherds and wise men populated the children's reenactment of the nativity scene. Jacob's heart was blessed as he gained a new understanding of the miracle of Jesus' birth.

He joined the Schultzes at home on Christmas Day. As Mrs. Schultz was still mourning the loss of her daughter, she hadn't had the heart to put up a Christmas tree. To pass some time, Jacob and his in-laws took a carriage drive that afternoon in the snow to look at the happy decorations on other homes. It was a day under the shadow of grieving, remembering past Christmases with Amelia. They hoped next year would be better.

December 30, 1883

Jacob was at work at his desk in the mansion's former library when he first saw the man Mrs. Sterling had invited. Artemus Blackstone checked in at three o'clock in the afternoon and was given the best room in the house. Jacob studied him through his office door as Mrs. Kemper put the guest register before him. The man signed with a flourish.

"Is Marguerite in the house?" he asked in a strong voice.

Mrs. Kemper answered, "No. Is she expecting you?"

Blackstone rested his elbow on the front desk and leaned in to give Mrs. Kemper his best smile. "She's expecting me. Can you telephone her at home and tell her I'm here?"

Jacob kept his eye on him while Mrs. Kemper dialed Mrs. Sterling at home. He instinctively did not like the man. But, he thought perhaps his attitude had been affected by knowing he was staying for free and worming his way into Mrs. Sterling's affections. He decided to give Blackstone the benefit of the doubt. Even better, he would try to make friends. He rose from his chair and strolled into the lobby behind the front desk.

He thrust out his hand. "Welcome, Mr. Blackstone. We've been expecting you."

Blackstone shook his hand. "Ah, Mr. Bishop. I met you at the party in November." His smile was friendly, but his eyes were cold. Something was off. Jacob shoved that feeling aside as irrational.

"I'll show Mr. Blackstone to his room while you make that telephone call, Mrs. Kemper." Jacob hoisted the guest's two bags and showed him up the stairs.

"I had rather hoped for a downstairs room," the man said.

"I'm sorry you're disappointed," Jacob said. "All the rooms are upstairs. I'm surprised Mrs. Sterling forgot to mention that."

With a heavy sigh, Blackstone followed Jacob to his room. He was given the most comfortable bedroom in the mansion, which had been Mrs. Sterling's bedroom when she lived there.

"Do you have someone to take me to Mrs. Sterling's house?" he asked.

"No, sir, I'm sorry," Jacob replied, "but we can call for a hansom cab. Why don't we wait and see if we can reach her by telephone first? She may not even be home."

Blackstone pulled his clothes from his bags and arranged them neatly in the bureau drawers. "I'll wait here for your message," he said.

Jacob descended the stairs, leaving him alone in his room. *I'll be glad when his stay is over,* he thought. *Already, he's rubbing me the wrong way. I wonder what she sees in him. I hate to think this of her, but maybe money attracts money.*

At the front desk, Mrs. Kemper hung up the phone. "Mrs. Sterling is on her way here," she said. "She's eager to see Mr. Blackstone."

"Thank you for making that call," Jacob said. "Would you ask the housekeeper to go to Room 1 and tell Mr. Blackstone that Mrs. Sterling is on her way?" He returned to his desk, wondering what the next few days would hold. The more he thought about Blackstone and his pushy manner, the more irritated he became. Who else would feel entitled to a free stay, a downstairs room, and a free ride to Mrs. Sterling's house?

Within the hour, Mrs. Sterling entered the lobby in a beautifully tailored new dress, covered with a long hooded cloak to protect her from the December weather. It was clear she had made a special effort with her appearance. Her cheeks were rosy from the cold, and her eyes sparkled. "Good afternoon, Mrs. Kemper," she greeted cheerily. "Would you go upstairs and tell Mr. Smith I'm here?"

As Mrs. Kemper left to deliver the message, Mrs. Sterling glanced at Jacob behind his desk. He kept his head down in his paperwork and didn't look up to greet her. She walked to his door and stuck her head in. "Hello, Jacob."

He raised his head, looking her in the eye, but said nothing.

"I see you're angry. Well, never mind. I expect you to be pleasant to the guests, all of them, and not let your emotions cloud your work."

"I will keep a professional demeanor," he said in clipped tones.

She entered the room and stood in front of his desk. "I told Mr. Blackstone he could put his laundry in the hall, and the housekeeper will take care of it. We won't charge him."

Jacob stood. "So now he expects free laundry, too. I will keep my opinions about the guests to myself, but I am concerned about the December financial report. You know our business has been down lately because of the depressed economy. If the report shows a loss because of the lack of income and extra expense for the housekeeper to do a guest's laundry for free, I won't be responsible. The responsibility will be yours."

He probably shouldn't have made that last statement, but it was out, and he wouldn't retract it.

She glared at him. "Jacob, I never thought I would hear you speak disrespectfully to me."

"Ma'am," he began, with his stomach churning. He had never called her 'ma'am' before. "I apologize for my tone. But I spoke the truth. I hope we don't show a loss this month, but the fact is, we may. So if that

266

happens, please don't lay the blame at my feet. I'm doing the best I can."

Her eyes softened, and she sank into the chair beside his desk. "I know you are, Jacob, so when I look at the December report, I'll be aware that it would be higher if I hadn't promised . . . Oh, look, there's Artemus." A smile lit her face, and she stood.

She forgot her conversation with Jacob and abruptly left his office to greet the guest in the lobby. He was of average height but impeccably dressed in an expensive suit with a vest and ascot. Holding her skirts away from her hurrying feet, Mrs. Sterling swept toward him. She stretched out a hand to him, which he took and leaned over with a kiss.

"My dear, it's so good to see you," he said. "I'd like to take you to dinner this evening. Would you accept my invitation?"

"Of course, but it's too early for dinner. Let's sit in the great room and pass some time."

He lowered his voice. "We would have more privacy if we sat upstairs in my room. There are so many ears down here."

Jacob heard every word from his desk and looked up in shock at that unseemly suggestion. His eyebrows were raised when Mrs. Sterling glanced at him. She knew by the look on his face he had heard, and she blushed.

Her voice took an urgent tone. "Artie, stop. You know that's not proper."

"But we're practically engaged."

She grabbed his hand and led him to the great room. "We're not married. I'll not have the employees gossiping about me."

Mrs. Kemper turned from the front desk to face Jacob and rolled her eyes. After the two disappeared into the great room, she turned to Jacob. "What could she see in him?"

He shrugged. "It's not our place to question her personal decisions, Mrs. Kemper."

She turned. "Yes, sir. You're right."

Jacob left the mansion at six o'clock after a long workday and went home to cook dinner for himself. Mrs. Sterling and her escort hadn't yet returned, and Jacob was grateful. He didn't want to deal with that man when it came time to serve the complimentary wine in the evening. He would probably request an entire bottle.

***

The following morning, Mrs. Kemper tallied the guests who came to the dining room for breakfast. They were all there except for Mr. Blackstone.

Mrs. Sterling arrived. "Good morning, Mrs. Kemper. I came to join Mr. Blackstone at the breakfast table this morning. Has he come down from his room yet?"

"No, ma'am, not yet."

"I'm sure he'll be down soon." Mrs. Sterling joined the guests in the dining room, saving the chair beside her for Mr. Blackstone. She chatted comfortably with Mr. and Mrs. Powderly, the Butlers, and other guests while she waited. Mrs. Butler's fame as Annie Oakley made for stimulating conversation. When the cook served breakfast, Blackstone was still in his room. Mrs. Sterling began to worry that perhaps he was ill or still asleep from their late dinner last night. She asked Mrs. Kemper to knock on his door and find out why he was late. "Tell him he's missing a chance to meet Annie Oakley."

When Mrs. Kemper approached his door, his clothes were lying on the floor in the hall. She kicked them into a pile before knocking once, twice, and then a third time. In a moment, he cracked the door and peered through the narrow opening.

"What is it?"

"Mr. Blackstone, everyone is being served breakfast downstairs in the dining room. Mrs. Sterling is there waiting for you. She wonders if you're coming down. Annie Oakley is among the guests."

He huffed and pointed to his pile of clothes beside her. "I left my clothes there last night for the housekeeper to wash, and they're still there. I have no clean clothes. How can I come down in this state?" His voice conveyed anger and frustration.

"But, Mr. Blackstone," she said, "the housekeeper goes home at four o'clock in the afternoon. She just now came in. There was no one here to do your laundry. She'll do it when she washes the sheets from the outgoing guests."

"Would you send Mrs. Sterling up here? I want to file a complaint. And have her bring my breakfast. As soon as you leave, I'll have to get some clothes out of that pile, and I'll be dressed when she gets up here. But my clothes won't be fresh."

Mrs. Kemper's worst nightmare was an angry guest. She scurried down the stairs to deliver the message. Stopping at the dining room door, she signaled Mrs. Sterling to come away from the other guests so she could give her the message privately.

Mrs. Sterling saw her signal and rose from the table, leaving her breakfast. "Is anything wrong?"

Mrs. Kemper lowered her eyes. "It's Mr. Blackstone. He's quite upset because his laundry wasn't done last night, and he has to wear dirty clothes today. He also wants you to come upstairs with his breakfast. He wants to make his complaint to you directly."

Mrs. Sterling patted her arm. "It's alright, Mrs. Kemper. I'll handle it. He owns several hotels, so he probably expects the kind of service he gets with a large staff. Everything will be fine." She smiled reassuringly.

***

Mrs. Sterling went to the kitchen to speak to the cook. "We have an important guest who wishes to have breakfast in his room. Would you make a breakfast plate for a late guest? I'll take it to him." While she waited, the cook dished up a generous portion of scrambled eggs, sausage, and half a sliced banana. She loaded a serving tray with the full plate and a cup of coffee, silverware, and a napkin.

Mrs. Sterling carried the tray upstairs to Room 1. Stepping around the pile of laundry in the hall, she rapped on the door.

"Come in," Artemus called from inside the room.

"It's me," she said. "Please open the door."

"Marguerite, just come in. You can leave the door open if you're worried about your reputation."

She hesitated, considering what people would think if she went in there. It was most improper. Her staff, and especially her friends, would be shocked if they knew. Gossip would be spread like wildfire. She didn't

269

want to be in a man's room, but leaving the tray on the bureau would only take a few seconds. The other option was turning around and taking his breakfast back downstairs. That seemed foolish and would no doubt irritate him, so she opened the door and stepped inside. She gasped to see him standing there in an open shirt and underwear.

"Artemus, this is uncalled for." Angry, she turned to leave, but he grasped her hand and pulled her back. He inserted himself between her and the door and closed it.

"Now we have some privacy," he said, leering at her. "Put the food on the dresser." As she tried to pull away from him, he said, "Never mind, I'll do it."

He tugged the tray out of her hand, spilling everything on it. Scrambled eggs, hot sausage, and banana slices scattered to the floor, and the coffee spilled down Mrs. Sterling's skirt. She struggled to get away from him. "Art, let me go." Her breathing was heavy in the physical effort to pull herself loose. She wanted to scream but didn't want to raise the suspicions of the guests if she could end this quickly. She continued to struggle, even though her wrist was being bruised. She got one hand loose and pounded his chest, hoping it would make him let go.

But Artemus was able to get control over her. He pulled her against his chest and wrapped his arm around her, kissing her neck roughly. Then he dragged her to the bed, forced her down, and put his weight atop her. Finally, the seriousness of her situation burned itself into her brain. She was frightened enough to scream. She took a deep breath and shrieked as loud as she could. Artemus tried to put a hand over her mouth, but she was struggling mightily and turned her face quickly to let out another scream. She tried to kick, but he restrained her legs and pulled at her dress.

"Stop fighting," he said through gritted teeth. "You know you want me to do this."

Anger at that insulting comment gave her new energy. She found the opportunity for one more piercing scream before he clapped his hand over her mouth. *This is it,* she thought, losing hope but still struggling. Her thoughts raced wildly. *He's really going to do this.*

Feet pounded up the stairs, and the door burst open. Jacob flew in with

270

a fury and jerked the man off her. Jacob was younger by twenty years and was five inches taller. He threw a punch that caught Blackstone in an uppercut to the jaw, knocking him to the floor. He turned to help Mrs. Sterling off the bed, but the attacker managed to pick himself up and take a swing. Jacob whirled and threw a vicious punch that caught Blackstone in the abdomen. He went down again, this time in a fetal position, moaning.

By this time, Mrs. Sterling had struggled to a sitting position on the edge of the bed. Her eyes were wild with fear. She was bruised, her hair a mess, and her new dress was streaked with coffee. When Jacob turned to her, she flew into his arms, shaking and sobbing.

"It's alright," he said. "I won't let him hurt you."

After several moments, she gathered herself and pulled away from him. She wiped at her tears with the palms of her hands. Her voice still quivered. "Thank you, Jacob. I don't know what I would've done—" Her hand went to her neck, and she shuddered. "He kissed my neck. I need to wash it off. And look at this mess on the floor."

Smith was still curled up on the floor in his underwear.

Jacob asked, "Would you like me to call the police?"

She glared at the half-undressed man clutching his stomach, lying in eggs and banana. "He looks pathetic down there on the floor, doesn't he? No, don't bother the police. Mr. Smith will be checking out this morning."

Jacob chuckled. "Are you going to fire me for punching a guest?"

She managed a chuckle, her eyes still red and her hair unkempt. "No, but I might give you a bonus. Artemus, you have fifteen minutes. Get your clothes packed and get out of here, or we will call the police."

"At least give me a chance to eat my breakfast."

Her eyebrows raised, and she pulled herself to her full height. "I can't believe you're worried about breakfast. You're welcome to eat your eggs and sausage off the floor if you're out of here in fifteen minutes. And if I ever see you again, I'll press charges."

She and Jacob left him to scramble for his pants and whatever breakfast he cared to eat.

On the way downstairs, Mrs. Sterling said, "You'd think the owner of several hotels would be more understanding of how the staff works. He

271

was complaining about not getting his clothes washed last night."

Jacob shook his head. "No, that was just an excuse to get you up there. Are you sure the man owns hotels?"

Mrs. Sterling sighed. "Now I'm not even sure his name is Artemus Blackstone."

At the bottom of the stairs, she turned to Jacob. "I'm a mess, and I don't want the staff to see me this way. I don't want to have to explain myself. Will you shield me from view while I walk to my carriage? I'm going home. And will you see that Mr. Blackstone is out of here in fifteen minutes? If he's not, you can throw his things out on the lawn or call the police. I'll leave that decision up to you."

Jacob responded, "Here's your cloak. Put it on and pull the hood up over your head. Are you in any condition to drive? I can call a cab for you."

"I think I'm just about through shaking, so I'll be fine to take the carriage. Oh, and that mess upstairs. How can we explain that to the housekeeper?"

"Don't worry, Mrs. Sterling. I'll go up and get most of it cleaned up before she gets there."

She turned and gazed up into his eyes, putting a hand on his arm. "Thank you again, Jacob. I can never thank you enough."

"You need to thank God, too," Jacob said. "If he had tried that where no one could get to you, he might have seriously injured you . . . or worse."

Chapter 36: A Long-Distance Phone Call

Late that afternoon, Solomon was at his drafting table when Miss Farnham put on her coat, getting ready to go home for the day.

"Miss Farnham, do you have any plans to go to a New Year's Eve party tonight?"

She turned to him with a smile. "Yes, Mr. Hawk. Some girls are getting together at a friend's house to wait for midnight. We'll be ringing in 1884 together."

The phone rang, and Miss Farnham said, "I'll get that." She lifted the earpiece from its hook and spoke briefly into the mouthpiece. "It's a long-distance call for you, Mr. Hawk."

"Have a good time tonight, Miss Farnham," he said. He quickly put the last touch on the window he was drawing and rushed to the phone as Miss Farnham left the office.

"Solly, it's me, Jacob. How are you?"

"Jacob! Talk louder. I can't hear you very well. Are you calling to tell me you're coming to Connecticut?"

Jacob sighed and raised his volume. "No, I'm not coming. Not yet, anyway. We had a terrible experience yesterday, and I need to tell someone about it. I can't tell the staff here. Mrs. Sterling told me to keep it to myself."

"What happened?"

Jacob recited the story about Artemus Blackstone, the budding romance with Mrs. Sterling, and how it now appeared that Blackstone was setting her up to take advantage of her.

"What kind of advantage? Was he after her money?"

"We don't know what all he wanted, but yesterday—I hesitate to say this—he tried to rape her." Jacob told him about the scene in the bedroom when he burst through the door and the ensuing fight.

Solomon gasped. "I can't imagine someone trying to do that to such a fine lady. Is she alright?" Solomon's line began to crackle. "You'll have to shout."

Jacob yelled into the phone, "She's badly shaken up, but she's fine. She'll get over the emotional shock eventually, I suppose. I'm praying for her." Then he chuckled. "When we left the room, the bounder was lying on the floor in his underwear and had the nerve to complain he hadn't had breakfast. She told him he could eat anything he wanted off the floor."

Solomon threw his head back and laughed. "Good for her."

"So, Solly, what's going on in Bridgeport? And speak up."

Solomon shouted, "You know how bad the economy is. Fortunately, some people can still afford to build, but work has been coming in slowly. I don't have the reputation here that I had in Chicago. Thank God I'm covering expenses."

"Why don't you come back to Chicago?"

"I can't. Mother doesn't want to leave the city, and Father is too sick. They're too old to move that far, and they depend on me to watch over them. But there is a bright spot."

Jacob heard static on the line. "Do talk louder, Solly. I can't hear you over the buzzing."

Solly shouted, "I can't hear you, Jacob. I'll call you—"

The line went dead.

Solomon tapped on the mouthpiece, but there was no sound. Disappointed, he hung up. He wanted to tell Jacob about the new opportunity. Dean Woodhouse at Yale wanted him to speak at a college convocation about setting up a business. He chuckled to think of the irony.

Chapter 37: Father's Final Words

July 1883

On Saturday, Solomon went to visit his mother and see how Father was doing. As he rode toward the house, his heart raced at seeing a white horse-drawn vehicle with a large red cross on the side. It sat in front of his parents' house. He ran inside, shouting, "Mother! Mother."

"We're in here, Solomon," she called from Father's bedroom. When Solomon entered the room, he found the ambulance attendants sliding Father onto a stretcher. It was clear that he had been coughing up quantities of blood. It stained his face, bedclothes, and pillows. One of the attendants wiped his face with a cloth.

Father's color had gone gray. His eyes were wide open, and he was gasping for air through his mouth. Solomon had never seen such a desperate look on anyone's face.

He moved toward his mother, wrapping his arm around her shoulder. Her face was drained of color, and her body trembled.

"This is more than just a cough," she whispered.

Events were moving too fast for Solomon to process them in his mind. He experienced so many emotions in that moment that he couldn't sort through them.

Father turned toward him, calmed somewhat, and reached for him. Solomon stepped toward him, not knowing what to expect, and took his hand.

Father's mouth moved, but nothing came out. He tried again. "I . . . I am . . . proud . . . of y—"

Tears poured down Solomon's cheeks. "Thank you, Father," he said.

The ambulance attendants tucked his blankets around him and lifted the stretcher. They carried him out to the street while Emeline walked beside him, holding his hand. Solomon couldn't hear what Father said to her, but his heart was moved. He stood at the door with his hand over his mouth, his face wet with tears. Hearing Father say he was proud of him was all he had ever wanted. Why couldn't he have said that sooner?

Once Father was deposited in the back of the ambulance, it took off toward the hospital built recently by P. T. Barnum. Solomon was grateful it was so close.

He and his mother went to the barn and hitched a horse to the carriage. She was still pale and trembling but calm. On the way to the hospital, Solomon asked, "What did Father say to you?"

"He said he loves me," she said. "He hasn't said that in years. The last time may have been at our wedding. I don't think he'll ever come back home."

The fact that their marriage was such an emotional desert had been hidden from Solomon until now. His heart ached for her.

At the hospital, Rev. Hawk was put into a ward with several other sick men. There was no privacy, but that didn't seem to matter to Emeline. She pulled up a cold metal chair beside his bed and planted herself there, refusing to leave. The smells and sounds in the ward were horrific: men moaning and crying for morphine, bleach fumes and bed pan odor permeating the air.

"Mother, you need something to eat. Come with me to get a bite, and we'll come right back afterward."

"I'm not leaving, Solomon. You get something to eat. Keep your strength up. You may need it. I'll be fine."

There was no convincing her. Solomon returned to his parents' house, made sandwiches, and brought her one. The two of them sat by Father's bed for hours, and she held her husband's hand much of the time.

Father didn't make it through the night. At about one o'clock in the morning, he expired.

Emeline gasped and leaned over to kiss her husband's forehead, dripping tears on him. "Have a good rest, Geoffrey." She sat, then turned to Solomon. "Even when you know it's coming, it's still a shock, isn't it?"

Solomon didn't reply, stunned in his grief and regret. He choked back a sob. "We could have had a better life."

They sat in silence for a while. Eventually, Emeline stopped shaking. "Please take me home, Solomon. When we wake up, we'll come find out where his body is, and we'll make some funeral arrangements."

They took the carriage home in silence, then walked into the house. "You'll stay with me tonight, Solomon?" she asked.

"Yes, Mother. Will you be all right?"

"Yes. It's an odd feeling, having been married to your father for thirty years. He was the one person I spent most of my time with. I had few other friends. But now that he's gone—you won't tell anyone I said this, will you, Solomon? —now that he's gone, I don't think I'm crying over the loss of someone I cherished. I'm crying for myself for fear of what the future holds. Oh, what has become of the bright-eyed bride I was when I married him?" She hung her head.

Solomon's heart wrenched. "Mother, there's no need for you to feel guilty about that. Father was hard on you. After all these years, it's no wonder—"

"He wasn't so bad."

His voice was gentle. "You can tell yourself that if you want to. I know better, but go ahead and believe that if it helps get you through this crisis. He did soften at the end, didn't he?"

She lowered her eyes and nodded. "If only he could have done that years ago."

***

Two days later, a large, impressive funeral was held for the Rev. Geoffrey Kingston Hawk. He was loved and revered by his congregation. Crowds came to his funeral at St. Matthews Church, then moved to the cemetery for the burial. Emeline was pale and a little thin. People gathered around her and Solomon, offering gifts of food and money. They expressed relief that Solomon was there with his mother.

Emeline stood for the line of well-wishers at the cemetery as long as she could, but her knees became wobbly, and she paled. "Solomon, I need to sit down. I'm afraid I'll pass out."

Solomon's eyes searched in desperation for a place for her to sit, but there was nothing, only a concrete tombstone a couple of feet away. It bore the name "Barnabas Harper, 1841 – 1863."

He could have been a soldier in the war, Solomon thought. *I can't seat her there.* But it was an emergency. He took her elbow and drew her to Barnabas' tombstone while the people in line continued to talk to her. He helped her get seated on top. The line of people continued.

When the well-wishers dispersed, he escorted her to the carriage. Then, they went home together to rest.

Solomon made a light supper for them from among the food gifts. His mother ate a little, then wanted to go to sleep.

"Solomon, one thing before I get ready for bed. Would you move into the house with me? I need someone here."

"Yes, Mother. I was thinking about that myself. But we'll have to have an understanding. Sometimes, I work late at the office or on a job site. My hours are irregular, according to the needs of my clients. Will that upset you?"

"No. If you're not here at mealtime, I'll eat something and expect you to get your own when you come home."

"Fine. We'll work out the details tomorrow. Sleep well, Mother, and God bless."

***

At daybreak, Solomon woke to the inviting sizzle of bacon and eggs. He entered the kitchen to find his mother looking stronger and calmer. Over breakfast, they discussed the future.

"You don't have to worry about money, Mother. I have enough to take care of both of us."

"Not necessary, son." Her mouth turned up in a conspiratorial smile. "I have a dress with a hundred-dollar hem." She told him about Maude sewing the money into the hem of her dress before they left Grandfather's house. Solomon grinned.

"I'll take the carriage and move my clothes into the house today," Solomon said. "I'll sell some of my furniture so that if Jacob comes, he can have his own office."

Emeline's eyes sparkled for the first time in a very long time. "Why can't Jacob live here with us? It wouldn't be a permanent situation, I know. For instance, if you meet a lovely girl and marry her, it wouldn't be fitting for Jacob and me to live in the same house together. But we would have a great time, the three of us. I loved Jacob for the little time I spent with him at Grandfather's funeral."

Solomon chuckled. "So that you know, he's not the same Jacob. He's not a blacksmith hoping to make something of himself. He's already made something of himself. He has charm, confidence, and a surprising amount of sophistication. And, he told me he gave his life to Christ after his wife and baby died."

"That's wonderful news. We'll make a place for him here until life events change."

"He'll be glad to know that."

Chapter 38: The Reunion

June 1884

It took much longer for Jacob to leave Chicago. He went back to work at the Sterling Mansion and fell back into a routine, but he visited the grave of his wife and child every day for months. A year later, with the pain in his heart dulled, he resigned from his job and said a sad goodbye to his in-laws.

"Jacob," Mrs. Schultz implored, "I wish you would change your mind. You're the only child we have now."

He put his arm around her shoulders, knowing they were grieved to see him go. "I promise to stay in contact by letter. When I get settled, I'll send you a number you can call if you decide to get a telephone. It would be good to hear your voices from time to time. And you could come for a visit if you're up to traveling."

Mr. Schultz stood by, grief written on his face. His arms hung loosely. "I'll miss you, son. Anna, let's think about getting one of those telephones."

They visited Amelia's grave together one last time. Jacob sank to his knees in front of her marker and whispered, "My sweet Amelia, I'm going to Connecticut to work with Solomon, but I'll be back to visit. And, dear heart, I will see you and the baby in heaven. We'll have plenty of time to spend together then. So goodbye for now." He touched the tombstone, and his body shook. His father-in-law laid a gentle hand on his shoulder, and Jacob stood, wiping his face. His mother-in-law embraced him, knowing it may be years before they could be together again.

The three left the cemetery in silence.

Jacob sold everything he owned in Chicago to the auction house, except for two things: He tenderly wrapped Amelia's wedding dress and gave it to her mother, and the baby's crib went to Mrs. Sterling for use at the bed and breakfast, should guests come with an infant. But before he took the crib to her, he turned it over and carefully carved "Estelle Bishop" in small letters on the bottom.

He packed only his clothing and took his horse to the livestock car on the train, arriving in Bridgeport in late June.

***

Solomon waited for Jacob at the train station, listening with anticipation for the puffing of the steam engine before it chugged into view around the curve. It blew a long blast of its whistle and slowed, its wheels squealing on the iron rails. As it came to a stop, there was an enormous hiss as the steam escaped from under the belly of the engine.

Solomon spotted Jacob stepping out of a coach, towering over the other passengers.

"Jacob!" Solomon waved his hand to get his friend's attention. Jacob's face lit up, and he hurried toward him. They grabbed each other, slapping one another's backs in greeting.

"It's great to see you, old friend," Solomon said. A grin split his face.

"And you, Solly. It's good to be back in Connecticut, although . . . I will miss Chicago."

"I know you will. I do, too. But Mother is here, so I'd like to stay unless we can't make a living here."

"My family is up near Beacon Falls. I can make that a day trip. They'll be glad to see me once in a while. Won't they be surprised to see me in these duds?" He laughed, a deep, joyous laugh.

"Come on, let's get your bags into the carriage. Things have happened here that I haven't had a chance to tell you about. Since Father died, I've gone to live with Mother, and we'd like you to come share the house until circumstances change."

"What circumstances?"

"Like one of us gets married and moves out. Or one of us finds a private house we'd rather live in."

"So we're living with your mother for right now?"

"That was her request."

"Suits me."

Solomon smiled. "Fine. I'll take you there to get you settled. After lunch, I'll show you the office. You'll have your own private office and a receptionist."

Jacob grinned. "Perfect. I'll be able to concentrate on 'bringin' in the scratch.'"

The two laughed and joked together all the way to the house, but Jacob's cheerfulness was accompanied by an underlying sadness. It made him seem older. Solomon hoped his heart would heal in time.

"Here's where we make a new life for ourselves, Jacob . . . the way we planned all along."

"I'm ready for it."

The two picked up Jacob's bags and headed for Solomon's carriage, shoulder to shoulder, chatting as if they had never been apart.

Yes, they would be dynamite together.

TO BE CONTINUED . . .

More Books from This Author...

Teacups and Lies
The Rippling Effect
The Man With a Mask
The Phineas Fletcher Mysteries

Coming in the Autumn of 2025:

Brothers by Grace, Book 2

Find these books and other stories at:

www.CherieHarbridgeWilliams.com

Also available on Amazon,
Goodreads, Barnes & Noble,
and other bookstores.